WILLIAM E. THOMAS

William Edward Thomas was born in West London in 1925.

He left The Brompton Oratory School when he was 14 and started work as a messenger at the BBC. When war broke out, he went to work with his father at a factory in Harrow. While still a teenager, William joined the army and was soon recruited in to the Parachute Regiment. By May 1945, he had been "dropped" in to a number of key battles and become a much decorated soldier. He was still only 19 years old. Following the war, William served in Palestine until 1948.

William has six children. As they were growing up, he was working and studying in shifts as a merchant seaman and an engineer. In his mid fifties, he decided to work full time as a lab technician at his Alma Mater, The Open University and remained there until his retirement. It was during his retirement that he decided to set himself the challenge of writing a novel. *The Cypress Branches* is the result.

William was diagnosed with Alzheimer's disease in 2006. His health has since deteriorated to the point where he can no longer live at home and he is now cared for at a home in Milton Keynes where he is visited by his wife Sheila and family members daily.

PEGASUS
FALLING

Part 1 of the *Cypress Branches* trilogy

WILLIAM E. THOMAS

To Ray and Esther

Wishing you both the very best
and happy reading!

Mike Harris

acuteANGLE books
London

FOREWORD

William Thomas, my grandfather, started writing *The Cypress Branches* shortly after his retirement in 1990. Having become quickly bored of the life of a pensioner, he looked around for something to keep him occupied. A lover of the arts, in particular music and literature, he bought himself an electronic keyboard (he is an excellent jazz pianist) and a word processor, having decided to sit down and write a book.

The book became a work of passion, taking him nearly two years to complete. Working from dawn till often way past dusk, he would tap away for hour upon hour, the story seemingly flowing from him in an unstoppable stream. At the end of each day's efforts, the new pages would be printed out and handed to his wife Sheila for review. He became besotted with his characters, and by all accounts, so did Sheila.

As the last pages were finished, the manuscript was handed to a select few family members and friends. Having seen my grandfather poring over this epic work for so long, I was eager to get my hands on it myself. Having just finished studying for my A Levels at the time, it finally arrived (via my mother) and I spent a very happy summer devouring its pages.

Like my mother, grandmother and indeed William himself, I fell in love with the characters and sobbed, often with laughter, but also with genuine anguish as the story unfolded. At the time

I had no doubt that this was a story which had to be told. Some efforts were made by William and Sheila to contact publishers, but as is often the case with first-time authors, none took it up. We begged William to keep trying but he became disheartened. I was determined to help but as university life beckoned, somehow the book was pushed to the back of our minds.

But it never truly left my thoughts. The manuscript went with me to university and has stayed with me wherever I've lived since, always with the thought of pursuing that dream of publishing it one day.

Shortly after finishing the book, William's health started to deteriorate. His memory was failing him and he was finding it harder and harder to do the things he most enjoyed. First he gave up driving, then the cryptic crossword, which he'd completed every day for decades, went blank. His normally exquisite cooking faltered, reading his beloved books became impossible and then even watching films became difficult – the 90 minute narratives too long to follow.

Six years ago he was diagnosed with a form of Alzheimer's Disease, confirming what the family already suspected. It was difficult for us all to watch a man so vibrant in life, such an intellectual, continue to deteriorate and slowly become a shadow of his former self.

One day, quite by chance, I found myself picking up the manuscript and dusting it down after many years of it sitting undisturbed on a high shelf. Suddenly the thought struck me that perhaps now was the time to set the wheels in motion again to see if we could get it published.

I explored many avenues, but finally decided on self-publication, the main reason being that William's health was deteriorating rapidly and I wanted to get the book published as quickly as possible in the hope that it would still mean something to him.

The Cypress Branches was published in its full length form as a hardback book in 2009. The entire family gathered on launch day to see William be presented with the first book and copies were duly distributed.

In its full length, the novel is epic. I struggled to fit the whole manuscript into one volume, and only managed by making several sacrifices. It was a large, heavy tome - a treasure to have on the bookshelf, but not exactly an ideal companion for the daily commute.

Even as a paperback, in its full form it would have been imposing – and prohibitively costly to produce. Thankfully, the episodic structure of the book lends itself to being split into smaller novels, so the decision was made to adapt it into a trilogy of paperbacks. *Pegasus Falling* is the first of three parts to be published.

I have endeavoured to stay as true to William's original vision as possible, however, those familiar with the original will notice that *Pegasus Falling* does not start where *The Cypress Branches* did. When editing the manuscript, I noted that the individual volumes would make much more sense as if I changed the order slightly. Seven chapters from the beginning of *The Cypress Branches* have been omitted, as they feature other characters and will appear in the second instalment instead. The minimum of editing has taken place; some small scenes have been deleted entirely, but only for the sake of clarity. Nothing has been added – what you read in this book is all William's work.

I hope you enjoy reading William's incredible story. If you do, please tell your friends and family about it. After all, but a third of the saga is contained between these covers and the remaining two books will only be published – and therefore the story concluded – if this one is a success.

Mike Harris
London, February 2012

ACKNOWLEDGEMENTS

The publisher would like to thank the following for their invaluable help: Dewi Clough for his excellent photography; Becky Potter for her incredible hair, makeup and design skills; Duncan Macmillan, Clare Lizzimore and Nina Clark for their star turns; Katie Harris, Dennis Harris and Kim Harris for helping in their many ways; Will Martin for his continued support; Vince Van Der Kraan for his guidance; and last but never least, the entire Thomas family for believing in this project and supporting it all the way.

PEGASUS
FALLING

PART ONE

CHAPTER ONE

The doctor cycled quickly up the path, raised himself on one pedal and, swinging his leg over the frame, dismounted on the run, letting the bicycle fall onto the path. He bounded up the front steps and into the house.

'Marie! Marie Doorn, where are you? They are here, they have come, they have come at last!'

His wife came out of the kitchen, wiping her floured hands on her apron. She looked with surprise at her husband. Rarely had she seen him so animated, nor heard him shout like this.

'Jan, what on Earth's the matter with you? Who has come at last?'

'The Allies, they've landed, thousands of them.'

'What do you mean landed? Landed how, where, on what?'

'Landed, my darling. Parachutists. Thousands of parachutists. I was over at old Mrs Mees's place near Apeldoorn...she's had another fall by the way...we heard the noise of aircraft, very loud. We thought at first it was another big raid on the Ruhr, but they sounded too low and anyway, they usually go for them at night. So we went out to see what was happening and there they were, flight after flight...big transports dropping thousands of paratroops. The sky was thick with them. I came back as fast as I could.'

He followed his wife into the kitchen and sat down at the large oak trestle table then watched her back as she busied herself at the stove. She had become very quiet and he shook his head in frustration.

'Don't you see what this means, Marie? It's over, those swine are finished. They will be driven out with their tails between their legs and we will be free at last.'

She shook her head slowly. 'Oh yes? Go back, will they? Without a fight, will they? Jan, we're talking about the Wehrmacht. They won't give up without a fight, they never do. And what about all those Panzers over at Elst? Do you really believe they will run back to Germany with their tails between their legs?'

'Well, the Allies know about them. The underground reported their presence already. That is why they dropped all those paras close to Apeldoorn.'

'You may be right, but you've always been an incorrigible optimist, Jan.'

He pulled a large Hunter from his pocket and looked at the time. 'Where is Druschke?'

'She and young Pieter went out together, down to the river, I think. I told them to be back for dinner.'

He nodded, frowning. 'I had better go and look for them. Things could get hectic around here soon.'

She watched through the window as he cycled away toward the river. When he was finally out of sight, she sat at the table and gazed at her pretty garden. A warm breeze rustled the autumn turning leaves, breaking the fragile hold of the first fall. She remembered she must gather the rest of the fruit before the first frost. She sighed. Two SS Panzer divisions at Elst and thousands of British paratroopers at Apeldoorn. Two concentrations of the most highly trained and battle-hardened troops in the world and only twenty kilometres apart. This was not the stuff of which balmy autumn evenings were made. Why was Jan so stupid? Did he really believe the Bosche would simply pack up and leave? She looked at the wall clock, breaking her contemplation. She must get the dinner started or they wouldn't be eating tonight. She smiled to herself. 'The condemned men ate a hearty last meal.'

The girl contemplated her reflection in the mirror, wrinkling her nose. 'I really must do something about my hair. I'll go to a proper hairdresser in Arnhem and have it cut and set.'

The boy looked up. 'Why, what's the matter with it?'

'Oh Per, for God's sake, look at me. I'm sixteen years old now, much too old for these stupid plaits. All I need is a bonnet and a pair of clogs and I'll look like the girl on that stupid Edam cheese poster.' She giggled. 'God, that awful stuff, like warm rubber, and that ghastly red wax...ugh! Do you remember how we used to roll it into balls and throw it at each other and how Mummy would go mad when it made greasy marks on the wallpaper and ceiling?'

When he made no reply she glanced at him in the mirror. Good old Per, head stuck in a book again. She returned her gaze to her own reflection.

The jeep screeched to a stop by the café across the street making the girl jump suddenly. She ran to the window, attracted by the noise. 'Per, quickly, look at this soldier.'

But the boy was already beside her. 'He's a para, Drush. Those are the British paratroops.'

They looked down, their young faces alive with excitement. The soldier climbed from the jeep and leaned on the canopy of the vehicle. He looked around cautiously then spoke to his comrade.

'What are they doing, Per?'

'I don't know.'

The second soldier climbed from the jeep and made directly for the house. The first straightened up, removed his red beret and began to scratch the back of his head with both hands, his elbows held out wide. He looked toward the house and, noticing the two youngsters at the window, raised his hand in a diffident greeting. His head tilted curiously and he smiled.

'Oh God, Per, look. Isn't he gorgeous?'

The boy shrugged indifferently but before he could respond they heard the doorbell. They darted from the room, racing for the stairs.

They opened the front door to a broad-shouldered soldier who fixed them both with a stern expression. He wore a green and brown camouflaged smock over his British khaki uniform, a round, rimless helmet was secured to his head by a thick padded chin strap and a large pistol hung from his belt. He resembled the pictures of German Falschirmjäger which appeared on propaganda posters in Arnhem and who were regularly seen on route marches around the local lanes. His whole attitude was intimidating and this reflected in the frightened faces of the two young people.

'Don't be afraid, I'm not going to hurt you. Oh Christ... Sprechen Sie Deutsche oder Englisch?'

'Both,' replied the girl.

'Yes, of course you do. Dutch people do, don't they? Probably French and Serbo-Croat too, I shouldn't wonder. You have to, I suppose, after all, who else speaks bloody Dutch?' He smiled, changing his whole countenance. 'Are your parents or any other adults around?'

'I am an adult,' said the girl haughtily. 'I am sixteen years old.'

'Well, that's good,' said the soldier, laughing. 'So this is your house, is it?'

'Yes, it belongs to my parents.'

He turned on his heel and shouted across to the first soldier. 'Sergeant, over here and bring the maps.'

'Sir.'

He turned to the girl. 'Where are your parents?'

She did not reply. Her eyes were fixed upon the sergeant as he crossed the road.

The officer smiled. 'You boy, go find them.'

'Where are they, Drush?' Per tried to hide his fear.

'They must be in the garden, otherwise they would have heard all this commotion.' Per turned quickly and headed for the back of the house.

The sergeant approached and stopped behind the officer. The girl looked at him and he saw her fear. His expression softened with just the trace of a smile and he gave her a barely perceptible wink. 'The maps, Captain.'

'Thank you, Sergeant.' He took the map case and appeared to relax slightly. 'Right, when the platoon is mustered tell Ernie to get them dug in around this bridge. Mount MGs and mortars at both ends and start checking for explosive charges.' He gazed at the structure. 'Not much of a bridge, is it, for all this fuss?'

The sergeant smiled. ''Tis a poor thing, but 'twill serve.'

The captain laughed. 'Well, let's hope we can hang on to it. I've sent for the owners. When they get here stay with them and don't let them move until I get back. We are going to commandeer this house as a command HQ. OK?'

'OK, Sammy.'

The captain turned and looked at the girl. She was still staring at the sergeant, wide-eyed, open-mouthed, transfixed. He shook his head slowly, smiling.

'Watch it, Bill, I think you have an admirer.'

'What?' He looked at the girl. 'Leave off, Sammy.' He smiled and turned to her as the captain busied himself with the maps. 'Don't mind him, love, it's just his way...er Miss?' She stared at him, unmoving. 'Miss? Hello, anybody home?' He leaned forward slightly and waved his hand before her eyes. 'Miss?'

She blinked and appeared to gather herself. 'Yes?'

'Ah! Welcome back.' The soldier began to laugh. 'Look, are your parents coming, love?'

'Yes of course, Per has gone to fetch them.'

'And who is Per?' he asked. 'Your brother, the boy I saw in the window?'

'He's not my brother, he's just a friend.'

'Boyfriend, is he?' The captain smiled.

'No he is not,' she replied indignantly. 'Pieter is just a neighbour.' She was relieved to hear the sound of footsteps approaching from inside the house. 'Ah, good, my parents are here. Papa, these men wish to speak to you.'

'Captain, Sergeant, welcome, welcome.' Jan Doorn beamed with delight. 'Welcome to our house. Come in, come in. Allow me to introduce myself. I am Dr Jan Doorn and this is my wife, Marie. You have already met our daughter Druschke, we call her Drush. And this is Per, Pieter van der Aar, the son of a dear friend and neighbour.'

The boy, still animated with excitement, asked, 'Is that a jeep?'

'Well, an English version, yes,' Bill replied.

'Why is the steering wheel on the wrong side?'

'Didn't you know they drive on the wrong side of the road in England, Per?'

'No, the doctor is not quite right, we drive on the *left* side of the road.'

The doctor laughed. 'My apologies, Sergeant, I knew it was the opposite of right.' He turned to Sammy. 'Now Captain, what can we do to help?'

'Thank you, Sir.' Sammy regarded the doctor for some moments. 'My commanding officer will be here directly. He has asked me to inform you that he intends to establish his battalion HQ here.'

'What...in my house?' The doctor appeared shocked.

'That's right, Sir. It is ideal, being so close to the bridge.'

'The bridge?'

'That bridge. That is why we're here, to secure the bridge for the army.'

'Army? Which army?'

'The British Second Army, advancing from Nijmegen.'

A huge smile lit the doctor's face. 'You see, Marie, what did I say? You wouldn't believe me, would you? These brave boys are going to stop those Panzers getting back to Germany. They are going to trap them here and the army are going to destroy the swine. Isn't that right, Captain?'

Sammy stared intently at the doctor. 'What do you mean stop the Panzers getting back? Back from where?'

'From here, of course. Good God, surely you knew there were two Panzer Divisions and a Falshirmjäger Brigade at Elst. The underground informed your people weeks ago.'

'Elst? Where is Elst?' He pushed passed the doctor, crossed to a large hall table and spread his maps upon it.

The doctor crossed to the door and pointed. 'It's over there, about eight kilometres.'

Sammy nodded without looking up from his maps.

'Bill, come here.' The sergeant joined him and studied the map. Sammy pointed. 'There's Elst and if he's right, there are two Panzer divisions and three thousand Kraut paras between us and Thirty Corps.'

Bill stared at the map, his eyes growing cold. 'Jesus H. Christ. Those bastards. They've screwed us again, Sammy. We've just force-marched ourselves into a trap, we're surrounded.'

'We are paratroops, Bill, we're supposed to be surrounded, goes with the turf.' Sammy shook his head slowly then rallied immediately. 'I must get back to battalion. Frosty will go berserk when I tell him about this. Keep this lot here, Bill, and don't let them go blabbing to the blokes, especially those two kids. I don't want anything interfering with their work. I want that bridge made secure.'

'Right...but Sammy...given what we now know, mightn't it be a good idea to keep the option of blowing the bugger ourselves?'

Sammy gave a wry grin. 'You're a devious bastard, Sergeant Grant, but we've got our orders. We are going to hold it and we are going to cross it in one piece, if it's the last thing we bloody well do...OK?'

'OK Sammy.'

The captain crossed the road and climbed into the jeep. He sat for some moments studying the maps, then drove off at high speed.

Bill turned and gazed at the bridge. He lifted his head to the bright blue sky with its tracery of high mackerel clouds. 'There's a better than even chance it will be the last thing we bloody well do,' he muttered.

Marie Doorn could not sleep, an aching anxiety heavy in her chest. She could not rid herself of the apprehension that something terrible was about to befall them all. She turned her head towards the window. A heavy silence had descended upon the village now. The paras deployed around the bridge and throughout the village had settled into their positions, quiet and alert, to await the inevitable onslaught. She knew the Germans would not allow the British to deny them access to the bridge and they would come to destroy them. The sergeant confided to

Jan that the presence of the Panzers had been unknown to them and that it would not be possible for the lightly armed paratroops to hold out for more than a couple of days against an armoured attack.

She eased herself up and leaned back against the headboard. Her husband woke with a start. 'What is it, my love? Can't you sleep?'

'I'm afraid, Jan. Terribly afraid. The Germans are going to tear into those wretched boys and I believe there is going to be the most awful bloodshed. Those are not Italians, they are British paratroops and I have been listening to them. I don't think they even consider the possibility they might be beaten. They have been conditioned to believe in their own invincibility and the possibility of defeat does not figure in their calculations. I think that captain is a madman. He is violent, lonely, and convinced of his own superiority. A typical medal-chasing psychopath. The only one who seems to appreciate the danger they are in is the sergeant who has so bewitched our daughter.'

Jan chuckled. 'Poor Drush does seem to have a crush on him, doesn't she? I think it is harmless though. He seems a very level-headed boy and I think you are being too hard on the captain. He is a good officer. According to the sergeant he is not a professional soldier, nor a wartime conscript. He was a scientist at Cambridge University and volunteered for the paratroops because he hates Fascism.'

'Which proves my point exactly, he is mad. Jan, can't you see they're all the same, the British, the Germans, the French? They have been at each other's throats for centuries and it is small countries like ours who get dragged into their madness.'

'But they are here to liberate us, Marie.'

'Yes, Jan, I know, you keep reminding me. They will wreck our house, raze our village to the earth and kill most of our neighbours, then we shall all be free, shan't we?'

'You may be right. I know you have no love for any of them but there is nothing we can do about that now. Try to get some sleep. We may not get the chance once the fun begins.'

She shook her head slowly. 'Fun,' she whispered.

'What?'

'Nothing, Jan. Go to sleep.'

The explosions blew the windows in. Had the heavy blinds not been drawn the girl would have been lacerated by flying glass. She bolted upright and began to scream uncontrollably. The doctor rushed into the room, gathered her in his arms and tried to calm her terror. 'Alright, my darling, shush now, Papa is here. Come now, stop crying. We must all go to the cellar. It was foolish to go to our beds as if everything was normal. Come, sweetheart, come.'

There was pandemonium in the street below and he knew he must get them all into the cellar, safe from stray fire and shrapnel. He tried to raise his daughter but she was stiff with terror and had begun to whimper softly.

His wife entered the room. He could see she was making every effort to compose herself but she was obviously terrified too. She crossed to the window and drew back what was left of the curtains. A cry came up from the pit of her stomach. 'Oh God! Oh dear, sweet Jesus. Jan, they're on fire, these men are on fire, oh God, oh God.' She repeated the words over and over, not crying out now, but almost to herself. She had clutched the lapels of her dressing gown together and held them tightly under her chin as if to claim protection and as she moaned she moved up and down on her toes, rising and falling gently in rhythm with the words.

The doctor released his daughter and crossed the room to where his wife stood. He took her in his arms. 'Marie, for God's sake, come away from the window, you'll be killed.'

He looked at the horror below. A German light armoured unit had attempted to force the bridge. The paras, retreating before it, had enticed the leading vehicles to pursue them on to the bridge and hit them when they had no room for manoeuvre. An armoured car had been struck by an anti-tank shell. Its cargo of ammunition had exploded and it was burning fiercely, blocking the bridge. The following column of assorted armoured personnel carriers, trucks, machine gun carriers and armoured cars backed up into the darkness beyond. The leading personnel carrier had also been hit and was ablaze, its human cargo already dead or burning to death as he watched. The paratroops, concealed behind the parapets and newels of the bridge, were raking the column with anti-tank and machine gun fire.

His attention was drawn to some activity immediately below in the street. The captain was kneeling in the middle of the road. Beside him lay two paratroopers operating a small mortar which propelled its charge horizontally. One pulled the stock close into his shoulder whilst the other loaded the small bomb into the apparatus. The captain raised his arm then as he let it drop, the trooper with the bombs gave his comrade a pat on the head. There was a loud report from the weapon and immediately a second personnel carrier exploded in flames. Another bomb was quickly loaded and the process was repeated until the whole bridge seemed to be aflame.

He felt his wife suffer a small spasm. He turned to look at her and saw that she had vomit running down her chin, over her hands and nightdress. Her glassy, staring eyes were empty of any expression and he knew if he didn't get her away and sedated quickly she would go into severe shock. Moving her back, he pushed her down onto their daughter's bed. She was also in shock, rocking back and forth, her arms wrapped in a self-embrace. He lifted the corner of the sheet and wiped the dribble from her mouth. 'Drush, listen to me, darling. I want you to take your mother to the cellar, quickly. I have to help the injured. There is no one else I can depend upon. Please Drush, come along now.' He thought to get her occupied she might avoid the consequences of shock.

She turned to face him and smiled. 'All right, Papa, don't worry, I'll take care of everything.'

She moved over to her mother and embraced her, but he knew she was also very close to the edge.

Bill Grant and the girl worked together in the cellar pantry arranging medical supplies. The numerous jars of bottled fruit and other assorted comestibles were heaped in the corner of the small room and the shelves were now piled with bandages, dressings, ointments, all the pathetic paraphernalia of the unequal struggle between a first aid station and a battlefield. He wondered how long they could last against the rising tide of casualties which the battle was inflicting.

'Another MO bought it today. If we lose any more medics your dad will be buried under the bodies.' He sighed. 'We still have plenty of morphine though, which is something.'

'Are you a medic, Sergeant?'

'No Miss, I'm what's called the orderly room sergeant, sort of head clerk. I was an accountant on civvy street.'

'I don't understand.'

'Accountant, you know, bookkeeper.'

'You worked in the Bibliotek, the er...library?'

'No, Christ, what's the bloody word...I deal with books about money, you know, firms' accounts...'

'Ah! Ein Büchhalter...that's the German word...you wouldn't understand the Dutch.'

He laughed. 'What makes you think I understand the German?'

'What is the orderly room?' she asked, frowning.

'It's the administrative office of a military unit. It's where the colonel runs the battalion, like your front room right now, Miss. It's the room where a lot of people who have no idea what they are doing make a bloody mess. That's why it's called the orderly room, as opposed to the mess, which is a bright, shiny, well-ordered sort of canteen, usually run by people who know exactly what they are doing.' They both began to laugh. He looked at her and saw her differently now. It was the first time he had seen her smile and he was touched as it lit her lovely young face. She had a fine, broad forehead which sloped up gently to where her hair, now loose, fell to her shoulders in tow-coloured waves. Her eyes were palest blue, big and clear and shining with an expectation which filled her cheeks with colour. He saw how pretty she was.

She peered up into his face. 'What is your name, Sergeant? You've been here five days now and we only know you as Sergeant. You must have a real name. What is it?'

Still smiling at her, he shook his head slightly. 'Tommy Atkins, Miss. It's Tommy Atkins, but you can call me Tommy.'

'Tommy. That's what the Germans call the British soldiers, isn't it?'

'Among other things, Miss.'

'Tommy Atkins, that is a nice name...Tommy.'

'And very famous, Miss. I've had a song written about me, a ballad.'

She looked at him smiling at her and she was overcome by an emotion she had never felt before. She yearned to touch him and for him to embrace her. She felt uncertain, afraid, yet she wished the excitement of this strange new experience would last forever. 'You are teasing me, Tommy. Don't tease me, please.'

He looked at her, at her tender yet expectant expression. He wanted to take her to him, to hold her, to feel the warmth of her. But he knew he could not. 'Oh Drush.' He felt the first acid tears burn his eyes. 'Don't do this to me love, not now, not in this terrible place.'

'Tommy...please.' Her young heart opened to him as a spring flower touched by the sun. She stretched out both her hands and touched his roughened cheeks. He drew her to him and they kissed, clumsily, almost gingerly, their teeth striking, but then more warmly. 'Tommy, I love you, I love you so much. Please tell me you love me too. Tommy, please.'

He pushed her gently back, holding her by the shoulders at arm's length. She watched his eyes well with tears and as he spoke his voice broke in despair. 'Look at me love, just look at me.' Her head tilted slightly, curious. 'I'm a British paratrooper. I've been sent here by a bunch of silly old men to yet another bullshit battle where I'm expected to fight Tiger tanks with a bloody machine pistol. I'm barely twenty years old, my comrades are being killed and mutilated in droves, I'm tired, I'm bloody filthy and I'm so scared I'm shitting myself.' He stroked her face. 'You are so beautiful, Drush.' He sighed. 'You are a joy and the one thing keeping me from going stark raving mad in this maelstrom. It would be so easy to love you, sweetheart, but it isn't right.' As the tears seamed his grimy face the two of them drew together again.

She began to sob against his chest and he stroked her hair gently. He was calmer now and his voice became more tender. 'You must try to understand, Drush, I have only known you a week and I care for you so much it hurts, but it's for the wrong reasons. Drush, I want to be loved so much now because I am probably going to die, can't you see that, sweetheart? And it isn't right, is it? It just isn't right.'

'Please, Tommy. Please don't let them kill you. I would die too if you were killed.'

'Alright, stop crying now, nobody is going to be killed. Well, not yet anyway, it's tea time.' He smiled, kissing her gently.

'Come on love, let's tidy this lot up before old "Ted" starts up again.'

The 'Bold Plan' had failed. Insufficient resource and bad logistics resulted in the airborne assault being spread over three days, thus losing the element of surprise. The Germans reinforced quickly, denying XXXth Corps it's hoped for dash to Arnhem across a 'carpet' of airborne troops. Faulty and incompetent intelligence had delivered the British paratroopers into the eager maw of two refreshed Panzer divisions and a parachute brigade. Second Para secured the bridge but were quickly isolated by the encirclement of the main elements of the division in and around the village of Oosterbeek where, surrounded on three sides and with their backs to the river, they were systematically pounded into submission within what the Panzers called 'Der Hexenkessel', the 'witch's cauldron'. The ferocity of the conflict for possession of the bridge increased by the hour. The Panzers deployed bulldozers to shove the stricken half tracks into the river in an attempt to clear the bridge, but were constantly harassed by the paratroopers whose marksmanship took a heavy toll. Finally, unable to resist the withering artillery of the German Tiger tanks, the British paras withdrew into the houses, sheds, cellars and gardens of the small hamlet and watched helplessly as their relief supplies of food and ammunition were dropped just beyond an ever-shrinking perimeter to be carried off by laughing German paratroopers who waved to them and called them comrade.

Sammy sat slumped on the hard flagstone floor, his back to the wall. His head had fallen forward as he slept, his arms hanging limp at his sides. Utter, bone-weary exhaustion rendered him impervious to his discomfort. The guns had fallen silent, the only sound now the soft, fitful groaning of the heavily sedated wounded.

He raised his head slowly and rubbed the back of his neck, easing out a painful sigh. He pitched forward, kneeling, then dragged himself to his feet. He licked his parched lips and crossed to the sink where he doused his face in refreshing cold water. He pulled off his red beret and began to dry his face with it. 'Ouch, shit!' He rubbed his face vigorously, spreading the blood seeping from the deep scratch he had inflicted upon his cheek with the sharp point of his winged parachute cap badge. He gazed round the room. The seriously wounded lay upon stretchers whilst those with more superficial wounds sat propped against the walls. He scanned the scene for some moments, estimating there were perhaps some fifty or so survivors together with the ten medics, Bill Grant and himself. He picked his way to the door and stepped into the sunshine. In the garden the unburied dead lay in rows covered by their ground sheets. He walked round the house, moving slowly through their quiet ranks, his face expressionless. He was beyond grief now, devoid of emotion, his anger buried deep within him. He glanced upwards and saw Bill with Doctor Doorn, his wife and young daughter. The girl was crying bitterly and Bill held her tight in his arms while her parents looked on helplessly. He raised his head and, seeing Sammy, spoke to the girl. He kissed her then released her into her mother's arms. He approached his platoon officer. 'You alright, Sammy?'

'Of course I'm not alright, I feel like a fucking spit roast. Did I suffer a direct hit or something? I ache in places I didn't know I had.'

'What happened to your face? It's covered with blood.'

Sammy gave a wry laugh. 'Jerry has spent the last nine days trying, without success, to dismember me and I nearly gouge out my own eye with a bloody cap badge.' He looked again towards the doctor's house. The beautiful old red brick residence was heavily damaged. The deeply raked mansard roof was badly holed and almost bereft of tiles. All the windows had been blown in and the rags of curtains flapped sadly in the soft warm breeze. The shelling had stripped the trees of most of their top foliage and the lawns were deeply rutted and cratered. The smell of cordite and fire and especially of blood filled his senses, making him want to heave. He raised his face to the sky and took a deep breath. 'How many dead, Bill?'

'Almost four hundred. Take the wounded and missing, I reckon about another two hundred. About three hundred got away. We took a right hammering, Sammy.'

'And C Company. How many of us survived?'

'Seventeen, including us. Fifteen got back.'

Sammy stared at the ground, slowly shaking his head as though trying to refute this grim arithmetic. 'What did they call this, Operation Market Garden, wasn't it? Operation fucking Abattoir is more like it. Bloody shambles.' He looked up. 'I can't believe I said that.'

Bill smiled. 'Begone tautology, that's what I say.'

'What happened to the Twins?' The 'Terrible Twins' were two inseparable and irrepressibly ebullient privates who played piano duets together in the NAAFI or wherever they could find a piano and who, together with Sammy, had knocked out seven armoured personnel carriers with an anti-tank mortar and blocked the bridge for days.

'They're not around here, they must have made it.' Bill laughed. 'What's the betting they have found a piano somewhere and are knocking out a few old favourites.'

Sammy nodded. 'No takers. Can you believe their signature tune is "Ain't Misbehaving"? Crazy pair of bastards.' He looked towards the house. 'How's the girl?'

'Terrified.'

'Poor little bitch. What about you?'

'Me?'

'Well, you hung your hat out, didn't you. I have to say you picked a bloody funny time and place to have a love affair.'

'I didn't have a love affair, Sammy. Christ, she's only sixteen. But she did stop me going crazy.' He gazed at Druschke, still clinging desperately to her mother. He snorted loudly, swallowing the salty mucus. 'Who knows, Sammy. Another time, another place?' He appeared to rally. 'Doctor Doorn says Jerry will be here in about an hour.'

Sammy looked at him sharply. 'How does he know that?'

'He biked over to talk to them about the wounded.' He shook his head and sighed. 'We might have a small problem. It's the Waffen-SS and you know what bastards they can be. They don't like us, Sammy, not one little bit.'

'The feeling's mutual. What about the Panzers?'

'SS too. Well, one of the divisions is.'

'Jesus Christ! So it ain't over yet.'

'Right, although the Falschirms might be friendlier.' Sammy scowled. 'Look, I said might.'

The young SS officer walked across the garden and stopped before them. 'Who is in command here?' His English was heavily accented but otherwise good.

Sammy stood to face him. He looked straight at the man with ill-disguised contempt. 'Stanley Adam Malcolm Parker. Captain, 14435175, 2nd Battalion. The Parachute Regiment.'

'Sir!'

'What?' Sammy looked at him.

'You have to call me Sir.'

'I don't have to call you anything, chum,' Sammy growled at him. 'You do not hold a rank which is recognised by any convention. Furthermore you belong to an internationally defined criminal organisation. Now, I have over three hundred dead to be buried and some sixty wounded to be taken care of, so stop fucking about and bring me to an officer of the Wehrmacht that I may formally surrender my men.'

'You will surrender to me.'

'Not a bloody chance, mate,' Sammy said adamantly. 'I'm not handing my blokes over to a bunch of criminal psychopaths.'

'You wish to resume the fighting?' the German asked contemptuously.

Sammy stared at him. 'Do you?'

The German smiled. 'Be very careful, Captain, remember you lost this fight and you are now a prisoner of war.'

'And as such, I and my men are formally protected by the terms of the Geneva Convention.'

The officer seemed unsure how to deal with Sammy. He looked at him for some moments then, turning on his heel, called to one of his men. 'Scharführer Netzkau.' The NCO ran over. The two men spoke quickly and then made off together.

'You were taking a bit of a chance there, Sammy.' Bill smiled at his friend. 'I thought any minute the bastard was going to draw his Luger and shoot you.'

Sammy looked at his friend. 'If I was going to be shot I was going to take that little shit with me. If he had made one move for his holster I would have given his face a nut massage.' He smiled. 'We've got a reputation among these idiots, Bill. They've been told we're some weird breed of murderous villain. It's all bollocks, of course, but if they believe it we have an advantage.'

Bill shook his head. 'You always were a crazy bastard, Sammy Parker. Thank Christ this war's over for us, I feel safer with the bloody SS than you.'

They looked up, attracted by the noise of traffic. The main column had arrived consisting of armoured personnel carriers and infantry in trucks, preceded by a large Mercedes staff car.

To Sammy's relief, the troops were dressed in the familiar uniform of the Falschirmjaeger, not SS. The car came to a noisy halt on the gravel path and an elderly officer climbed out. Sammy saw the stripe running down the man's trousers indicating an officer of General rank. He looked at Sammy, unsmiling, then nodded. Sammy stood to attention and saluted. 'Captain Parker, Parachute Regiment, Sir. I am the senior British officer present. My unit has withdrawn and I have elected to remain with our dead and the sick and wounded, along with my platoon sergeant and ten medical orderlies.' The general still did not respond but looked directly at Sammy who gave a slight frown. 'Ich bitte Sie um Entschuldigung, Herr General, Sie haben vielleicht kein Englisch. Ich bin Kapitän Parker...'

The general smiled and held up his hand to stop Sammy. 'Thank you, Captain, that will not be necessary.' He looked around at the scene. 'How many dead and wounded do you have?'

'About four hundred and fifty, Sir. In accordance with convention, I surrender myself to you together with all the men under my command. We are unarmed, all our weapons have been stacked and are now under guard and at your disposal.'

'Thank you, Captain. Do you have any other effectives apart from you and your medical staff?'

'No Sir.'

'Very well.' He turned to his adjutant and speaking softly gave him a series of orders.

'Jawohl, sofort Herr General.' The officer made off in the direction of the column.

The general looked at Sammy then extended his hand. Sammy took it uncertainly and felt the general shake his hand with a firm grip. 'Oberst General Rudolf Wissig, Commander 3rd Briagde, Hermann Goering Parachute Division. You had bad luck, Captain, finding us here.' He smiled. 'You should have come three weeks earlier, we were still in Russia. We came here to rest, you know, and you made us fight. That was most inconsiderate of you.'

Sammy returned his smile. 'My apologies, General, a small matter of faulty intelligence.'

The general nodded. 'I have asked my adjutant to arrange a burial party for your dead. We cannot have brave comrades lying unburied. My chaplain will hold a short service, unless you have any objection.'

'None, Sir. You are by contrast most considerate.'

'Good.' He smiled. 'Now, as far as your casualties are concerned, they will be handed over to our medical people. They will receive good treatment.'

'Thank you, Sir.'

'As for you, Captain, I fear I must hand you and your effectives over to the Kriegsgefangen Abteilung. Your war is now over. It has been an honour to meet you, good luck.'

'Thank you, Sir, but do you intend handing us over to the SS?'

The general fixed Sammy with a cold stare. 'Why?'

'Because, Sir, they have a Führerbefehl to shoot us.'

He looked steadily at Sammy. 'The German Army does not shoot its prisoners, Captain.'

'I know the German Army doesn't, General, I'm talking about the SS.'

'You have my word, Captain, you will not be harmed.' He turned on his heel and walked to his car.

In accordance with the general's instructions the seriously injured were driven away in ambulances, while the remainder, including those with minor superficial wounds, were left to the care of the regimental medics. They waited in the hot September sun, without food, water or adequate medication, in increasing distress.

Bill approached his friend. 'We've got to do something, Sammy. These SS bastards are doing this deliberately. I'm going to see if I can get some water from the kitchen. They've got the arsehole because that para general gave that little SS prick a bollocking.'

Sammy smiled. 'You have a rare gift for scatological medley, Sergeant. OK, if you have any trouble let me know.'

Bill walked toward the house and entered the kitchen by the back door. Several SS troopers were sitting at the large wooden table with the remains of a meal strewn before them. He saw Drushke standing by the sink looking terrified. He crossed the room and smiled at the girl. 'Can you give me a bucket of water, love? My men are parched.'

The girl looked at him and began to cry. 'Oh Tommy, what are they going to do? Are they going to shoot you?'

'No, of course not. Now stop it, don't let them see you cry. Get me a bucket, there's a good girl.' She went into the scullery to fetch the pail.

One of the troopers rose and approached Bill. He looked at him quizzically. 'Was machen Sie hier?'

Bill smiled at the man. 'Sorry mate, no sprecken zee doich.' Drushke returned with the bucket and gave it to him. 'Ta, love.' He began to fill it at the sink.

The trooper grabbed at the bucket and turned off the tap. 'Nein, kein Wasser.' He pushed Bill roughly away from the sink. 'Raus! Kein Wasser.'

Bill wrenched the bucket from the man. 'Leave go, you bastard. I've sick men out there, dying of bloody thirst and I'm going to get them some water if it's the last thing I do, so piss off.' He pushed the trooper violently and he staggered back against the table. He charged at Bill, his face distorted with anger. Bill lifted the bucket threateningly. The other troopers rushed forward and grabbed him. They punched and kicked him and then threw him bodily out of the house. He landed in a heap in the garden. Sammy ran over to assist him.

'Still getting chucked out of bars, Sergeant?'

Bill stood up, wiping the blood from his mouth. 'Those bastards,' he said through clenched teeth. 'What the fuck's the matter with them? I only wanted some water, for crisake.'

Sammy strode towards the kitchen. 'Follow me, Sergeant.' The two men entered the room and the troopers looked at them in amazement. Sammy picked up the bucket and pushed it violently at one of the troopers.

'Hohlen Sie mir Wasser, sofort,' he barked. The man leapt to his feet in confusion.

The senior trooper rose and approached Sammy. He looked at him, eyes narrowing. 'Sind Sie verückt?' he asked, incredulous.

Sammy smiled at the man. 'Es ist doch möglich, ich bin Fallschirmjäger.'

The man continued to stare at Sammy for some moments then he began to laugh loudly. He handed Bill the bucket and waved toward the sink. 'Hohl. Wasser wenn Sie muss.' Still laughing, he turned to his comrades, cocking his thumb toward Sammy. 'Er trinkt kein Wasser, das ist doch klar.'

The sergeant filled the bucket and the two paratroopers left the house. Bill looked at his friend. 'What was all that about?'

Sammy laughed. 'Well, I ordered the first ape to fetch some water, then Corporal Shithead asked me if I was mad and I said yes, it's possible, I'm a paratrooper, which seemed to tickle him, then he told his mates he thought I must be pissed.'

Bill shook his head. 'And he wasn't far out, was he? Jesus Christ, Sammy.'

Forced to stand for hours in the sun surrounded by heavily

armed troopers, the ragged, limping column was finally marched away from the small iron bridge for which they had struggled for nine long, blood-soaked days, to the train station in Arnhem. There they were loaded into cattle trucks and hauled off into captivity. They were taken to Celle, a small town north-east of the city of Hanover. The journey of some three hundred kilometres took three days, during which time neither food nor water was provided to the prisoners. Sammy lay on the floor of the truck and tried to suck clean air through a gap round the door. He felt the train slow, then heard the engine whistle. The brakes screeched and the train shuddered and ground reluctantly to a halt. He heard shouting and the barking of dogs. When the doors were finally thrown back, the smell of blood, sweat, vomit and ordure was overpowering. The guards fell back in disgust. Sammy screwed his eyes up for some moments in the glare of sunlight then jumped from the truck. He looked around and spotted the same young SS officer standing back viewing the spectacle before him, his face betraying his disgust. Sammy approached him.

'Remember me, Captain Parker, the senior officer of these prisoners of war?' The German officer did not respond. 'My men have been treated abominably by these SS guttersnipes. They have been locked in cattle trucks for three days without food or water or any opportunity to relieve themselves. Many of them are wounded and some have died. The actions of your men is an outrage and in direct contravention of the Geneva protocols. I demand you take immediate action to relieve my men and to discipline that rabble. I also wish to know your name and rank as I intend to make a formal complaint to the International Red Cross about this atrocity.' Throughout this tirade, the German still did not move. He fixed Sammy with a cold stare for some moments then his mouth twisted into a contemptuous grin. Bill watched this exchange from the platform and although he could not understand what Sammy was saying, the manner of his saying it left him in no doubt about the general drift.

'That mad bastard's off again,' he said to the medics. 'I'd better get over to him, just in case.' He started to move toward Sammy.

The German nodded in the direction of the train and waved his hand dismissively. 'Get back to your men, Captain,' he sneered, 'you smell like a pile of shit.'

Sammy's eyes narrowed. 'Don't speak to me like that, you dung-brained little bastard,' he spat. 'I asked you for your name and rank, that is my right. Now do as I ask and bring me to your superior at once.' The officer turned, his face distorted with rage. He began to unclip his holster. Despite exhaustion and general debility, Sammy's reflexes were like lightning. He rushed the officer, head down, driving him back against the wall. Bill heard the man groan as the air was driven from his body. In what seemed like a single movement Sammy straightened up, crashing his head into the jaw of the officer and driving his knee into his stomach. The man dropped like a sack. As Bill ran forward he heard the clicking of rifle bolts. Fully expecting to be shot in the back, he turned quickly. He stood in front of Sammy, facing the onrushing troopers. As they pulled him roughly aside, one of them hit Sammy in the face with his rifle butt. He fell, unconscious on top of the SS officer. The troopers were kicking Sammy and shouting excitedly but he could not follow what they were saying. He looked down at his stricken friend and watched helplessly as his blood spread darkly across the grey jacket of the unconscious SS man. As he was dragged away by the troopers, Bill Grant feared he would never see his friend alive again.

CHAPTER TWO

As he dragged slowly back to consciousness, Sammy felt the cold from the stone floor eat into his bones, filling his every move with pain. It was pitch dark, he felt gut sick, disorientated, his head raged, pressing more pain into his face and he tasted blood. He tried to lick his swollen lips but his parched tongue had thickened. Pulling himself to a sitting position he tried to wipe his nose and mouth. 'Argh, shit.' He winced with pain as his hand touched his puffed and lacerated face. He began gingerly to explore it with his fingertips. His nose seemed to have burst and he moved his head painfully, moaning at the swell of pain rising from his bruised and battered body. As his eyes gradually adjusted to the gloom, he became aware of a dim relief to the darkness reflected through a fanlight high above him and hauling himself slowly to his feet, he made towards it. After only a few steps his shins barked against a hard object and he cried out again. He reached down, feeling for the obstruction and found he stood beside a low cot. He turned dizzily to sit but fell backwards onto the bed. 'Well, Sammy my son,' he croaked hoarsely, 'you're really in the shit this time, you're in the choky and any minute now they'll be along to ask what you would like for your last meal.' He began to chuckle, softly at first, but his laughter grew louder until it became hysterical. The door burst open, streaming light into the room. He lifted his hand to shield his eyes and peered through his fingers at the approaching shadows. He felt himself grabbed roughly by the arms and hauled from the room.

He stood unsteadily, flanked by two guards. An officer, whose rank he was unable to determine, sat gazing up at him, his elbows propped on a large wooden desk, his chin resting on his clasped hands. He regarded Sammy pensively for a few moments. 'What is your name?' he asked softly.

'Cabtain Barga...Barachoo...Bara.' Sammy mumbled through swollen lips, trying painfully to swallow.

There was a ripple of laughter which the officer quelled with an icy look. He pointed quickly to the side of the room and then to Sammy. One of the guards brought a chair and, grabbing Sammy roughly, pushed him down into it. The officer poured water into a glass and handed it to Sammy who swallowed the contents greedily in one long draught. 'Noch ein.' He proffered the glass and the officer refilled it.

The German waited until he had gulped the second glass. He sighed heavily. 'I am Hauptstürmführer Alfried Gräber, Commandant of Konzentrationslager Matthausen. The rest of your men are now in Stalag Wälle, but you have been sent to me for disposal and I must decide what to do with you.' He paused, looking at Sammy. 'Why did you attack a German officer?'

Sammy felt much refreshed by the water and his voice returned stronger, more confident. 'What do you mean disposal? Where am I?'

'I have already told you, you are in camp Matthausen. Now answer my question.'

'Is this a prisoner of war camp?'

'No.'

'Then why am I here?'

'Because you attacked a German officer.'

'I didn't attack him. It was self-defence.'

'Explain.'

'I formally surrendered my men to a parachute general at Arnhem. We were then delivered into the hands of the SS who locked us up like cattle on a train which took three days to reach its destination, during which time my men, most of whom were wounded, received neither food, water nor medical assistance. Three of them died. I complained to the officer at the station about this atrocity, pointing out it was contrary to the Geneva Convention and he pulled a gun on me. I had been made aware that the SS had a Führerbefehl to shoot all paratroopers, so I hit him...in self-defence.'

Gräber sighed again, shaking his head. 'You hit him,' he repeated, his voice tinged with sarcasm.

'Yes.'

'Yes, Sir,' Gräber demanded.

'Bollocks.' Sammy tried to smile, his mouth smarting painfully. 'I'm not sure of the exact translation...Hoden vielleicht?'

A guard made to strike Sammy but Gräber lifted his hand to stop him. He slowly shook his head, smiling. 'You are a very arrogant man, Captain, which is perhaps unwise given your situation. I suppose you are going to tell us next that you too are a personal friend of Churchill.' His men joined his laughter.

'No, but I do know Sarah quite well,' Sammy said nonchalantly, unsure whether they would grasp the significance of the remark.

'Who is Sarah?' Gräber asked, turning to his officers.

'I believe she is his daughter,' one of them whispered to him.

He looked at Sammy, his eyes narrowing. Sammy shrugged. 'So how do you know this Sarah quite well?'

'We were at Cambridge together, before the war.'

'So!' Gräber nodded. 'Oxford and Cambridge...Oxbridge... the breeding ground of the English upper classes, eh Captain?' Sammy gave another shrug. Gräber returned to his notes. 'Are you aware...er...Captain Parker, who was at Cambridge with Churchill's daughter, that the good Oberstürmführer Held is at present in hospital with severe concussion, a ruptured spleen and a fractured jaw? You didn't hit him, you almost killed him.' Sammy did not reply. He looked at Gräber. The man had the familiar double ess flashes on his jacket collar, but he was no Aryan superman. He was dark, swarthy and slovenly overweight. He appeared apathetic, tired, as though the effort was all too much. Finally he stood and rounded the desk. He sat on the desk top in front of Sammy, his legs dangling. He stared into his face. Sammy noticed his eyes were dull, his pupils dilated. He thought he was probably drunk, he could not detect alcohol but thought he smelt garlic. 'The state my nose is in right now, I doubt I could smell hot pig shit,' he thought.

'Your face is a mess.' Gräber spoke quietly, emitting another weary sigh.

'Well it would be, wouldn't it?' said Sammy. 'Somebody drove the butt of his rifle into it and then these heroes,' he cocked his thumb backwards, 'kicked the shit out of me.'

Gräber smiled. 'They could have shot you.'

'No they couldn't.'

'Why not?' Gräber frowned.

'For one thing, it's against the Geneva Convention and for another there is the order of a general expressly forbidding it.'

'Which general?'

'Oberst-General Wissig, of the Falschirmjaeger Division.'

'The Wehrmacht has no jurisdiction here,' Gräber said dismissively, 'and whilst we are on the subject, it is also against the Geneva Convention for a prisoner of war to attack an officer.' Again, the tired smile.

'And for an officer to attempt to shoot an unarmed prisoner.'

He touched Sammy's arm in what was almost a friendly gesture. 'Also. Wir haben einer Stillstand. It is what the Ami's call a Mexican stand-off,' he added smiling, switching to poorly enunciated English. He paused and stared at Sammy. 'We must get your face looked at. Your nose is broken, I think. Do you object to being treated by a Jew?'

'What?'

Gräber laughed. He turned to the guards and issued a series of instructions. One of the guards replied rapidly in a dialect Sammy found difficult to follow. They lifted Sammy by the arms again and dragged him from the room.

He was taken to a clean, well-equipped first aid room and handed over to the medical officer. The guards then left. The German looked at Sammy and gently touched his swollen face. 'Sprechen Sie Deutsch?' he asked.

'Ja, aber nicht Seine Mündart,' Sammy replied, nodding toward the retreating guard.

The man laughed. 'I didn't understand him either, he's probably a Lithuanian or one of those Ukranian swine. Now, let's have a look at this.' He pressed gently at the contusions around Sammy's eyes and nose. Sammy winced with the pain several times. 'It probably looks worse than it is, although I think your nose is broken and there is not much I can do about that. When the swelling goes down and you've lost those two shiners you'll look like a prize fighter. I'll get the Jew doctor to set your nose and give you the once over to see if those lunatics have broken anything else.' He crossed the room and opened a connecting door. 'Jude, komm' hier, schnell!' he called gruffly. An elderly man entered. Of medium height, grey hair, very thin, he walked with a slight stoop. He wore a black and white striped twill suit comprising a loose tunic buttoned to the neck, baggy trousers and a round mop cap made of the same material. He looked at Sammy through dull rheumy eyes. He did not smile or appear to express any emotion. 'This is a British prisoner of war,' said the officer, 'he has been "wounded".' He shrugged, shaking his head. 'He has a broken nose which I want you to set and I want you to examine him for any other injuries he may have suffered. He speaks German so he will understand what you say to him.'

The old man worked quickly and expertly, apologising quietly whenever Sammy winced. Finally, when Sammy's nose was set, dressed and strapped with sticking plaster, he took his instruments to the sink and began to clean them.

The medical officer inspected the work, nodding approvingly. 'You wait there,' he said, 'I won't be long.' He left the room.

The old doctor put the instruments away in the cupboard and returned to Sammy. 'Now, let's have a look at you. I take it you have already met the reception committee?' He examined Sammy thoroughly and tested his reflexes. He nodded. 'I've seen worse but there is still a lot of water in the tissue and you will hurt like hell for a few days, my son,' he said. 'I shall ask the Oberleutnant to give you some aspirin. I'm sure he will agree, he is not a proper doctor you see, he is an osteopath, from Hamburg by the sound of him, but he relies on me.' He shrugged. 'It's the best I can do. They have morphine here but it is terribly addictive so I would not recommend it.' He sighed and nodded toward the window. 'They use most of it themselves, anyway. Die Rauschgiftsüchtigen,' he added.

Sammy looked at the man. 'So, you are the doctor. How come you have to ask permission of this bone-bender to prescribe medicine?'

The man smiled sadly. 'The world is different here, my son. Sort of topsy-turvy, as you will see.'

'What is this place?' Sammy asked.

'Don't ask.' He looked around furtively.

'Why are you wearing those clothes? Is that regulation dress for medical staff?'

'No, I am an inmate, a guest of the Führer.' The doctor's wheezy laugh gave way to a fit of coughing.

Sammy waited for him to recover. 'This is a prison?' he asked, amazed.

'In a way, except you never get out.'

'You mean you're all serving life sentences?'

'No my son, we are all serving death sentences.'

'Jesus Christ!' Sammy shook his head. 'What kind of a bloody place have they sent me to? What did you all do, for Christ's sake, mass murder?'

'What is your name, Englander?'

'What? Oh...Sammy...Sammy Parker.'

'Well, as I said, Sammy Parker, this place is topsy-turvy. You see, here we get locked up and they do the mass murder.'

'What do you mean?' Sammy asked, frowning. The doctor crossed to the window and beckoned Sammy to follow. He pointed to a high wire fence, away across the compound, beyond which were rows and rows of low wooden buildings which seemed to stretch to the horizon. As he stared at the barracks, a vague gleam shone through the fog, high in the sky, capped by a pall of black smoke. Now that his nasal airways had been cleared, he became aware of a nauseating odour which hung in the air, different from the stagnant smell of ordure. 'What do they do in there?' he asked. 'Is it some kind of factory?'

The doctor looked around nervously again. 'Look, he'll be back in a minute, if he finds me talking to you about the camp...well...' He paused. '...and he's not SS, he's one of the nicer ones.' Hearing the officer's voice he immediately scuttled into the back room.

The Oberleutnant entered the room, smiling at Sammy. 'Well, Englander, I have saved your neck, you have been assigned to me as a nurse. I don't suppose you have any experience?' he inquired hopefully.

Sammy looked at the man. 'Sorry, chum, no bedside manner, but I was a scientist.'

'Oh!' The man brightened. 'And what science was that?'

'Biochemistry, genetics.'

'That's just great, so you'll know how to keep a laboratory clean, won't you?'

'Which laboratory?'

'This one.' He laughed. 'You can assist Rhadski.'

'Who's Rhadski?'

'The old man who fixed you up. By the way, where is he?'

Sammy nodded toward the door. 'He went in there, I haven't seen him since.'

The officer looked at Sammy then asked, 'What's your name?'

'Captain Parker, Parachute Regiment.'

'Don't you have a forename?'

'I have three, but my friends call me Sammy.'

The man smiled wryly at him. 'Well, Sammy,' he said sarcastically, 'you can skip all that captain of the Parachute Regiment shit, you're just another prisoner here and as long as you keep your trap shut and do as you are told, you'll be fine, OK?'

'And what do I call you?' Sammy's face was expressionless.

The officer frowned slightly. 'I am Oberleutnant Müntzig of the Heeres Gesundheitsdienst. At all times you will call me Sir.'

Sammy stared at him. He realised that with his face swollen and black and blue from his beating and his nose covered with sticking plaster he must cut something of a comic figure but he adopted his most menacing tone. 'Now you just listen to me,

Ober-bloody-Leutnant Müntzig, my rank is captain, which is superior to yours, so you will call me Sir, alright? I am a bona fide prisoner of war protected by the Geneva Convention and as an officer I am not required to work at all. However, though I personally prefer to be occupied, I am not prepared to be treated like a piece of shit by some half-arsed Platt-Deutsche Chiropractor in the bloody Army Medical Corps.' He smiled at the shocked officer. 'Now, as this war is nearly over and as my side is going to win, why don't you be sensible and be nice to me? You can start by telling me your name, because I'm buggered if I am going to dislocate my jaw with Oberleutnant bloody Müntzig all day.'

Like most non combatants, the Oberleutnant was easily intimidated by front line soldiers and he was terrified of the SS, under whom he was forced to serve. He had also been encouraged to believe all British paratroopers were quite literally homicidal and the behaviour of this particular specimen did little to disabuse him. He tried to maintain his composure. 'Look, Captain, please don't try and play the hard man, not here. This is no ordinary prison camp. They send people here to be killed and they almost killed you, didn't they? I still can't understand why Gräber didn't just shoot you, after all he kills some poor wretch almost every day, but he didn't, so count your blessings.'

'He thinks I am playing bumsen with Churchill's daughter.'

'What?' Müntzig gave a short nervous laugh.

Sammy laughed. 'I'm kidding. He just likes me, what can I say?'

Müntzig looked pleadingly at Sammy. 'Listen, Captain, I'm not a fool, I know Germany is finished, but don't you see? That's the problem. These SS are all crazy. When the end comes they'll kill everyone, not just the bloody yids. So for God's sake, Sir, don't make a fuss about your rights, this lot doesn't give a shit about the Geneva Convention.'

'You still didn't tell me your name.' Sammy stared at him, unblinking.

'It's Müntzig, I mean...it's Karl.'

Sammy smiled and put his arm round the man. 'Charlie boy, I think we are going to need each other if we are to survive this lunacy. Now tell me, what the fuck is going on here?'

In the weeks that followed, Sammy was to learn much about the camp, that Matthausen was a Vernichtungslager, an extermination camp. That thousands of people, mostly Jews, were herded into large hermetic chambers and gassed with Zyclon B, a derivative of a cyanide-based insecticide. Believing they were simply taking a shower, they were processed, by what Karl called Vernichtungswissenschaften, scientific annihilation. That there were also other so-called enemies of the state, socialists, communists, gypsies, Jehovahs Witnesses, mongols and other mental retards, homosexuals, criminal recidivists, anyone in fact whose life was adjudged to be of no value to the Reich. He was kept in the headquarters block, a sector separated from the main camp by a high electrified barbed wire fence. The small medical facility in which he was put to work catered only for the military and SS personnel and a number of men and women from the main camp who appeared to enjoy certain privileges. These individuals did not wear the striped 'pyjamas' of the inmates, but black tunics and trousers, both men and women. They were Kapos, or trusties, a particularly nasty variant of the slave driver. There were others, such as Doctor Rhadski who, although dressed as inmates, were employed in the central compound because of their special professional skills. They were, however, all returned to the main camp at night. He was surprised to learn that the doctor was not a Jew, but a respectable GP from Heidelberg whose only 'crime' was his friendship with a certain dissident German pastor suspected of being implicated in the notorious 'July' plot to assassinate Hitler.

His attention was also drawn to one particular woman inmate who appeared to spend her time in the camp commandant's quarters. She sometimes came to the dispensary to collect aspirins, cough mixture and other medications. She rarely spoke, simply handing Karl a note or requisition signed by Gräber, waiting, head bowed, while he filled the prescription. That she was an inmate was clear from the identity number tattooed on her arm, but she appeared better fed than the rest and wore pretty dresses. She was dark with the light olive complexion common to many Ashkenazim, tall and full figured, with broad hips which swayed seductively as she walked. Her jet-black hair hung below her shoulders in long tresses, unlike the quarter-inch crop of the other inmates.

'Who is that woman, Karl?'

The doctor smiled. 'That is the gorgeous Noami, she's quite a performer by all accounts.'

'Performer? What do you mean performer? She looks scared to death.'

'Officially she's Gräber's Putzfrau, but she does a little more than just the dishes and she certainly does more in the bedroom than turn back the sheets.'

'You mean she screws for him?'

'Of course. Nobody's sure if he is married or not, he doesn't keep a wife here, that's for sure. Rumour has it he fucks Gisele Höchst from time to time, but Naomi is his current Geliebte.'

'But she is a prisoner.'

'Sure she is. She came here from the east, Poland I think, with her man and a couple of girls. They are dead now, of course. She survived by moving in with his nibs.'

'Christ almighty! He murders her husband and kids and now he's fucking her. Some master race, you lot, aren't you. What happened to all that racial purity shit?'

'It's shit! Listen, if you could stick your old man into that would you worry about racial purity? She's not the first either, he's had a couple before her, he picks out the pretty ones, but she's the best looker so far.'

'So what happened to the others?'

'They went for a shower. He got fed up with them, I suppose, or something tastier turned up, like Naomi.' He began to laugh.

'But how does she relate to the other inmates?' Sammy asked. 'Isn't she ostracised for fraternising with that bastard?'

'She's not fraternising, Captain, she's simply staying out of the shower...and she is able to bring things to the others from time to time, bits of food, clothing, that sort of thing. She has no choice, it's fuck or die.'

'You mean he gives her stuff to take back to her friends in the camp?'

Karl laughed. 'Gräber? Are you serious? No, she shares her favours a bit, you know, people like me and a couple of the Kapos.'

'You mean you have used this woman?' Sammy was unable to disguise his utter contempt.

'I gave her some penicillin once. There had been an outbreak of clap in the compound and one of her friends had become infected. VD is a death sentence here. She was...well...willing to pay.'

'What would happen to her if she became pregnant?'

'Curtains. But she's OK, she can't have kids.'

'Why?'

'She just can't, she's had the Mengele treatment.'

'Mengele?...What?'

'Mengele...Der Weisse Engel...he's the camp surgeon at Auschwitz.'

'Auschwitz?...Where the f...you mean they sterilised the poor bitch?'

'Well, there's not much point...you know...' Karl began to look shamefaced under Sammy's contemptuous stare.

'How can you behave like these bastards?...What the fuck's wrong with you?' Sammy demanded reprovingly. Karl shrugged and walked out of the dispensary.

Sammy and Doctor Rhadski worked together in the small storeroom sterilising the instruments, grateful for the opportunity to huddle close to the hot water boiler. The cold northerly winds now sweeping down across the north German plain brought the first flurries of fine dry snow which blew like salt across the compound, driven by the icy gusts. They had listened stoically to the news on their illicit radio, that a German offensive had smashed the American front in the Ardennes and halted the Allied advance, adding perhaps a further six months to the war and as Christmas approached Sammy wondered how much longer he could sustain himself in these conditions. His health had suffered from the effects of the cold and poor diet and Karl had allowed him to move his bunk into the dispensary to spare him the nightly ordeal of shivering, sleepless in his freezing cell. Yet compared to the inmates of the main camp he knew he was living in comparative luxury. He looked at the doctor. His eyes gazed hopelessly out of a cadaverous face and his breathing became ever more strained. Sammy tried to share his meagre rations with him but he invariably declined.

'It is important that you survive, my son.' He wheezed painfully. 'You must live to tell them about this place and what they did. Good Germans must know and understand what has been done in their name.'

'But if you don't eat you will die and that is foolish. The war will soon be over, Germany will need men like you.'

The old man smiled. 'I am dying already, it would be foolish of me to take food from you and put you at risk.'

'You are being foolish and stubborn,' said Sammy. 'You're not dying, you are killing yourself.'

'You are a good man, Sammy. You remind me of some English friends I had before the war, good people. Our two sons were as close as brothers.'

'You were in England?'

'I have visited England, of course, but no, these were doctors from London whom I met at the university in Heidelberg. We were post-grads there. I fell in love with the woman. We were lovers for a while, until her Englander arrived.' He shrugged and gave his wheezy laugh.

Sammy touched his arm. 'You will see them again, Rudi, I promise, but you must eat.'

The old man looked at Sammy affectionately. 'No Sammy, I shall not survive the winter. I have TB.'

Sammy looked at him sadly. 'How can you be so sure?'

'I'm a doctor, for God's sake, but it's rife in the camp, and there is dysentery and pneumonia. The consequence of all this good living, I guess.' He tried to laugh again. 'You know it's ironic, but the gas chambers are a merciful release for most of us.' Sammy looked away, chastened by the old man's suffering.

The klaxon sounded for the evening roll call. Sammy gazed through the window of the dispensary at the shivering prisoners huddled together in groups on the arctic Appellplatz. He knew the SS guards would keep them there until they almost froze, before returning them to the main camp for the night. He saw Rudi, his hands tucked under his folded arms, coughing into the icy wind and as he watched he felt the bitter tears of frustration running down his face. He turned wearily and slumped into a chair. He felt crushed by despair at his impotence in the face of such infamy. Suddenly the door burst open to admit two SS guards.

'Komm, Englander, on your feet, the boss wants to see you, now.'

'What for, what does he want?'

'You don't ask the questions here, you piece of shit, you just do as you are told. Now move it, nobody keeps Gräber waiting.'

He was taken under escort to the commandant's office. He wondered what he had done. Perhaps Gräber had discovered he was sleeping in the dispensary instead of freezing in his cell. He determined to brazen it out.

Gräber pointed to a chair. 'Setzen Sie sich.' He looked at Sammy, his cold shark's eyes expressionless. 'Do you know what today is, Captain Parker?'

Sammy held his gaze. 'No, and why should I care?'

Still unsmiling, Gräber said, 'It is Weihnacht, Das Christfest, the last of the war.'

Sammy smiled broadly then said softly, 'Geronimo.'

'What did you say?'

'It doesn't matter.'

Gräber smiled. 'You don't understand, my friend, the Wehrmacht will be in Antwerp within the week. Von Ründstedt's Panzers have smashed through the American lines in the Ardennes, the allies are in full retreat and our secret V weapons are levelling Paris, Brussels and London to the ground as we speak.' He rose and walked to a large wall cabinet. He lifted a large stone flask and poured thick yellow Korn schnapps into two glasses and offered one to Sammy.

He raised his glass. 'Sieg Heil. To victory.'

Sammy smiled. 'I'll drink to that.'

Gräber laughed aloud. 'Come, my friend, let us go and eat.'

'Eat?' Sammy echoed with some surprise and followed as the SS man made off into a connecting room.

Several SS officers were standing round a table laden with a dazzling variety of delicacies looted from the occupied countries. Polish ham, Norwegian herring, smoked salmon and pâté de foie gras from France, lobster and langoustine and Viennese pastries. Sammy's gaze fell upon a woman dressed in the uniform of the SS. It was clear she had been beautiful once. Her thick blonde hair framed a finely boned face which was now growing plump. She had a dissolute appearance, her expression vacant. He thought she was probably drunk. 'Be careful, Liebchen,' Gräber laughed, 'I think our guest fancies you.' Turning to Sammy he said, 'Allow me to introduce my adjutant, Leutnant Höchst, but watch yourself Captain, die schöne Gisele eats men like you for breakfast, don't you, meine Süss?' He bent to kiss her. She gazed up at Sammy, leering stupidly. 'Meine Kameraden!' Gräber addressed the gathering. 'It is Christmas, the last of this war, for Germany is on its way to final victory. So in the spirit of magnanimity to a gallant enemy, I have invited our gallant British Bulldog and...' He tapped his nose with his finger, winking suggestively. '...friend of Churchill's daughter, to celebrate with us.' He paused, grinning. 'Before we return him to his kennel, that is.' They all laughed heartily and sycophantically. 'Come, Captain Parker, eat.'

Sammy looked at the assembled company. They stood around, arrogant, loud and contemptuously self-assured in their leather and steel. He looked at the repast laid out before them and thought of the conditions barely a kilometre away in the compound. The cold, the hunger, the disease, the hopelessness and the assurance of a painful, unjust and premature death at the hands of these philistines. He turned his gaze finally to Gräber. Slowly and deliberately he turned his glass over, causing the yellow liquor to patter noisily onto the carpet. 'I don't think I care to,' he hissed. 'It is enough that I have to witness your sickening barbarities every day, listen to the cries of children and see the hopelessness in the faces of their elders as they try to ease what's left of their short miserable lives, to watch the casual beatings and murder of people who have done no more than try to survive this hell. What I will not do is share any of this loot with you.' He flicked his hand contemptuously at the assembled officers. 'Or these shitbags.' He placed the glass on the table and wiped his hands on his jacket as though trying to remove all witness of contact with his captors. He scowled at them. 'If I live through this, Gräber, I swear to God I shall see you pay for all you have done here, you bastards. Now, I have no doubt that you will arrange for a couple of your simians to beat the shit out of me before I go to sleep tonight, so let's get it over with, shall we?' He turned and walked from the room.

Gräber shouted after him. 'But I can't have you beaten, Parker. You are protected by the Geneva Convention, remember. And Germany is a civilised country.'

He heard their laughter as he made his way out of the officer's block. Trying to understand why Gräber had not immediately placed him under arrest or had him beaten, he hurried to the dispensary hoping they would not look for him there, but he found the administration block empty. Then faintly, drifting across the icy Appellplatz from the guard's quarters, he heard singing and carousing. He sat on his bunk. 'You're OK, Sammy my son, at least until Boxing Day. They are all having a good old Christmas piss up.'

He smiled and lying back, pulled the thin blanket over himself. The fire had died in the stove and he knew he would not be able to fetch more fuel until morning. As he lay, weary from hunger, he felt the cold gradually begin to eat into his limbs and he wondered how much more he could take. He drifted into a fitful sleep, waking to rub the hurt from his freezing feet. As he drifted back into sleep he felt the warmth gradually spread through him and he felt a weight against him. He wanted to turn over but could not move. He tried to sit up but felt himself pushed back.

'Shush Liebling, ruhe.' The woman kissed him softly upon the lips and began to caress his face.

'Who are you? What do you want?' he whispered.

'I am Naomi. I have come to wish you a merry Christmas.' She began to unbutton his jacket and she pushed her hand into his shirt. He twisted free of her and jumped up, switching on the light. She sat on the bunk eyeing him defiantly then she winked coquettishly and beckoned him with her forefinger.

'Good God, woman,' he cried. 'Do you want to get us shot? If Gräber finds us here together like this we'll be right in the shit.'

She threw back her head and began to laugh. 'I am a Jewess in a German concentration camp and he says I will be in the shit.' She regarded him, her eyes wide and curious. 'Now how much more shit do you think I can get into, Ivan? Anyway...' She winked saucily, cocking her head toward the door. '...there's no need to worry about him, he couldn't get it up if he tried, he's already paralytic.' Her coarseness surprised Sammy. She laughed as she pulled him down to sit beside her upon the bunk. She still held his hands and he smiled back at her.

'Why have you come here tonight, Naomi? What is it you really want? And who the hell is Ivan?' She dropped her head, clasping her hands together in her lap. He thought at first she was engaging in some act of demure, kittenish foreplay, but then he saw the tears begin to fall onto her hands. Placing his arm around her shoulders, he pulled her to him and she clung desperately, leaning into him. Her crying became more agonised and intense and he clasped her firmly as she sobbed against his chest. He kissed her upon the forehead and crossed the room to fetch a towel. He gently wiped her eyes and as he looked into the sad, battered prettiness of her face, he saw the effects her suffering had wrought. Her skin betrayed the effects of poor diet and was further roughened by hard water and ersatz soap. Deep lines accentuated her mouth lending her full lips a sensual prominence and she had small crow's feet around her eyes. Her dark, almost black irises accentuated the whiteness of her eyes which revealed a tracery of small blood vessels. She smelt faintly of carbolic. Taking her hands, he said, 'You want to talk, is that it?' She looked up at him, her face drawn and pained. He felt his heart grow heavy as he looked into her desperate, pleading eyes and realised now, this was probably the first real affection she had known since coming to this dreadful place. 'Oh Christ, love,' he said softly. 'What have they done to you?'

She fell against him again, sobbing piteously. He held her tight, stroking her hair until at last her grief subsided. She looked into his face then asked quietly, 'Wie heisst du, Ruski?'

'What?' He smiled. 'I am not a Russian.'

'You are not a Russian soldier?'

'No, I am a British paratrooper. Why do you think I am Russian?'

She smiled sadly. 'You have a red hat.' His hand went instinctively to his head, which was bare. 'I have watched you.' She smiled. 'And I have seen you watching me.' She looked at him for some moments. 'What is your name?'

'My friends call me Sammy.'

She smiled. 'Sammy, that is a happy, friendly name. May I be your friend?'

'I should like that, Naomi, very much.' He brightened. 'So, tell me about yourself.'

He wrapped the thin blanket around them and as she cuddled into him on the hard, narrow bunk, she told him her story.

She was from Dresden, the only daughter of a bookseller who specialised in books on cartography and exploration. Her father, a gentle, introspective man, attracted the attention of the authorities through the reputation of his elder brother Stefan, a prominent left wing political activist who became notorious during the periods of civil unrest during the Weimar Republic, fighting in the streets of Berlin and other German cities, first against the Freikorps and then the Brown Shirts. Following the election of Adolf Hitler's Nationalsozialistische Deutsche Arbeiterpartei as the largest political group in the Reichstag and the murders of Rosa Luxembourg and Karl Leibnitz, Stefan decided to quit the field before he too ended his days in the murky waters of the Spree. He emigrated to the United States with his family and Naomi's family prayed things would settle down. At first Naomi missed her cousin Lotte, to whom she had been very close, until she married David, her childhood sweetheart. She bore him two daughters and soon adapted to life under the Nazis until her family, dispossessed of their property by the anti-Jewish property laws, were arrested and deported to Poland. As the Russians advanced she had been sent West, to various concentration camps. She did not know what had become of her parents or her brother. She finally arrived at Matthausen with her husband and children, but her family was immediately separated by the SS guards. Her husband, sent to work in the Buna synthetic rubber works, died beneath the snow-covered rubble when the RAF razed the factory during one of its huge air raids. Her daughters were taken to the Kinderlager and she never saw them again. She had been forced to give herself to her captor after he had picked her out of the line to become his housemaid. She submitted because she wanted to live.

She related these terrible events quietly, without emotion and when she had finished she turned and looked at Sammy. He touched her face gently and she smiled at him.

He shook his head in disbelief. 'Naomi, how could you bear such pain? How could you see them destroy everything you loved and still allow them to use you this way. How?'

She sat up. 'What else can I do? He will kill me too if I refuse, but I have learned to survive. At first I wanted to live to see the pig punished, but now...' Her head dropped and she hardened her grip on his hand, as if to assuage some terrible, unendurable pain. Wrestling with her agony she spoke softly. '...I had to force myself not to notice what he was doing to me, to somehow put myself beyond the experience.' She looked down at him. 'Sammy, when you have lost everything, your man, your children, your whole family, all the things which made you what you were, you die inside. You look the same, but what you once were is gone, it is no more.' She laid her head back, eyes closed. 'But then it begins again.' She sighed heavily. 'You crave affection. Every touch, every caress, every kiss, every smile is precious, is necessary to you until finally you turn to your tormentor because there is no one else. Like a child terrified by a brutish father, you try to please, not just because you fear his cruelty, but because you need someone, anyone, to like you. In desperation you begin to cherish even the smile on the face of violence. But it is a trick of the mind and when you think you have nothing left to lose, it is then you lose your very soul.' Her head dropped and she sat motionless, staring at her hands. 'It is a strange thing, you know,' she said softly, 'we are all victims of this madness, even them.' She shook her head slowly, as if the thought puzzled her. 'When Gräber forces me to take him, I feel for him, because I can feel his loneliness, his craving to be loved. He needs desperately to be loved, but knows that will never be because the only emotion he is able to inspire is fear. There is a terrible emptiness within him which I am only now beginning to understand. You see, I had always been loved, as a child, as a woman, as a mother, but I do not believe he has ever known love, it is missing from his life and it is this which makes him so brutal. You do not have to be beaten and brutalised yourself to become like that, it is that total absence of love, the denial of feeling which leaves you so completely empty and without compassion. Sometimes I think I shall weep for him, but I know my tears will freeze as they drop.'

'Has he ever hurt you?'

'He struck me only once.' She shook her head slowly. 'It was very strange, I had done nothing wrong, you see. I was in the kitchen preparing his coffee and he came in. He said nothing, just stared at me. I thought I saw him smile then suddenly he hit me across the face so hard I thought I should faint.' She sighed. 'I sometimes wish I had died with my family, but I am afraid of death. I want so much to live.' Her head dropped again and she fell silent.

Naomi's story forced Sammy to confront his own predicament, brought him eye to eye with its sheer hopelessness. Despite his determination never to yield, he felt he was close to the end, had exhausted his own capacity to resist. He cried out angrily at his weakness and in pity for this desperate woman who sought solace from him and had come to him, to lie in his arms. He could no longer contain his anguish or hold back his tears.

She asked quietly, 'Do you think I am a bad woman, Sammy, to accept this instead of death?'

'No, no, no,' he cried desperately. 'These bastards are not going to beat us, Naomi, we will survive this, you and I, and we shall see them all hang.' He pulled her down and hugged her in his despair. 'Oh, dear God!'

She turned to face him. She took his face in her hands and looked into his eyes. 'Sammy, my sweet kind Goyim, you have given me your love this night and asked nothing of me in return. You have grieved for my loss and wept for my suffering. Most of all, you have touched my heart and shown me that I am still able to love and to be loved. I cannot lose that love now. I can

51

not ask you to love me, Sammy, but I do ask that you let me love you so that I shall never again need him. Will you give me that, Sammy? Will you help me to be free and to know joy again, if only for the short time left to me, will you Sammy?'

He took her in his arms. 'Come on, love,' he said softly, kissing her eyes. 'Don't cry any more, there's a good girl. We are going to make it, right?' Her bowed head bobbed slightly. He lifted her face and kissed her cold, roughened lips. She responded passionately and they came together, huddled for warmth throughout the bleak Christmas night.

Soon they became inseparable and in their desperation clung to each other. She showed him her special route through the wire into the main camp. She came to him after curfew and they stole into the compound together, expressing an almost childish exuberance at their defiance. Karl discovered their secret and remonstrated with them, warning them of the terrible consequences they risked. 'Sammy, for God's sake, you'll get us all shot.' He turned to Naomi. 'Sister, talk to him, he's mad. Why risk your lives now you've almost made it?' But they knew only that the joy they brought to each other must be cherished before it was crushed. As winter turned to spring, rumours began to abound and, risking their lives, they listened in to the Voice of Freedom on an illicit makeshift radio. They learned that a huge Allied offensive had thrown the Germans back across the Rhine, that thirty thousand paratroopers had landed behind enemy lines to the east of the great river and that the war was at last drawing to its terrible close. The weather grew warmer and Sammy felt himself recover. He grew confident that he would, after all, survive. Karl seemed more morose by the day yet rather than exult, Sammy expressed regret at his plight and tried to comfort him.

'Karl, I'm sorry mate, not that the war is ending and our side has won, it's just that...well, I know how I would feel if it were me on the losing side and I know how much you lot have suffered. You have simply fought your guts out for a rotten cause, but it will be better for you too in the end.' He nodded toward the window. 'We couldn't allow this to go on, Karl. You must see that. We will hang all these Nazi bastards and then all you decent Germans can pick your lives up again, you'll see.'

Karl grinned wryly. 'Who will decide who is a decent German and who is a Nazi bastard, Sammy?'

'Well, they don't exactly disguise themselves, do they?' Sammy answered. 'Like all bullies they crave attention with their bullshit uniforms, their Totenkopfen, the SS flashes and all the rest of that atavistic bollocks.'

Karl stared at him. 'Don't you know what's going on here, Sammy? Haven't you seen what the bastards are doing?'

Sammy frowned. 'What do you mean?'

'They're getting out, like rats leaving a sinking ship. They are bringing in ordinary troops, poor buggers wounded at the front, and they are drafting them into the SS in droves.' He pointed to the wall where his jacket hung on a peg. 'I'm in the SS now, Sammy. Didn't you even notice?'

Sammy looked at the jacket, incredulous. He saw the infamous double ess on the epaulettes. 'Jesus Christ, Karl. I'm so sorry, I didn't know. But you must tell the Allied troops when they get here.'

Karl looked at him, shaking his head in disbelief. 'And they will believe us? Sammy, they will take one look at this place, shoot us all out of hand then ask the questions.'

'I shall tell them, Karl, I know.'

'And how will you survive, Sammy?'

'Oh, I'll survive, Karl, you can count on it.'

They rushed to the window attracted by the noise. Across the square a group of SS troopers were dragging a woman from Gräber's quarters. She was screaming at them as they beat her. Gräber and Gisele Höchst followed and joined a group of officers waiting in the compound. As the woman was thrown down in front of them, Höchst kicked her viciously and then began to beat her with her leather crop. After some moments Gräber bent down and, grabbing the woman by the hair, dragged her to her feet. Sobbing and bleeding, she looked up at her tormentors. Sammy's heart leapt as he recognised Naomi.

'Those bastards,' he screamed and turning, ran towards the door.

Karl grabbed his arm to restrain him. 'Don't be a fool, Sammy,' he shouted. 'There is nothing you can do. Do you want to be shot?'

'But it's Naomi, for Christ's sake. Why is that whore beating her like that?'

Karl opened the window and called to a trooper who was enjoying the spectacle. 'What's going on? Why are they walloping that prisoner?'

The soldier laughed. 'It seems she's got religion, Herr Oberleutnant, she doesn't want to fuck any more. Gräber's got a hard on up to his chin but she's closed her legs and told him to jerk off.'

'What will he do to her?'

The man laughed even more loudly. 'What do you think? He'll probably let that lot gang bang her, then blow her lousy Jew brains out.'

Karl turned to Sammy but he was gone. He looked back through the window and saw Sammy racing across the compound toward the crowd. He called out, 'Sammy! For God's sake don't, it isn't worth it, she is going to die anyway...oh what's the point?' His voice trailed away in despair.

As Sammy approached, Gräber looked up, stunned at his

temerity. Several troopers raised their rifles but he lifted his hand to restrain them. He still held Naomi by the hair as Sammy stopped before him. He looked at the Englishman, smiling. 'Well, well, come to join in the fun, Captain? Do you want a poke at this stinking Jew whore before I slit its throat?'

Sammy glowered at him. 'Let her go, you bastard,' he gritted through clenched teeth. He reached out to take hold of Naomi's arm. An SS trooper raised his Schmeiser machine pistol to strike him but Sammy sidestepped quickly causing him to stumble forward. Sammy swung his arm up viciously and with great force smashed the man's windpipe with the heel of his hand. As the trooper collapsed, choking, he expertly disarmed him. Quickly cocking the weapon, he turned on Gräber. The action had been so quick that nobody had the time to react. Sammy pushed the barrel of the gun into the officer's stomach. 'Right, I said let her go, or so help me I'll cut you in half now.'

Gräber released Naomi and looked at Sammy. 'You are a fool, Captain,' he snarled. 'You might just have survived this lot, but you paras always have to play the hero, don't you?' He pointed to the assembled soldiers. 'How far do you think you will get? As soon as I give the order they will shoot you down like a dog.'

Sammy glowered at him. 'Listen to me, you lousy Nazi Scheisser, if you so much as nod your head I shall kill you.' He turned to face the troopers. 'Listen to me, you lot,' he shouted. 'I know what's been going on here, I know very few of you are real SS men. You have been drafted in by these cowardly bastards to face the music for what they have done.' As he turned his head to scour the crowd he saw one of the officers begin to reach for his revolver. In one rapid movement he struck Gräber with the butt of the gun, dropping him unconscious to the ground. He placed the heel of his boot on Gräber's throat and pointed the weapon at the officer. 'Don't even think about it, you shithead,' he called to the man, 'or so help me, I'll kill both of you.' The officer slowly backed away. He turned to the troopers again. 'Listen to me, Allied troops will be here any day now and I'm the only chance you have. If you let them kill me, no one will believe your story. You will all be shot out of hand. British paratroopers are on their way here as I speak and I assure you they will show you no mercy. Without me your lives are not worth shit.' Throughout this entire fracas Naomi had remained at his side, dumbfounded and frozen with fear by his actions. She had seen thousands of her people rounded up like cattle and taken to their slaughter almost without demur. They had believed there was nothing to be done about their fate. But this one man, her Goyim, had felled the mighty Gräber before his own men and had cowed the rest into quiet submission. Gräber began to stir on the floor and Sammy grabbed him by the hair, just as he had to Naomi and dragged him to his feet. 'Now, you wicked bastard, tell this lot to back off. I'm taking this woman to the dispensary.'

Gräber nodded to his officers and they stepped aside to allow Sammy to pass. The troopers looked on apathetically as the two of them backed slowly away. Suddenly Gräber shouted to the men. 'Shoot them, now, shoot them!' But they looked on, unmoved. He began to scream. 'Shoot them! Do you hear me? Shoot them or I'll have you all shot.' Sammy turned to face him, pushing Naomi behind him. He raised the Schmeiser and took aim at Gräber.

An elderly trooper stepped forward and approached. He stood before them and saluted. 'Oberfeldwebel Holz, 323rd Infantry, Sir.'

Gräber stared at him in amazement. 'Do your duty!' he screamed at the man.

The soldier looked at him, his face impassive. 'Shut your gob,' he said. 'It's over, you bastards have had your day and I'm fucked if we're going to take the can back for what you've been up to here.' He turned and addressed his men. 'He's right, men, this Englander, he's the best chance we have of coming out of this alive.' He pointed to the group around Gräber. 'If any of these try anything, shoot them.' He walked up to Sammy who smiled at him. He did not respond, but stared glumly at Sammy. 'Who the bloody hell do you think you are, lad, Bulldog Drummond?' He allowed only a brief smile. 'You're a prisoner of war, don't forget that, and the German Army doesn't like its prisoners knocking its officers about, not even these SS bastards.' He paused. 'But I have a problem. I have to keep you alive for my own good, otherwise I would have shot you myself.'

Sammy smiled. 'Of course you would. That's army discipline for you, softens the brain. You should give it up, old son. Oh and by the way,' he added, 'it's Sir, I'm a captain.'

The Feldwebel shouted to his men and two of them ran forward. 'Place the captain under arrest and then take him and this whore to the Jew camp. He can spend what's left of the war with them as he seems to like them so much.'

The men disarmed Sammy and grabbed his arms. He struggled free and looked at the warrant officer. 'At least let me take her to the dispensary and fix her up, they've knocked the hell out of her.'

The man looked at Naomi for some moments then nodded. 'Alright, SIR, clean her up but then to the camp. I don't want to see you again, versteh'?'

Sammy nodded. 'Versteh'.' He frowned. 'What if I die in there?'

'That's a chance I shall have to take.' The German stared at him impassively. 'You are not the dying kind, you lunatic.' He continued to stare, unblinking, into Sammy's eyes. 'You haven't won yet, you know,' he added.

Sammy smiled. 'Oh yes we have, Sergeant Major, but thanks anyway. I'll see you get a fair hearing when this is over.'

Karl and the doctor patched Naomi up, bathing the weals from Gisele Höchst's whip and stitching a gash above her eye. The German guards looked on impassively as they worked and then, when the medics had finished, escorted their charges together with the doctor to the main camp. The three prisoners were pushed through a gate in the wire and it was locked firmly behind them.

Hard-pressed by the Allies, the Germans retreated eastwards. Acting under superior orders to recover at all costs every able-bodied man fit for work, the rest were abandoned to their fate. The Germans took no further interest in the two lovers. No guards, either SS or regular army, entered the camp, nor was any provision made for the needs of the inmates. Neither food nor medicine was provided and the water to the barracks and the infirmary was disconnected. The water supply for the more than two thousand surviving inmates was limited to three standpipes. Sammy tried to get back into the HQ compound but found that their secret route had been discovered and effectively sealed off, the gates welded shut. He watched impotently as starvation and disease took its inevitable toll on the inmates. Rhadski quickly succumbed to TB, finally dying from a massive haemorrhage. In the infirmary Sammy witnessed terrible extremes of physical stress and suffering. Sick old men and women plucked from their homes, madmen taken from asylums, women in childbirth and starving purulent children, their pinched little faces deformed by the venomous bites of bedbugs and rats. All the time the long barracks' rough cement walls echoed to the complaints of the dying and the desperate words of comfort from the yellow-starred nurses who contemplated the rows of triple-decked bunks with impotent, terrified, almost blind expressions. He felt sick as he watched bent and emaciated men and women fighting around the garbage cans for scraps of putrid food. He saw the starving drop and he wept as he watched them die and lie unburied. At night he would cover his ears to deaden the groans of the dying and the scuttling of the over-fed rats. Inexplicably he felt a terrible, overbearing shame, the kind of shame a decent man experiences at the crimes of others, a heavy burden of guilt that such a crime could exist, that it could have been introduced into his world and that irrevocably his own will for good had not prevailed. Finally, broken in body and spirit, he fell silent and prepared to face his own death. He did not leave Naomi's side, but followed her quietly wherever she went like an apathetic child. When she stopped to tend the sick, he stood patiently until she was ready to move on. At last, when she too became too ill to carry on, they waited together for the end.

He awoke, his head on Naomi's knees. He tried to focus, he wanted to be sick again but there was nothing left. 'You were crying in your sleep again, Liebchen.' He heard Naomi's voice, remote and faint. 'Your tears never stop. Why do you dream so much?' She lifted his head. 'Here, let me wipe your face.' She spat on the hem of her dress and wiped her lover's inflamed eyes. He looked at her, expressionless, and she pulled him to her breast. She watched as his eyes turned up and the lids slowly closed again then she too drifted into an exhausted sleep.

She woke to the noise of vehicles. She shook Sammy violently to wake him. 'Sammy, come my darling, you must wake up quickly, they are coming back, those swine are coming back to kill us all.' She tried to drag him to his feet but he was too weak and she fell back exhausted, watching as the column of trucks came through the gate.

The troops clambered from the trucks and stood in groups

surveying the scene of horror before their eyes. The officer from the leading truck looked at his sergeant then back at the camp compound. 'Jesus Christ!' He turned back to see the sergeant leaning against the truck, retching violently. He recovered, wiping his mouth on the sleeve of his jacket.

'Are you alright, Sergeant?' He looked at his NCO. The man nodded slowly. Aghast, disbelieving, they began to walk slowly through the compound, through the heaps of hundreds of cadavers, piled up pell-mell, their skeletal limbs intertwined, their skulls knocking together; through the groups of silent emaciated inmates who stared at them through wide, mad eyes, sunk deep and black, unable to comprehend what this invasion of their particular hell meant; through the dying who sat or lay on the ground unable to move. And they felt sickened by the overpowering, all pervading smell of wickedness.

The sergeant looked around then frowned quizzically. 'Look over there, Sir.'

'What is it, Sergeant?'

'Those two, over there by the fence. They're not in these striped clothes.' As he began to run towards the couple, he shouted back. 'He's a squaddy, Sir. He's in bloody battle dress.' The two soldiers stopped, looking down at Sammy and Naomi.

'Good God, Sergeant, he's a parachute officer.'

'Right, Sir.'

'What the bloody hell is he doing in a place like this?'

The sergeant bent down and touched Naomi's arm. She looked at him and smiled. 'Who are you, love?' he asked. 'And who's this officer?' Still smiling, she shook her head. 'I don't think she speaks English, Sir. Either that or she's too far gone.' He shook Sammy gently but there was no response. 'I don't think he's going to make it either, Sir. Jesus, look at the poor sod, he's all skin and bones.' Gently, he prized Naomi's arm away from Sammy and sat beside him. 'Can you hear me,

Captain?' he shouted directly into Sammy's ear. 'It's the British Army, Sir. You're free now, do you understand?' Slowly, Sammy's eyelids lifted and he stared vacantly at the man in front of him, then his lips began to move slightly as he tried to speak. The sergeant bent closer, putting his ear to Sammy's face. 'Who are you, Sir?'

He heard Sammy's breath come in a faint hiss as he whispered into the sergeant's ear. He stared at his officer with a surprised expression.

'Well, Sergeant, what did he say?'

'I'm not sure, Sir, but it sounded like, "About bloody time."'

CHAPTER THREE

At midnight on April 12th 1945 Dr Joseph Göbbels, Reichsminister for Propaganda, telephoned his beloved leader. 'Mein Führer!' he called exuberantly, 'I congratulate you. Fate has laid low your greatest enemy. I have just learned that the Jew lover Roosevelt is dead. God has not abandoned us.' This was the 'miracle', it seemed, for which Hitler had been waiting, a repetition of the death of Catherine the Great at the critical moment of the Seven Years War. Hitler became convinced that what Churchill had named 'The Grand Alliance' between the Soviet Union and the Western allies would now be broken in the clash of rival ideologies. His hope was not fulfilled. By April 25th the city of Berlin was completely surrounded by the armies of Marshals Zhukov and Konev and on the 27th Konev's forces joined hands with the Americans on the river Elbe. On April 30th, the day after his marriage to the devoted Eva Braun, Hitler committed suicide along with her and their petrol-soaked bodies were burned amid the ruins of the German Chancellery.

The war in Europe came to an end officially at midnight on the 8th May 1945. In reality that was merely the final and formal recognition of a finish which had been happening piecemeal during the previous week. On May 2nd all fighting ceased on the southern front in Italy. On May 4th the surrender of all German forces in Northwest Europe was signed at Montgomery's headquarters on Lüneberg Heath. Finally, overwhelmed by the industrial might of the United States and its allies and the numberless divisions of the Red Army, their country in ruins and almost seven million of their people dead, missing or displaced, the German High Command signed the instrument of unconditional surrender of all German forces to the Allied Powers at Eisenhower's headquarters in Rheims.

The Royal Army Medical Corps established its HQ in a well-equipped former military hospital in Bielefeld, an army garrison town in the region of Westphalia. This comfortable country town which sat among the wooded hills of the Teutoburger Wald had been chosen, with no small sense of irony, as the headquarters of the British Army of Occupation. In the year 9 AD, in the reign of the Divine Emperor Augustus, the Cherusci, a Teutonic tribe led by the legendary hero Hermann, Arminius to the Romans, trapped and annihilated the legions of the Roman governor general Quinctilius Varus in these dark forests, thus ending forever Rome's attempt to conquer the Germanic tribes. Hermann's monument still dominated the town.

The chief medical officer looked up at the small group of specialist medical staff gathered in his well-appointed office for the daily case conference. 'I am still worried about this poor devil Parker. The clinical reports suggest that physically he is recovering well, albeit very slowly, but it is his mental state which is still causing a deal of concern. He remains apathetic and morose and is frequently found crying to himself. He rarely speaks, sometimes nods when addressed but generally makes no response at all. What concerns me particularly is the fact that our conclusions are based almost entirely on vital signs, heart rate, blood pressure, reflexes, the usual stuff...nothing very sophisticated.' He considered his colleagues for some moments. 'Could it be possible, some outside chance, that he may have suffered a degree of brain damage, perhaps as a consequence of malnutrition or from the beatings they seem to have routinely administered? One has only to look at some of the other inmates to see that would not be entirely untypical. Inhibited catatonia, is that a possibility? Or manic depressive psychosis? Bones, what do you think? You've been all over him since he got here.'

The surgeon looked up from his notes. 'I think you are suggesting some very worst case possibilities, if you will forgive me, Sir. One has to bear in mind that we are not dealing here with an ordinary inmate. Most of those poor wretches had been locked away in ghettos for ages before being sent into the camps. They were half-starved before they arrived. Our boy, on the other hand, was from among some the fittest men in the army, those paras are like young bulls. Oh he's a wreck now, of that there is no doubt, but his reserves of strength are enormous. Given proper diet and exercise, he'll be as good as new in no time, physically that is. For what it's worth, and remember I'm no trick cyclist, I think we can rule out any serious clinical mental disorder such as schizophrenia, or any of the other possibilities to which you have already referred. But he has no enthusiasm for life, he's in a state of extreme melancholy and is clearly suffering some form of reactive depression, some psychological trauma, the result perhaps of the loss of something or someone vital to him.'

'Go on.' The CMO waited for him to continue.

'People in conditions such as those in the camps, long-term prisoners for example, bond strongly, often in homosexual relationships. It's a form of self protection. Unable to cope alone with the enormous physical and mental stress of such an experience, they attach themselves to someone, usually a person of stronger character, or perhaps superior position. Often they will empathise with the very people who are persecuting them. It is a sort of dependency, a need to be liked. This dependency may become virtually total, such that when they become separated, the loss is too much for them to bear. Try talking to him again Sir, see if he had a friend in there, someone special to him...perhaps even a lover.'

'A lover? Jesus Christ, Ian.'

'I don't mean a bed partner, Sir, although the sex drive often transcends the most appalling physical conditions. Did anybody see the reports of experiments carried out on some inmates in the camps? Diabolical. One field of inquiry was into the effects of extreme hypothermia on long-term recovery. I suppose they were concerned with survival on the Russian front. They immersed the poor wretches in tanks of water and exposed them to the elements in the depths of winter. According to the experimental notes recovered, in some cases, where both men and women were immersed together, coupling actually took place...it's extraordinary!...No, what I mean is something probably much deeper than that. I think he may have formed a very special bond with someone in there, a bond which saved him and gave him a reason to survive and now that bond is broken, he is lost.'

The CMO nodded. 'Thank you, Ian, I suppose it's worth a try. Bob, this is your field, I think. See what you can get out of him, will you? I don't want to recommend a medical discharge unless it's absolutely unavoidable.'

'Right, Sir.' Bob Parsons nodded. 'But like Ian, I'm not a psychiatrist, I'm a psychologist, often confused, I know.' He smiled at his chief. 'I think I might be able to get through to this chap, though. You see, I worked for a time at Hardwick Hall.'

'Where?'

'Hardwick Hall, Derbyshire.' He grinned. 'It's a stately home, just outside Chesterfield. For reasons only the military could explain, it was chosen as a training camp for the paras. Part of their qualifying programme was a psychological assessment, to ensure they were all of a similar character type, all equally bloody mad, I suppose. I may even have examined him, I don't remember, but of course I'll talk to him.'

Bob Parsons regarded Sammy who sat slumped in his chair. The extent of his appalling maltreatment was apparent. Severely wasted from starvation and dehydration and barely two thirds his normal body weight, he appeared gaunt and cadaverous. His clothes hung loosely on his large bony frame and his eyes stared blankly from deep, black orbits.

'How are you feeling today, Captain Parker?' Sammy shrugged but made no reply. The doctor pushed a pack of cigarettes across the desk. 'Smoke?' Sammy shook his head. 'Captain Parker...' He paused. '...look, do you mind if I call you by your first name? I think we might feel more relaxed.' Sammy shrugged again. 'Fine, well...' He consulted his notes. 'Er... Stanley. Or is it Stan?'

'Sammy.' He whispered, but did not look up.

'Sammy?' The doctor's brow furrowed. 'OK, that's fine. Sammy it is.' He paused. 'Sammy, we have been discussing your case and the CMO, that's the chief medical officer, has asked me to talk to you.' Sammy fixed him with a cold, unblinking stare. 'Look, I know this must be very difficult for you, but I have to ask you some questions about your time in the camp.' He looked for some response but Sammy just stared at him disconcertingly. 'Sammy, it's obvious from your injuries that you suffered most awfully at the hands of those swine but you are a strong chap and we are reasonably happy with your physical state. We are, however, extremely concerned about your mental condition...'

'I know,' he muttered. 'You think I'm nuts.'

'No, of course I don't, but...'

'Yes you do, and you're right. Of course I'm fucking crazy, I'd have to be, wouldn't I?' He became agitated. 'If I'd had any fucking sense I'd have stayed where I was. Those bastards, those fucking bastards, they had no...' He began to sob again.

'Take it easy, old son.' Bob touched his arm gently. He pulled a handkerchief from his pocket and offered it to Sammy. 'Here...' Sammy wiped his sleeve across his nose and mouth and looked straight at him. He decided to take a chance. 'What happened to her, Sammy?' he asked directly. 'Did they kill her?' He watched, fascinated as Sammy's eyes narrowed with suspicion giving way to a look of intense bewilderment. His mouth opened slightly as though he was about to speak then his head slowly dropped and his shoulders heaved as he wept. The doctor watched him for some time then he asked, 'Who was she, Sammy?'

Sammy's head rolled slowly from side to side. 'It's no good talking about it now,' he said in a hoarse, barely audible whisper. 'She's gone.'

'They killed her?'

He shook his head. 'I don't know. They took her away from me. I've lost her.'

'Where did they take her, Sammy? To the gas chambers?'

'No, not those bastards.' Sammy's head fell. 'The army. They handed her over to the civvy people. They took her away and now I'll never find her.'

The doctor was elated. He knew he had broken through. 'Who was she, Sammy?'

Sammy wiped his nose again with the back of his hand, like a child, sniffing loudly. He raised his head. 'Naomi. Her name was Naomi.' Sammy's nightmare was over, but his agony was about to begin.

The doctor wrote quickly as Sammy related his experience of

life in the camp; of Gräber and Höchst; of Doctor Rhadski; of the beatings, the hangings, the shootings; of the filth, the disease and the terrible selections of those who would die quickly in the 'showers' and those who would succumb more slowly to starvation and overwork; of Karl and the innocent Wehrmacht troops drafted into the SS; and he told him of Naomi and how he had come to love her for her strength and for giving him the will to survive and how they had become separated when the camp was liberated. The doctor's report was sent to military intelligence who immediately stopped Sammy's repatriation until he could be interrogated.

'I'm sorry, Sammy, but there it is, I'm afraid. They want to talk to you. They are sending some bod over from the Foreign Office to ask you some questions. In the meantime, we have been looking for that woman friend of yours, Naomi wasn't it?'

'Yes, any luck?'

'Not really, old boy. It appears all the non-Allied inmates were sent to one of these Displaced Persons camps. There are dozens of them. Bloody awful places. Nobody knows who these people really are, least of all themselves, poor sods. They have no homes, no families and no hope, most of them.'

Sammy looked at Bob. 'Perhaps she went home, maybe someone in her family survived. There may have been friends who would remember her.'

'Where's home, Sammy?'

'Dresden, she came from Dresden.'

'Well she wouldn't go to Dresden, would she Sammy?'

He frowned. 'Why not?'

'Why not?' Bob laughed. 'For Christ's sake, Sammy, think about it. For one thing Dresden is in the Russian Sector and for another, it ain't there any more, is it?'

'What do you mean, not there?'

'Jesus, Sammy, where have you been?'

Sammy scowled at him. 'Where the fuck do you think I've been, Bob?'

'Shit...I'm sorry Sammy, that was stupid, of course you won't know, will you?'

'Know what?'

'Dresden was completely destroyed. The RAF firestormed it last February, totalled it.'

'Destroyed...but why, for crisakes? It wasn't a strategic target, surely to Christ. Did they think Jerry was going to bombard us with china fucking dolls?'

Bob looked away. 'They say the Russians wanted it taken out, it was in their line of advance.'

Sammy sighed. 'That poor bloody woman. Those Nazi bastards murder her whole family and then we smash her home town to bits. Where will she go? I'll never find her now.'

'Do you love her very much?' Bob looked closely at Sammy, gauging his response.

'Love her?' He shook his head slowly as if confused and his eyes misted over. 'I wish I could answer that. I know I want to, with all my heart I want to. I have this overwhelming, crushing need, this longing for her, but I don't know if what I feel is love, not in the usual sense. That place was not exactly Memory Lane, was it? But we became close, you see, so very close, so much a part of each other that love was essential to us and to our survival. That's how we got through. I can't explain what I feel. Perhaps it's not easy to understand. I have never experienced such feelings before. I'm no bloody poet, I don't have the eloquence to describe them. I know only that she is a part of me, Bob, and I feel lost and empty without her. I want to see her, to touch her, to take her in my arms again. I know if I can just do that, just know she is safe, then I can pick myself up again and get on with my life.' He looked up, snorting back his tears. 'I

69

know it all sounds like a lot of schmaltz, a sentimental lot of old bollocks...' He laughed, sighing sadly. '...not what you would expect from a hairy-arsed paratrooper, is it? But I can't help that...fuck 'em.' He turned his head away. 'Perhaps I can live without her if I must, but only if I know where she is, only if I know she is safe. That is why I have to find her.' He looked at Bob. 'She can't die, Bob. She mustn't die, not now, not after all that she has been through. She has earned the right to life and the right to love, yes to love, she has the right to be a woman again. She is beautiful, Bob, in every sense and she deserves to be loved, if not by me...' He snorted, pressing his eyes tight. 'She needs to love and to be loved.' He lifted his head, beating back the tears. 'I just can't bear to think that she might be dead.'

Moved by Sammy's confession, Bob was unable to respond at once. He turned away, taking time to recover. He looked at Sammy. 'There is one other possibility.' Sammy looked up, his interest stirred. 'Palestine.' Sammy tilted his head. 'There's an outfit called the Jewish Council, part of the Zionist movement, I think. Well, they are going round the DP camps recruiting people to emigrate to Palestine. It's all very unofficial, of course. You know, against government policy, but the Yanks are stirring the shit at the UN so the government looks the other way.'

'You think she may have joined one of these groups?'

'It's possible.'

Sammy grinned broadly. 'So, how do I get to Palestine, Bobby, my boy?'

'How indeed, Sammy.'

CHAPTER FOUR

Lesley Anne Carrington was, as a consequence of her mother's obduracy, born in Liverpool. Her father, Sir Marcus Carrington, the Conservative Member of Parliament for one of that city's more affluent suburbs, was paying a routine visit to his constituency accompanied by his heavily pregnant wife. The Hon. Lady Anne Carrington, entitled in her own right as the eldest daughter of an Earl, being a woman of determined and cantankerous stripe, chose to ignore her husband's stern and oft repeated admonishment to remain at home and had gone into her accurately predicted labour in the official car. Ignoring her rebarbative insistence that she be returned at once to the family seat in Rutlandshire, Sir Marcus ordered she be driven immediately to the city's Royal Infirmary where, after laying siege to the maternity department, she was finally delivered of a daughter. She expected a son and in a fit of pique at being thus frustrated, proceeded to name the unfortunate child Lesley, her only concession to gender being in regard to spelling.

Sir Marcus, besotted by his dark-haired, beautiful daughter, lavished upon her every advantage his ample means were able to provide. She repaid him, equally lavishly, achieving all he could have wished in any child. After preparatory and public school and a Swiss finishing academy she went up to read Greats at

Oxford. Having done with philosophy and the classics she mastered French and German and when it was suggested she sit the Diplomatic Examination she did so and passed, again with distinction. Finally, assisted by her father's not inconsiderable influence, she gained direct entry as a high flyer into the Foreign Service. Notwithstanding her manifest advantages and the progressive revision of more traditional attitudes, it was a notable achievement for so young a woman.

She spent the war at several 'desks' including that of the United States. Liaison with the Americans was considered vital to the successful prosecution of the war in Europe and she found liaising with the Americans, particularly the younger staff officers, a less than arduous duty. Lesley was a striking woman whose appearance rarely failed to turn a head. Her thick dark hair; her soft hazel eyes, which appeared to darken beneath the curve of her long lashes; her perfect, finely boned face and full sensual mouth complemented to perfection an unblemished, delicately sun-kissed complexion. Her voice was rounded and mellifluous and she spoke eloquently, without hesitation and when amused, would beguile all but the most cynical with a deep, slightly husky chuckle. Tall, elegant, she stood erect with the confident assurance of one born to privilege yet lacked all conceit. She used her considerable gifts with charm and with delight. Generous, at times passionate, she appeared often to overflow with exuberance, yet it was a restrained vivacity and at the age of twenty-five she had not yet known love.

As the war drew to its close Lesley was posted to Brussels. Although she had experienced some of the later self-propelled bomb and rocket attacks upon London she was shocked by the extent of damage wrought by these weapons upon the Belgian capital. She would later discover, as she was driven through the shattered towns and villages of the battle zone, that beyond the horizon the devastation was all but total. She reported at the newly reoccupied embassy and amid a pandemonium of painters, plasterers, wallpaper hangers, furniture deliveries and a frenetic horde of scurrying staff, she was escorted to the office of her section head. A secretary held the door open for her. 'Miss Carrington for you, Sir Andrew.'

'Come in, come in, my dear girl.' He rose to greet her, kissing her lightly upon the cheek. 'I was, in fact, just reading your file. Sit you down, please and allow me a moment to finish.' Sir Andrew Morton, every inch the professional diplomat, had pursued a long and distinguished career devoted to the interests of his nation and thirty or more years of high governmental service had polished him to a Mandarin wisdom. Tall, urbane, he enunciated received English in a refined, delicately modulated voice whose soft throaty quality betokened a liking for fine malt whisky. A long-time friend and alumnus of Marcus Carrington, he had known Lesley since she was a child, an especial and much-loved child. He looked up. 'Your record is, of course, exemplary.' He regarded her with a look of concern. 'But what of Germany? How do you think you will cope with the now vanquished master race?'

'I shall be magnanimous, of course, that is official policy.' She smiled at her chief. 'They do not appear to be the masters of very much at the moment, do they? They look a pretty sullen lot to me. I am sure I can hold my own. But...why me?...A woman, I mean?'

'We have, for some time, considered moving you up and the moment is opportune. It is a considerable promotion and well deserved, I hasten to add. But there are other considerations.' He paused, reflecting. 'You may know our troops have liberated a number of camps. Peculiar places, not prisons exactly. Conditions within them are dire and if early reports are to be believed, the most appalling atrocities have been perpetrated against political dissidents and other perceived undesirables such as homosexuals and Gypsies but more particularly...' He sighed, shaking his head in disbelief. 'There appears to have been a policy of mass extermination, mainly of Jews. Our involvement at an early stage is therefore essential if we are to prevent them from eradicating the evidence. You are clearly capable of handling the situation diplomatically and anyway, you will have the full authority of the Secretary of State, but...' He hesitated.

'But?'

'Those dreadful shouting foot-stamping soldiers are on the rampage and we thought the presence of a woman, particularly one of senior rank, might serve to cool their ardour, exercise a calming influence, if you will.'

'I see.' She wondered if the presence of a woman might serve only to confuse the thrust of their ardour. She smiled briefly. 'You mentioned Jews.'

'Yes...' He hesitated. 'Lesley, we appear to have forced the gates of hell. The Germans, it seems, have been systematically murdering these prisoners. The situation is by all accounts diabolical, the dead and the dying are everywhere in their multitudes. Conditions are appalling and although we will not be asking you to go into the camps yourself, your duties will include the interrogation of survivors, former inmates, those who are fit enough, that is. There are also a number of British POWs who were forced to work in these camps. You may wish to interrogate them about anything they may have seen which may assist your investigations.' His regard softened. 'This is an arduous assignment, Lesley, so please, feel free to decline. No one will think the worse of you.'

'Well, if what you say is true, magnanimity will not come easily, will it?' She regarded her chief seriously. 'But no, I want to do it. We must discover why a highly civilised people could have been so beguiled by such a nasty, common, unlettered sociopath, how they could perpetrate such barbarities.' She gave a wry little shrug. 'I also want to get away from Brussels for a while, the place gives me the bloody willies. Uncle Andrew, why couldn't you have been given Paris?'

Sir Andrew laughed. 'That's settled then, I cannot begin to describe how grateful I am to you, my dear girl. Dear Lady Anne must be so very proud of you.'

'You know Mummy, she expects nothing less of her favourite son.'

He threw back his head. 'Right, off you go. And Lesley, as soon as you feel you have had enough, you must tell me and I shall bring you out, you must promise.'

'I promise.'

Lesley reported to the sector garrison HQ in Langenhagen, near Hanover. The staff headquarters was situated in a pleasant, well appointed Kursaal set in a small wood. An orderly escorted her to the Garrison Commander's office. She walked straight in. A plump, red-tab staff colonel looked up, surprised at her impertinence. 'Colonel Hewitson?' He nodded, perplexed. 'Lesley Carrington, Foreign Office, I believe you are expecting me.'

The officer rose to his feet awkwardly. 'Er...yes...er Miss Carrington, I er...'

'Don't tell me, you were expecting a chap. Believe me, Colonel, I know the lines by heart. Here are my papers.' She smiled. 'Colonel, forgive me, it's been a long day and a bloody awful journey, may I sit down?'

'Of course, please excuse me...You are right, of course, I had somehow expected a serving officer.'

'From the Foreign Office?'

'Yes, that's all very well but...you see, things are pretty damned awful here too and well...I er...it's not the sort of thing...er...'

She regarded the man. Forty-something, she thought, too clean and well manicured to have seen many shots fired in anger. A staff idiot sent out to run the show now that things were quiet. Any minute he's going to say something about worrying my pretty head. This is not the time to stand on ceremony. 'Colonel Hewitson, my brief is quite straightforward. I have to ascertain, as quickly as I can, what the situation is in our sector with regard to foreign nationals, in particular citizens of Allied or other friendly nations who have been held in these so-called concentration camps. My purpose here is not a military matter. If you would care to examine my credentials you will see that I come with the full authority of His Majesty's Secretary of State for Foreign Affairs and that I report directly to his Principal Secretary. I have full authority to determine my own programme of work and I shall decide with whom I wish to speak and when. As garrison commander you are required to afford me every assistance and facility to enable me to complete my task as quickly and as effectively as possible.' She smiled disarmingly at the colonel. 'This need cause you no problem, it is a mere formality, so why don't we dispense with the formalities and start acting like adults? You can begin by calling me Lesley and showing me to my quarters.'

The colonel, clearly discomfited, tried to smile. 'But, er...I'm afraid, er...you see, we had expected an officer of somewhat more junior rank. I fear your room may not be entirely suitable er...Miss...er, Lesley.'

'Got a bed and a bog, has it?'

'What?...Oh yes, rather.'

'Then that's fine.' She chuckled, touching his hand. 'Colonel, please stop fussing...what's your name, by the way?'

He looked at her, nonplussed. 'Colonel Hewitson, of course.'

'Married?'

'Well...yes.'

'So, every morning your wife calls up from the kitchen, "Colonel Hewitson, breakfast, dear".'

'Oh, I see.' He managed a strangled titter. 'It's Anthony...er Tony.'

She smiled. 'Right, Tony, let's go, at the double, I need to pee.'

'Good heavens...right...this way.'

At her insistence the colonel reluctantly agreed to accompany Lesley to the concentration camp at Matthausen, some sixty kilometres north of Hanover. Covering about seventy hectares and completely surrounded by a six-metre high electrified razor wire fence, the camp consisted mainly of single storey wooden huts arranged in rows. A large area in the centre of the camp, which she was told had originally sited the camp offices and work facilities, had been cleared by army bulldozers. German prisoners and civilians, pressed into labour by the occupying forces, were busily pushing thousands of emaciated corpses into mass graves. The stench of putrefaction was overpowering and all were compelled to wear masks to protect them from infection. The bulldozers raised huge clouds of dust in the warm summer sunshine and the air immediately above the graves was black with flies. She felt physically sick but managed with difficulty to retain her composure. When she was satisfied she had seen enough she nodded to the colonel and they began to retrace their steps.

'How many were held in this terrible place?'

'It is impossible to say at the moment. You see, they had a large turnover of prisoners during the several years of its operation.'

'Turnover? You mean some were released, transferred...?'

'No, not exactly. You see...' He glanced back at the main camp. 'They murdered them there.'

'Murdered them? How?'

'In large gas chambers disguised as communal shower baths.'

She recalled Andrew Morton's remarks about extermination. 'Good God Almighty. Tony, I had forgotten about that. But I don't recall seeing any...where?'

'We were forced to demolish them, they were a health hazard, you see. The place was alive with rats and the medics feared the spread of plague. But we have hundreds of photographs and there is film footage of the gas chambers and crematoria.'

She closed her eyes. 'Great God alive, what happened to them?'

'The prisoners?'

'No...it doesn't matter...who was responsible, the SS I suppose?'

'Theoretically, yes. But, and this is quite extraordinary, one of our men was held here...as an inmate...a Captain Parker, Parachute Regiment chap. He insists the SS made off when they knew Germany was finished but before they fled they brought in ordinary line troops to man the camps. Transferred the poor beggars into the SS en masse. We may find ourselves punishing the wrong people.'

'What in heaven's name was a British officer doing in a place like this?'

'He fell foul of the Hun, it seems. Attacked one of their officers, nearly killed the poor beggar according to eyewitnesses. Bad show, really...bad example to other ranks. But as I said, he is a paratrooper and they are a funny lot. Not a proper regiment, you see, no tradition.' He frowned as he pondered his digression. 'However...it seems he worked first in the HQ section and then for some reason they put him in the main camp when they evacuated the place. It nearly did for him. The poor devil still hasn't properly recovered. You may wish to talk to him.'

'Yes.' She looked at him, shaking her head. She turned again to look at the main camp and suddenly felt cold and sick. 'Right, I've seen enough, let's get out of here.'

They climbed back into the staff car. Lesley laid back and closed her eyes, fighting to rid her mind of the images of the horror she had witnessed. 'Tony, I'll go up to my room when we get back. I want to tub. I don't think I shall ever feel clean again. Be a dear, make my apologies to the others, please?' He touched her hand and his gentle intimacy released the flood of emotion which welled within her. She began to sob. He put his arm round her shoulders and she leaned against him. 'I'm so sorry, Tony. I really didn't want this to happen.'

He hugged her gently. 'Not at all, my dear young lady, and you are by no means the first. I only regret that you have been assigned to such unenviable duty. Have an early night, by all means. I'll have something sent up.'

She pushed the file away and sat back in her chair, rubbing her eyes with forefinger and thumb, pinching tightly at the bridge of her nose. She sighed heavily. The horror of what she had seen in the camp was still fresh in her mind but these official reports, with their cold clinical account of planned industrialised murder, of routine gratuitous cruelty, human degradation, appalling physical conditions, and the medical prognoses of the major proportion of the survivors defined the real dimensions of atrocities beyond imagination. She returned to the file of Stanley Adam Malcolm Parker, DSO and bar, Captain, the Parachute Regiment. How had he survived? Eyewitness accounts of his encounters with the German authorities, in particular that of a Sergeant William Grant, of his vicious attack upon a Waffen SS Oberstürmfürher, should have lead one to expect his summary execution and disappearance from relevant record. The copious medical and psychiatric reports on his condition could persuade one to the view that perhaps that might have been more humane than his ultimate experience. Yet his almost miraculous survival was undoubtedly seminal in bringing the hard evidence necessary for the prosecution of those responsible.

She looked up at the orderly sergeant, a burly sergeant major in the Gordon Highlanders.

'This Captain Parker, what sort of chap is he?'

'Difficult to say, really, Miss. He's no a talker, know what I mean? When he first came here he was like a bloody zombie, ye couldnae get a word outae him. Nearly drove the medics crackers. Then the trick cyclist, Major Parsons, managed to get through tae him somehow. He talks to the Major quite a bit now. Seems very fond of him, does the major.' He paused, shaking his head. 'But he's a funny bugger, d'ye ken, Miss? He unnerves a lot o' folk. Ye have to mind what ye say. He flies off in te a paddy for nothin', know what I mean? And he can be a right nasty bastard, if you'll excuse me, Miss. If it was me, I'd talk to Major Parsons before I went anywhere near him.'

'I already have, Sergeant Major. But it's all doctor-patient stuff, very helpful, of course, as are these reports. He appears to be a very violent man. Well, let us say he is capable of violence.'

'Oh Christ aye, he's that alright. Well, he is a bloody para, Miss and ye ken what mad buggers they are, them and the commandos. They're taught some very nasty tricks, that lot and as for the SAS...Jesus Christ.' He shuddered.

She looked at the warrant officer. 'I want to know how he is regarded by the rank and file, not doctors or intelligence wallahs, but chaps like yourself.'

'Well, as I say, Miss, he doesnae say much. Mind you, he's no so hard now, is he? I mean they bloody nigh killed him in there.'

'You say he is prone to quick temper, is there anything in particular one should avoid?'

'Well, he hates the regular army, Miss, so don't try to come the old soldier wi' him, y'ken? Don't try tae pull rank or any other kenna bullshite. And whatever ye do, don't tell him what a wonderful war leader Churchill was. Like a red rag tae a bull, that one. Got in a proper paddy wi' a guy in the mess who was runnin' doon the Labour Government, saying Winnie should be Prime Minister. Tipped a billie o' Chinese wedd'n cake all over the poor bastard's heed.'

'Chinese wedding cake?'

'Rice pudd'n, Miss.'

'Oh my God.' She paused, then asked quizzically, 'Why Chinese wedding cake?'

'It's got currants in, Miss.'

'Ah well, that explains it.'

The sergeant major laughed. 'I'm sure he'll be fine wi' you. He can be very nice when he wants. Polite, y'ken, but...be careful, Miss.'

Lesley completed her notes. Satisfied, she laid down her pen and looked up at him. Despite his sallow complexion and generally dissolute appearance, she thought him rather attractive, his broken nose giving him a faintly audacious air. He stared back at her, expressionless, his pale blue eyes unblinking.

'Thank you, Captain Parker, your statement has been most helpful, I regret you were forced to endure such a dreadful experience. How do you feel now about confronting Gräber and Höchst?'

His eyes narrowed menacingly. 'They're here?'

'Yes. Is that a problem?'

'Not for me.'

She smiled at him but he still made no response. She thought she would try a change of approach. 'By the way...' She looked down at her notes again. '...what do you prefer to be called? You seem to have so many Christian names. I guess it's Stan, right?'

'No.' He spoke softly. Clearing his throat, he spoke more loudly. 'The initials spell SAM, everybody calls me Sammy.'

'Everybody?'

'If they want a bloody answer.'

'I see.' She chuckled. 'But how clever. Well, Sammy Parker, your war is over at last, you can go home now. How long were you a POW, by the way?'

'I wasn't a POW. That shithole wasn't an oflag, it was a concentration camp. I was an inmate, a political prisoner...look, I'm sorry, I...'

'No, please, it is I who should apologise.'

He looked away briefly then returned his gaze to her. 'As it happens, not long. I was one of the lucky ones. I only did eight months.'

'Lucky?' she asked, dumbfounded.

He shrugged. 'The unlucky ones didn't make eight hours.'

'Yes, I see...and where were you captured?'

He stared at her, expressionless. 'I wasn't captured, we quit.'

She felt discomfited by his unremitting stare, his terse and aggressive manner, but maintained her composure. 'Oh, really? And where was that?'

'Arnhem.' He looked away through the window.

She recovered quickly. 'Yes, but my God, Sammy, what more could you do? You were surrounded.'

'We're paratroopers, we're supposed to be surrounded,' he replied quietly as he continued to gaze through the window.

'But Sammy, you didn't quit. It was a magnificent show, you are all heroes.'

He turned his head slowly back and stared into her eyes. 'What's your name?'

'I beg your pardon?'

'I asked you your name.'

'I'm sorry, Captain...Carrington.'

'Yes, I know that,' he snapped impatiently.

She smiled. 'Lesley, Lesley Anne Carrington. My mother expected a son and refused to compromise. Doesn't make a nice convenient acronym like yours, I'm afraid. LAC's a certain something?' She gave a short laugh. 'Most of my friends call me Carrie, you know, short for Carrington. It avoids confusion,' she explained.

'Carrie.' He repeated the name and then he smiled at her, for the first time, a warm, friendly smile revealing his even, white teeth. The smile slowly faded. 'Carrie,' he said quietly, 'you are talking standard, king's regulations, rule Britannia, Rudyard Kipling jingo-bollocks and you really must try to do better. We lost, love. They kicked our proud arses to kingdom come. We were not all heroes, more than half of us were killed. It was not magnificent, it was an obscenity and it was not a show, it was a fucking abattoir.' He closed his eyes briefly then lowered his head. 'I'm sorry,' he said, 'that was out of order, it's not your fault.'

She stood up and, leaning across the desk, touched his arm. 'Hey, come on, Sammy Parker, stop apologising. Show me that smile again.'

He looked up and nodded. 'What are you doing tonight?'

'What?' Lesley tried to restrain a nervous giggle.

Surprised by his own remarks he also began to laugh, lightly at first, but then yielding to a hearty chuckle. He wiped a hand across his eyes. 'Oh Christ, I've been away from humanity too long. I'm losing my manners, forgetting the rules. You must forgive me, Miss Carrington.' He smiled and self consciously allowed his head to fall. 'Have you any idea how long it is since I smelled anyone quite like you?' he asked softly.

She felt herself choking but she remained calm. 'Did you say smelled?' she asked.

He looked up. 'I'm sorry, that too was gauche, but...your perfume, it is so delicate. In the camp people smelled either of piss or carbolic.'

She looked at him steadily then said, 'Not a thing.'

'What?' He looked puzzled.

'Nothing, I'm not doing anything tonight.'

He appeared to grow in stature. He sat up, smiling. 'Geronimo,' he said aloud.

Lesley stared at him, puzzled. 'Geronimo?'

'We always shout Geronimo before a jump.' He paused then closed his eyes sighing with exasperation. 'Christ all bloody mighty, what a thing to say.' He fidgeted uncomfortably. 'Carrie, I'm so sorry, I didn't mean...you know...Jesus.' He gave her a sad smile. 'I think all that opulent living must have softened my brain. Perhaps...if you could bear to spend a little time with a complete imbecile...I thought we might go somewhere, for a drink, perhaps. What about the officer's club?'

She smiled. 'There's a much better place in town. Have you been to Hanover yet?'

He began to laugh. 'No, I haven't felt much like mixing lately. I can't think why.' He paused. 'Sorry, don't mind me. I'll find it, OK?'

'Scrounge a lift,' she suggested. 'There is transport into the city and the place isn't too badly damaged. Go to the Combined Services Club. It's an old Bier Keller, all barrels and oom-pah-pah. Ask for the Nienburger Strasse. It's close to the park, Der Grosser Garten. But first to business, I'm afraid we must get our SS friends out of the way. Can you be back here at two?' He nodded. 'Good, see you then.'

'Time?'

She frowned. 'I told you, fourteen hundred.'

'Not that, our date.'

'Date?' She chuckled attractively. 'I'll try to get away. Shall we say seven?'

He nodded and left the room.

Lesley pressed the buzzer and the orderly sergeant appeared. 'I'm ready for those two beauties now, so wheel 'em in, Sergeant Major. But not too quickly, I don't want them sans culotte, certainly not before lunch...right?'

He frowned, curious. 'Aye, right Miss.'

'Is Captain Parker standing by?' He pointed to a connecting door, she nodded.

After some moments the door swung open and the sergeant major pushed a man and a woman into the room. 'Right, stand still and stand straight, and speak when you're spoken to and no before,' he bawled at the couple. Lesley lifted her hand to conceal her smile. It was clear neither understood a word of his broad Glaswegian accent but he left them in no doubt about his temper. He looked at Lesley. 'Major Grabber and Lieutenant Hock, Ma'am.' He mispronounced the names in a stentorian barrack square bark.

'Thank you, Sergeant Major. I'll call if I need you.'

He looked at her anxiously. 'Will ye be alright, Miss?'

She regarded the two Germans. Both wore the uniform of the Adolf Hitler SS, the familiar insignia on their collar. All buttons had been removed from their clothing and their jackets hung open. Gräber gripped his flies together in a desperate attempt to contain a well developed beer gut and Höchst's breasts hung, unsupported beneath a grubby cotton vest. Belts, laces, ties, stockings, brassieres, anything that could be tied or knotted had been removed. They stood, hopelessly clutching their clothing. She stared at them for some moments then smiled. 'Sergeant, if they took one angry step they'd fall arse-over-head. I'll be fine, thank you.' He left the room laughing at her exquisitely enunciated obscenities. As the door closed behind him the smile vanished from her face as quickly as the sun leaves the land before a storm. 'Setzen Sie sich,' she said sharply, indicating the two chairs. They sat quickly. Lesley consulted her notes then said quietly, 'Hauptstürmführer Alfried Gräber?' She looked up at the man.

He shifted in his seat. 'Ja.'

She turned to the woman. 'Unterstürmführerin Gisele Höchst?'

'Ja.'

She interrogated them thoroughly in fluent German for about an hour. They answered her questions readily and fully, showing little comprehension of, or genuine remorse for the horrors with which Lesley confronted them. When asked why they had committed such atrocities, they simply shrugged and repeated the mantra, 'Ja, Wir sind beiden sehr leidvoll, aber, Befehl ist Befehl, nicht war?'

She wrote rapidly, hardly glancing at them, then she asked almost casually, 'And what of Captain Parker?' Gräber started in his chair and looked anxiously at his comrade. The woman dropped her head and stared at her hands. Lesley looked up. 'Well?'

'Who is Captain Parker?' Gräber fidgeted.

Lesley withdrew a large file from her tray. She opened it slowly. 'Captain S.A.M. Parker, 2nd Battalion. The Parachute Regiment,' she read. 'This officer has made a long and considerably detailed statement about the conditions in Matthausen where he was illegally incarcerated, being a prisoner of war. According to his evidence you knew him very well. In fact, you ordered he be shot.'

'That is nonsense.' Gräber fidgeted on his seat. 'Matthausen was not a Kriegsgefangenenlager, a British officer would not be placed in such a place.' Lesley reached down and pressed a buzzer under her desk. The door opened and Sammy entered.

Höchst began to snivel, but Gräber looked up and emitted a resigned sigh. He smiled at Sammy. 'So, Fallschirmjäger, you made it. You survived after all?'

'Oh yes, Gräber, I survived. I had to see you this one last time.' He smiled but his eyes reflected an unremitting hatred. 'Don't you think it rather ironic? If you hadn't been such a wicked and cowardly bastard and spirited all your SS thugs away to safety, I would be dead. They would have obeyed your orders to kill me without hesitation. And the woman too, wouldn't they? You should have killed me yourself when you had the chance, because as promised, I am going to see you hang.'

Gräber leered at him. 'And what about my Jüdischer whore, did she survive too?'

Before Lesley could react Sammy reached across and lifted a heavy glass ashtray from her desk. 'You bastard,' he grated, 'you never give up do you? I'll smash your fucking...' He lunged forward.

Realising this madman was about to attack him yet again, Gräber stood up quickly and tried to back away. As he raised his hands to protect his head from Sammy's threat his trousers fell to his ankles and he toppled backward, crashing into Gisele Höchst, knocking her from her seat.

'Oh God, no!' Lesley cried out, terrified by Sammy's violent reaction. 'Captain Parker, please, you can't do...Oh Christ...'

The sergeant major burst into the room and looked with horror at the bizarre, Rabelaisian tableau before him. The two SS officers lay sprawled on the floor caught, their buttocks exposed, in flagrante delicto and standing over them like an avenging angel stood Sammy Parker, brandishing the huge glass ashtray. Lesley began to giggle hysterically. The sergeant major lifted an admonishing hand. 'Now come along, Captain Parker, put the ashtray down, Sir, please. You donnae want to go getting into any more trouble over these bastards. Look what ye're at, Sir, you're spilling dog ends and fag ash everywhere.'

Sammy looked at him, incredulous. He gazed down at his quarry and as his anger appeared to subside, he began to laugh. He looked at Lesley, struggling to regain her composure. 'Christ Almighty, there I go again,' he said softly. He handed the ashtray to the warrant officer. 'You're right, Jock, it's against the rules to strike a prisoner, isn't it?' He looked down at the terrified Germans and, still laughing, added, 'Ah! Fuck the rules.' As he spoke he kicked the SS man several times viciously to the stomach and head. He then switched his attack to Höchst.

'No Sir, ye musnae,' the sergeant major shouted. 'She's just a wee lassie.'

'Just a wee lassie? This sadistic homicidal whore?' He drove his foot into her back, driving the breath from her body. 'Wee lassie...Gisele-fucking-Höchst...a wee lassie?' Three more vicious kicks punctuated this litany. 'Jesus-H-Christ.' He shook his head in disbelief and strode from the room. They heard him laughing raucously. 'Dog ends. Fag ash. God save us from the regular army.'

The sergeant major turned to Lesley. 'Are ye alright, Miss?'

She was visibly shaken but recovered quickly. 'Eh...yes, I think so. My God, what a terrible man, is he quite mad?'

'Oh aye, Miss.' He looked at Gräber. 'I mean, he would have to be, wouldn't he. And she's nae much better, is she? But I had to stop him, Miss, the captain, I mean. He woulda killed the pair a'em otherwise.'

'I'm speaking of the captain, not these...these...things.' She waved her hand at the Germans, visibly disgusted.

'Oh aye, right Miss, he's outa his head right enough, but I did try tae warn ye.'

She bobbed her head towards the still terrified prisoners. 'Get them out of here, will you please, Sergeant Major, before the good captain smells blood again and returns to his kill. I think we've had enough excitement for one day.'

'Right, you two, on your feet, come on, look sharp, quick march, left right left right left right.'

She watched them shuffle from the room and suddenly felt very cold. She closed her eyes and gave a slight shudder. 'God in Heaven,' she whispered.

The rules of occupation forbade all fraternisation with Germans, but, as with most prohibitions, it spawned a thriving underworld. There was particularly heavy traffic in black market cigarettes, soap, chocolate, as well as items of food and other luxuries. German money having no value, the ultimate currency, inevitably, was that ultimate casualty of war, the woman. Sammy rode the 'passion wagon' into Hanover. The city, as Lesley had observed, had suffered only superficial damage during the final pursuit of the Wehrmacht to its defeat. Certain prime sites such as hotels, restaurants and hostelries had been commandeered by the army to serve as headquarters as well as for accommodation and recreation. A large and by all accounts popular local Bier Keller had been converted into a club. Managed by the Expeditionary Forces Institute, it provided food, drink and entertainment for the Allied forces in the area.

Sammy unscrewed the stopper of his third bottle of Newcastle Brown Ale. After almost two hours he had surrendered all hope of seeing the beautiful diplomat again, resigning himself to yet another evening alone. He felt disappointed and not a little angry, but as he reflected upon his encounter with Lesley and upon his uncharacteristic presumption, he smiled to himself. 'Bit of a bloody cheek when you think of it, embarrassing the poor bitch like that. I guess she felt obliged to agree. Hairy-arsed paratrooper, off his nut, locked up for eight months, terminally horny...refuse and the bloody lunatic would start rearranging the furniture. Almost did too, doing my nut over those bastards.' He began to chuckle. 'Ah, so what. Fuck 'em, it felt great.'

'And what do you find so amusing, Sammy Parker?' Lost in thought, he had not noticed her approach. He leapt up, spilling his beer. She chuckled throatily at his surprise. 'I say, steady on old thing, you'll smell like a beer mat.'

'I'd almost given up hope. Christ, you scared the hell out of me, creeping up like that.' He smiled. 'Sorry, I'm not being very gracious, am I? I really am out of touch. Please excuse me, but it is lovely to see you. I didn't think you would come, particularly after...'

'A date's a date, right, Captain?'

He nodded. 'What would you like to drink?'

She pointed to his glass. 'What's that?'

'Newky Brown.'

'Ugh, really!' She wrinkled her nose. 'Leave this to me, I won't be a jiff.' She approached the bar and spoke to the bartender who nodded and disappeared into the back room. Lesley returned to the table. She smiled and she sat facing Sammy. 'Right, talk to me,' she demanded. Her manner took him by surprise. Pleasant, sociable, above all confident. She appeared quite unaffected by the events of the afternoon.

'What about?' he asked, diffidently.

'What about?' She raised her eyebrows. 'Dear God, I have a date with one of the Young Lions of popular fantasy, a gallant paratrooper, veteran of many battles, hero of Arnhem, prisoner of war...sorry, political prisoner...subduer of evil and he has nothing to say to me? Sammy Parker, show some imagination. Enough of this false modesty. Thrill me, make my girlish heart flutter with tales of your many exploits. It shouldn't be difficult, after all, it isn't as if you have to resort to romancing is it?'

Before he could respond the waiter arrived with a bottle and two wine glasses. He placed them on the table. 'Ihr wein, Gnädige Fräulein,' he said.

Lesley smiled up at the man. 'Vielen Dank.'

'What in God's name have you got there?'

'Möselwein.' She chuckled, hunching her shoulders like an excited child anticipating a treat. 'Aren't I clever?...Newky Brown, indeed.'

He laughed with her, shaking his head. 'You know, Miss Carrington, you are really quite a girl.' He paused, dropping his gaze. 'Look, I'm sorry about the fracas this afternoon, my behaviour was inexcusable, but those bas...'

She reached across and placed a finger to his lips. 'Shut up, Sammy Parker. That was then, this is now. Let's change the subject, shall we?'

He nodded gratefully. 'Your German is faultless, where did you learn?'

'Oxford mostly, then some further advanced stuff courtesy of the FO. How about you?'

'Cambridge.'

She laughed. 'I knew there was something fishy about you, young Parker. A light blue, eh? You must have read German too, or did you pick it all up in the calaboose?'

'Not exactly. I read biochemistry and if you are going to research that field, German is almost mandatory.'

She regarded him seriously. 'Yes, they've always been the world's most inventive industrial chemists, haven't they? As recent events have only too graphically demonstrated.'

He struck her hand lightly, almost playfully, causing her to start in surprise, but he glared back at her through cold, hard eyes. 'Who said forget the war?' His voice was edged with menace. She felt herself grow cold with fear, she tried to smile. He recovered quickly and took her hand. 'I'm sorry, I'm making you feel awkward again. I don't mean to, but after my performance today I realise I need more time to get myself sorted out, you know, rehabilitated. Those bastards tend to bring out the worst in me. Please forgive me.'

She touched his face, her relief tangible. 'Oh Sammy, you poor old thing. I do babble, don't I? You must think me crass but I was attempting a perhaps somewhat misplaced levity, trying to make you feel a little better. I'm sorry too.'

He looked at her gravely. 'So shut up and pour that bloody wine.'

She sighed, smiling happily as she teemed the pale yellowish liquid into the glasses. 'Zum wohl, Sammy Parker.'

'Prost, Carrie Carrington.' He held her gaze as he sipped the wine. 'You know, you are very beautiful.'

She felt herself flush and dropped her head, momentarily embarrassed. She inclined her head, smiling demurely. 'Thank you. And you, kind Sir, are not so bad yourself...except, tell me, who gave you that awful pug nose?'

He laughed aloud, spilling some wine. 'You're really saying I'm an ugly sod, right?' She stared at him, her expression feigning innocence. 'I used to box for the varsity,' he explained.

'Any good?'

'Good enough.'

'Then why did you let them bust your nose?'

'I didn't...I'm fibbing...I tried to deflect a rifle butt with my face.'

'I don't get it.'

'My late hosts disapproved of my attitude.'

She laughed at him. 'Will you please stop talking in riddles.'

'The SS knocked me about a bit. You know, like one of the ruins of Cromwell.'

She looked down at her hands. 'Oh God, I'm so sorry, Sammy. I just cannot begin to understand what you must have been through, please forgive me.'

He took her hand and gave it a squeeze. 'I'm acting like a bloody fool again. Let's change the subject before I say something outrageous.'

'Like Geronimo?'

'Oh Christ!' He threw back his head. 'I can see I shall not live that howler down.'

'You're nothing but a thug, Sammy Parker.' She laughed. 'Now tell me about your research at Cambridge.'

'Well, it was interrupted when I joined up, of course, but I was doing some interesting stuff in biochemistry and genetics.'

'Really? How fascinating. What, mucking about with cells?'

'That sort of thing, yes. Bragg is very keen not to let London steal the march on DNA.'

'Bragg? You were at the Cavendish?'

'Yes.'

'I'm most impressed.' She frowned. 'What the hell is DNA?'

'Deoxyribonucleic Acid. It is one of the basic nucleic acids present in all living cells. We believe it is concerned with genetic replication and the current theory holds it is the key to understanding heredity. The problem is we don't yet know its exact structure. King's London is also on the trail and Maurice Wilkins has already presented a paper on it.'

'Sounds like very heavy stuff to me.'

'Carrie, when this lot is sorted out there are going to be some very dramatic discoveries. Electronics will transform research.'

'Electronics?'

'A new science completely, arising out of war work, mostly. Radar is one of its applications.'

'Oh, I've heard of that.'

'Right! We will be able to look right into the cell itself and make changes.'

'What is the practical application of that? It has the smack of the sinister to me, particularly after all that Nazi eugenics nonsense.'

'Eugenics isn't nonsense, Carrie.'

'I don't understand. Are you saying selective breeding should be permitted?'

'It already is, where do you think pedigree animals come from?'

'But not among humans, surely?'

'Why not? Suppose it were possible to genetically eradicate mongolism or hydrocephalus or muscular dystrophy, would you object to that?'

'No, of course not. I was thinking more of the Nazi's preoccupation with the master race. I mean, we don't want pedigree humans, surely?'

'Don't we?' He laughed. 'Christ, look at the bloody royal family and some of the older lines of the aristocracy. Don't you think they have been selectively bred?'

'Maybe.' She laughed. 'But they don't look much like Bloodaxe or Eric the Viking any more, do they?'

'No more than a Pekinese looks like a wolf, but it's still a pedigree dog.'

'So what is the advantage?'

'Well, take insect pest control for example, we might be able to mutate some species to make them infertile so that in time they will die out. If we could so eradicate some of the more voracious bugs, we could treble food production.'

'Do you really think that is possible?'

'Well, some of my colleagues seemed exercised about it. I had a different approach myself.'

'You did, you clever old thing? Would I understand it? I would love to know.' She stared at him, engrossed.

'Well, mine was a purely empirical solution. I argued against getting involved with electronics and genetics and all that malarkey.'

'So what would you do?'

'I'd just spray the bugs with a very strong aphrodisiac, wait ten minutes then swat the sods two at a time.'

'Oh you rotter, Sammy Parker!' She squealed with delight as he parried her blows. 'And I was taking it all so seriously.'

They talked and laughed the evening away. She warmed in his company, delighted in his conversation and humour, yet still felt a chill of apprehension. She recalled his violence against Gräber and marvelled at how he was able to change so dramatically from a ruthless and obviously accomplished fighter to this pleasant, urbane and amusing companion. She knew she must avoid any reference to the war. 'Do you have a girlfriend back home, Sammy?' His eyes clouded briefly. He appeared to become anxious. She said, 'I'm sorry, old thing, I didn't mean to pry.'

'No, not at all.' He smiled. 'I did have a girl back home, her name is Sarah.' He paused. 'I say girl, she was very much a woman. A lovely woman, beautiful in fact. A teacher of English. We met at the university, she was doing a late Ph.D.' He chuckled. 'I chatted her up in the refectory. We discovered we were almost neighbours and somehow became very good friends.'

She smiled. 'Just good friends, Sammy?'

'A bit of a cliché, I guess, but...' He laughed. 'I suppose we loved each other in a way. I was very attached to her. As I say, she was a lovely person.'

'There is a lot of past tense flying around here, young Parker. Are you saying it's over?'

He considered her question, all the while staring at her without blinking, then he said, 'She was considerably older than I. Somehow it didn't seem to matter then, but now...' He paused thoughtfully. 'I've changed, Carrie, too much I think for a lady like that. All the nice, comfortable ambiance that made our relationship possible, made it so attractive, so amenable, so natural if you like, it's all gone now. The world is a different place, I'm a different person.' He smiled. 'Her young Stanley died in the war. It wouldn't be fair to inflict Sammy Parker on her now, would it?'

Lesley tried to imagine Dr Sarah. A middle-class, almost middle-aged teacher of English. The older woman with her quiet, bookish young boyfriend. Then she recalled her experience that very afternoon when this same young man, aged by terrible ordeal, had come close to murdering two German prisoners by beating out their brains with a glass ashtray. 'No, I suppose not,' she replied quietly. She looked at him pensively.

His voice interrupted her thoughts. 'Well, all good things come to an end. We'd better be getting back.'

She smiled at him. 'Yes, but we still have some time before the last truck, unless you don't mind riding with me, I have a jeep.'

'A jeep?' He laughed. 'My God, such power and influence, how can I refuse? Carrie, I'd love to ride home with you.'

'How about a stroll first?'

'Please, I should like that.'

They walked quietly through deserted streets, past the neat substantial houses of this neat substantial town. He looked at his companion and recalled her reaction when he had remarked upon her looks. He would not have been the first to comment upon her beauty, he thought, yet in spite of her confidence and obvious social skills, she had been confused and almost demurely bashful. 'Not many natives about.'

She looked at him. 'Curfew. They can be shot on sight.'

'Has anyone been shot?'

'Not by us, but I read a report that the Yanks had killed one of their top composers, a chap called Webern. It seems the poor devil was wandering the streets turning some new theme over in his head and ignored the warning. They say he was shot in error. Can't see how you can point a gun at a chap and blow his brains out by mistake, can you?'

'Well, you did say it was a Yank. Those trigger-happy bastards spend most of their time shooting each other, why should they make a special case of some Kraut tunesmith?'

'You appear very critical of our gallant allies. Are they really such incompetent soldiers?'

He laughed. 'It's all part of the act, a necessary constituent of the special relationship. We have never forgiven them for beating us in 1776. Since then it has been almost de rigueur for each side to rag the other. Of course, being a para I have perhaps a different perspective on yanks.'

'Why being a para?'

'We always fought together. All the big airborne assaults were carried out by the so-called Allied Airborne Army. Three Yankie divisions, the eighty-second, the one-o-one and the seventeenth, and two Brits, the first and the sixth. I have more in common with some Eighty-second Airborne "Screaming Eagles" redneck than I do with a bloke from, say, the Coldstream Guards. We depended on each other when we were in the shit, which was frequently.'

'What on earth is a screaming eagle?' she asked, frowning.

'A bloke from the 101st Airborne. Their regimental icon is an eagle's head with its beak ajar...hence screaming.'

'Of course, how silly of me.' She chuckled.

They found a bench beneath a tree in the park and sat side by side, he staring silently into the night. She looked at him with a slightly quizzical tilt of her head. 'Feeling better now, Sammy?'

'Much.' He sighed and took her hand again. 'Better than I've felt for a long time...thank you.'

'And thank you, Sammy.'

'Me? What for?'

'For not being boorish. You see, after your impressive and terrifying exhibition of backstreet brawling in my office, I was more than a little apprehensive about this date. I almost stood you up, you know.' She smiled. 'But I am glad I took the chance. Back there, in the club...it was in such contrast and when you said I was beautiful...well, it completely threw me. I thought, oh God, here we go again, but when I looked at you I could see you were merely making an observation, an opinion. No motive, no bullshit, just an opinion.'

'No I wasn't, I was stating a fact. You are very beautiful.'

His directness was disconcerting and she felt embarrassed again. She smiled. 'Yes, but you didn't push it and I found that refreshing. Look, I love flattery as much as the next girl and I know I've got the right parts in the right places but it can be a bit of a bore sometimes when a chap gets pushy. My God, it's often like wrestling with an octopus.' She chuckled. 'But you have behaved with exemplary propriety, Sammy, and I am grateful to you.'

He stared at the ground for some moments, as if abashed then he looked at her. 'I'm not sure it has much to do with propriety, Carrie. Who knows, perhaps at some other time I might have pressed my suit with all the ardour of, what did you call me, a young lion? But right now...' He sighed heavily. '...believe me, this is no reflection on you, you are, I think, the most beautiful woman I have ever seen, but I have been through too much. I saw my comrades killed and mutilated in their hundreds and then I was subjected to abuse from those SS bastards. They had orders from that maniac to shoot us, did you know that? No Fallschirmtruppen to be taken prisoner. If a certain Falschirm-jaeger general had not threatened to shoot the bloody lot of them, they would have done it too. Then they brought us to that awful place, my God.' His head dropped and he closed his eyes tightly. She did not touch him, did not intrude into his grief. He recovered quickly. He made no apology or excuse. He looked at her. 'I met a woman in there, Carrie. A good woman, a decent wife and mother.'

'Was that the "Jew whore" to whom Gräber so injudiciously referred?'

'She was no whore,' he grated angrily. He would not sully her memory, would not admit even to himself what she had been compelled to do. 'They murdered her whole family and they almost murdered her.' She heard the tremor of rage in his voice. 'She saved my life in that place, forced me to hold on. We became close, inseparable, we depended upon each other.' He choked again. 'We were separated when they liberated the camp and I don't know where she is. She gave me her love, Carrie. She took me to her heart and I couldn't repay her, I couldn't thank her, I couldn't even tell her goodbye. We have looked everywhere, the DP camps, the refugee organisations, the Zionists.' He sighed, dropping his head. 'Now I'm just too tired. I seem to have lost the zest for life I once knew, the capacity for love. I feel gutted, Carrie. Those bastards took away my manhood.'

She regarded him sadly, deeply affected by the tragic poignancy of his story. She began to comprehend the enormity of what had been perpetrated here. Sammy's individual human tragedy, one of millions, compounded and aggregated into the horror she had witnessed at the camp. She began to understand what had happened to him, to appreciate why and how poor Sarah's young academic had so changed. 'Did you love her, this woman?' she asked quietly.

He stared at the ground then slowly shook his head. 'You are not the first to ask me that and I have tried many times to answer. Perhaps...I don't know if I love her in the usual sense of the word. I only know I must find her. She became a part of me and now I'm lost.'

She squeezed his hand. 'If your reaction to Gräber's gratuitous insult is any indication, I think you love her very much and in the usual sense of the word.'

He sat quietly for some time, then taking her hand he said, 'I'm sorry love, I seem to be spoiling an otherwise perfect evening.' He lapsed into silence again. He sat up suddenly. 'Perhaps...' he smiled at her. 'No, that won't happen.'

'What Sammy? What won't happen?'

'I thought how nice it would be if we should meet again, you know, some time in the future when I've got this out of my system...'

She touched his hand. He took hers in a firm grip and she squeezed. 'Sammy, you are a sweet man. I wish I might have known you better. I cannot possibly understand what you have been through, but I do understand what you are saying. You will get over this, Sammy. You will never forget it, none of us must ever forget what happened here, but you will recover. Find your woman, Sammy. Find her and love her, take everything that life has to offer, you've earned it. Now come, we must get back.'

They drove in silence until she pulled into the transport compound. 'Well, here we are.' He made no reply, staring straight ahead. He took her hand. On an impulse she kissed him gently, a simple goodbye kiss upon the cheek. He turned suddenly, surprised and curious.

'Au revoir, Sammy Parker.' She smiled.

'So long, Carrie Carrington.' He climbed from the jeep and walked away without looking back.

'So, how bad was it?' Andrew Morton looked over his spectacles at her.

'Abominable, Uncle Andrew, those swine must be made to

pay. It's all in my report. It is not something I can discuss yet without becoming emotional.'

'Quite so. How were our chaps? This statement by...er...yes... Captain Parker, very damning, very damning indeed. These two charmers...' He consulted the notes again. 'Ah yes, Gräber and Höchst, did you see them?'

'Yes I did, it's all there.'

'Of course, but you can't get the feel of them. What were they like?'

'Just a couple of ordinary service erks, scared out of their wits at what might happen to them. "We're both very sorry," they kept repeating, "but orders are orders, aren't they?" Sammy, however, said they were totally different in the camp. A couple of arrogant strutting psychopaths, absolute monsters.'

'Sammy?' He smiled. 'And what was Sammy like?'

'Oh Uncle Andrew, he was so pathetic. He was a paratrooper taken at Arnhem. One could imagine him: tough, fearless, but they had knocked the stuffing out of him, eviscerated him, he was an absolute basket case. Gräber insulted a woman he had known in the camp and he went berserk, attacked him, and Höchst too, with a huge glass ashtray. I thought he was going to kill them both. He frightened the life out of me. God knows what he's like when he's fit. I'm sure he'll recover then God preserve whoever upsets him.'

'But I had assumed he was some species of intelligent life, one of those Bletchley Park types. If he was a POW what on earth was he doing in a concentration camp?'

'Apparently he attacked one of the SS officers who captured him at Arnhem for ill-treating his men. He almost killed him. They smashed him up pretty badly then threw him in that place to die. But he confounded them.'

'It would seem he routinely assaults SS officers. Good for him.'

'Not a view shared by some of the regular army types. They think striking an officer, even an SS psychopath, is a "pretty bad show". Bloody imbeciles.'

'But you liked him?'

'I couldn't help it, really. I spent an evening with him, we went for a drink. He was a lovely chap, simply charming. A Cambridge research Fellow, articulate and with a wonderful sense of humour. I felt so sorry for him. He shouldn't have had to suffer like that. He was still very sick...had the most dreadful halitosis.' She paused, deep in thought. She looked up. 'I must have some leave, Uncle Andrew. I know I could sit in a bath for a month and still not feel clean.'

He stood up and, rounding the desk, put his arm around her shoulders. 'Of course, my dear, sweet girl. You have done a magnificent job yet again, just as I knew you would. Then...' He looked at her gravely.

'What?' she asked suspiciously.

'Palestine.'

'Palestine?' she cried.

'There is mounting illegal immigration into the country by Jewish survivors of those terrible camps. The security forces are being overwhelmed and of course we are getting no help from the Americans. We will inevitably relinquish the mandate, that is not for public consumption, you understand, and the Jews will establish a homeland there.' He sighed. 'If only that idiot Balfour had kept his mouth shut. The whole area will be a war zone, it will be a blood bath.'

'Well, thank you for thinking of me, Uncle Andrew.'

He laughed, hugging her affectionately. 'They've appointed Alan Cunningham High Commissioner for Palestine and Pi-force, what we used to call Mesopotamia. You know him, of course, which should help you to settle in quickly and not be bothered by the natives.' Bending, he kissed the top of her head paternally. 'When things get too hectic, out you come, so don't fret. Now, go home for a few weeks. I'll call you when your brief is decided. By the way, how's your Russian?'

'Russian?'

'Yes, a number of these poor devils are of Russian origin, or speak some other Slavonic tongue.'

'Apart from Bolshoi, vodka and orange and Tchaikovsky, non-existent.'

'Then we must give you a crash course. Now scat, go home.'

During the period of convalescence following his repatriation, Sammy began the slow recovery from the physical consequences of his incarceration. He was eventually pronounced fit for active service, but in consideration of his outstanding war record and the unusual nature of his capture and subsequent ill treatment, the Army Council approved his immediate demobilisation. His first encounter with civilian life was a disaster. Upon returning home, he exhibited severe disorientation. He became morose, uncommunicative, found it impossible to re-assimilate, to accept or express affection, found all concern for his well-being unbearable. He ignored suggestions from his parents and friends that he get in touch with Sarah and tersely refused their entreaties to accept her calls. Any expression of interest in his exploits, any question concerning his ordeal caused him to fly into uncontrollable tantrum when the hapless inquisitor would invariably be invited to, 'take your morbid curiosity elsewhere,' or more usually, 'why don't you just mind your own fucking business?' He began to drink heavily and despite numerous, sincere, albeit ephemeral bouts of contrition, his volatile temper, his irascibility, his foul language and his tendency to rage at the slightest pretext, imposed an unendurable strain upon family and friends alike. After only two weeks of a six week demob leave, he sullenly packed his kit and returned to barracks.

*

Alone, and with time to reflect, he knew he must find Naomi. He did not know how he could achieve this, or if it were even possible, but he knew in his soul that unless he discovered what had happened to her, where she was, whether she was alive or dead, he could not know peace and his life would be forever filled with despair. He recalled Bob Parson's suggestion, that if Naomi had survived, and knowing she could not return to her home in Dresden, she might choose to emigrate. He declined his discharge and requested an immediate return to active service. The army, desperately short of experienced active service officers, was happy to accommodate him. Posted to the Sixth Airborne Division, his rehabilitation began when he found himself reunited with many of his former comrades and on his way to Palestine.

CHAPTER FIVE

The Red Cross doctor consulted her notes and looked up. 'So, Frau Blomfeld, as far as your physical condition goes you appear to have recovered well. How do you feel in yourself? Do you have any questions?'

Showered, head shaven, deloused, dressed in a plain green twill frock several sizes too large for her, Naomi stood, head hung. She raised her head briefly, staring listlessly from large sightless eyes.

The doctor regarded her for some moments then, speaking loudly, if haltingly, asked, 'Wie geht es Ihnen, Frau Blomfeld? Haben Sie vielleicht etwas zu fragen?'

Naomi shook her head slowly. 'Nein.' Her reply was barely audible.

The doctor turned to a medical orderly. 'There is nothing more we can do for her here. Anyway, we need the beds. Get her over to DPs, I think she is fit enough to be repatriated. Where is she from, by the way?' She leafed through her notes again. 'Oh Christ.' She glanced at the orderly, shaking her head. 'Look, get her over there, Sarge, she is not our problem any more.'

Discharged from hospital, Naomi became the responsibility of the United Nations Committee for the Resettlement of Displaced

Persons. The Committee had taken over several former German Army barracks and she found herself quartered with hundreds of other refugees, forced labourers, survivors from the camps, ex-soldiers from the Soviet Union who had either defected to the Nazis or had been forced to fight for the Germans on pain of death. Whole 'families', defined largely by nationality, lived in a great hall divided into 'apartments' by chalk squares drawn on the floor. Cutting the hall in two, an aisle barely a metre wide gave the 'tenants' access to the door. Each resident feigned ignorance of his neighbour's existence. To cross a chalk line was to cross a border, scale the wall of a private existence. To pay a visit, one said, 'knock knock,' with a forced smile and waited politely to be invited into a square. It was as though they had all been driven to the point of madness by their hopelessness. Some attached cords to the ceiling to hang a mirror or a family portrait. Only the children obstinately refused to respect the borders erected by their elders, which occasioned such squalling and squabbling. She had been there hardly a day when she felt an overwhelming compulsion to flee. She felt as though she were caught up in some sort of grotesque game. The squares, named of the countries from which their occupants came, Russia, Ukraine, Latvia, Poland, Hungary, Romania, lands scorched, pillaged, ravaged, wasted and now lost beyond the cold eastern marches, seemed as little serious, as fantastic as those other squares traced out by the playing children in the peculiarly Jewish version of the game of hopscotch. Squares which represented a loaf of bread, a pound of peas, a bowl of chicken soup. She tried to imagine fantastic squares of her own representing love, a lingering kiss, a tender caress. Then others, a spitting insult, a slap in the face, the lash of a whip, Typhoid, TB, and finally, the 'shower'. The hop stone rolled about in her mind, crossing in turn each of the chalk squares drawn by the Jewish Committee for Refugees. Repatriation, emigration, resettlement. Sometimes the stone rolled quickly to the square marked America but then quiet reflection surveyed the ocean that would separate her from all she knew. As for the square marked France, it suffered the inconvenience of association with the names of Laval, Barbie and...Dreyfus? Didn't they send this poor Jew to Devil's Island for something he didn't do, just to protect the honour of an Österreicher? The mere thought forced a shudder. Often it rolled and lingered pleasurably in the square marked England. England! She would sigh and smile, eyes closed, but as she tried to recall his face she would feel again the pain of loss, the chill of loneliness and she would cry quietly.

The Red Cross officer looked away, discomfited, turning his gaze to his companion who leaned against the wall at the back of the room. 'Michael, I cannot seem to make her understand. Perhaps it's my college German, I don't know, but she will not accept that she cannot return to Dresden. Can you try?' Michael crossed the room and sat before Naomi. He grasped her hands and gazed into her sad face. Her shaven head made her dark eyes appear large and slow moving, the heavy shadows beneath them accentuated by the pallor of her skin. Her face and her body were still wasted making her look excessively delicate and fragile as though she were made of some material other than flesh, a material so brutally wrought there seemed little possibility of it ever changing and yet...there was a sort of pathetic, grating sensuality about her.

He smiled at her. 'Frau Blomfeld, isn't it?'

She made no reply.

'May I call you Naomi?'

She shrugged.

'OK. Naomi, I am Michael Berkovitz and I am a Palestinian.' He saw her eyes flicker briefly. 'I know this uniform looks like that of a British officer, but I am in fact a major in the Jewish

Brigade, at least I was until we defeated these swine. I now work for the Jewish Council and I am with the Zionist Committee for Refugees.' He looked hard at Naomi to see if he could detect any interest. 'Captain Parr of the Red Cross here has been trying to explain why you cannot go back to your home in Dresden. Naomi, I realise it must be hard for you to understand. You have been dispossessed by the Nazis, your family has been murdered, you yourself almost died and now that you are free at last you find you cannot return to your home because of incomprehensible restrictions placed upon your movements by the very people who fought to rid you of your oppressors. Do you understand what I am saying to you?' As she stared at him, he saw her eyes slowly begin to regain their vitality. She straightened up in her chair and raised her head.

'Yes, I understand you, your German is good...better than his.' She cocked her head toward the Red Cross man. 'But I understood him too. The trouble is, neither of you tell me anything. You are wrong, Palestinian, this man has not told me why I cannot go home to Dresden. He says it is impossible. I want to know why.'

'So, you can speak, after all.' Michael smiled. 'Now we can make progress. Naomi, after all you have endured, the last thing you want to hear is more bad news. But if you are to understand I fear there is no alternative.' He hesitated, glancing briefly at his colleague. 'Naomi, your home is gone.'

She frowned. 'What do you mean, gone? Is somebody else living there now? I know the Nazis stole our home and all our possessions for some Gestapo swine and his family, but now I want it back, it is my right.'

Michael shook his head. 'No, Naomi, please try to understand. Your home is gone, Dresden is gone, obliterated. The Allied air forces bombed it to rubble last February, very little remains. Unless you lived in one of the outer suburbs, you no longer have a home.'

'Obliterated?' She seemed not to comprehend. 'The Allies obliterated Dresden? But why?'

He shrugged, sighing. 'It was part of their strategy to destroy the morale of the German civilian population by massive bombing raids. Most of the major cities have suffered the most appalling destruction. Unfortunately, Dresden was the worst.'

'Then we must rebuild it,' she asserted defiantly.

'Who?'

'Who? We, of course, we Germans.'

He looked at her sadly. 'Naomi, there is nobody there to do it.'

'What do you mean? Where have they gone? Have the Russians driven them all out?'

'No, Frau Blomfeld,' Captain Parr intervened, 'the few who survived are most probably refugees, like yourself.'

'Few?' Her face betrayed her anxiety. She turned to Michael. 'How many died there?' she asked.

'There are no accurate figures...some estimates say around one hundred thousand. These figures are always exaggerated, of course,' he added urgently. He sighed heavily. 'It was bad, Frau Blomfeld, very bad, I am so sorry.' As Michael looked into her eyes he saw the despair return to dull their fragile brightness. The enormity of his revelation gradually penetrated her consciousness and he watched the blood drain from her face. She shivered slightly and closed her eyes. She seemed to withdraw, to shut out the scale of her predicament. She began to rock slowly back and forth. He pulled her to him and held her close. She did not resist. He looked up at the Red Cross officer. 'Captain Parr, with your permission I would like to take Frau Blomfeld back with me to Darmstadt. We have a facility there for German Jewish Nationals who cannot be repatriated. She is clearly in need of further treatment before she is able to make any decisions about her future. I fear for her sanity if she is left here, she has suffered enough.'

'They have all suffered too much,' Captain Parr said patiently, 'but of course, if Frau Blomfeld wishes to accompany you, I have no objection.' He turned to Naomi. 'Go with Major Berkovitz, Frau Blomfeld, let him advise you. He will know what is best for you. Get away from this place, get out of Germany altogether, there is nothing for you here. After what the Germans did to your people, why would you wish to remain?'

She raised her head slowly and gave him a sad, puzzled look. 'I do not know what you mean by "your people"', she said softly. 'I want to stay, to go home, because I am a German. This is my country too.'

Darmstadt, a garrison town in the province of Hessen, enjoyed, as far as the interests of the Committee for Refugees were concerned, the advantage of being in the American sector of occupation. The Committee occupied the small cavalry barracks at Rheilgen, where it began quite openly to organise parties of Jewish refugees whose ultimate destination was Palestine. The Americans, whilst not overtly assisting this endeavour, made no attempt to interfere and ignored all representations by the British who protested the American action was contrary to their government's policy.

Naomi recovered quickly in the excellent garrison hospital. She regained weight and her hair grew long. But though the bloom returned to her cheeks, she rarely smiled and remained persistently apathetic, about herself and about her future. Having been persuaded that a return to Dresden, now in the Russian zone, was virtually impossible, she acquiesced to Michael's suggestion that she join the next band of survivors to make the journey to the Promised Land. But she showed no enthusiasm for the idea, she still pined for her home and could not understand why the Russians would not allow her to return. Many of the camps had been in the east, in the Russian sector. Many refugees had returned to homes in the west. But she had been compelled to accept that such an undertaking would be fraught with danger and inadvisable in the new political situation. The advice, not only from Michael, but also from most of the American officers who had interviewed her, at first bewildered her. 'Don't go east. It isn't over, even now. They still hate the Jews. In the west it's not as bad, there are laws, but in the east you will have nothing.' Michael understood her desire to return to the familiar, her need to reaffirm her identity, but he also knew this would never be possible, for the familiar was gone forever. She would return only to loneliness, despair and possibly danger.

'What is it like, this Palestine of yours?' She regarded him solemnly.

He smiled at her. 'I was born there, I'm third generation Palestinian, so naturally I am biased. I think it is the most beautiful country in the world.'

She looked at him sternly for some time. 'My father had books about Palestine in his shop, big books with photographs. I often looked through them. It is not a beautiful country, it is a harsh and barren land of rock and sand and poor, miserable people living in mud houses amid rubble. Oh, I know you Russians have built a couple of cities, but they are ugly places, like most cities built by Jews with American money. You are simply talking patriotic rubbish, blödsinn.' She waved a hand. 'Go look out of the window, look at those beautiful green hills and neat clean towns. That is a beautiful country. But as you look, remind yourself what an arrogant, mindless nationalism did to it.' She looked away, as though impatient with the subject. When he did not reply she asked, 'So how do we get there?

When do we leave?'

He laughed. 'Are you so eager to get to this barren, ugly land of mine?'

She turned to him and her expression softened. It was the first time he had seen her smile and he felt himself strangely attracted to her. As he stared at her she felt his anxiety. 'Forgive me, Michael.' She reached forward and gently touched his face. 'You have shown me such kindness since we met in that awful barracks and I have been so ungrateful.' She dropped her head as if shamed by her behaviour. 'It is not easy for me.' She sat nervously playing with a handkerchief, twisting it round her finger until it was tight. 'I do not mean to be surly.' She would not look at him. 'I am afraid, Michael, still terrified of authority, of loud men in uniform. They took everything I had, everything. My world is gone forever, I must start again and I am afraid. I thought if I could go back to my home in Dresden I could pick up the pieces of my life, begin to remind myself of what that life had been like for me. I was a person there, Michael. I had a life, an identity, I had been loved there, wanted and respected. But it's all gone. I know that now and I feel empty and lost.' She closed her eyes and sighed deeply as she contemplated her fate.

Once her life had been secure, almost predetermined. Born into a middle-class Jewish family in Dresden, she had been part of a close, insular group whose identity was defined and whose customs seemed immutable. She had never considered the possibility that she would do other than follow those customs which demanded she respect her elders, obey her parents' wishes and eventually marry one of her kind. Her friendship with David Blomfeld, the son of her father's best friend, whom she had known since childhood, had seemed as unremarkable to her as that she should one day marry him and bear his children. But the holocaust of Nazism had ripped her existence apart. Secure, comfortable, happy as a wife and mother and respected within the only society she had known, she had found herself suddenly the object of an irrational, incomprehensible hatred which systematically destroyed the vibrant, creative culture which had made her what she was. Her family murdered, beaten, brutalised, shamed, her body defiled, she had finally yielded to her fate in order to survive. Then a miracle had occurred. At her nadir, stripped of self-respect and of hope, she had found love. Unexpected, spontaneous, unselfish love. A bittersweet, desperate interlude which had so briefly lifted her heart and restored her dignity. But it was not to be, she knew that now. She began to shake her head slowly in resignation. She smiled sadly and thought of Dresden, now crushed and desolate, as a poignant metaphor for her own tragic life. She dropped her head and shivered slightly. 'I am cold, Michael, so cold.' She sighed, looking toward the window. 'I want to feel the sun again, to smile, to hear laughter. I want to be loved again.' She looked directly at him. 'Oh Michael, I wanted so much to be loved.' She held his gaze for some moments then, turning away, she said quietly, 'But I have lost him. He is gone and he will never find me now.'

He took her hand to comfort her. 'He is dead, Naomi. Nothing can change that.'

She looked back quickly, her eyes cold. 'Who told you that?'

He frowned, puzzled. 'You did, when we processed you in Brunswick, you told us your husband had died when the Buna factory was bombed.'

She nodded, looking away again. 'Ah yes, poor David,' she said mechanically then affirmed, 'yes, he's dead.'

Michael looked hard at her, trying to understand, but she gazed blindly out, lost in thought. He touched her hand to attract her attention. 'Naomi, what did you mean, "he will never find me now"? Who? Who will never find you?'

She shook her head slowly then sighed deeply. 'I know he

would look for me, he would not let go. But he will not know where I am now. He was very sick, they would have sent him home.' She dropped her head and Michael saw the tears fall on to her hands.

'Who, Naomi? Who is "he"?'

She pulled the knotted handkerchief from her hand. She wiped her eyes and blew her nose loudly. 'If I go to Palestine, Michael, how will he ever find me?'

He lifted her face but her eyes remained closed. 'Naomi. Look at me, please. Tell me who "he" is.'

She opened her eyes and he saw they were dull with anguish. 'Sammy,' she said softly. 'My Sammy. Oh Michael, I love him so much and I have lost him.' She began to sob and she cried out. 'I want him, oh dear God, I want him. I want him back, to love me, he is my life.'

Michael embraced her and she clung to him desperately. As she grew quiet, he pushed her back gently and, taking the handkerchief, began to wipe her face. 'Now tell me, who is Sammy?'

'Sammy,' she explained, 'he was in the camp with me.'

'He was an inmate?'

She nodded.

'But what happened to him? Didn't he go to the DP camp with the rest of you?'

She shook her head. 'The army took him away.'

'The Americans? Was he a German guard?'

'No, a British Falschirmjäger. The British Army took him away.'

'Falschirmjäger...British Army?' He gaped at her, disbelieving. 'What in God's name was a British paratrooper doing in Matthausen?' She began to cry again, so bitterly he could not console her. 'Please, Naomi, you must not do this, you will be ill. Lie down, I'll fetch the doctor.'

Throughout the ensuing days she told him of her encounter with Sammy and how and why she had come to love him with such passion. 'And did you not try to trace him?'

'How? How would I do that? There were no means. I tried explaining to the British authorities that I had known this man and that I wished to find him, but there was always a reason to ignore my requests. It was clear to me they did not want me reunited with Sammy.' She paused, reflecting. 'He was a British officer, after all, and I was just another camp whore, wasn't I?' She emitted a short bitter laugh. 'Did you know, at first they treated me almost as a collaborator?'

Michael took her hands. 'They did not understand, Naomi. They were shocked and bewildered by what they found. Only gradually did the full horror of what had happened become clear to them.'

She nodded. 'I know, Michael. I know it wasn't their fault.' She gazed through the window, weeping silently.

'And you still love him, this Englander?'

'Yes.' She did not look at him.

'You came together in the most terrible and extraordinary circumstances. You were desperate, it is natural you should feel as you do. But your time together was short, perhaps your feelings do not go deep. Time will heal, you'll see, you will forget.'

She turned to look at him, her gaze defiant. 'No, you do not understand. I shall always love him.'

'How can you know that?'

'Because he was not an ordinary man, he was very special.' She sighed then sat quietly with her thoughts for some time. She spoke softly. 'He knew what I was, he had seen me about the camp, leaving Gräber's house. But when I came to him he took me for myself. He did not care what I had been or what I had become, he did not judge nor condemn me, he took me to his heart asking nothing in return. He raised me up and made me feel clean again. He restored my dignity, gave me back my self-respect and when he had done all this, he stopped Gräber from killing me. He fought them to save my life, Michael, and he almost died himself.' Michael reached forward and touched her arm. She covered his hand with her own. 'You are right in what you say, I shall have to accept that I may never see him again. But you are wrong, also. You see, he made me understand the true meaning of love and now I love him in my very soul. I shall never forget him, Michael, never.'

As the weeks passed Naomi grew close to Michael. His innate, spontaneous generosity comforted her, eased the pain still throbbing deep within her. He helped her to draw it forth, to confront it. He listened with patient attention to her ramblings as she repeated her story over and over and by sharing her anguish, helped her heal the wounds inflicted by her ordeal. He did not subdue his desire as his attraction for her grew stronger and he rarely left her side. She saw that he loved her, was even flattered by his attentions. At first she rejected him, determined to resist his advances. But she craved a reaffirmation of her life, of her womanhood, and gradually, because she was lonely and needed affection, she responded temptingly then finally yielded to him. Once they became lovers, her release was absolute and palpable. She revelled in their intimacy, taking him ardently and physically and he was overwhelmed by the sheer joy of her being. Yet he knew she gave him nothing. She lived only with the dream that one day she would be reunited with the man she truly loved.

The Committee for Refugees had established a network of camps and safe depots across Germany, Austria and Italy through which the emigrants were passed until they reached the Adriatic port of Trieste. Its territory was disputed by the claims of both Italy and Yugoslavia and nominally under UN control. It had no formal, organised government and no troublesome bureaucracy. It was perfect. From Trieste the route took them through the Adriatic to Greece where they waited patiently until a local ship owner or fisherman could be persuaded with enough money to run the gauntlet of the Royal Navy to the shores of Palestine. Once there, and if they escaped arrest and deportation to Cyprus, they were quickly dispersed and assimilated into the Jewish communities. As they waited in the port of Piraeus for a passage, Michael began to detect a change in Naomi's demeanour. She became nervous, irritable and frequently fell into moods of deep melancholy. They had taken a room in a seedy waterfront hotel and as he entered he could see she had been crying again. He sat beside her on the bed and placed his arm around her shoulders.

'Darling, what is it? Please let me help you. I can see you are desperately unhappy and my heart is breaking because I do not know what to do. Please tell me what I must do to make you smile again.'

She yielded to him, pushing her face into his chest. He kissed her hair and she lifted her face to him. 'Oh Michael, I am so afraid.'

'Darling, nothing is going to happen to you, I promise.'

'How can you say that? As time passes here I become more terrified. How much longer must we wait?' She looked at him, her face drawn with pain. 'Michael, I could not bear to be locked away again, not by the British. I understand why you cannot be with us on the journey, but I know I cannot make this voyage alone. If we were stopped and I was captured and deported I know I could not survive another camp. I would go mad and I would kill myself.'

'Shush, my darling.' He drew her to him and kissed her cheek. 'You must not be afraid, everything that can be done is being done to ensure your safe arrival.'

'I know, Michael, you will all do your best, but the British have a huge navy and an army to stop us. There are already thousands of Jews in the camps on Cyprus, you know that.'

He sat quietly, unable to reassure her. He knew she was right, the camps were already filled to bursting point and the Royal Navy was intercepting ships far from the coast of Palestine and actually returning their cargoes to German ports. After some time he hugged her tightly. 'There is a way you could come with me,' he said, his voice full of encouragement.

'What? How? How could we do that?' She looked at him, wide-eyed.

He stood up and, taking her hands, pulled her to her feet. He lead her to the window. 'Look, my darling, look at this harbour, look at all those ships, every one with a captain who would sell his mother for a few drachmas and every one of them has the power to perform marriages.' He grasped her by the shoulders, excitedly. 'Naomi, listen to me. I love you. I know you love another man, one who saved your life, but my angel, he is gone and though you have hope in your heart, you know in your head you will never see him again. My darling, have you not endured enough? Suffered agonies beyond imagination? Is it not time for you to begin to live again? Naomi, you are a beautiful woman yearning to be loved. I can give you that love, and though I pray you will one day come to love me, I shall ask nothing in return. My darling, marry me. As my wife you will be a Palestinian citizen and can return with me legally. Please say you will, I know I can make you happy.'

She looked at him, smiling. She pressed against him, resting her head on his chest. She felt the beat of his heart, she smelled his sweat. Her heart cried out for Sammy, to have her, to hold her, yearning to believe that some day he would find her. But her head knew Michael was right. She would never see Sammy again. She prayed for time to heal the wound, to dull the pain as he slowly faded from her memory. She prayed this would be her last heartbreak, the end of her suffering. As she looked into Michael's expectant face she prayed to her God to help her to love him. 'You want me to marry you?'

'Oh yes, very much. Do I ask too much?'

'No Michael, it is I who ask too much.'

'Then you will?'

'Yes Michael, that would make me very happy. I shall be a good wife to you. I will do everything I can to make you happy, I promise.'

He kissed her. 'You have already made me the happiest man in creation, my darling. I love you so much.' He gazed at her, smiling. Then, straightening quickly, he pulled her toward the door. 'Come, we must lose no more time, let us go home.'

PART TWO

CHAPTER SIX

Sammy sat on a large weapons crate, indolently banging the heels of his calf-length jumping boots against its side. He watched a new draft of reinforcements crab unsteadily down the gangway of the troopship, weighed down by heavy kit bags and equipment. He was bored, impatient to get away. He watched Sergeant Grant tick the names from the roll as the men reported, handing each an allocation card. The sun was hot on the back of his neck. He turned his beret round and pushed it back on his head to afford some protection then he vaulted from the crate and walked over to join his sergeant.

'How many, Bill?'

'Forty-eight, Sir, including two corporals.'

He looked up at the troops. They stood, shifting uncomfortably in the midday heat. 'We'd better get them out of this as quickly as we can. We don't want the sods going crook with sunstroke. I'll say a few words of welcome then you can get them loaded up and away.'

'OK Sammy.' Bill strode quickly over to the squad. 'Right lads, fall in, the captain wants to say a few words then we are going to board those trucks. Go to the one marked with the number on the card I've given you. Come on now, look sharp or this sun will burn you to a frazzle.' He turned to Sammy and saluted. 'All present, Sir.'

'Thank you, Sergeant.' Sammy turned to the men. 'Right, settle down, I shan't keep you long. I know you must be feeling like shit after nearly three weeks at sea and standing around in this heat is not going to improve your temper. You've already met Sergeant Grant, I am Captain Parker. You have been assigned to Eight Battalion. Some of you will be joining "C" Company and some my platoon. Don't bother to check your cards now, you will be told later where to go. You are probably already aware you have arrived at the port of Haifa. Your destination is Ramat Gan near Tel Aviv. I'm sorry, but you have another two hour journey before you can relax. Today is Thursday, you have the rest of the week to settle in and unpack your gear. On Monday, HQ Company will complete your allocations then you can look forward to a whole new lifestyle. Welcome to Palestine and to Eight Battalion. Get plenty of rest, try to eat in the mess and touch neither fruit nor women unless they are thoroughly clean. Any questions?'

'Yes Sir, which of those two should we avoid the most?'

Sammy smiled. 'What's your name, son?'

'Private Caine, Sir.'

'Let's put it this way, Private Caine, unclean fruit will give you amoebic dysentery, an unclean woman, syphilis. These are both unpleasant but entirely treatable conditions. The choice is yours. If you are a fruit case you might prefer the first option, if on the other hand you are a nut case go for the second, the consensus is it's more fun. Right,' he shouted above the laughter, 'that's enough, mount up now and hit the road.'

The sergeant loaded the troops into the trucks then climbed into a jeep beside Sammy. 'All rookies, Bill?'

'Yeah, except er...' He consulted his manifest. '...Manders and Challis, the two corporals. Another pair of Aldershot hard-arses, I shouldn't wonder. I wish to Christ the mob hadn't gone all regimental, Sammy, talk about bullshit baffling brains. Bloody shower. Why doesn't the "Arsehole" Cavalry back in Blighty let us appoint our own NCOs?'

'What do we know about these two, Manders and...who was the other one?'

'Challis...bugger all, but don't worry, Sammy, I'll soon knock the sods into shape if they try coming the old soldier with me. I hate these bloody snot-nosed regulars coming in and ordering vets about, particularly when they come all that regimental bullshit. I just hope they don't fall foul of the Twins.'

Sammy laughed. 'Now that would be worth watching. But that's your bailiwick, you handle it.' He paused. 'I'm skiving off for the weekend, Bill. I should be back Sunday afternoon. I'll give you a knock, OK?'

'Where are you staying?'

'Usual place, but I don't want any bugger to know, unless it's absolutely necessary.'

Bill climbed from the jeep, grinning. 'I hope she's worth it, Sammy.'

'Oh she is, Bill, she is. Now sod off.'

Bill watched, shaking his head as the jeep roared out of the dock and merged with the traffic. 'Mad bastard,' he muttered, smiling, then climbed into the lead truck.

Since their arrival in Palestine a heavy duty had been placed upon the paratroops. Maintaining public order, searching for guns, ammunition and other ordnance, carrying out patrols, intercepting illegal immigrants and pursuing and arresting terrorists had afforded Sammy scant opportunity to pursue his search for Naomi. Then miraculously, the military authorities decided to use the port of Haifa exclusively for the disembarkation of reinforcements, a decision which delighted Sammy. There was a branch of the Jewish Council in the city which included an office of the Committee for Refugees and he quickly made himself known to their bureau personnel to elicit their help tracing Naomi. They had been pleasant, helpful even, but did not conceal their suspicion.

'You say her name was Naomi?' The Jewish-American accent was unmistakable.

'Try "is", it makes me feel better.'

'OK, it is...and that she was, er, came originally from Dresden?'

'That's right.'

'But you know neither her married nor her family name?'

'No, sorry.' He paused, shifting uncomfortably in his chair. 'Listen, I know this seems a bit weird, but well...names didn't carry much weight in there, they were just numbers.'

'Yes Captain, we know all about the camps,' she said loftily. 'Now, you say you encountered this Jane-Doe Naomi in camp Matthausen, that she had been married with two children and that her family had been exterminated.'

'Yes.'

'So, how did she manage to survive?'

'She had er...' He turned his head away to avoid her inquiring look. 'Call them special duties.'

'She was a doctor, an artist, a musician? What special duties?'

'Let us say she was...how can I put this?...Exceptionally desirable?'

The woman frowned briefly then, grasping the significance of his words, clasped her hand to her mouth. 'Oh dear God.' She stared at him, horrified. Recovering, she asked, 'You discovered this poor woman when your outfit overran the camp, right?'

'Not exactly.' He sighed. He had wanted to avoid explanations, detail, but he knew he could not. He was a British parachute officer, a member of a force currently engaged suppressing public demonstrations, searching Jewish towns and villages, entering homes, pursuing illegal immigrants, many of whom were camp survivors. He marvelled they were talking to him at all, but to overcome their understandable mistrust, ensure their confidence and obtain their assistance, he knew he would have to reveal exactly how he came to meet Naomi. He held the woman's gaze, smiling. 'I'm sorry, love, I realise my inquiries must look, shall we say...not quite kosher...but you see...' He sighed. 'I was there too, in the camp, I mean. I had a spot of bother with the master race and...well...they threw me in the slammer.'

Her mouth fell open with a sharp intake of breath. She looked at him aghast. 'You were in Matthausen?...An inmate?'

'Guilty, I'm afraid.' He squeezed her hand but she continued to stare at him. He leaned forward. 'You see...what's your name, love?'

'Rosie,' she whispered, awestruck.

'You see, Rosie, Naomi saved my life in that place, I owe her so much, I must know that she got through. She couldn't go home to Dresden, could she? So I thought she might have come here.'

She shook her head, disbelieving. 'But why? What did you do to the Krauts, for crisakes?'

He laughed aloud. 'I'm a paratrooper, sweetheart. In return for clothes, food, lodging and the guarantee of a reasonably soft landing, my government insisted I kill the sods.'

She recovered, laughing weakly at his quip. 'Yeah, I can see that, but why weren't you an ordinary prisoner of war?'

'I beat up an Oberstürmführer. Almost killed him.' She frowned. 'After I was captured,' he explained. 'I think that's what pissed them off, actually.'

'My God, they could have shot you.'

'Nah.' He shook his head, dismissively. 'As I told them at the time, it's illegal.'

'Oh my God!' Rosie began to laugh, a raucous strident whooping. 'You told 'em it's illegal, the goddamn SS? You told 'em...my God, Captain...'

'Sammy,' he offered. He too was laughing.

'...holy shit, Sammy, you sure got some nerve, or are you just plain nuts?'

'I gotta tell ya, Rosie, my brand a' nuts are pretty fancy,' he mimicked.

Their laughter attracted the attention of a colleague in the rear office. 'What's goin' on, Rosie, what's with the Mardi Gras?' A small, dark, very morose man approached, peering disapprovingly over his spectacles.

'Oh Willie!' Rosie laughed, shaking her head. 'We gotta help this guy. He's lookin' for his girl. He beat up on a goddamn Nazi storm trooper, for crisakes, just so he could get himself thrown into Matthausen to be with her. Now he's come all the way to Palestine to find her. Willie, it's the least we can do.'

The little man looked bewildered. 'You're telling me this Limey was in Matthausen?' His accent was nasal and unmistakably New York. 'Some bill o' goods you're selling me here, Rosie.'

'What's with you, Willie?' She regarded him reproachfully. 'You're calling Sammy here a liar? Listen, I'll explain later.' She waved a peremptory hand. 'So...say hi to Sammy,' she ordered.

'Hi Sammy.'

'Hello Willie.'

He checked into the Carmel Hotel. He bathed, dressed quickly then made for the 'Council' offices. Rosie smiled broadly as she saw him enter. He bent and kissed her affectionately on the cheek.

'Hey, what am I, your goddamn mother?' She grinned. He

kissed her again, this time on the lips. 'Enough already, heartbreaker,' she chuckled, 'you got ten minutes to quit that...Oh Willie,' she sang loudly to her chief, 'Sammy's here.'

He came to the door of his office polishing his glasses with the hem of his shirt. He regarded Sammy myopically and with his usual forlorn expression. 'Hi Sammy,' he said, sighing.

'Willie! My God you look positively luminous. What happened?'

Willie shrugged sadly, replacing his spectacles. 'My ol' lady's threatenin' to walk out on me.'

'Wonderful, that would explain your exuberance. But why, Willie? What did you do right this time?'

'She heard I spent the weekend with Lana Turner when she came with Stars and Stripes.'

'That's good, she should always listen to idle gossip.'

'I told her, already.'

'What's she like?'

'My ol' lady?'

'No, you klutz, Lana Turner.'

'Sammy, gimme a break. Go look for Naomi.'

Rosie said, 'Sammy, it's impossible, I need a name. Your description has all the precision one would expect of a scientist, but sweetheart, have you any idea how many beautiful, dark-haired, black-eyed Jewesses there are called Naomi?'

'Not too many got out of Matthausen, Rosie.' He watched her eyes shut briefly. 'I'm sorry, love, that was crass.'

'No, that's OK, sweetheart, you're right, of course you're right.' She sat silent for some time, deep in thought. 'Sammy, how often do you go to Tel Aviv?'

'Often. I go to the PPO concerts.'

'Then you know Dizengoff.'

'Sure.'

'The Café Delilah?'

'I don't know, it's possible, I rarely look at names.'

'OK listen, go to the Café Delilah, ask for Ben. His ol' lady owns the joint. Ben comes from London England, well Germany originally, but he was sent to England as a kid.'

'How can he help?'

'Sammy, I don't know if he can, but his wife's folks live up near Nathanya. There's a huge kibbutz up there, at a place called Rosh Pinnah, and you can bet a lot of illegals pass through it.' She paused and smiled at him. 'I shouldn't be telling you all this, you know, you Limey son of a bitch. How do I know you're not a spy?'

'If I were a spy would I be dressed like this? No!' He flounced. 'I'd have a long black cloak, a floppy black felt fedora and I would look like Aristide Bruant.' He touched her arm gently. 'You don't have to worry about me, love, I promise.'

'I know, sweetheart.' She covered his hand with her own. 'Go talk to Ben.'

Sammy glanced up from his desk upon hearing the knock. 'Come in.'

The sergeant entered carrying a single sheet of paper. 'Today's platoon orders, Sir.'

Sammy flipped the foolscap over quickly and raised his eyes in surprise. 'Short list today, Bill.'

'Yeah, just this bit of bother with Private Povey and the interview with Corporal Manders.'

'Any idea what he wants?'

'Manders? He wants to discuss discipline. Apparently the blokes won't take any notice of him.'

'Isn't this your department?'

'I have already spoken with him, but he is not the easiest of men to communicate with.'

'Why?'

'He's an imbecile.'

'Tortuously ambiguous as always, Sergeant. Try to be more specific?'

'He insists on giving orders which, quite frankly, knowing our lot, are at best only going to excite amusement.'

'And at worst?'

'Someone is going to thump the prat.'

'Give me an example.'

'For example, the other day he went into the NAAFI, latish, everybody's tanked up and he musters a parade outside, to call the roll.'

'Call the roll?' Sammy looked nonplussed.

'He said he was checking for deserters.'

'Deser...but we are in the middle of a fucking desert, where did he think they were going to go? Or is he perhaps confused about the etymology of desert?'

Bill laughed. 'Then this morning, during tea break, he ordered the Twins to stop playing at the piano.'

'Why did he do that? Is he crackers?'

'Good question, and you are really going to enjoy the answer. But it must come from Manders himself.'

Sammy sighed aloud. 'Why do I have to do this?'

'Because you are an officer, it comes with the turf.'

'OK, you had better show him in.'

'Er...I think you should deal with Povey first, Sir, the doctor's been waiting some time.'

'Doctor? What's it got to do with the doctor?'

'He's got the pox.' Sammy's jaw dropped. 'No not the doctor,' the sergeant hastened to explain, 'Povey!'

'Right.' Sammy nodded slowly. 'But how does this concern me? Why doesn't he just put Povey's prick in a sling, or whatever they do, and mark him fit for duty?'

'He's put him on a charge..."occasioning a self-inflicted injury".'

'Self-inflicted injury! How the fuck do you self-inflict the pox?'

'Oh, that's very good, Sammy,' laughed the sergeant, 'I suppose the answer must be yes.'

Sammy laughed with the NCO. 'Jesus, what a bloody place. Show the doctor in, Sergeant.'

'So, what do you want me to do with him, Doc?' Sammy struggled not to laugh.

'Well Sir, as, like most of us, he is new out here, I thought you might advise him how to behave when off duty. I mean to say, it's up to the older chaps to give guidance in these matters. Damn it all, the chap has syphilis, which as you know is against King's Regulations...'

Sammy could contain himself no longer and both he and Bill collapsed into gales of laughter. 'Oh Christ, Doc, you are the bloody end. How is syphilis against KRs, for Christ's sake?' He turned to the sergeant. 'It's those bloody spirochaete, not a bloody clue about good order and military discipline.'

The doctor raised himself haughtily. 'Just because you seem familiar with the pathology of the disease, Captain, that is no excuse for twisting my words.' As Sammy and Bill resumed their laughter, the doctor grinned sheepishly at his unintended pun. 'I was referring to the act itself, you know, all those awful women.'

Sammy recovered. 'What do you expect, for Christ's sake? We feed them a diet of red meat and violence and you expect them to behave like Trappists.' He turned to the sergeant. 'What's he like, Bill?'

'Bit of a yokel, deepest Devonshire by the sound of him.'

'Oh shit!' Sammy sighed. 'You'd better wheel him in.'

'Right, Sir.' He turned on his heel and opened the door. 'Right, Povey, on your feet, get in here now! And you two, stay put. The platoon commander may want a word with you later.'

Private Povey, a large, ponderous, tow-headed youth, appeared in the doorway and looked uncertainly at Sammy. 'Right! Off cap, come to attention before the platoon commander and clearly state your name and number,' commanded the sergeant.

'I ain't got no cap, Sarge,' Private Povey whispered nervously, 'I only got this berry.'

'Improvise, lad!' the sergeant suggested.

Private Povey snatched at his red beret and quickly stuffed it into his trouser pocket. He stopped before Sammy's desk. '767354, Private Povey, R. reporting, SIR!' he roared then, lifting his right foot to knee height, crashed it to the floor.

'Jesus Christ,' Sammy said, visibly shocked by this assault. 'Must you make such a bloody racket? Calm down, for Christ's sake, Private Povey, R...what's the R for, by the way?'

'Bob, Sir.'

'Of course it is, silly of me. Now, the doctor says you've been a naughty boy with the ladies and should be punished...' He frowned suddenly and turned to the sergeant. 'Who were you talking to out there, Sarge? Who's "you two"?'

'The Twins, Sir.'

'The Twins? What do they want?'

'The accused has called them as character witnesses, Sir.'

'Character witnesses? Those two! What's the matter, have Burke and Hare reported sick? Jesus Christ, that's all I need.' He looked at the private who began to nod his head, smiling expectantly at Sammy, as though seeking approval for his choice of allies. 'So what's the story, Povey? The doctor here says you've got a dose of Bombay Crut, is that right?'

'No Sir.'

'No? Are you saying the doctor is mistaken, that he doesn't know the pox when he sees it?'

'Oh no, Sir, but tweren't Bombay see, twere Beirut. I were on R and R and they two buggers led I on and...'

'Yes, well, if we are going to involve "they two buggers", as you call them, we shall have to hear their side of the story. But before we go into the sordid details, I want to hear what the MO has to say...Doctor?'

'Yes Sir. Well, the accused attended my sick parade complaining of a discharge and considerable discomfort in his...er...his...'

'Wedding gear?'

'Quite so, Sir...and upon examination, I discovered a well-formed chancre, that's a sort of ulcer, and I diagnosed syphilis. The accused admitted having recent intercourse with a prostitute, contrary to all existing advice, so I placed him on a charge for occasioning a self-inflicted injury.'

'Yes, I see,' said Sammy, trying desperately to keep a straight face. 'But are you sure a clinical condition such as venereal disease actually constitutes an injury? I think perhaps what the army had in mind was some sod shooting himself in the foot to get Blightied, not catching carnal flu.'

'I can assure you, Sir, the consequences of untreated syphilis are far more severe than an injured foot...' He shook his hand angrily at the young soldier. 'Did it never occur to you that you might catch something dire from such a creature? Do you realise you could become insane, man?' he cried.

Private Povey looked pleadingly at Sammy. 'I didn't know she were mad, Sir. They two said I'd be alright.'

Sammy gripped the wings of his nose painfully between finger and thumb, suppressing his mirth. 'Sergeant, bring "they two" in, will you?' he uttered nasally.

Bill moved to the door and called the two waiting soldiers to attend their platoon commander. 'Privates Walters, C. DCM and Williams, T. DCM, Sir.'

'Thank you, Sergeant.' Sammy looked up at his two favourite veterans and detected at once the familiar glint of mischief in their eyes. He smiled. 'Good R and R?' he asked in a friendly tone causing the doctor to gasp in surprise.

'Bloody great!' replied Calvin Walters. 'Wasn't it, Tommy?'

'Absolutely bloody wonderful, Cal,' confirmed Thomas Williams. 'You should have been there, Sa...er...Sir.'

'Not a bloody chance,' said Sammy. 'The last time I was fool enough to attend a party with you lunatics I had the distinct impression someone was trying to kill me. Now, you may have had a wonderful time, but what about poor Povey here? I suppose you know he is in trouble with the doctor?'

Tommy looked at the MO. 'What's he done, Doc?'

'What's he done, SIR!' bawled the MO.

'Eh?' asked Sammy, frowning. 'How the bloody hell would I...oh...right.'

'...What's he done?' the doctor persevered. 'I'll tell you what he's damned well done, he's contracted the pox, that's what he's done, and no thanks to you, it seems.'

Tommy turned to his friend. 'I thought anyone could catch the pox, I didn't know you needed a contract, did you Cal?'

Calvin shrugged. 'First I've heard of it.'

Everybody began to laugh except the doctor. 'With all due respect, Sir,' he said, his face flushed with anger, 'this is a very serious matter and I do believe we should address it with a little more gravity...I'm sorry.'

'No, Doc. You are right. It is I who should apologise.' Sammy turned his attention to the Twins. 'Right, tell us how you managed to get this young soldier, who has only recently joined us out here and is quite inexperienced in these matters, into this bloody mess.'

'Inexperienced? Him?' Calvin was incredulous that he and his old comrade should be held responsible for Povey's predicament. 'All he thinks of is shagging, it's an obsession with him.' He turned to the hapless Povey. 'Come on Pove, you asked us to help you out here, not take the can back for you.'

'And how did you propose to do that?' asked Sammy. 'Did he deliberately catch the pox or not? And if he did, what did you do to discourage him?'

'Discourage him? Povey? God almighty himself couldn't discourage him when he smells crumpet, so when he told us he wanted to get his leg over, we thought we'd better take him to the Sans Rival...'

'What is the Sans Rival?' asked the doctor.

'I was wondering what a rival is, and why this place hasn't got one,' said Sammy.

'It's a sort of music hall,' said Tommy, 'you know, singing and dancing, like the Moulin Rouge. It's also a licensed brothel where the bibbies get regular medicals...we do a turn there, don't we, Cal?'

'You do a turn in a brothel?' The doctor turned desperately to Sammy.

'I think they mean the music hall, Doc. They are both very accomplished pianists.'

'Are you telling me this sort of thing is officially sanctioned?' The doctor was clearly shocked.

'Oh yeah, they love English dance music, don't they Tommy?'

'I was referring to the brothel!' the doctor snapped testily.

'Oh absolutely, Sir, well it is in Beirut, it's French, see. But they're very strict about hygiene, the Frogs.'

'Then how did he manage to contract syphilis?' the doctor asked haughtily.

'Who said he got it there?' asked Tommy. 'He more than

likely picked it up around here. I mean, the English don't approve of shagging, do they? So they don't allow licensed knocking shops...so they don't have any medical controls...so when poor bastards like Povey here get a dose of knob rot, people like you can't wait to put them on a charge.'

'How dare you speak to an officer like that!' cried the doctor. 'I have never heard such insolence.'

Tommy looked at his platoon commander. 'We're not being insolent, Sammy, you know that's not our style, but...well, I don't think the MO understands what things are like out here, I mean he hasn't got his knees brown himself yet, has he? We thought Povey would be alright as far as that was concerned.'

'My God...' spluttered the MO.

'Alright Doctor, calm down,' said Sammy. 'You are not in bloody Aldershot now and this is the Middle East not Middlesex. Now...' He switched his attention back to the Twins. '...did you attempt to make sure that he was ok?'

'Not really, Sir...I mean you can't just barge in...right?'

'We did look in for a minute when she started leading off at him, remember Cal?'

'What do you mean "leading off"?' asked Sammy. 'Why was she leading off?'

'Well, it seems old Pove dozed off on the job and she got the hump,' said Calvin.

'Dozed off?' repeated the doctor, his eyes wide with amazement.

'Yeah, well...he was well pissed,' said Tommy. 'But when we woke him he got going again and she was alright.'

'On the large side was she?' The sergeant suddenly joined the discussion.

'Large!' exclaimed Tommy. 'She made Sophie Tucker look undernourished.' Sammy looked puzzled.

'Povey has an obsession with convex women,' Bill explained.

'A sort of endomorph fetish. Just exactly how big was this specimen, Tommy?'

'Let's say she was taller on her back than she was on her feet. We were afraid he was going to burn his arse on the light bulb and do himself an injury...'

'Why do you always pick them fat old dogs, Pove?' asked Calvin amid the laughter. 'After all, there's lots of nice slinky bints in Beirut, not like round here.'

'I likes the big'uns, they skinny ones is no good...anyway, they's too dear. I could 'ave all night with Lerah for the same price as a short time with that other one.'

'Lerah...you know this woman personally?' asked the doctor, causing yet more laughter. 'What I meant to say was...' he flustered then, affected by the empathy between the four veterans and their light-hearted, almost burlesque badinage, he too began to laugh. 'Oh shit,' he chuckled, 'why do I bother> You are all clearly incorrigible.'

'One of these days, Povey,' said Sammy, 'unless you attenuate your sexual appetites, you are going to disappear without trace and quite frankly I won't know how to inform your unfortunate family. I mean, it's not exactly a hero's death, is it? Hardly in the proud tradition of the Parachute Regiment. What could I possibly tell them?'

'I don't know, Sir.' Povey dropped his head, shamefaced and shuffled his feet.

'Missing believed swallowed?' suggested Calvin.

'Injuries suffered following a drop?' added Tommy.

'Yes that's all very funny,' said Sammy above the laughter, 'but, God help him, this idiot looks to you two for guidance and example and above all to make sure he doesn't get into trouble... right?'

'Sammy's got a point, you know, lads,' said Bill. 'The next time you catch him astride another beamy odalisque, try tying his foot to the sink.'

'Alright, alright!' Sammy raised his hands to quell the laughter. 'Let's put this one to bed. How long will your course of treatment take, Doctor?'

'Six weeks should clear it up, Sir.'

'Right, Private Povey. Confined to barracks for eight weeks...'

'He said six,' protested Povey.

'But he's not the judge, is he? Would you prefer twelve?'

'No Sir, eight's fair.'

'Good! Now bugger off, and Povey...'

'Sir?'

'Take yourself in hand, lad.'

'Do you need us any more, Sammy?' asked Calvin.

'Not any more, thank God,' answered Sammy. 'And I certainly don't deserve you, so you can bugger off too.' The two paratroopers left the office laughing.

'Are those two usually so insubordinate?' the doctor asked Sammy.

'Only when it doesn't matter, Doc,' replied Sammy, smiling. 'I think that's it, right?'

'Yes, thank you, Sir.'

Sammy waited for the door to close. 'Right Bill, let's see what Manders wants, shall we?'

The sergeant opened the door. 'Come on Manders, look sharp, the Captain's waiting. Corporal Manders to see you, Sir.' Sammy could tell by his barely suppressed amusement that Bill was enjoying himself.

'Thank you, Sergeant Grant. Come in, Corporal.' He looked up at the man. 'You wanted to see me?'

'Yes Sir...It's personal, Sir.'

'I see, will you excuse us, Sergeant?' Bill turned at the door and gave Sammy a broad wink. Sammy watched the door close.

'Right Corporal, shoot.'

'Am 'avin' trouble wi' some o' the blokes, Sir.' The man spoke in a slow, ponderous Black Country accent. 'I wanted to put two ov 'em on a charge and they tow'd me to fook off. Then when I ordered two others to put 'em under close arrest they aw started laffin'.'

Sammy tried to focus his social skills and constrain his own laughter. 'Tell me, Corporal, why did you want to charge them?'

'They was playin' the pianner after time, Sir.'

'After time?' Sammy was clearly bemused.

'The NAAFI was shut, Sir.'

'Presumably the piano was open?'

Manders appeared unsure quite how to field this question. ''Scuse me, Sir?'

Sammy, realising the corporal had had his first encounter with the Twins, decided it was time to lay down some rules before the climate worsened. He pointed to a chair. 'Sit down, Corporal Manders.' He waited until the soldier seated himself. 'Manders, I have a problem and I need your help.' The corporal squinted. 'You see, our wartime chaps are not accustomed to the sort of regular army discipline to which you have been subjected. Take the two men in question, for example, Williams and Walters, they volunteered for the commandos during the war precisely to avoid it. When their commando converted to airborne duties they were among the first ever paratroopers. You see, Manders, the wartime Parachute Regiment was a far more relaxed affair when it came to things like square-bashing and spit and polish. In fact there was none, there was neither the time nor the need for it. That in no way affected their ability to fight. Every man jack acquitted himself in battle far beyond what is normally referred to as "the call of duty". The "Twins", that's their nickname by the way, both hold the Distinguished Conduct Medal for bravery. I fought beside them at Arnhem, Corporal. I saw what they did and had it been left to me they would have been awarded the VC. These men fought a hard and bloody war and now they are waiting to be demobbed, to return to their families. They are first class soldiers who do not require such mindless barrack square, spit and polish bullshit to make them do what is asked of them in the line of duty. Do you understand, Corporal?'

Manders fidgeted in his chair. 'They 'ave to learn to obey orders from their superiors, Sir. They made me look a right prat and I wan' 'em charged for insubordination under KRs.'

Sammy closed his eyes and sighed. 'Oh Christ.' He looked straight at the corporal. 'Now Manders, I want you to pay close attention to what I am going to say. I want you to read my lips very carefully. Leave my bloody men alone. And by my men I mean all those who served with me in the war. You will not charge Williams and Walters with anything and for the following reasons. One; playing the piano, after time, as you put it, or at any other bloody time, come to that, is not a chargeable offence under King's Regulations. Two; you will never at any time give orders which are simply the issue of some illiterate, mindless whim. Three; you are not, nor could you ever be, their superior. Four and finally; when it comes to looking like a prat you need no help from them, or indeed anybody else.' He paused, fixing the corporal with his cold unblinking stare. 'Corporal Manders, you are my worst nightmare incarnate. You are a thick, ignorant, bullying, bullshitting oaf and if I don't put a stop to your stupidity right now you are going to cause me a great deal of trouble and I don't want trouble, not now, not when it's nearly all over for us. When we have worked our way through the system, Manders, and have all been demobbed, you and your ilk can have the Parachute Regiment and you can fuck it up to your hearts' content. In the meantime, and if you want to stay healthy, keep away from us. Do I make myself clear?'

141

'Are you threatnin' me, Sir?' Manders grinned at Sammy defiantly.

Sammy smiled back. 'I would not wish to deceive you, Corporal, but yes, that is precisely what I am doing and I would advise you to take me seriously...OK?'

Manders finally averted his gaze. 'Yes Sir, but if I ca' tell the blokes what to do, I dunno why they made me a corporal.'

Sammy smiled at him. 'That makes two of us, Manders. Now...piss off.'

Norman Manders was a large, strong, dim-witted man who had worked on the assembly track of the Austin Motor Company in Birmingham. A working class Englishman, he was aggressively xenophobic, declaiming loudly to any with the patience to listen that, 'All wogs start at Calais.' He was also violently and irrationally anti-Semitic. 'Fookin' yids,' he would proclaim. 'Best thing Adolf ever did, wipin' out those bastards. We shoulda waited till 'e'd bloody finished the fookin' job.' Fascinated by the wartime exploits of the paratroops, he volunteered for parachute training within days of being drafted for National Service. He imagined himself adorned in his red beret, lionised by his friends and pursued by beautiful women. Discovering his class was to join the Sixth Airborne Division in Palestine, he was overjoyed. 'Great mob, the Sixth, D Day, the Rhine and now Palestine. Those fookin' yids' feet won' fookin' touch, you watch.'

Following his encounter with Sammy Parker and other veterans of the very battles which had so inflated his ego, he felt a deep resentment. 'Fookin' shower, laffin' like a bunch o' fookin' tarts and playin' the fookin' pianner. Fookin' paratroops? Oi've shit 'em.' He was, however, careful to heed Sammy's warning and avoided the veterans.

He quickly attracted a cadre of sycophantic admirers, like-minded individuals who also resented the veterans and their reputation. His overt hatred of both Arab and Jew and his brutal and violent behaviour while on patrol earned him the appellation 'Gräber the Jew Baiter', after the notorious concentration camp commander whose name had been much in the news during the trials of German war criminals in Nüremberg.

'Kicked a few wog arses today, eh lads? Fookin' shower. I bet those shit bints don' arf stink. Must be ugly bastards too the way they 'ave to cover up their gobs. 'Ere, did you see that fookin' yid's face when I kicked his fookin' door in? He nearly shit 'iself. I ca' stand the bastards, any on 'em, we ought to send 'em all back where they fookin' come from.'

'And where is that, exactly, Corporal?' Bill Grant looked at the man with ill-disguised contempt. He had, yet again, to reprimand Manders for using excessive force while carrying out the routine search of a Jewish settlement near Petah Tikva.

'Well, you know, they don' belong 'ere, do they?'

'So, where do they belong?'

'Well I don' fookin' know,' he shouted aggressively. 'But we got orders to keep 'em out of 'ere, so it ain't fookin' 'ere, is it?'

'Did you understand the purpose of today's patrol, Corporal?'

'Yeah, course I did.'

'Which was...?'

'To seek and find an underground press.'

'Right, so why did you think it necessary to smash that family's home to matchwood and beat up an old man?'

'He wouldn't tell me where the fookin' cellar was.'

'Cellar?...' Bill looked bemused at first then he closed his eyes, shaking his head. 'Oh my God.'

'Any road, it's about time we showed 'em who's boss.'

'Button your lip, Corporal.' Bill could barely conceal his hatred of the man. 'Or I'll take those stripes and stuff them up your useless arse.'

143

Manders grinned defiantly. 'You could try, Sergeant.'

'So what do you want me to do, Bill?' Sammy looked at the sergeant's reflection in his shaving mirror.

'Nothing, Sammy, I'll handle it. I just thought you should know. He's a nasty piece of work, that one, an utterly detestable bastard with absolutely no redeeming features. And he is so unbelievably thick. As I have said, it is virtually impossible to communicate with him. But it is his attitude to the Jews which worries me the most. He absolutely detests them and I'm not talking about the usual derogatory joking around. This is the real thing, you know, like the Nazis. He is completely irrational and I believe it's only a matter of time before he goes ape and does something really stupid.'

Sammy smiled. 'Then we'll have him, won't we, Bill?'

'God, I hope so...look, that's not why I came to see you.' Sammy turned from the mirror and began to dab cologne on his face. Bill smiled. 'I hope you haven't anything planned for tonight.'

'I was going to pop into Tel Aviv.' He winked. 'I have a secret assignation.'

'Oh yeah, who with?'

'Someone called Ben.'

'Ben? Short for what?'

'Benjamin, I suppose.'

'That's original.'

'What do you mean original?'

'Well, you know, "Do you Benjamin take this man Sammy", don't sound right.'

Sammy smiled. 'Consider the possibility I'm going to meet a bloke.'

'You're not going to meet anyone, we've just pulled another patrol.'

'Tonight? Bill, tell me you are joking...Shit!' He threw down his shirt in disgust. 'Who told you this?'

'Burty Burns. There's an "immigrant" approaching. Spotted by the RAF coastal boys.'

'Where?'

'Well, they say it's too close to shore to run down to Gaza and the only other beach with enough draft is the one between Herzliya and Nathanya.' Bill looked at his friend. 'Still no luck, Sammy?'

'Not yet, Bill, that's why I wanted to see this chap Ben.'

'Cheer up, mate, you'll find her one day.'

'Of course I will...thanks Bill.' He regarded his friend. 'How about your little Dutch clog dancer? Still writing to each other are you?'

'Yeah, I had a letter today, in fact.'

'Good for you. Any plans?'

'I can't do much from here, Sammy...anyway, she was just a kid...'

'So was Juliet.'

'So she was.' Bill chuckled. 'A bloody fine Romeo I'd make, eh? But she was so lovely...I'll definitely go and see her when I get back...who knows?'

Sammy smiled. 'I'd better get briefed. See you at the motor pool in half an hour.'

The platoon deployed, concealed among the groves at the top of the cliffs. Lookouts had been posted to watch the road in both directions. Sammy raised his night glasses and watched the shallow waves roll silently across the white sandy beach below. He raised his sight to look further out to sea. It was clear to the horizon. He heard a footfall behind him and turned to face the sergeant.

'Anything?'

'Nothing, Sir. Palestine Police intelligence says the Haganah are covering this landing.'

Sammy nodded then scanned the beach again. 'I hate this, Bill,' he muttered. He lowered his glasses and leaned against the squat, leafy orange tree. 'We sit here in the dark waiting for some rusty shit freighter to run aground then we ambush a bunch of poor, half starved, demented sods who have lost all that once made them human in some Nazi concentration camp and hand them over to the navy who take them over to Cyprus to be locked up in yet another bloody concentration camp. Why in the name of God don't we try to rehabilitate them in their own countries?'

Bill smiled. 'They say this is their own country.'

'Well that's obviously bollocks, isn't it, Bill? The Arabs have been here for almost a thousand years.'

'Tell that to...shush, hold on, Sammy.'

'What is it?'

'Trucks...listen...up there, towards Nathanya.'

The noise of the engines grew louder and Sammy deployed his platoon to intercept them on the coast road. They saw the lead truck make the bend and head for the beach trail. 'Right, now!' Sammy shouted. The searchlights rang loudly as their switches were thrown, flooding the road with light and causing the trucks to grind erratically to a halt. He lifted his megaphone and looked in the direction of the lead truck.

'This is a British Army patrol. Dismount now, place your weapons on the ground and put your hands on your heads. You will not be harmed.' He watched as they dismounted from their trucks to stand bewildered in the road, some shielding their eyes against the intense light. He walked forward, followed by the sergeant and two armed paratroopers. The people looked at the soldiers, their faces betraying fear.

'Who is in charge here?' Nobody moved. They stood frozen

before the soldiers. He approached a small group standing in the road. They wore blue twill shirts and overalls, men and women alike. 'These people don't look like Haganah to me,' he said. Turning to the group he asked, 'Who are you people and what are you doing here after curfew?'

A man stepped forward. Sammy judged him to be about thirty-five, above medium height and stockily built, his fair hair bleached by the sun. He doesn't look much like a Jew, Sammy thought. 'Who are you?' he asked. The man kept his hands on his head, shifting uncomfortably. 'Lower your hands,' said Sammy. He looked at the others. 'Put your hands down and relax, nobody's going to hurt you. Now you, I asked you a question.' The man stared back, still uncertain. 'Which organisation are you from?'

'Organisation?'

'Yes, this uniform, what is it?'

He tilted his head slightly. 'This is not a uniform, these are our working clothes. We are kibbutzniks, from Rosh Pinnah.'

Sammy started at the name. 'What is your name?' He looked up at the other people gathered at the roadside. 'What are so many kibbutzniks doing here?'

The man raised his palms and shrugged. 'I am Michael Berkovitz and these are my brothers and sisters. We have come to meet other kibbutzniks who are going to join us. We are not armed.'

Sammy looked at the man then shook his head. 'Michael Berkovitz, you know and I know that you are here to meet illegals and that I cannot permit that.'

Again he shrugged. 'I know, you have a job to do, Captain.' He looked away for some moments then returned his gaze to Sammy. 'Captain, our people will be exhausted, they will be filthy and hungry, many will be sick. In God's mercy I ask you to let us at least feed them when they come.' He reached forward and touched Sammy's arm. 'I cannot expect you to understand what they have been through, but you seem like a decent man. What difference will one night make?'

Sammy turned his gaze again out to sea. In the blackness beyond the lights he heard the gentle surf washing the beach. He closed his eyes and her voice came to him out of the darkness. 'I will never leave you, Sammy, you will remain forever in my heart.' He choked back the pain of his loneliness.

'Sergeant Grant.'

'Sir.'

'Check the positions, I don't want any cock-ups tonight. Report to Sergeant Major Burns, make sure he understands my orders. I want no shooting or any heroics. These people are not Haganah, they are farmers. Tell the men to stand easy until we get sight of the boat.'

'Right Sir.' He made off into the darkness.

Sammy turned to Michael and asked softly, 'Why are kibbutzniks assisting illegal immigration and how do you know that a ship is due here?'

Michael stared back at Sammy for some moments before he replied. He could not explain why, but he detected something unusual in this officer's manner. His attitude, though firm, was sympathetic. He appeared to show real concern for what was to come. He smiled. 'Our people keep us informed. We have known for some time about this party. We have relatives among them, as well as friends. Rosh Pinnah is a large kibbutz, we need many hands to work it and defend it. We thought we would be safe, someone must have betrayed us.'

Sammy looked away quickly. 'Nobody betrayed you, you had bad luck. The ship was sighted by an RAF patrol. From its position and speed this is the only place it could beach safely.' He returned his gaze to Michael. 'How long have they been at sea?'

'Three weeks.'

Sammy sighed heavily. 'Bloody hell.'

'Yes Captain, you can be sure it is just that.'

Sergeant Grant approached, accompanied by a Palestine Policeman. 'What is it, Sergeant?'

'This officer has just had a radio message that a patrol of Haganah has been stopped at Herzliya, Captain.'

Sammy looked at the policeman. 'Are our people there, Officer?'

'Yes Sir, the lot from Qastina.'

'Ninth Battalion?'

'Yes Sir.'

'Right. Get back to the men, I'll be with you in a minute.' He turned to Michael. 'You say you are from Rosh Pinnah, where is that?'

'It lies east of Nathanya, about thirty miles.'

'On the Plain of Sharon?'

'Yes.' Michael smiled. 'You know the country?'

Sammy did not reply at once. He stared intently at Michael and the man felt a strange empathy with him. Sammy's head bobbed. 'How do I get there?' he asked.

Michael was surprised by the question. 'You want to search our kibbutz?'

'Search?' Sammy seemed bemused.

'You will come with your soldiers?'

'No, alone. I want to talk to you.'

'What about?'

Sammy fell silent and gazed out across the sea again. He stood, unmoving, detached, deep in thought. He raised a hand and appeared to brush his eyes. He turned suddenly and Michael began to feel strangely apprehensive under his intense and unremitting stare. He shifted uncomfortably.

'From Nathanya you take the road to Nablus, for about thirty miles. But why, what do you...'

Turning suddenly, Sammy walked away from him, back to his troops. Michael looked at his retreating figure, frowning, until he disappeared. He heard his voice come out of the darkness.

'Sergeant Grant.'

'Sir?'

'Round up the men, we've been had, that lot was a decoy. Christ knows where that ship is going to ground, but I'll wager it's not Herzliya.'

'No arrests, Sir?'

'What would be the point? Wrap it up, Bill, let's go home.'

'An absolute shambles, Parker.' Lieutenant Colonel John Hackett looked angrily at Sammy. 'A boatload of illegals lands exactly where predicted and its cargo is spirited away to God knows where after you have decided to quit the field. What in God's name were you thinking of, Sir?'

'I had to make a decision based on my judgment of the situation, Sir.' Sammy spoke without emotion. 'And it was my judgment, given the position of the immigrant ship as reported by the RAF, that it would arrive at the rendezvous beach at around seven in the evening. Weather conditions were ideal and even allowing for other unforeseen circumstances, an overshoot of nearly four hours made me suspicious. The Palestine Police expected the landing to be assisted by the Haganah, which is not unusual. Instead, four trucks of kibbutzniks showed up. Men and women, unarmed and seemingly frightened out of their wits by our presence. It was the demeanour of the leader which most aroused my suspicions. He, of all of them, seemed not in the least disturbed by our presence. He appeared to expect us and tried hard to detain us as long as possible. The report from the Palestine Police that a Haganah patrol had been intercepted at

Herzliya lead me to conclude we had been the victims of a very successful double bluff.'

'Well it isn't going to look very good on your report, Captain Parker, not very good at all. I have been meaning to speak to you about your general attitude to your duties. I'm far from satisfied, very far from satisfied.'

Sammy did not respond. Why does the stupid bastard keep repeating himself, he wondered.

'Well?' The colonel stared at him.

'Well what, Sir?' He stared straight ahead.

'Have you nothing to say, nothing to say at all?'

'About what, Sir? Perhaps you could be more specific, a little more specific.'

The colonel's eyes narrowed. 'Be very careful, Parker, just watch it, right?'

Sammy lowered his head and looked straight at the colonel, his gaze cold and hard. 'Will that be all, Sir?'

'For the moment, yes.'

CHAPTER SEVEN

Sammy followed the coast road to Nathanya where long ago a fresh spring suddenly burst through the thick blanket of sand and bubbled its way down towards a desolate beach before being overtaken and smothered by the dunes. Here Bedou, yielding to that involuntary hunger for greenness which lies at the heart of all desert people, had planted palm and fig whose roots had taken a firm grip on the sandstone from which the crystal water sprang. The folded rocks formed a long shapely defile which descended to the salty desert at Tabah. He knew of the settlement at Rosh Pinnah. It had been built early in the century on sour land bought from a local Effendi by immigrants fleeing pogrom and famine in Russia. Through hard work and good husbandry it had flourished despite numerous attempts by local Arab tribes to destroy it. Its clean, neat buildings and its well-tended fields and groves now sat in open country behind piled concertinas of razor wire. He approached slowly to give the watchkeepers time to identify his jeep. An armed shomer came to the gate and eyed Sammy with ill-disguised disdain. 'What do you want here, soldier?'

Sammy gave the man a friendly smile. 'Would you be good enough to convey my respects to Michael Berkovitz. Tell him Captain Parker of the Parachute Regiment is here to see him.'

'What about?'

'It's a personal matter.'

'I asked you a question.'

Sammy, still smiling, said, 'Do you have a permit for that weapon?'

The man grinned then opened the gate. He pointed to a group of low buildings in the centre of the compound. 'Park your jeep beside those trucks then go to the building with the blue doors. That's the dining hall. Michael will be in class right now but I'll get a message to him and he will come as soon as he is free.'

'He is a teacher?'

'Among other things.' The man seemed surprised and suspicious. 'I thought you said you knew him.'

'I don't think so.' Sammy smiled at the man and accelerated away.

He parked the jeep and made his way to the dining hall. He entered a large, airy space with several rows of tables running down the middle. Behind the long counter, through the serving hatches, he saw the kitchen, quiet now, the gleaming pans and utensils hanging from their hooks. He looked around the spotless hall, its shiny floor reflecting the bright sunlight streaming in. Each of the tables had a bowl of flowers at its centre and the room smelled of fresh polish. The windows were hung with bright gingham curtains and on the wall between them were murals, portraits of kibbutzniks at various tasks and paintings of various camp activities; ploughing, reaping, bread making, tending animals. He walked slowly around the room, stopping to look at each picture in turn. As he looked up into her face his heart leapt in his breast. She stood, surrounded by a group of children. She wore the traditional blue denim dress and her head was bound in a spotted peasant scarf. She smiled silently down at him from the wall. He reached forward slowly, as if to touch her.

'Yes, they are all originals, we have several very good artists here.' He turned to face Michael Berkovitz. Preoccupied with the picture, he had not heard him approach. Michael frowned. 'Are you alright, Captain? You look as though you have seen a ghost.' Sammy tried to recover but, still overcome with emotion, he turned back to the picture. 'It's very well composed, isn't it? An excellent likeness too.' He touched Sammy's arm. 'Are you sure you're OK?'

'What is she doing here?'

Michael frowned, puzzled by the question. 'My wife helps in the Kindergarten. Why do you ask?' He turned his head as he heard the door open. He smiled broadly. 'And here she is, the lady herself.' He turned to Sammy. 'Now Captain, judge for yours.e..l...f...' His voice died away but Sammy did not hear him.

He stared across the hall, choked with emotion. Naomi stared back, eyes wide in shock and wonder. Michael looked from one to the other, unable at once to comprehend. Still staring at Naomi, Sammy touched Michael's arm, an involuntary gesture and she waited, motionless as he slowly moved towards her. He stood before her now, eyes closed, and breathed deeply, as if to draw her very presence into him. She too closed her eyes, swallowing painfully, then raising her hands, began to trace the contours of his face, blindly confirming his presence. She ran her fingers into his hair then across his closed eyes and down, brushing his cheeks. As her fingers moved across his lips he turned and a sigh caught in his throat as he kissed her hand. She took his head and pulled it to her breast. He stood silent and bowed as he felt the warmth of her body move through him again, reminding him of everything she had been to him. She bent and gently kissed his head. He pressed his face against her breast and placed his arms around her, crushing her to him in a desperate embrace, like an anguished child craving solace. 'Sammy?' she whispered. He lifted his face to hers. 'Is it really you, have you come to me at last, my love?' She felt his lips brush away her tears and knew that at last all those endless empty nights of pain, of frustration, of hopelessness had ended and her heart seized the day in this bright, warm place. 'Oh God! Sammy, oh my love, oh God!' she cried out, her voice muffled by his body as she pushed herself deeper into his arms. He laid his cheek against her head and waited for her passion to still. She raised her head at last and gazed longingly at him.

'So,' he said softly, speaking for the first time, 'you moved into the neighbourhood. Couldn't you at least pick up a phone?' His voice broke as he smiled at her, his eyes brimming.

She began to laugh through her tears and lifted the hem of her dress to wipe his eyes as she had so long before. 'Oh Sammy...' She shook her head, smiling sadly. 'Must I still wipe the tears from your eyes?' As he gazed at her he felt his throat contract painfully and he could not speak. 'But can this be true? Is it over...is my agony really over at last?' Almost imperceptibly their lips came together, softly, poignantly, then becoming more urgent. She grabbed his hair, pulling, not wanting ever to let him go.

He took her angrily into his arms. 'I have searched for you until I thought I would go insane. I believed my heart would break when I lost you. All this time, though they said you were dead, I would not believe them, I never lost hope, never, never.'

Michael watched, confused and helpless. He sensed their anguish and their ecstasy and he cried with them. He went to them, but they had eyes only for each other. 'So, he has come at last,' he said sadly. His voice seemed to wake them from their reverie.

Naomi turned to him, her eyes wet and bright with happiness. 'Oh Michael, why didn't you tell me?'

'How could I tell you what I did not know?'

She looked at him, puzzled. 'You mean you don't...? Michael, this is Sammy, my Sammy, from the camp. This is the man who almost died for me, who saved my life, who fought Gräber and stopped him killing me. Michael, this is my beautiful British Goy for whom I have wept such bitter tears...but how did you find him?'

Michael looked at Sammy. 'I didn't,' he replied softly, 'he found me.'

She looked from one to the other, bewildered. 'Found you, where?'

'On the beach, at Nathanya. I thought he had come to arrest me.'

Naomi paraded her hero through the kibbutz in triumph, introducing him to everyone with her version of events in the camp. 'He cowed them all, those strutting Nazi swine. They had beaten him and starved him, but he never bent his neck to them, never and when they were going to shoot me he said he would see them all hanged if they touched a hair of my head. He told the Wehrmacht soldiers he was their only hope and if they killed him his comrades would shoot them all and they believed him, he was incredible. You should have been there, he was magnificent, my Sammy.' Her enthusiasm at first excited much sardonic amusement but it quickly became contagious until finally they embraced this British soldier, Naomi's Goy, who had shared her agony, wept for her loss and eventually crushed her tormentor and they took him to their hearts.

Michael applauded with the rest, though with heavy heart, for he saw how much they loved each other still. He knew the day he had most feared had come at last and that he was about to lose the woman he adored. He had lived with her obsession with this man which had eaten into his heart but now, finally, he began to understand. This soldier held a unique, almost talismanic fascination for her. He was her hero, her champion, her legend. Her tormented heart had cried out for him and now he had found her at last. Her joy could not be denied.

They returned to the hall and shared bread and wine. Naomi glowed in the presence of her love. She repeatedly touched him, her eyes never leaving his face. Sammy just gazed back at her, lost in reverie. Michael looked at them and though his heart cried out, he smiled and said softly, 'I think you should spend time together. You have shared so much pain and terror and loss, now you must be alone to share your happiness. You shall go to the hotel, today, at once.'

Sammy stared at him, trying to comprehend. Naomi took her husband's hands and kissed them. 'Oh Michael, thank you, thank you.' She looked at Sammy. 'Come with me, my darling, please, we have so much to recapture. I thought I had lost you and now there is so much I want to say to you. Sammy, please say you will.'

He swallowed. 'Of course I will come with you.' He turned to Michael. 'But I don't understand, which hotel?'

'We have a family hotel, on the heights at Nathanya. My father built it and now it is ours, Naomi's and mine. You can be alone there.'

'I thought you were a teacher.'

'That is my labour of love. For a living I run a hotel.'

Naomi looked at her husband urgently. 'But you still have classes, my love, how shall we get to the hotel?'

Michael smiled tenderly at his wife. 'Are you too bewitched to think? I do not suppose your hero dropped on us today by parachute, I am sure I saw a jeep. Now come, you are wasting precious time.'

The kibbutzniks gathered at the gate to see them go. Michael grasped Sammy's hand and Sammy looked hard into his eyes. 'Michael, what can I possibly say? I know this cannot have been easy for you, but it has been a shattering experience for me. I cannot believe I have found her safe at last. I dreamed of this day and prayed a thousand times it would come and now that it is here I am overwhelmed. Meeting you all here today has been an honour and I am both bewildered and embarrassed by your generosity.' He pressed Michael's hand.

Michael inclined his head slightly. 'The honour has been ours, Sammy Parker. How could we ever repay you for what you did for Naomi in that terrible place? From this day you are our brother and our home is your home.'

They drove away leaving the shouting, waving kibbutzniks amid a cloud of dust. Naomi waved back at them like an excited child until they were out of sight. She sat back and at once began to laugh. 'What's so funny?' Sammy asked, chuckling with her.

'It is just like a wedding. Are you sure they didn't tie tin cans and old boots to the back of your jeep? Turn here.' She pointed upwards to a grove of trees high on the cliffs. 'Look there, above the cliffs.'

A miniature oasis had been created. The spring had been dug out, channelled and gathered into a marble cistern which formed the centrepiece to a courtyard, paved with terracotta and enclosed on three sides by a low white building. As the water grew so the green grew with it creating the spiny shapes of cactus, the exuberance of bougainvillea and poinsettia, the shade of fig and palm. Into the severe whitewashed walls of the hotel were set mullioned and grilled windows which offered sudden, slotted views of the sea. Tables were set beneath the trees and the court gave onto a terrace built on three levels looking out to the ink-blue sea and down to a rocky cove. A gentle sea breeze rustled the leaves and the quiet waves hissed among the rocks far below. He sighed. 'Naomi, this is so beautiful, what do you call it?'

'Beth Shalom.' She looked at him, her black eyes dancing. 'You think it's corny, don't you?'

As she laughed he wanted to seize her but he drew back. 'Only a little.' He smiled.

'Well, my cynical Goy, before I renamed it, they called it Casablanca.'

'Gotcha.' He chuckled. 'No, Beth Shalom is perfect. House of Peace.'

Taking his hand, she led him into the hotel. It was cool and dark in contrast with the bright sunlight outside. They came to a pleasant oblong room with a low, beamed ceiling. At one end stood a fireplace, massive and white with decorated lintels suggesting Arab ceramics. At the opposite end was a large stone table standing between stone benches like the refectory of a monastery. The severity of the room was relieved by a scatter of Persian and Afghan rugs. In one corner stood an old, still brightly polished Samovar which once served to remind the builder of his roots. They stood alone again, yearning to touch each other, reaching back for a love so distant now, which they had left in another life, in a dark faraway place so terrible that they had all but driven it from their minds. They could not speak. She laid her head against his chest as he took her gently into his arms. She sighed contentedly and taking his hands, pressed them to her breasts. They kissed and she moved her hands beneath his shirt and caressed the warm skin of his back. He did not move. She led him from the hotel and across the court to the terrace, he following mutely. They sat upon the warm grass and gazed out at the shimmering sea, far below. They moved together and as they drew close the bitter memories crowded his mind.

He was a soldier, weary, battle marked and bloodied, but heroically so. She was fascinated by his presence, by his mystery, until finally, unable any longer to resist her curiosity she came to him half terrified, half in awe. He was reluctant and inviolable and at first resisted, held her away, but she refused to notice and grew ever more urgent until gradually, as his caution yielded to wonder, he too came to accept the truth of what was happening to them. Their enforced separation almost destroyed him. He felt an unendurable sense of loss which he could not assuage and to mitigate its pain he filled his mind with dreams; confused, dramatic fantasies which served to dull experience and fill his imagination with brighter promises of hope.

He wanted desperately to communicate these images to her now, but there was nothing he was able, or dared to put into words. Something stood between them still, something real, not imagined. He looked at her and she met his gaze. 'Oh my love,' he whispered.

'Yes my darling, I know...I know,' she answered, sharing his anguish.

He pushed back her hair. 'I had almost forgotten just how beautiful you are.'

His sudden compliment caused her to drop her gaze and he watched her blush from the rise of her breasts to the roots of her hair. She glanced up, smiling then kissed him. 'Yes, I have my looks back now and I have regained some of my confidence. Do you remember how it was, my darling, as we began to die?' She looked away briefly then smiled. 'Isn't it funny? Amid all the horror, it was losing one's looks, feeling oneself grow daily uglier that had been the worst thing. When I got to the DP camp and saw myself in a mirror for the first time, I wept. No one who had not endured it could possibly know what it meant, yet they discuss it endlessly here, these Palestinians, these fat farmers. I have to try so hard sometimes not to despise these chatterboxes who did not experience such hell.'

He swallowed hard, shaking his head, unable to speak, to explain what was in his heart, to resolve his own confused and troubled emotions. His head fell till his chin touched his chest.

'Sammy.' She reached out and touched his face. 'Oh my love,

I wept for you so much I believed my eyes would be dry forever. Even though I had married Michael I could not forget you and I prayed you would come back to me. Sometimes I dreamed that you were dead and a part of me died too. Then I dreamed that you were alive and my heart sang, knowing one day you would find me. Now all I hoped and prayed for has come to pass, you have come to me, you are here, but...I don't know what to do...or how to tell you what my heart wants you to know.' Her head dropped and she squeezed her eyes shut. 'Sammy, you lived and our love drove you to search for me and you found me and made me want to live again. But is that all there is? Must I be content with this?' He took her into his arms and held her close. 'You are a part of me, Sammy, as I am part of you and we shall remain so for as long as we live, do you understand what I am saying to you, my love?'

'Yes, I know that, of course I know.' He shook his head violently. 'But you said it, my love. Is it enough? After all the pain, is this all there is? Naomi, what are we to do?' He turned his gaze back to the sea. 'What are we to do?' he pleaded, but he could not look at her.

'Sammy, you know I would not deny you anything you asked of me, I could not.'

He turned his gaze to her, his eyes betraying his confusion. 'Were we ever really lovers?' he asked softly.

She smiled at him. 'You don't remember, my poor sweet boy, did they hurt you so much?'

He took her hand, averting her gaze. He recalled how they had come together, frantically seeking release from the torment. He remembered how they had saved each other from madness, from death, from despair and a terrible hopelessness. He closed his eyes and shuddered as if an evil presence had passed between them. Their eyes met and he gave a wry grin. 'I cannot rid myself of the stench of that place. I shall never forget how much we stank ourselves. My God, love, we were rancid.' Their heads touched as they laughed.

'So what if we smelled,' she said, 'isn't it written somewhere that to the forests and the seas, every man and woman in the world stinks?'

He looked at her, sighing. 'And in this, we were lovers?'

'Yes, my darling, we were.' She raised his hand to her lips. 'Do you remember how we first made love, so desperately, so greedily? There was so much anger in us and we needed love to feel complete and human again in that filthy place, if only for a brief time. But then we began to fall in love and we drew together, tenderly, oh so tenderly, my darling, that I could not bear another hand to touch me.' She kissed his ear and whispered, 'That is why we came so close to death, you and I.'

'And now?'

'I had to marry,' she stated flatly.

He looked away. 'So, were we ever really in love?'

'Were we, Sammy?'

'I don't know. I know only that I love you now. Oh God, Naomi, I love you so much, but...' He looked at her and saw his image reflected in her eyes. He felt and shared her need. '...I am so confused.' He sighed heavily.

She stood and walked to the cliff edge. She looked down into the cove far below, to where the waves broke gently, filling the dark rock pools. She watched the shadows of the long dune grasses swaying sensually on the bright strand. She turned to him and extended her arms. He came to her and took her hands. She looked longingly into his eyes. But he dropped his gaze to the beach below. 'It seems so peaceful down there. Another place, another time.'

She pulled him towards her, suddenly excited. 'Come,' she said. She led him to the cliff path and they made their way laughing to the shore. She kicked off her shoes and ran to the water's edge. She turned and began to dance, tracing patterns with her feet in the soft wet sand, like a young girl again. She began to disrobe and he watched as she dropped each garment on to the sand until, finally, she stood naked before him. She raised her arms to the sky, throwing back her head. 'I am Aphrodite, goddess of love, risen from the sea.'

'Wrong beach, love,' he shouted back. He heard her laughter carried on the breeze and he closed his eyes, sighing with pleasure. When he looked again she had walked into the water.

She raised her arms again and called to him. 'Come to me, Sammy, come to me now, my love.'

Enthused by her joy, he undressed quickly as she watched then ran splashing into the warm water. He reached out to her and took her in his arms. She laced her fingers behind his neck and they jumped, turning in circles, dancing and shouting and kissing in the warm sea.

Attracted by the noise, Michael walked to the cliff edge and looked down at them. He felt the sharp, stabbing jealousy as he watched them, but gradually his expression softened and he smiled at her screams as Sammy splashed water into her face. They were as children at play, freed from the constraints of order and convention and freed at last from the bitterness of their past. They came together in an embrace. She kissed him then spoke urgently to him. He took her face into his cupped hands, shaking his head as he spoke to her. He kissed her gently on the lips. She nodded and smiled sadly at him. Michael turned and walked away.

They walked side by side, pushing out of the sea with long slow strides. As they reached the sand they placed their arms about each other, like strolling lovers at the close of day. They gathered up their clothes and climbed the cliff path then lay on the warm grass, she in his arms, as the sun dried their bodies. After they had dressed they embraced and kissed. 'I shall always love you, Sammy,' she said.

He nodded. 'I know, my love.' He sat, pulling her down beside him and they gazed down at the sea. 'Tell me about Michael,' he said suddenly.

'Michael? What is there to tell? He found me in a DP camp in Germany. He was working for the Zionist Commission for Refugees. He fixed a passage for me with a contingent bound for Palestine but I refused to leave, I was afraid of capture. So he suggested we marry so I could come to Palestine legally and here I am.'

'Yours is an arranged marriage, for convenience, that is what you meant by "I had to marry"?'

'He is a good man, Sammy.'

'But you do not love him.' She shook her head and looked away. 'Will you come to love him?'

'Would you be hurt if I did?'

'Oh no! Naomi, I would be happy for you, to know that you had found love and could give love in return.' She snuggled into him and he nuzzled her hair.

They watched quietly as the glow of the setting sun danced upon the golden, dappled surface of the sea far below them. She turned to gaze into his face. 'Sammy, I am so happy.'

'Yes, it is over for us at last, my love. Perhaps, who knows, we can get on with our lives.'

After a while she asked, 'Have you found anyone yet?'

'Not yet...though I did have a bit of a crush on a woman in Germany.'

'A German woman?' She looked at him reprovingly.

'I love only one German woman.' He smiled. 'She was English, a civil servant from the foreign office investigating war crimes and gathering information about the camps. She interviewed me when I left the hospital.'

'And you fell in love with her?' she asked, surprised.

'No, not love, more an adolescent infatuation.' He chuckled to himself. 'The military bods asked me to write a report about conditions in the camp. They had collared Gräber and Höchst and were collecting the evidence to nail them. I gave them what they wanted on that score, of course, but I also told them about the camp guards, you know, Karl and that Wehrmacht lot and how they had been drafted in as scapegoats as the SS progressively pissed off. They asked me to remove that part of my report. They wanted blood, anybody's blood. They weren't interested in innocence or guilt. Naturally, I refused. If they had settled for punishing those poor sods they would have closed the case on the whole affair and the real culprits would have gone scot-free, which is what they wanted, of course. But I had given those men my word and I was determined the SS should not escape justice. I told them to go fu...to sod off. Then in true army fashion, they passed the buck to the civvy authorities and I was summoned to appear before this Mandarinette. I went reluctantly. I didn't give a shit about anything, really. Naomi, I was at my nadir, I had almost died. I weighed about one hundred and ten pounds, my eyes looked like piss holes in the snow and my breath smelt like a drain. I was obsessed with finding you. I thought you were dead. I was on the verge of madness. So, I was ushered into an office and there she was. My God, Noami, I thought she was the most beautiful creature I had ever seen. She had the most exquisite face and her voice...it was like music, your ear followed its cadences up and down...and she wore the most delicate perfume I had ever smelt.'

Naomi feigned surprise. 'Carbolic you didn't like any more?' They fell into an embrace, laughing. 'So what did you do?'

'Do? I proceeded to make a total ass of myself.'

'How?'

'She went through my report line by line, hitting me with a thousand questions, then she switched to more personal things, you know, name, number, all that shit. Well...I asked her if she would like to go out with me for a drink and to my surprise, she said yes.'

'So you had a date with this shiksa...did you tell her you loved her?'

'Naomi! I had only known the woman for about two hours. I did tell her she was beautiful, though...no, that was later, after I told her I had never smelt anyone quite like her.'

'After you told her what?' Naomi asked, aghast.

'That just about sums up her reaction, too. As I said, I wasn't very well.' She punched him happily as they laughed. 'But she was so kind to me. She took me to a Bier Keller and we drank wine and talked, but not about the war or the camp. When she discovered I too was Oxbridge, she became interested in my post-doc research. She was extremely intelligent, well informed and very amusing. I actually heard myself laugh for the first time since we were liberated. She said she hoped we might meet again some day...she did it to buck me up, I'm sure.' He looked away.

'Sammy, what is Oxbridge?'

He laughed. 'Graduates of Oxford and Cambridge Universities, usually by way of English public schools, a sort of exclusive governing elite.'

'Like the Nazis?'

'Oh God.' He rocked. 'I had never thought of it quite like that, but...'

'And she was Oxbridge?'

'Oh she was most decidedly Ox, I was just marginally Bridge.'

'Could you have loved her?'

'I think of her sometimes. She was very beautiful. She made a deep impression on me when I was most vulnerable.' He shrugged. 'They're just dreams, love, and anyway, I am here, in Palestine.'

She squeezed his arm. 'Don't give up hope, Sammy my love, we Jews have an old saying remember, "Next year in Jerusalem".'

'And what do you turtle doves find so amusing?'

'Michael? I didn't hear your truck. Darling, come, sit with us.'

Michael sat beside them and Naomi kissed his cheek. He looked at them in turn, his lips set in a sad, almost wistful smile.

'So, have you recovered from your shock?' When neither of them spoke he turned to Sammy. 'Captain, why did you come to the kibbutz today? It couldn't have been to see Naomi, could it?'

'Michael...' Sammy looked at him, surprised by his tone. He touched his arm. 'I came for information, that's all. I have been searching for Naomi for over a year and when we met at Nathanya I thought perhaps you may have encountered her, as an illegal. I wanted your help to find her. How could I know she would be your wife and that I should find her here?'

'Then you didn't come to arrest me?'

'Arrest you? For what?'

'I broke the law.'

'Sod the law.'

'You are a very strange man for a British officer, Captain Parker.'

Sammy laughed. 'There are those who say I'm a very strange man, period.' He regarded Michael intensely for some time then averted his gaze. He spoke softly, as though to himself. 'When I came to, on the cold hard floor of that cell in Matthausen, I knew my life was not worth a cent. I was alone, I was injured and I was afraid, very afraid. My training enabled me to foolishly deny the reality of my situation and to defy my captors with an exhibition of false bravado but my head doubted that I could survive. As I sank deeper into despair...' He turned his gaze to Naomi and his expression softened. He laid his hand gently on her arm. '...she came to me, one cold Christmas night as I lay shivering and without hope and when I saw her and what they had done to her, I knew at once what I must do. We came together and together we found the strength to survive. We clung desperately to each other and tried to hold on until...finally, we began to die. But she was the stronger and refused to let me go.' He placed his arm around her and she laid her head upon his chest. He looked up. 'Michael, listen to me. From the day the camp was liberated I have been locked within my own private hell. I had lost Naomi and my life had no meaning. For a second time I had no reason to live because I knew I would not find peace until I knew what had become of her. As each day passed without her, as her image began to fade, I became afraid because I knew if I lost her from my mind a part of me would die. She is everything to me, Michael, she is essential to me because she gave me my life, do you understand? A miracle happened here today. I found her, she is alive and she is beautiful, but...she is your wife, Michael. We cannot be lovers, perhaps we never really were lovers. My need for her still fills me, but it is beyond love. Don't ask me to explain, I do not have the eloquence. I do not understand it myself. You are a good man, Michael, and I know that with you she will be safe and that you will love her. With that I am content.'

Michael looked at Naomi, lying quietly in Sammy's embrace. 'But what of you, you love him still, don't you?'

'Yes, I love him still.'

'And what of me?'

'Michael, I have never deceived you, you know that. He too gave me my life and as a result almost lost his own. Now, I must share that life with you, because you are my husband.'

They fell silent and gazed out at the sunset. They watched the evening sun paint its magic upon the sky from darkest violet to blazing red as it sat, huge upon the rim of the world before sinking swiftly, turning the surface of the sea to shimmering gold. They sat, silent, beneath the stars, each alone with their thoughts. Finally, Naomi spoke. 'Michael?'

'Yes, my darling?'

'Did you know Sammy's got a shiksa in the foreign office?' There was a stunned silence then Michael began to shake and soon the groves echoed to the sound of their laughter.

CHAPTER EIGHT

The ship, a rusted coaster, had beached upon a shallow sandbank about fifty yards from the shore and was listing dangerously. Sammy and Bill watched with increasing concern as the immigrants edged nervously down a makeshift ramp to a floating levee anchored alongside. There they waited, grabbing desperately at each other's clothing, to board any of the plethora of row boats, dinghies and other small craft tilting and riding upon a gentle swell. 'What a bloody mess, look at those poor devils.'

Sammy nodded. 'This is no good, Bill, that pontoon could capsize any minute. They'll never get them off at this rate. How many trucks are laid on?'

'About twenty, I think, not nearly enough.'

'Right, that's it, it's down to us! Bill, get a platoon to secure that landing and get a team of medics aboard now. I want kids, old people and the halt and the lame taken care of first. Make the fit ones help, but exercise discretion. I don't want anyone hurt here today and I certainly don't want anyone dying. Those poor buggers have suffered enough already.'

'Right, Sir.' He paused. 'Sammy, go easy, we are only here for security. The Palestine Police will want that lot locked up jildy in the compound at Gaza.'

'Fuck the Palestine Police,' Sammy grunted. 'Before they mount any high horses they want to get their arses in gear and clear this shambles, it is a bloody disgrace. Find the prick in charge and bring him to me, we need more transport.' Bill looked suspiciously at his friend. 'See to it at once, Sergeant, will you? We have a serious security situation here.'

'Who says so?'

'I do, so get on with it.'

Bill nodded then called, 'Bentley, Hill.'

'Here Sarge.' The two airborne medics joined Bill.

He pointed. 'We're going to board that ship. Get your blokes together with whatever you will need to assist the kids, the sick and the elderly. Remember, they've been at sea for the best part of a month, God knows what condition they're in.'

'If it's par for the course there will be malnutrition, dehydration and the shits from the lack of clean water,' said Bentley. 'Some of the old ones will certainly be suffering from heat stroke...Leave it to us, Sarge.'

'Thanks lads, get to it.' He looked about. 'Corporal Manders, over here, now!' he shouted.

The big man ambled over and looked at Bill. 'What's up?'

'I want you to get your section over to that ship, commandeer a boat if you have to. I want you to form a guard on that companionway, two rows of men, one either side to prevent anyone going off into the drink. We are going to bring off the sick. Do you think you can handle that?'

'If i' wus up to me, I'd leave the bastards on there.'

Bill shook his head in disgust. 'Yes, well fortunately for us all it isn't up to you, is it, you nasty misbegotten prick. Now just move and do as you are told.'

Norman Manders rounded up his men. 'Roight lads, we gonna board that yid bum boat. We're gonna need a boat to gerrus out there.' He looked about. 'There, that one, that's just the job.' He waded out to a small outboard powered fishing smack. A frail, elderly man sat in the boat, his arm on the tiller, waiting his turn to go out to the ship.

'Right you, owt! I'm commandeering this boat.'

The fisherman looked at Manders, the fear showing in his face. 'But I must go to the ship.'

'Don't fookin' argue wi' me you Jew-nosed bastard, I said owt!' Grabbing the man by the lapels of his reefer jacket, Manders lifted him bodily into the air. The terrified man tightened his grip on the tiller bar as he was lifted, pulling it from its spigot. There was a shout from the beach.

'Look out, Grabber, the bastard's got a fookin' great stick.'

Manders reacted swiftly. He head-butted the man viciously, knocking him unconscious then pitched him into the sea. Retrieving the tiller bar as it floated to the surface, he placed it back upon its spigot and started the outboard motor. He called to his men. 'Right, come on you lot, gerrin this boat.'

'What about this bloke?'

'Fook 'im, ler 'im swim.'

He steered the boat towards the ship without a moment's further thought to the fate of the old man, still floating, face down in the water.

Sammy looked up from the file. 'Corporal Manders, you have heard the charge brought against you by Sergeant Grant. Do you have anything to say?'

''E attacked me, Sir.'

Sammy frowned. 'Attacked you?'

'Yes Sir.'

'Manders, I have been to see this man in the mortuary. He was sixty-one years of age and weighed about a hundred pounds. He was more than twice your age and little more than half your size. What did he attack you with, a tank?'

'No Sir. 'E went for me wi' a big stick.'

'Stick? Where did he get a big stick from?'

'The boat, Sir, the steerin' stick.'

'Steering sti...you mean the tiller?' Manders looked puzzled. Sammy sighed. 'And did he strike you with this big stick?'

'No Sir.'

Sammy closed his eyes to temper his exasperation. After some moments he looked up at the corporal. 'Manders, your behaviour since you came here has made this day inevitable. You are a brutal and callous lout with the intelligence of a dung beetle and about half its charm. I should have expected such an event, it was clearly only a matter of time. My regret is that I did not have you broken down to the ranks sooner and have you RTU'd.' He paused, shaking his head. 'I cannot deal with this matter, it is outside my jurisdiction. I am remanding you to CO's orders and I shall recommend the matter be referred to the adjutant general and that you be tried by a court martial for wilful murder. You are remanded to the custody of the provost marshal. March him out, Sergeant.'

The colonel threw the file down on the desk in front of him. 'This is a bad business, Parker, a bad business indeed. Murder is a very serious charge, very serious. The man could be hanged, you do appreciate that, of course?'

'With respect, Sir, that is not a matter for me. I have presented the substance of the allegations as reported to me, together with my recommendation that the matter be pursued, prima facie, as a case of murder. Should you so decide, after your preliminary hearing, it will be for the adjutant general to decide, on the basis of the evidence presented, whether such a charge should be brought, not us.'

'But how did you conclude it was murder, Parker?'

Sammy nodded at the file. 'Eyewitness accounts by, among

others, Sergeants Grant and Pearce, say an old man weighing little more than a hundred pounds was attacked by Corporal Manders, a large, physically fit young paratrooper. He was lifted bodily into the air, battered unconscious and thrown into the sea where he was left to drown. It would be difficult, would it not, Sir, in the light of such evidence, to conclude that the man met with an accident? I had then to consider the character of the accused man himself. Manders is an illiterate sadistic bully who has been reprimanded by me on several occasions for using excessive and unwarranted violence toward both Jew and Arab whilst on duty.'

'Perhaps you should have considered more appropriate punishment at the time.'

'The man is an NCO, Sir. I do not have the authority to impose anything more severe than a reprimand. On the three occasions I have remanded him to CO's orders for acts of brutality which, only fortuitously, avoided the same terrible consequences, you have, in every case, referred the matter back to me.'

'Very well, Parker. I shall, of course, have to deal with this, but I don't like it, I don't like it at all.'

'Captain Parker, Sir!' The provost sergeant bawled into the corridor.

Sammy entered the CO's office. Manders stood bareheaded before the colonel, flanked by two military policemen.

The colonel looked up. 'Captain Parker, I have read your official report and recommendation but before I come to a decision in this matter I should like to hear your version of events.'

Sammy stared at him, incredulous. 'But my report is my version of events.'

'Yes yes, but it's all wrapped up in jargon, Parker. I want you to tell me, in simple English, exactly what you saw.'

'Saw, Sir?' Sammy frowned. 'But in my report I state quite clearly I was not an eyewitness to these events. The report and my recommendation are based upon the evidence of several material witnesses, including Sergeants Grant and Pearce, who have both sworn affidavits. My involvement is merely procedural, being the accused man's directly superior officer.'

'But you did not actually see anything yourself, did you, Captain Parker?'

Sammy felt his gorge begin to rise. Is it me, he wondered. Am I unable to communicate with this imbecile, or is he deliberately acting like a prat to stall the proceedings? He stared at the CO. 'Sir, a frail old man is dead. Witnesses, whose word I trust, have sworn on oath that he was killed by this man. Their affidavits clearly state that Corporal Manders viciously assaulted the old man then threw his unconscious body into the sea, whereupon he seized his boat and embarked, making no attempt to rescue the drowning man.'

The colonel looked impatiently at Sammy. 'I also have statements from members of Corporal Manders' section to the effect that the man attacked the corporal who reacted entirely in self-defence.'

'I am sure you have, Sir.' Sammy could no longer conceal his contempt. 'As I am equally confident the court martial will give due weight to their evidence in the light of all the circumstances.'

The colonel drummed his fingers on the table for some moments, staring at Sammy then said, 'Captain Parker, I am not of a mind to recommend a court martial in this case. I do not find the evidence conclusive either way. It is my view that courts martial have a bad effect on morale and should only be recommended when the circumstances point overwhelmingly and unavoidably to such a course. I shall deal with this matter myself.' He turned his gaze to Manders. 'Corporal Manders, I have to give weight to the possibility that you acted in self-defence but it is my view that you reacted somewhat over-zealously. You are an NCO and as such should show an example to your men. You are hereby reprimanded and admonished to temper and moderate your behaviour and to act in accordance with the best traditions of the Parachute Regiment. The charge of wilful murder is dismissed and the recommendation to a court martial is declined. You are dismissed. March him out, Provost Sergeant.'

Sammy stood dumbfounded as the prisoner and escort marched out of the office, leaving the two officers alone. The colonel looked at him inquiringly. 'Was there something else, Captain?'

'A reprimand?...For murder?' Sammy's voice betrayed his anger and frustration.

'The charge of murder was dismissed for lack of evidence, Captain Parker. The reprimand was to moderate behaviour.'

'Moderate behaviour? Don't you understand that you have given that Nazi thug the green light to be even more vicious than he is already?'

The colonel flushed angrily. 'Captain Parker, I have made my decision, so if there is nothing else.'

Sammy came to attention. 'Sir, I wish to be relieved of my duties as platoon commander and reassigned.'

'Request denied.'

'In the name of God, Colonel, I will not serve with men like that.'

'Your request has been denied, Captain Parker, that will be all.'

'Oh that will be all, will it?' His voice was heavy with contempt. 'Well, you listen to me, Colonel.' He gave a derisory emphasis to the rank. 'I can no longer present myself for duty if I am required to command an illiterate, xenophobic, anti-Semitic Cromagnon who revels in the name of Gräber. Yes, you heard me, Colonel, Gräber, God help us. Corporal Manders is an odious lout who, together with a bunch of like-minded thugs, routinely commits acts of violence toward both Jew and Arab and who commits murder without compunction or, it would seem, effective sanction. Now, do I make myself clear?'

The colonel glared at Sammy. 'Captain Parker, I am aware that your recent and terrible experiences in Germany, occasioned largely in my view by your own lack of discipline in striking an officer, may have unbalanced your mind and I am prepared to allow you a certain latitude, but you are sailing close to the wind, very close to the wind indeed.'

Sammy flushed angrily. He leaned, knuckles down on the colonel's desk, staring into his face, his expression cold and remorseless. 'Don't you dare patronise me, you supercilious Sandhurst wanker,' he snarled. 'I didn't strike an officer, I laid into a murdering SS psychopath who had tortured my men. So you can go fuck yourself with your latitude.'

'Do you realise I can have you court martialed for this?' the colonel screamed at Sammy, his face florid and distorted with rage.

'Of course you can,' Sammy sneered sarcasm, 'and you probably will. But it's such a chore, isn't it? So, let's see if I can help you out here. You carry on doing what you do best, old son. You just sit there for a minute with your finger up your arse while I pop out and murder an old yid, then you need only give me a reprimand...no wait, better still...why don't I just butcher a Wog, then you won't have to bother at all, will you? After all, we must think of morale, right Colonel?' He turned and walked from the room leaving the colonel agape.

Major General Mark Bradbury, Commander of the Sixth

Airborne Division and Military Governor of Palestine, closed the file and looked up. 'Well this is a bloody fine mess, Parker, platoon commander confined to his quarters under close arrest for refusing to take his men on patrol. Serious, won't do at all. What have you to say for yourself? Is this true?'

'Yes Sir.' Sammy looked straight ahead without expression.

'Your commanding officer wants you court martialed, you know that?'

'Yes Sir.'

The general sighed and turned to his adjutant. 'Would you excuse us please, Major Shoppee, I wish to speak with the captain alone.'

'Right Sir.'

The general waited for the door to close behind the major then flicked a hand. 'Sit down, Sammy.' He waited for Sammy to seat himself. 'Now, what the fuck is the matter with you, man? And I want the bloody truth, so don't try any flannel with me.'

'No Sir, but there isn't much I can add. The colonel's report is accurate as far as it goes. I have refused to take patrols...that's it.'

The general shook his head. 'I said no flannel, Parker. Don't take me for an idiot. For God's sake, man, we fought together, I know the kind of man you are. What you did at Arnhem was magnificent, you and those two lunatics of yours blocking that bridge and holding up the Panzers for days then staying with the wounded when you could have escaped with the rest. How you survived what those bastards did to you in that damned camp, I'll never know. That's why I recommended you for another bloody DSO, for Christ's sake. Do you now expect me to believe you are now so shit-scared of a bunch of ragged-arsed Levites that you want to dive under the bed? Now, once more, what the fuck is going on?'

Sammy looked straight at the general. 'You've always been straight with me, Sir, and I'm grateful...Yes there is more to this, but I can't go into it without dropping people in the shit. This is my decision and I am satisfied in my own mind I have no alternative.'

The general held his gaze. 'Off the record, Sammy, and no bullshit.'

Sammy regarded his old Brigade Commander for some time then nodded. 'Right Sir, off the record.' He gazed toward the window for some moments. He sighed, as though struggling with his thoughts. 'Sir, I don't know what the bloody hell we're doing here. It's barely a year since we finished the war and the experience is still fresh in my mind.' He paused, staring at the floor then slowly raised his head. 'I saw what those SS bastards did to the Jews in Matthausen, Mark. Indescribable, gratuitous cruelty and brutality. They beat them, starved them, flogged them to death for being late on the Appellplatz, hanged them slowly for the most minor infringements of the rules and when they were of no further use, gassed them, along with their kids. They gassed little children, Mark, in their mothers' arms...Jesus Christ.' He tried to compose himself. 'Well, we beat the bastards and I thought it was all over, that we could leave it to the courts to deal with them, that I could play my time out as a war hero until my demob group came up and then go back to Cambridge. But I came here.' He looked at the general who held his gaze.

'Go on.'

'Sir, something's happening to the mob, it's not our Parachute Regiment any more. We're getting a lot of young prats, replacements, national service wallahs and regulars, tough, hard, well trained, but they're not like our blokes. In fact, the old sweats...Christ...' He paused and grinned wryly. '...old sweats, some of them are still in their twenties...well they won't have anything to do with them. They're living in the reflected glory of what we did and, Mark, they're behaving like Nazis. I have a platoon corporal who revels in the name of Gräber, can you believe that? General, to this day I can't hear that name without breaking into a cold sweat. I can still hear the bastard's arrogant voice, smell his cologne. I still have nightmares about what he did to me and what he and that fat whore Höchst did to all those other poor bastards...and now? I have to put up with a lumbering brainless Brummagem guttersnipe disguised as a paratrooper who luxuriates in his name. It is not a name he has assumed himself, you understand. His friends have named him because of the brutal way he behaves towards the civvies. "Gräber the Jew Baiter" they call him. He is by no means an isolated case and it isn't just the Jews. They treat the wretched Arabs abominably as well. Their behaviour is appalling. I have tried to bring them to discipline, brought several of them up on charges, but my commanding officer consistently undermines my authority. When I advised my CO that Corporal Manders, that's Gräber, incidentally, should be arraigned for battering an old Jewish fisherman unconscious and throwing him into the sea to drown, Colonel Hackett refused to accept my recommendation for a court martial, said it would be bad for morale. Bad for morale, Jesus Christ. He reduced the charge and gave the brute a reprimand. No reduction in rank, not even bloody jankers. A reprimand, for murdering a helpless old man, for crisake.' He closed his eyes and sat quietly for some moments. Then he looked straight at the general. 'I'm sorry, Sir, but he leaves me no option. I will not command a gang of Nazis. I have only just finished fighting the bastards and if I am not permitted to maintain proper discipline, make them behave like real paratroopers, then I cannot command them. It is as simple as that.'

The general looked at him. 'These are very serious allegations, Sammy. If what you say is true there will be repercussions. The situation with the Americans over the treatment of Jewish immigration by the government is a political and diplomatic hot potato right now. If it were to become known that the British Army, indeed its very own elite Parachute Regiment, was acting like a bunch of marauders, the shit, as our American cousins would say, would surely hit the fan.'

Sammy looked up angrily. 'Fuck our American cousins. Look, it isn't just the way some of our young tykes are carrying on that is giving me pause. The Jews are no better, are they? They rush about banging the Bible, proclaiming all that promised land bollocks and they are not waiting for the UN, Mark. You must know what's going on, they are already occupying territory to which they have no legitimate claim. These Jews are not the descendants of Abraham, they're bloody Europeans, not Asians. We've got Poles, Czechs, Russians, you name it. I even know a couple in Haifa from the Bronx, would you believe. Yet here they are, throwing Arabs out of their villages, bulldozing their homes to rubble and killing them if they resist. They commit a Lidice every day of the bloody week, for crisake, and we do nothing to stop them. I know how they suffered, I was there, but it wasn't the poor bloody Arabs who gassed them, was it? It was the Germans. If they want a fucking homeland then let them build one in Saxony. Mark, I led a platoon of men during the war, real soldiers, genuine, hard, decent men, not these yobbos, and we fought the best that Jerry could throw at us. Now I'm expected to command a bunch of Nazis committing atrocities against another bunch of Nazis who are themselves committing atrocities against a lot of ragged-arsed poor buggers who have lived here forever. I was trained for war, Mark, not for this shit. I don't know who the enemy is any more, I could be shot in the back tomorrow by the fucking baker, or blown up by a tallyman in a pinstriped suit. I am bewildered, I am angry, but most of all I am tired. I have had enough and I don't give a baboon's blue arse about diplomatic hot potatoes, or how much shit hits what bloody fan...I just want to go home...I'm sorry, Sir.'

The general stood and crossed to a large cabinet. 'Scotch?'

'Please.'

'Soda?'

'As it comes.'

He returned with the drinks. 'You realise I can't let you go back to your battalion.'

'No, I suppose not.'

'I shall reject Hackett's recommendation for a court martial. From what you tell me he shouldn't have a problem with that. If he does, it will be with me. After all, you haven't actually killed anybody yet, have you? But before you do, I'll arrange to have you posted to HQ in Jerusalem, the King David. I often need the odd non-routine job done on the side. You speak German, don't you?' Sammy nodded. 'Good. You can drive a desk until your group comes up. By the way, what number are you?'

'Group 24.'

The general turned and looked at a chart on the wall of his office. 'They're doing 16 at the moment. About six months by my reckoning. Now, try to keep that nasty misshapen nose of yours clean until then, will you please, for me?'

Sammy laughed. 'I'll try.'

'You won't try, you awkward bastard, you'll do it. Right?'

'Right, Sir.'

'Right, Captain Parker, back on the record.'

'Yes Sir.'

'I want you to prepare a confidential report on the events you have described. I want names, dates, places, everything. You will not be mentioned and I shall take no retrospective action, but I intend to put a stop to this now. Too many brave young lives were sacrificed to make our young regiment what it is and I will not have a bunch of undisciplined louts sullying their memory.

Any more of this and I'll RTU the bloody lot. Good enough?'

'Good enough, Sir.'

'Good. Clear your billet, your orders will be with you within the day.'

CHAPTER NINE

'Miss Carrington?'

Raising her head, Lesley snapped her book shut and nodded curtly.

'Tom Beresford, Miss. High Commission. Sir Alan sends his regards and looks forward to meeting you again. Welcome to Palestine.'

She glared at the young man. 'Welcome, Mr Beresford?' she snapped. 'Welcome, indeed? I have been waiting for the better part of an hour in this flea pit. I am cold, I am tired and in my frustration have smoked far too many cigarettes. Added to which, it is pouring with rain, the wretched roof leaks and I have been forced to share this postage stamp of dry floor with half of Islam.'

The young man shifted uncomfortably. 'I am very sorry, Miss, but I was only given the job about a half hour since. Er...it's the rainy season, you see,' he explained weakly.

She considered the absurdity of his remarks for some moments then began to laugh. 'Oh this is too bizarre, you are simply the poor devil who had the misfortune to draw the short straw. You must forgive me, Mr Beresford, I am forgetting my manners, I am not usually so irascible.'

'Oh I say, no, not a bit.' He laughed nervously. 'I know how miserable it can be. Here, let me take your things, the car is waiting.' He picked up her suitcases.

Gathering her purse and briefcase, she followed him across the airport concourse into a dimly lit corridor. She looked up. The walls stretched interminably, converging at some distant point beyond the darkness. She realised she was going to have to walk its length and her heart sank. 'Great God, where are you taking me?'

He pointed into the murky blackness. 'It's just along here. We have to cross over to the military bit.'

'Military bit?'

'Yes Miss, Lydda is also used by the military.'

'And precisely where is this "military bit"?'

'It's at the end of this passage.'

She regarded him icily. 'You are quite wrong, Mr Beresford, Calcutta is at the end of this passage.'

'Look, let me take those other bags,' he offered desperately.

She pushed herself back into the deep leather upholstery of the big Humber staff car and closed her eyes. Tom Beresford stowed her luggage into the boot and climbed in beside her. The driver turned in his seat. 'High Commission, Sir?'

'No, King David please, driver.' He turned to Lesley. 'It's a nice hotel, Military HQ now, of course, but it's very comfortable.'

'Thank God,' she sighed. 'I'm absolutely whacked.' She smiled at him. 'Sorry Tom.'

'Not at all, Miss Carrington, I understand, really. It's a long rotten journey isn't it? Did you fly in one of those BOAC bone shakers?' She nodded. He leaned forward, fumbling through the pockets of his jacket. 'Would you care for a cigarette?'

'Not right now, thank you Tom. My mouth resembles the inside of a yak tent as it is.'

Tom glanced at her, trying not to turn his head. She lay back in the seat, her eyes closed. He could see she was exhausted by her journey, yet he could not help but remark upon her beauty. He had been advised by his section head to proceed with caution. 'She's a bit of a stunner by all accounts, but she is very senior and very well connected, knows the HC personally, so watch your step.' She opened her eyes and turned to look at him. He smiled. 'I'm sorry about the cock up meeting you, being so late but, well there's a bit of a flap on.'

'Flap?'

'Riots. Tel Aviv, Haifa, Gaza, all over.'

'Wonderful! How like me to arrive in the middle of a war. What are the riots about?'

'Petah Tikva. Haganah, Palmach, Irgun, Zvai-Leumi, they are...'

'Mr Beresford, there is absolutely no point you twittering at me in Hebrew like a damned rabbi. I am new here, remember?'

'What? Oh yes...I'm sorry. Well Petah Tikva is a small town near Tel Aviv, a strong Zionist settlement and a hotbed of dissidents. The Haganah, the Stern Gang, the Irgun, you name it. There's an army garrison close by at Ramat Gan and every so often the Jews attack the soldiers, try to break in, steal weapons and ammo, that sort of thing. But the place is well fortified so nobody takes much notice.'

'So, why all the fuss?'

'Well, the garrison changed hands recently. The Airborne took it over.'

'The Airborne?'

'Paratroops.' He paused.

'Go on.'

'The Jews decided to throw a welcome party, break in, shoot the place up, usual sort of thing...'

'And?'

'The paras killed most of them...shot them, slit their throats, broke their necks...'

'Good heavens.'

'...Yes indeed, Miss Carrington. But not content with that, they chased the survivors back to Petah Tikva and smashed the place up. There is the devil to pay. We have never seen anything like it.'

'I have,' she said softly.

'Sorry?' He frowned. The car drew to a stop. 'Right, we're here, the King David.' He escorted her to reception where she was greeted by a uniformed WAAC.

'Everything is ready for you, Madam.' The girl smiled. 'If you are hungry we can arrange to have dinner sent up to you.'

'What is your name?' Lesley asked, smiling.

'Private Hennessy, Madam.'

'Tell me, Private Hennessy, is everybody un-given when they join the army?'

'Excuse me, Madam?'

'What is your name, Private Hennessy?' She winked. 'As one girl to another.'

The girl laughed nervously. 'Sorry Madam...it's Margaret... Maggie...Maggs.'

Lesley sighed and looked at Tom. 'I simply detest multiple choice questions, don't you?' She turned to Private Hennessy. 'Now come on love, help me out here. What's the answer? Which do you prefer?'

'Oh!' she twittered, 'Maggs please, Madam.'

Lesley pressed her hand. 'Thank you Maggs, you have been very helpful. I think perhaps I will have something. A couple of sandwiches and some hot coffee, no...make that chocolate. After all, I don't suppose there's much to stay up for is there?'

'No...I mean yes, Madam.'

Lesley gathered her purse and room keys. She smiled at the

girl. 'Don't call me Madam, there's a pal. I am a civil servant, not a brothel keeper. My name is Lesley, by the way. Good night, Maggs.'

Maggs cut short a nervous giggle and stared at Lesley's retreating figure, wide eyed.

'Where do you want these?'

'What? Oh, anywhere Tom.'

Tom placed her cases beside the dressing table. He looked at her then began to laugh. 'Poor old Maggs, she didn't know whether to laugh or cry.'

'Nonsense.' Lesley chuckled. 'We will get along fine now, Maggs and I. I cannot abide bullshit, Tom. Now bugger off before I drop.'

He laughed. 'Get a good night's sleep. I'll pick you up in the morning at half nine, the HC is expecting you at ten.'

'Thanks Tom.' She closed the door and he stared at it for some moments before turning and walking away.

The following morning, Tom was punctual.

'Is it far?' She settled into the seat beside him.

'The High Commissioner's palace? Depends on the traffic. The roads are a bit circuitous to the Hill of Evil Counsel.'

'Where?' she asked, surprised.

'It is a strange name, isn't it? Sort of sinister.'

'What is the origin?'

'I'm not sure really, probably something in Jewish history.'

She regarded him icily. 'Was that an informed or just an inspired guess?' she asked. 'I hope to God the intelligence here is going to be a bit tighter than that.'

He tittered nervously. 'Yes, I'm sorry...I don't know really.'

'Quite,' she said. 'Then say so.'

She was ushered into the High Commissioner's study

promptly at ten. The tall general rose stiffly to greet her. 'Miss Carrington, how nice to see you again.' He looked at her, smiling approvingly. 'I have to say, my dear, you look remarkably different from when I saw you last. It was at your parents' home in Rutland, as I recall, er...'

'Redmile, Sir. I do recall the occasion, though vaguely. I must still have been wearing pigtails and braces. Revolting and precocious, according to my dear mother.'

He laughed. 'What nonsense, you were always a delightful gel. And how is the good Lady Anne, and your father of course?'

'Mummy is still dedicated to the overthrow of His Majesty's Government, whom she insists has been insinuated into the British body politic by the NKVD. And Daddy?...He still pretends it doesn't matter.'

Laughing, he turned to his aide de camp. 'Is Miss Carrington's brief ready, Bromley?'

'Yes Sir, I have it here.'

'Splendid. All right, Miss Carrington, er Lesley, I shall now hand you over to Wing Commander Bromley here. He will explain your brief. As an FO official you will not be under military jurisdiction. The territory is at present under martial law and you will liaise with the Military Governor's staff in Jerusalem, of course, but your direct line of responsibility is to me, er...through the wing commander, of course. This will afford you the degree of independence necessary to your task. I hope to have the pleasure of your company at the Palace from time to time and please convey my respects to your parents when next you write.' They rose and he shook her hand. 'Good luck.'

Lesley quickly acclimatised to her new surroundings and adjusted to her new duties. Reporting directly to the High Commissioner had its advantages, she was held in a sort of awe by the staff at GHQ. She was to liaise with the military and advise on the implications of settlement, in particular the proposed partition of Palestine and the consequences of the establishment of an independent Jewish state within the mandated territory. Her contact was to be a major in the Parachute Regiment and adjutant to the Military Governor.

'Come in.' She looked up as the man entered her office.

'Good morning.' His voice was loud and confident. He smiled. 'Sorry to bother you, love, I'm looking for Lesley Carrington.'

'Love? My, the natives sure are friendly around here.' She smiled sweetly at him. 'Look no further...sweetie.'

'You?'

'Right.'

'Well I think someone might have warned me. I expected a bod.'

She looked down briefly, appraising herself. 'This is a bod,' she confirmed.

He attempted a laugh. 'No, not that, I meant...I thought you were a bloke.'

'You did?' Her eyes widened. 'What's the matter, Ken? I thought all you airborne types were twenty-twenty.'

He was feeling distinctly uncomfortable. 'Good Lord no, that is yes, I say, look here, I didn't...' He paused, frowning. 'How the hell do you know my name?'

She chuckled happily. 'Don't mind me, old son, I'm just teasing.' She patted a pile of manila folders. 'I've read your confidential file. I know everything there is to know about you, Kenneth Shoppee, perhaps even things you didn't know about yourself. Now tell me, what's a nice bank manager like you doing in a crummy joint like this?'

He removed his beret and began scratching his head awkwardly. 'Being made to look a complete clot by the best looking bloke I've seen in years. There is a good side, however,' he added laughing.

She grinned. 'Which is?'

'I get to work with him.'

She stood up and extended her hand. 'Good to know you, Ken. And my name is Lesley, but you already know that, don't you? My friends call me Carrie, it prevents confusion.'

'Are we friends?' he asked. She smiled, inclining her head slightly. 'Right, Carrie it is. Look, I can see you're busy.' He pointed to the thick briefing file on her desk. 'I only popped in to say hello, perhaps you might make my day and join me for lunch?'

'I'd love that Ken, but I have barely scratched the surface of that lot, which as you can see, is a prodigious pile.' She contemplated the pile for a moment then said, 'Oh sod it, why not...one-ish?'

'Look forward to it. You know where to go, don't you?' She nodded. 'Right, see you then.' He waved his red beret at her as he left.

She began to read the file with a growing sense of frustration. It was clear that Palestine was descending into chaos. She could not see how the British could ever resolve the deep differences which existed between Arab and Jew, based as they were upon such fundamental hatred. She found she had sympathy with both sides, sympathy which was to become sorely tried during the periods of violence now recurring with increasing frequency. The Jewish settlers, their numbers swollen by illegal immigration, were putting more and more pressure on the High Commission and the security forces. All previous attempts by Britain to find a way out of the dilemma in Palestine had come to little. Caught between Zionist demands that Jews persecuted in Europe should be free to emigrate to Palestine and Muslim Arab insistence upon protecting the rights of the Arabs in Palestine, Britain had, over the years, tried many times to devise a scheme of self government for the region. In 1917 Arthur Balfour, the then foreign secretary, had issued a Declaration so exquisite in its irreconcilable ambiguity that it was to bedevil all attempts at conciliation in the region thereafter. It contained the statement: 'His Majesty's Government view with favour the establishment in Palestine of a national home for the Jewish people and will use their best endeavours to facilitate the achievement of this object, it being clearly understood that nothing shall be done which may prejudice the civil and religious rights of existing non-Jewish communities in Palestine, or the rights and political status enjoyed by Jews in any other country.'

The alarm caused by this declaration, and the subsequent publication by the Bolshevik government in Moscow of the hitherto secret Sykes-Picot agreement by which Britain and France colluded to partition the former Ottoman Empire in the Near East in their own national interests, drove the Arabs to revolt. The issue hung in suspense until 1944 when sympathy aroused by the Nazi's Final Solution to the problem of European Jewry and the pressure by the Zionists in the United States combined to produce a United Nations proposal for the partition of Palestine and the creation of a Jewish State in the former territory. Initially the British government had agreed to accept one hundred thousand Jewish refugees into Palestine but as civil unrest among the country's Arab population increased, they rescinded the agreement and declared an end to all further immigration. They ended all land sales to settlers or their agents and rejected all Jewish political claims in the region. The new Labour foreign secretary Ernest Bevin announced that in future, any refugee ship caught on the high seas would be escorted to the island of Cyprus and its complement interned in camps to be established there. British forces, recently reinforced by the Sixth Airborne Division, made a gigantic sweep of the country, arresting many hundreds of Jewish leaders including the heads of the Jewish Agency and the commanders of the Haganah. They were thrown into a camp at Rafah, while members of the Irgun and the Stern Gang, regarded by the authorities as little better than terrorists, were incarcerated in the notorious Napoleonic prison fortress at Acre. The newly arrived paratroopers pounced on kibbutz and village alike and Tel Aviv was isolated while they dragged the city for guns, illegal immigrants and Jewish underground fighters. Inevitably, outrages were committed by all sides. The Jews, in an attempt to pre-empt any United Nations decision on national boundaries, began a campaign of ruthless confiscation. Fighting broke out between the Jews and the Arab League as the Jews expropriated Arab land, driving people from their homes and razing their villages. The Arabs attacked kibbutzim, the Jewish farming communes, in reprisal, killing women and children indiscriminately and both Jew and Arab regarded the British forces as legitimate targets. Their camps and barracks were routinely raided to obtain arms and ammunition and the British paratroopers, fresh from their war in Europe and trained not to take prisoners but to pursue and kill until relieved, reacted ruthlessly and decisively.

She talked incessantly throughout lunch, bombarding Ken with questions and asserting her views on the various aspects of the Palestine problem. 'Ken, I simply can't see how this can ever be resolved politically. It's all very well for the Yanks to put pressure on the UN to give way to the Zionists, but within the reach of verifiable history this land is Arab. The population is largely Arab and the culture is predominantly Islamic and has been for hundreds of years. What's more, we promised them autonomy after their revolt against the Turks during the First World War. You just can't chuck people out of their homes and out of their country to accommodate the atavism of Chaim Weizmann's Zionists. The Jews have suffered terribly, as I know only too well, but how can we make it a problem for the Arabs? Let's face it, Ken, these Jews are Europeans, the tragic victims of a mad, nihilistic ideology and a European civil war. The European Gentiles simply want them out of their hair. It's the hypocrisy of it which really incenses me. This constant, crude and facile appeal to Biblical sources for authority to expropriate. I mean, my God, it's as silly as the people of East Anglia and Yorkshire laying claim to Saxony and Jutland on the basis of the Saxon Chronicles and the Norse Sagas. The poor bloody wogs are not just going to pack their camels and leave, are they?'

Ken smiled at his guest. 'You sound like our Sammy. But don't take it to heart, old girl, or you'll go bloody gaga like him. All we can do is try to make the hand over, when it comes, as smooth as possible. But don't look for just and equitable settlements, not here, not in this bloody charnel house and believe me, it's going to get worse, much worse.'

'But Ken, it is so unjust. We're supposed to be responsible for these people and we make one cock up after another. I remember my section head in Brussels saying it was a pity Balfour hadn't kept his damned mouth shut.'

'Amen to that.' He looked at her. 'What were you doing in Brussels?'

'Control Commission. Although I spent most of my short time in Europe working in Germany with displaced persons.'

'You certainly get around, don't you?'

'Yes, I suppose I do, but rarely to the salubrious bits. How about you? What did you do before you came here?'

'Well, as you have already discovered, I was a bank manager, in Brighton.' He began to laugh. 'How in God's name am I ever going to go back to that?'

'No, I meant before coming to Palestine.'

'Ah! Active service, in Europe.'

She looked at him closely. 'Arnhem?'

'No, luckily, I'm with the other lot.'

'Other lot?'

'Sixth Airborne, you know, D Day, Battle of the Bulge, The Rhine crossing. Arnhem was First Airborne. All gone now, of course, poor devils.'

'They didn't all die though, did they? I heard about half were casualties.'

'That's right, but the division was never reformed. We got most of the survivors and the rest went into a special service brigade, like the SAS. But why the interest in Arnhem? Lose someone there, did you?'

'No.' She paused thoughtfully, smiling. 'I met one of the survivors when I worked out of the Brussels office.'

He looked up. 'Oh really? What was he doing in Brussels?'

'Oh he wasn't in Brussels. I met him on an assignment in Germany.'

'P.O.W?'

'In a way.' She looked away momentarily.

He frowned. 'Which Oflag?'

'What?'

'Which camp?'

'Oh...Matthausen.'

Ken's spoon clattered noisily into his plate. He looked at her, dumbfounded. 'Matthausen? Did you say Matthausen?'

She stared at him, her eyes narrowing suspiciously. 'Just now, when we were talking about the situation here, you said I sounded just like your Sammy.'

'That's right.' He became excited. 'Sammy was in Matthausen, he worked in the hospital, I think. You met Sammy Parker, didn't you? Jesus Christ, you know our Sammy.'

She shook her head, disbelieving. 'He's here? In Palestine?'

'He's not only here, old thing, he's in this very building. He works here, since the awkward sod blotted his copybook, that is.'

Her eyes brimmed and she fumbled in her handbag. She blew her nose loudly. 'How is he?'

'Sammy? He's fine. You know Sammy, indestructible. There are no flies on Sammy Parker.' He looked at her, curious. 'I say, I'm so sorry, old girl, I didn't realise. Did you and Sammy have a...well you know...were you...?'

'No Ken.' She smiled at him. 'Captain Parker and I did not have a "well you know". I met him, very briefly. He helped me with my inquiries, as they say. He had a lot of useful firsthand information about conditions in Matthausen, about Gräber and Höchst in particular. My recollection of that time and particularly of Captain Parker is, well, somewhat poignant.' She dabbed her eyes dry. 'He was in a very bad way, Ken. They almost killed him. That is why I am so surprised, I really expected he would have been discharged, he was an absolute wreck. We spent an evening together before I left Germany. I think I even managed to make him smile. I liked him.' She raised her head and smiled. 'He was a basket case, though. I'm so pleased to hear he has recovered. I thought him quite charming.'

'Charming...Sammy?' Ken guffawed loudly. 'My God, charming is not the epithet which springs to mind when thinking of Sammy Parker and who said anything about recovery? He's still a basket case, which has nothing to do with Matthausen, of course. That's Sammy, he's bloody mad. Look, you'll want to say hello, I'll have him paged.'

She started nervously. 'No, please! I would like to see him again, but not yet, not here. I know if I see him now I'll go to pieces. Matthausen was extremely distressing for me, Ken and devastating for the Captain, of course...Do you mind not telling him...please?'

'Of course I don't mind, old girl, good heavens. I say it must have been absolute hell. He won't talk about it, you know. You say he was in a bad way, that they ill-treated him?'

'Abominably, you see he almost killed one of their officers.'

'Oh Christ,' he laughed, 'that's Sammy to a tee. What happened?'

'He didn't tell me. Another POW, his former platoon sergeant, made a statement, pretty anecdotal stuff. It appears Sammy complained to an SS officer about the treatment of his men after they were taken at Arnhem. An altercation broke out between them, insults were traded and Sammy got the better of the exchange. He hated them with a passion, of course, and it is entirely possible his language was, shall we say, colourful. Then in true SS style, the idiot went for his pistol.'

'Oh dear, not a wise move. Sammy has a punch to fell a mule and a temper to match. You know he boxed for Cambridge? Well, I say boxed, if his style in the inter-regimental milling tournaments is anything to go by I think brawling might be a better description. I don't think the Marquess of Queensberry would have approved. You say he clobbered this officer?'

'Seriously, hospitalised him.'

'Bad show, that.' He shook his head disapprovingly. 'But, as I say, that's Sammy. He doesn't know when to stop. So, he was up before the head Boche.'

'No, they beat him terribly and threw him into the camp to die.'

'Why didn't they just shoot him out of hand?'

She looked at him, shaking her head. 'That question bothered me at the time. Ken, did Sammy ever mention a woman?' She examined his reaction.

He appeared surprised. 'A woman?'

'He told me he befriended a woman inmate when they threw him into the main Lager with the Jews. They were together until the camp was overrun. He seemed very concerned about her fate, I just thought...as you say, Ken, he is excessively reticent on the matter and as most of the inmates were either dead or in DP camps, we could not ascertain exactly what happened. I know he almost died from starvation and neglect. When I interviewed him he had only begun to recover, he still looked like a skeleton.' She blew her nose again to quell her tears.

'Poor old sod!' Ken squeezed her hand. 'He's far from a skeleton now, as you'll see.'

Lesley smiled. 'Please let me find him in my own time. I'll contact him when I'm ready, OK?' He nodded. 'Ken, what did you mean by "since he blotted his copybook"?'

He frowned slightly. 'Can't go in to details, you understand, but he had a bit of a run in with the top brass, as in Germany, I guess. It's the usual thing with Sammy, of course. He's an undisciplined thug, you know,' he added, laughing.

She flushed angrily. 'Nonsense, I don't believe it. He got into the most awful trouble trying to help his people. I don't know what happened here or what he has done to blot his copybook, but I'll wager it wasn't entirely selfish.' She stared at the major impatiently. 'When I met him in Hanover he was very ill. His behaviour was at times unpredictable and his remarks were sometimes a little gauche but his conduct was beyond reproach.'

Ken shrugged, smiling. 'Yes, well, I am sure he was on his best behaviour, as you say but then he would be, wouldn't he? I mean he wouldn't have been on top form after eight months in that camp, but I assure you he's recovered now and I can only urge caution. Look, I won't say another word, you look him up yourself. That's if he's around, of course.'

She frowned, tilting her head. 'Why wouldn't he be around?'

'He goes off, on his own.'

'What do you mean, goes off? Goes off where?'

'Tel Aviv, Haifa. He has friends up north, somewhere on the coast.'

'Friends? You mean local people, Palestinians?'

'Yes, Jewish folk. He visits them frequently.' He began to

chuckle. 'Perhaps he has found another little yiddisher doxy to take his mind off things.'

Lesley looked at him steadily. 'Why don't you like him, Ken?'

The question surprised him and he stared back at her defiantly. 'I didn't say I didn't like him, but he is a bloody maverick. Oh, he has a good war record, DSO and all that, but he simply will not obey orders...or let us say he picks the orders he thinks he prefers to obey. As I have said, he has no sense of discipline, calls his men by their Christian names, Bill, Wally, Ernie, that sort of thing. Bad show, very bad.'

'It didn't seem to affect their capacity to fight, did it, Ken? I am sure they didn't get their medals for "conspicuous familiarity".'

'As it happens, the MG does think very highly of him...bit of a blue-eyed boy, but then the General's an Arnhem veteran too, you see. That's why our lad is finishing out his time in this cushy billet instead of facing a court martial as he jolly well deserves.' He fidgeted with his napkin. 'I'm sorry, Carrie but that needed to be said.'

'Only by you, I think.' Lesley's face betrayed her contempt. 'You know, Ken, you are a typical bank manager.'

He stood, embarrassed. 'Yes, well, be it on your own head and don't say I didn't warn you. I wash my hands of the whole affair.' She watched him stride haughtily from the mess then gathered her bag and followed him out.

She returned to her office and dropped into her chair. She felt unsettled and unable to concentrate. She lit a cigarette and puffed nervously a couple of times before grinding it out angrily. She stared down for a while at the remains smouldering in the large glass ashtray then closed her eyes as she recalled the terrible experience of Hanover and her first meeting with Sammy. She had been disconcerted by the knowledge that he was in Palestine, in the same building, and still angry with Ken for bringing her such news and for his gratuitous remarks about Sammy. 'Pretentious, sanctimonious shit,' she muttered. She regarded the heap of correspondence spilling from her in-tray. She reached across and took a file from the top.

1.Daniel Aaron Asche.
2.Itshak Scharm.
Subject: Appeal by defendants against sentence of death by hanging. Transcript of proceedings of Military Tribunal. 14.5.1946.

She read the file quickly, closed it and pushed it across the desk. Two Jewish terrorists, members of the notorious Irgun Zvai Leumi, were due to be hanged in Acre gaol for the murder of five British soldiers during an attack on an army motor vehicle park in Tel Aviv. During the attack the accused had been wounded and captured. Despite long and rigorous interrogation by the Military and Palestine Police, they vigorously resisted all attempts to compel them to name their accomplices. Subsequently tried and convicted of murder, they were sentenced to death by hanging. The Americans pressed the British Authorities to commute the sentences but public opinion in Britain had been aroused by the nature of the attack, in which the sentry had been knifed and his sleeping comrades shot. Lesley was to prepare a report for the Appeals Tribunal.

'What a bloody mess,' she muttered to herself. 'The poor devils will be damned if they do and damned if they don't.' She fully expected the Irgun to carry out reprisals. Their leader, Menachem Begin had vowed to avenge his colleagues if the sentences were carried out. She reluctantly completed her report with the conclusion that there were no superior political or diplomatic considerations which should influence the verdict of the court. She cleared her desk and headed for reception.

'Anything going anywhere remotely pleasant tomorrow, Maggs?'

Private Hennessy looked up, smiling. 'Hello Lesley.' She frowned. 'You look tired, lovey.'

'That's why I'm taking a couple of days off...transport, Maggs?'

'Pleasant,' she mused, tapping her teeth with her pen. 'Let me see.' She slowly turned the pages of her desk diary. She brightened. 'How about a day at the seaside?'

'Sounds wonderful. Where?'

'I've got to run some reports over to Ramat Gan after lunch. I can drop you off at the Ark Club if you like.'

'Ark Club?'

'Combined services place in Tel Aviv, bang on the beach.'

'How long will it take to get there?'

'The way I drive, about an hour, once we're out of the city, that is.'

'Great, what time?'

'About one?'

'Maggs, you are a princess.'

CHAPTER TEN

The jeep bounced heavily along the desert road. 'Sorry, I've got to put me foot down, Pet, but it helps to even out the ruts, know what I mean? Not only that, it don't pay to hang about, you could easily get ambushed in these passes.' Maggs giggled. 'Just imagine, eh, being ravished by a black-eyed Sheikh in flowing robes on one of those lovely big white horses, you know...what do they call them?'

'Arabians.'

'No, not them, the horses.'

'If that's what turns you on, Maggs, and if you really cannot distinguish between Arabs, you could find the experience hugely exhilarating. I can't say the idea of being ravished by a horse of any breed or colour appeals to me. I could never trust a creature that walks and shits at the same time.' She smiled. 'So why don't you stop lusting after black-eyed Berbers and put your foot down a bit farther, I want to get out of this wretched place.'

She gazed out across the shimmering desert landscape of Judea as the jeep sped toward the coast. An ancient land, mysterious, prehistoric, inexact, scarcely touched by the scurrying feet of centuries, its life evolving in complete seclusion. Among the rocky wastes, clover patches of green, swarming with snakes and clouds of mosquito. A landscape devoid of songbirds yet full of kite and vulture, hunting by day and preening their plumage on precarious, craggy outcrops. In the pitiless sun whole segments of the sky and land displaced to open like a box or heel over and turn upside down. A great confluence of pastoral mirages from the forgotten history of an old world which still lived on, side by side with the new which man was determined to impose. 'My God, why would anyone shed blood for such a God forsaken place? It looks like the dark side of the moon. What a dump.'

Maggs laughed. 'You sound like Bette Davis, Pet...you know, in The Petrified Forest, with Humphrey Bogart and that. Makes you think though, don't it? They say it's their country, given to them by God thousands of years ago.'

'Who, Bette Davis and Humphrey Bogart?'

'No, don't be daft,' she giggled. 'The yids.'

'And they haven't seen the joke yet.'

'You're right there, love.' She chuckled. 'The coast is nice, though, you'll like the coast.' Following the curve of the sweeping cliffs, the jeep came out of the pass of Latrun and she saw the coastal plain stretched out below them. The orange groves were heavy with fruit, converging lines of squat trees, their still-green harvest ripening in the blazing sun. The distant Mediterranean, black against the long drawn white strand, lay in quiet contrast to the lush plain. 'There it is, Lesley, Tel Aviv.'

She looked toward the bright white buildings set against the blue sky. 'The Hill in the Sun, eh. Looks beautiful, doesn't it?'

'Yeah, well, looks can deceive. Those poor bloody Airbornes didn't find it too beautiful, did they? Those lovely boys, shot to bits in their beds. I hope they hang, those Jewish bastards, slow.' Lesley glanced quickly at Maggs, shocked by her tone, but she stared straight ahead at the winding dusty road, whistling tunelessly. They completed the journey in silence. As they wound through the outskirts of the city Maggs asked, 'Where would you like to be dropped, lovey?'

Lesley gave her a quizzical look. 'You said something about a club.'

'Oh right, sorry, so I did.' She giggled. 'Have to start going to bed at night...well...' She nudged Lesley. '...going to sleep, anyway.' The jeep turned on to a wide esplanade running parallel to the sea front. Lined with palms, its buildings draped with bougainvillea, she thought how exotic it all seemed after the drabness and destruction of post-war Europe.

'Here we are, Pet, the Ark Club.'

Lesley leaned over and kissed her cheek. 'Thanks Maggs. I repeat, you are a princess.'

'And so are you, love.' Maggs smiled broadly. 'I think you're smashing.'

'Well!' Lesley smiled, taken aback. 'Praise indeed, thank you.'

'I mean it. When they briefed me about you coming, you know, being upper class and a friend of the high commissioner and all, I was shit scared, I don't mind telling you and then you told me off for calling you Madam and said you didn't run a brothel...well, I didn't know what to call you, did I? No one told me. Then you asked me my first name and told me yours and treated me decent...well, I think you are a lovely person.' She sighed, smiling. 'When will you be going back?'

'What?...er...I'm not sure, don't worry, Maggs darling, I'll go to the consulate if I get stuck.'

'Right, cheerio then.'

'Bye Maggs.' She watched as the jeep roared away and disappeared into the traffic. She took a handkerchief from her handbag and blew her nose loudly. 'How very extraordinary,' she said to herself.

She entered the club and, waiting for her eyes to accustom to the light, she was immediately approached by a young lieutenant. 'Excuse me, this is the British Combined Services Club for Officers, I'm afraid civilians aren't allowed in here.' She stared impassively at the young officer while reaching into her bag for her identity pass. He opened the heavily embossed document gingerly and as his eyes scanned...'To whom it may concern, The High Commissioner for Palestine requires, etc, etc,' he began to fidget. 'I'm so sorry, I didn't realise. I thought, you know...'

'And you are?' she asked haughtily.

'What? Er...oh, sorry. Lieutenant Carlton, Sir.'

'And your first name?'

'Er James, that is Jimmy.'

She smiled suddenly, touching his arm. 'Jimmy, be a darling and fetch me something long and cool, will you?'

'What? Oh, rather. John Collins?'

'Perfect.' She smiled. 'And Jimmy...'

'Yes?'

'...don't call me Sir, there's a dear, I find it most demoralising. My name is Lesley, by the way,' she added. He looked puzzled and she feigned surprise, arching her brows indignantly. 'Well?' she said.

'Lesley?'

'With a "Y".'

'Ah...yes of course. Look, I'll fetch your drink, er, Lesley.'

She smiled as he hurried off to the bar.

He returned with the tall cool glass filled the American way with ice. 'Thank you, Jimmy. Now sit down and talk to me.'

'What? Oh yes, glad to...'

She sipped her cocktail. 'Mmm! That tastes good, thank you, Jimmy.' She placed her glass on the table and, reaching into her handbag, withdrew an elegantly tooled, wafer thin cigarette case. Removing one of the oval Turkish cigarettes, she tapped it slowly on the case. 'Light?' Startled to attention, Jimmy fumbled in his pocket for matches. He lit her cigarette and watched as she blew a plume of the heavily perfumed smoke towards the ceiling. 'Not drinking, Jimmy?' she asked.

'What? Well yes I was, it's, er...'

'You really shouldn't leave a girl to drink alone, you know,' she interrupted, 'it's not gallant, not gallant at all.'

He bolted up. 'No, right, I'm sorry.' He rushed to the bar to fetch his drink. She smiled as he returned.

'There, that's better, much chummier. Now Jimmy, I'm the new girl here and I should like to have a look around, take in the sights, places of interest, you know, galleries, concerts, theatre, whatever...'

He grinned. 'I can help there, I'm the entertainments officer for the club, you see. We have a bureau for that sort of thing, but this is not London or Paris, you know, you won't find much doing here...unless you like classical music.'

She laughed. 'You obviously haven't taken a close look at London or Paris of late, but as it happens I love classical music. Are you telling me there is good music to be heard here?'

'Oh, rather,' he enthused, 'we have the Palestine Philharmonic. It has most of the former Jewish members of the old German and Austrian orchestras. You know, Berlin, Vienna, Dresden, Leipzig. They're all here, well, let's say the lucky ones, those who got out in time.'

She nodded. 'Jimmy, that sounds wonderful, but is there anything on today?'

'I'll go and find out. Won't be a jiff.' He made off across the room. She looked about her. It was a large room, predictably furnished with large rattan chairs set about low tables. She was reminded of the colonial novels of Somerset Maugham, or Joseph Conrad. A bar ran along one side, at which were seated several officers dressed in khaki drill and in the corner was a counter at which an elegant, grey-headed patissiere was serving coffee and Viennese pastries to young servicemen and women clad only in beachwear. She gazed out through the large French windows which stood open to the beach. The ink-blue Mediterranean rolled gently in then bubbled back across the white sugar-sand. She watched the tanned sunbathers, some playing volleyball, others swimming in the warm shallow water or just lying on the beach and she thought how strange it all seemed amid the turmoil about them. Her reverie was interrupted by Jimmy returning with a handful of flyers. 'Here we are, Sir...oh gosh, sorry.'

She looked at him sternly. 'Jimmy, really, are your reflexes terminally conditioned? Look at me, for God's sake, do I look even a tad like one of the chaps?'

'Oh I say, God no, absolutely not.' He blushed hugely.

She began to chuckle. 'Poor Jimmy, I am teasing you inexcusably, forgive me. So, what have you found?'

'Oh, bundles! There's more happening here than I imagined. I have all the "gen", in fact, there's a concert this very night, at the Dizengoff Hall.'

'Jimmy, you're a wonder. May I see?' He handed her the flyer. She read aloud. 'The Palestine Philharmonic Orchestra conducted by Leonard Bernstein. Richard Strauss, Tone Poem "Don Juan". Gustav Mahler, Symphony No. 5 in C minor.' She looked up. 'Two questions, Jimmy, old scout, who is Leonard Bernstein and who the hell is Gustav Mahler?'

He smiled confidently. 'Leonard Bernstein is an up-and-coming young conductor and composer from New York. He's Jewish and a very extrovert showman. Gustav Mahler was an Austrian composer and conductor of the late Romantic period. He was also Jewish, but he converted to Catholicism.'

'Why?'

'To keep his job, I suppose...and to get Alma Schindler between the sheets of course. Oh gosh! Sorry, Miss.'

'And who was Alma Schindler?' She chuckled at his embarrassment.

'Is, she is still alive. She lives in California. Her father was a famous artist but she was also very beautiful and...'

'My God, Jimmy, what a gossip you are!' Lesley laughed. 'Wasn't poor Mahler at all renowned for his music?'

'Oh rather, he was a leader of the German Viennese school until it fell under the influence of Arnold Schönberg and his 'Atonal' revolution. He wrote nine symphonies, including three set for voices, as well as 'Das Lied von der Erde', a symphonic setting of early Chinese poetry for contralto, tenor and orchestra. These are all very large-scale works, very evocative and sensual.'

She looked at him, wide-eyed. 'Jimmy, I am impressed. Such erudition, where did you learn all this?'

He laughed. 'From the little Jewish lady who runs the bureau. She knows absolutely everything...she helped me to mug up so I wouldn't look a complete clot.'

She laughed with him. 'You are a cheeky sod, Jimmy Carlton, but at least you try to do your job. We could do with a few more like you around here. Right, how do I get to...what's it called...ah yes, Dizengoff Hall?'

He pointed through the open front door. 'Straight up that road, Allenby Street, go right to the end, you can't miss it. You will come to a big square, that's Dizengoff, shops, cafés and you will see the concert hall.'

'Walkable?'

'No problem. Ten minutes, no sweat.'

'Thank you, Jimmy, you have been more than helpful. Now you may return to your friends.'

'My pleasure, Lesley.'

She watched him rejoin his friends at the bar, gossiping avidly of his encounter. She smiled as they took turns to glance obliquely at her, feigning indifference to her presence.

She made for the street and as she passed through the door she heard the inevitable guffaw of laughter. She strolled slowly, window gazing, as she made her way along Allenby Street. She was surprised at the variety of shops and cafés and by the general demeanour of the people. The whole ambience suggested a modern Western city in perhaps California or Florida rather than a Middle Eastern city riven by the ancient enmity of Jew and Arab in a life and death struggle for the possession of an ancient land.

She entered a bookstore and began to browse. Most of the titles were English but she noticed a large section devoted to Hebrew texts. She remarked, perhaps not surprisingly, there were no German Language editions although she heard many people speaking German, obviously as their mother tongue. The wounds went deep. She picked up a second-hand edition of 'The Seven Pillars of Wisdom' by T. E. Lawrence, bound in red leather with gold blocking. She looked at the price pencilled on the flyleaf, 'two hundred mills'. She converted the price quickly, four shillings. She ran her fingers over the finely tooled spine, slowly shaking her head. She paid for the book then continued her stroll in the warm afternoon sunshine. She stopped at a small pavement kiosk for a glass of freshly pressed orange juice.

'Bik oder liddle?' the owner asked in very broken English.

She smiled. 'Ein grosser bitte, es ist Heute sehr heiss.' The man looked at her, surprised.

'Sie sind Deutscherin?'

'Nein, Englisch.'

'Aber Ihre Deutsch ist sehr gut, sehr deutlich.'

'Danke.'

'Ein bischen besser als mein Englisch, nicht?'

'God, I hope so.'

He laughed loudly. 'English humour, nicht?'

She drained her glass and smiled at him. 'How much?'

'On the house.' He grinned. 'You can pay for the next one.'

'But I don't want any more.'

'You will be back, I insist. You made me laugh and that's not easy.' He gestured at the passing crowd. 'Ask anyone.'

She laughed with him. 'It's a date, and thanks.'

'Nichts zu danken, 'wiedersehen.'

The vendor's easygoing manner, his genuine friendliness made her feel at ease for the first time since her arrival. She walked a little way then looked back. He was still looking at her. He waved and she waved back and felt a strange contentment. She came at last to the square and headed for a pavement café opposite the concert hall. She ordered coffee and, opening her book, was soon engrossed in the exploits of Lawrence of Arabia. She was constantly drawn back to Lawrence's own introductory chapter, a chapter filled with the pathos of betrayal. She returned again to one particular passage in which Lawrence so eloquently encapsulated her own view of the Arab dilemma. He wrote:

'We lived many lives in those whirling campaigns, never sparing ourselves: yet when we achieved and the new world dawned, the old men came out again and took our victory to re-make in the likeness of the former world they knew. Youth could win, but had not yet learned to keep: and was pitiably weak against age. We stammered that we had worked for a new heaven and a new earth, and they thanked us kindly and made their peace.

'All men dream: but not equally. Those who dream by night in the dusty recesses of their minds wake in the day to find that it was vanity: but the dreamers of the day are dangerous men, for they may act their dream with open eyes, to make it possible. This I did. I meant to make a new nation, to restore a lost influence, to give twenty millions of Semites the foundation on which to build an inspired dream-palace of their national thoughts. So high an aim called out the inherent nobility of their minds, and made them play a generous part in events: but when we won, it was charged against me that the British petroleum royalties in Mesopotamia were become dubious, and French colonial policy ruined in the Levant.

'I am afraid that I hope so. We pay for these things too much in honour and in innocent lives.'

She placed the book on the chair beside her and gazed out with unseeing eyes as she reflected upon the implications of what she had read. The Arabs now faced a newer and different aspect of that same betrayal as another generation of Europeans tried to salve their consciences and safeguard their interests. Horrified by the Holocaust and its consequences, they sought to wash the guilty blood from their hands by allowing the survivors to increase their settlement of a land promised to the Arabs and for which they had so bravely and innocently fought. By this policy they could so destabilise the region that they could continue to dominate and exploit these contested lands unhindered.

Gradually the noise of the busy, crowded square insinuated itself. She saw that people were beginning to arrive for the concert and she stood and began to collect her things. She started across the square but stopped short as she caught sight of him.

He sat alone at a pavement table of a large café beside the concert hall. He had regained weight and his muscular arms filled the sleeves of his olive drab drill shirt. He wore drill shorts and his stout legs were deeply tanned as was his face. The red beret was pushed to the back of his head and the quiff of his fair hair was bleached almost white by the sun. A waiter came to refill his cup from a steaming coffee pot, some banter passed between the two men and the waiter departed laughing. The grin lingered as he stirred his coffee and she recalled the smile which softened an otherwise rugged appearance.

She smiled. 'That shit Ken Shoppee is right, he does look something of a brute,' she thought. She was at first reluctant to approach him. Their encounter in Germany, though brief, had been dramatic. He had been sick, demoralised and vulnerable and she had felt the pain of his suffering and pity for his frailty. But pity was not an emotion he aroused in her now, nor was frailty apparent in his indifferent, almost arrogant demeanour.

Suddenly he stood, draining his cup. He placed it on the table. She felt a fascination and could not turn away from this warrior with his strong, sunburned limbs and his blond hair, standing astride like Flaxman's Achilles. He stretched upwards and, removing his beret, began absently to run his fingers through his hair. He looked straight at her, not seeing at first. Slowly, as he began to focus, his eyes opened wide with incredulity. He remained still, his hand resting on his head. She walked slowly towards him, smiling. As she drew close his hand dropped to his side and he too began to smile.

She stopped before him. 'Well, well! Captain Stanley Adam Malcolm - Sammy to his friends – Parker. And I thought this just might be a cushy assignment.'

He began to slowly shake his head then, whacking his leg with his folded beret, he pirouetted like an excited boy. He looked down at her. 'I don't believe it. I just do not believe it.' He laughed. 'Lesley Carrington, what in the name of God are you doing here in this nut house?' He peered into her face, frowning suspiciously. 'You haven't come to interview me again, I hope. You always seem to show up when I'm in the shit with the Goons.' He smiled. With his confidence now completely restored he looked rudely, almost forbiddingly healthy, but in his voice she thought she heard again the gentle man with whom she had spent that strange, hauntingly memorable evening. She looked into his eyes and felt a sudden, inexplicable surge of emotion and she felt its excitement and its pleasure, but there was also the qualm, the stab of apprehension. He smiled wistfully at her. 'Hello Carrie Carrington.'

'Hello Sammy Parker,' she replied and before he could respond she added with an impetuosity which surprised her, 'Well, don't I get a kiss?'

He placed his hands on her arms, squeezing gently yet affectionately then, leaning forward, he kissed her cheek and she felt and shared his pleasure. He stood back, still gripping her arms. 'My God, you've made my day, what a wonderful surprise. Carrie, you look marvellous.'

'And so do you, old sport.' She punched his arm playfully. 'Just look at you. What happened to the seven-stone weakling?'

He grinned. 'He decided he'd had enough sand kicked in his face.'

She touched his face and said seriously, 'When I left you in Hanover I expected never to see you again. I was convinced you were destined for the knackers yard. What happened?'

He laughed. 'Ah, well, the army has some special stuff for blokes in that condition, you see. Bloody miraculous it is too.'

'What?' she inquired.

'It's called food,' he replied, laughing.

'Oh, you idiot, you did it again. I never know when you are serious.' She began to feel at ease. 'But what are you doing in Tel Aviv? Are you on leave?'

'No, I often come down to the coast. It only takes a couple of hours. I'm stationed in Jerusalem, you see, at GHQ. But I can't stand the bloody place, it's got more pricks and brass than a team of dray horses.' He struck his forehead with the palm of his hand. 'Jesus, there I go again.' He offered a contrite shrug. 'I'm sorry, love, still out of touch, I'm afraid.'

She laughed. 'You do have a gift for the mot profane, as I recall, Captain Parker. But please don't apologise, I am a big girl now.' She sighed. 'So, what were you planning to do?'

'I was going to the concert at the Dizengoff tonight.' He tilted his head back toward the concert hall. 'But I had not anticipated meeting you...which rather alters things.'

'Really?' she said, surprised. 'But so was I, going to the concert, I mean. Oh Sammy, let's go together, please.'

'Of course, that would be great. Do you have a ticket?'

'Not yet. I was on my way to buy one when I spotted you, but you have this infuriating habit of diverting my attention.'

He smiled at her. 'I already have one, but let's see what we can do.'

'Oh Sammy, let us please try to sit together.'

'You leave this to me, these folks will do anything for the paras.'

She looked at him quizzically. 'They like the paras?'

'No, they hate us really, but we scare the shit out of them.'

He went to the booking office and spoke to the clerk, explaining the problem to her. Speaking to her in German, he very soon had her laughing at some quip. She exchanged his ticket for two adjacent stalls and said she hoped that he and his lovely lady would enjoy the concert.

'Danke vielmals,' said Sammy.

'Nichts zu danken,' replied the clerk.

'Well, you certainly scared the shit out of her,' said Lesley.

Sammy laughed. 'She's lovely isn't she? A typical yiddisher mama. She knows me quite well now, I'm a regular here. Look, we still have about an hour before the concert. Fancy a drink?'

'That would be lovely.'

They returned to the café and settled themselves at a table. He gazed at her. 'I still can't believe this.' He sighed. 'Carrie Carrington, I never dreamed...' As he hesitated she began to feel slightly discomfited by his gaze. Then recovering, he said, 'What would you like to drink?'

'A beer, I think.'

'Have you tried the local beer?'

'Not yet.'

'Well, there's Gold Star or there's Stella.' He pulled a face, shrugging.

'That bad?'

'Gold Star isn't too bad, brewed at Beth Horon by an immigrant brewer from Bohemia.'

'That sounds wonderful. Pilsener?'

'Er, not exactly. I don't think they use real hops.'

'What do they use?'

'Expert opinion is divided between onions and owl's piss.'

'Parker, you're disgusting.' She was laughing heartily. 'And what about the other one?'

'Stella? Not sure really, but I don't think it's owls.'

'Why not?...No, don't tell me, I'll try Gold Star, please.'

A waiter approached, grinning widely. 'Back again already, Sammy? I thought I'd gotten rid of you.' He turned to Lesley, smiling his approval. 'And who's this? Hello pretty lady.'

'Right, enough already,' said Sammy. 'She's my date, so roll up your tongue, cut the bullshit and fetch us two Gold Stars.'

The man laughed. 'OK Sammy, two nice cool Gold Stars coming up.'

Lesley had been struck by the waiter's obvious affection for Sammy. She looked at him quizzically. 'Well, you certainly are on very friendly terms with the natives, young Parker. Who is that man?'

He smiled. 'That's Ben. This is his wife's place, but he's just a waiter.' He paused, staring at her for a while. 'One of his relatives got into a bit of a scrape some time back and I was able to help...they're a nice bunch of people.'

'He speaks very good English.'

'He lived in Paddington when he was a kid. His folks sent

him over from Germany in the thirties with his sister. They stayed with an aunt. The sister married an Englishman. Ben was called up and served out here with the Eighth Army. When he was demobbed he stayed on.'

She looked across the café and watched Ben teeming beer into two glasses. She nodded in his direction. 'What happened to his family? Or is that a silly question?'

'Auschwitz.'

'Oh no, poor man.'

Ben returned with their beer. 'We're out of Gold Star, so I fetched a couple of Buds.'

'Budweiser?' Sammy asked, surprised. 'The genuine stuff?'

'Sammy, don't be a putz.' Ben grinned. 'I said Buds, not Budweiser. This is Milwaukee, Mister, not Pilsen. But it is slightly better than Beth Horon owl's piss.'

'How did you manage to get hold of American Budweiser, you crafty sod?'

'Marshall aid, Sammy. They love us, those Yanks. They have to otherwise Morgenthau will close all their fucking banks...oh, excuse me, Miss.'

They all laughed at Ben's joke and he joined them at their table. Sammy nodded towards Lesley. 'This is Lesley Carrington, Carrie to her friends. We met some time back. In the line of duty, as they say.'

'Duty clearly has its rewards.' Ben took her hand and kissed it gallantly. 'Carrie, your beauty shines intrinsically fair. No gems, no gold you need to wear.'

Lesley threw back her head to laugh. 'And you would be my Lover's Choice too, Ben.'

'Aha! Literate as well as beautiful, and a lover of poetry too.' Ben laughed, turning to Sammy. 'So, where are you taking this lovely girl, you hideous sod?'

'The Philharmonic, you schmaltzy bugger.'

'What's playing?'

'Mahler Five.'

'Ah wonderful,' Ben said wistfully. He turned to Lesley. 'Do you know Mahler, Carrie?'

'I fear not, until today I had never heard of him.'

'But you'll love the fifth, you are obviously a romantic. Believe me, once you've heard that adagio for harp and strings, even Vlad the Impaler here will look good to you.'

She chuckled. 'Then I shall look forward to the experience...I don't think they play his music in England, well certainly not on the wireless.'

Ben laughed heartily. 'What, Lew Stone and his old wind up gramophone? You're expecting a bit much, aren't you? Listen, as long as the musical establishment in England is run by that same bunch of desiccated medievalists and faggots, anything later than Beethoven will be considered vulgar and likely to frighten the horses. I mean to say, we can't have the British getting all emotional and slack upper-lipped like Continentals, can we? I'm telling you, Uncle Gustav is very big with the Germans, as are Bruckner and Schönberg.'

She took a draft from her glass and the beer's foamy head stuck to her lips. She licked it away. 'I've tried Schönberg. Horrible noise, I can make neither head nor tail of it.'

Ben laughed. 'That's exactly my point. Those sods wouldn't dream of letting you hear any early Schönberg, the Gurrelieder, Pelléas and Mélisande, good sexy romantic stuff to get your blood racing. Verklärte Nacht, now there's a piece. All about a bloke giving succour to a fallen woman with child. Such stuff as would give those BBC transvestites the vapours. They regard the late Romantic oeuvre as Biedermeier music, the worst kind of nineteenth century Gemütlichkeit, the Impressionists as deranged and decadent and any informed definition or discussion of modernism is entirely beyond them. So they prat on about the

New Viennese School and twelve note serialism and atonality and all that esoteric shit which is, as you say, a bloody noise. Music should be enjoyed, Carrie. Tasted, savoured, rolled around your senses like fine wine around your tongue, not analysed...or do I mean anal-ised? Most of them talk out of their arse anyway.'

Sammy laughed with Lesley. 'Why did you have to switch him on? For God's sake, stop encouraging him with questions or we'll be here all night. Can't you see what an ingrate he is? We take him in, give him aid and succour when he's in the shit and he repays our altruism by alleging our wonderful BBC is run by a bunch of nancies and transvestites.'

'Only the music department,' protested Ben, 'only the music department. The rest are Nazis.'

'Oh Ben, really,' said Lesley laughing.

'Piss off, Ben,' Sammy said, then turning, he touched Lesley's arm. 'Come on love, or we'll miss the overture.' He stood and walked to the edge of the pavement. Lesley rose and to his utter surprise, kissed Ben on the cheek.

'Goodbye Ben,' she said. 'It has been such a pleasure meeting you...I hope things go better for you here.'

'Shalom, pretty lady.' Ben smiled. 'And do me a favour, will you? Try to keep that lunatic out of trouble, at least until he goes home. He's very special to us, you see.' His words caused her to frown, quizzically. He walked away quickly.

She joined Sammy and took his arm as they crossed the square. 'I like your Ben.' She glanced at him. 'He seems very fond of you.'

He nodded. 'Yes, I am also fond of him, he is a Mensch.'

'A Mensch?' She chuckled. 'What's with the Yiddish already? I guess it must be the company you keep.'

'Come on.' He ignored her comment. 'I want a programme before they sell out.'

They settled into their seats. The hall felt cool in contrast to the heavy atmosphere outside in the square. The chatter from the largely Jewish audience was, as usual, cacophonous but Lesley seemed not to notice, engrossed as she was in the detail of her programme. Sammy watched her, a soft smile set upon his lips. He recalled their first encounter. Broken by his ordeal and crushed by the loss of Naomi, he had no mind for anything beyond an obsession to find her until he entered an office in Hanover and faced Lesley for the first time. He recalled how she had excited within him a desire, unexpected yet irrepressible, which brought with it a sense of confusion and self reproach. Believing his devotion to Naomi absolute he had tried desperately to suppress these strange and alluring emotions, to rid himself of his infatuation. But the images of their encounter remained with him to remind him how, for one brief moment, he had felt again the touch of intimacy and the brightness of joy when all had seemed so dark. He felt that same contentment now, like the reprise of an enchanting melody and felt again that same desire quicken within him. He sighed softly as he contemplated her beauty. He wanted to touch her, to stroke her hair, to kiss her. She turned to him, smiling and raised her programme.

'According to this, your Mahler was not exactly a bundle of laughs.' He held her gaze, smiling wistfully. She tilted her head quizically. 'Sammy?'

He nodded slowly. 'Perhaps not, but wait till you hear his music.'

She studied the programme again then said dismissively, 'He looks like a Jewish pawnbroker.'

He laughed, snapping out of his reverie. 'And what does a Jewish pawnbroker look like, compared say, with a Presbyterian pawnbroker?'

She punched him playfully. 'You know what I mean, don't

pretend to be obtuse. Just look at this picture, look at those awful little specs.'

He nodded. 'You are right, that is obviously why Ben calls him "Uncle Gustav".'

Chuckling happily, she found herself warming once again to his boyish humour. She recalled how, while still recovering from the brutal treatment he had received in Matthausen, he could still crack a joke.

He smiled at her. 'Happy, pretty lady?'

'Oh poor Ben, he was so sweet. Yes I am, very happy. This is nice, such a lovely surprise, not at all what I expected when I left Jerusalem today.'

He frowned and a question began to form but a ripple of applause diverted his attention. 'Look out, here comes the Konzertmeister, we're off.'

She sat up expectantly. 'What's this conductor like?' she whispered.

'Bernstein? Young, very energetic. Nice Jewish boy from New York.'

The conductor approached the rostrum to rapturous applause. 'He's very popular.' Lesley looked at Sammy.

'Well, he's almost a local boy, keeps a house on the edge of town, I believe.' His voice dropped to a whisper as a hush fell upon the hall.

Bernstein took up his baton and stood for some moments, posing theatrically, head bowed, hands clasped before him. He looked up suddenly and with a flourish of his baton, swept the orchestra into the frenzied opening bars of Richard Strauss's Don Juan. Lesley had not heard the music before, Strauss being effectively expunged from the English musical repertoire for the duration because of his perceived allegiance to the Nazis. She sat, transfixed. She had never experienced orchestral sound like this, the belling brass contrasting with tender woodwind melodies and sumptuous strings. She clapped enthusiastically and squeezed Sammy's arm in her excitement. 'Wasn't that wonderful?' she shouted above the applause.

He looked at her face, so animated with pleasure and he wanted to crush her to him. He simply smiled. 'And the best is yet to come.'

It took her ear a little time to attune to Mahler. Gradually, she found herself swaying in her seat to the rhythms of marches, waltzes, ländler, then laying back, eyes closed, drinking in the rich, sensuous orchestration. Bernstein took a rest after the third movement, standing again, head bowed on the rostrum. She glanced sideways at Sammy. He smiled at her. 'Like it?' She nodded, sighing. Then suddenly, as she gazed at him, she heard a harp and the strings, following its meter, began to play the most beautiful and poignant love music she had ever heard. She glanced at Sammy again. His eyes were closed and his face bore a quiet, wistful expression. She recalled Ben's remark, 'even Vlad the Impaler will look good', and she felt herself being irresistibly drawn to him. Not to the fearsome, violent man she had first encountered in Germany, a man consumed with hatred and anger, but to a gentle, sensitive man, compelled by cruel and intolerable circumstance to act against his true nature. She turned to face the orchestra again and slowly pushed her hand into his. At first he did not respond, but then gradually his grip tightened and she leaned into him.

After the concert they left the hall in silence. He had taken her hand again and as they crossed the square they looked at each other. She knew at once that something extraordinary was happening to her. They reached the café and sat, staring at each other. She was the first to speak.

'Oh Sammy, that was absolutely the most wonderful experience I have ever had and I want to do it again soon, please.'

He smiled at her then asked flatly, 'What do you do in Jerusalem?'

'What?' His question had taken her completely by surprise. She shook her head at him impatiently. 'Sammy Parker, you are the most infuriating man I have ever known. I have just spent two of the most extraordinary hours of my life having my emotions put through a shredder and all you are interested in is my bloody job and what I do in Jerusalem.'

'Well?'

'Sammy, for God's sake! I work there, with the High Commission. I'm on Alan Cunningham's staff, I have an office in the King David.'

He noted the familiar "Alan Cunningham". 'Then you must know I too have an office in the King David?'

'Yes.' She avoided his gaze.

'How long?'

'Nearly a month.'

'You have been avoiding me?'

'Yes. I mean no, not avoiding...Oh Christ.' She began to fumble in her handbag for her cigarette case.

'Why, Carrie?'

She looked into his face. 'Sammy, when Ken told me you were here, I didn't know what to do. He wanted to page you so that we could meet at the club, but I just couldn't. I can't explain. After Hanover...oh I don't know...it was such a terrible time, that awful business in my office, all that violence. I know you had every reason and that you were very ill...I was assured you would be discharged. As I have told you, I expected never to see you again. But you came at me suddenly, unexpectedly, out of the past, out of a bad experience and I knew that if I were to meet you it would have to be in my own way, in my own time. I knew I should want to see you, Sammy, to renew our acquaintance, but I knew I could not face you then...not then.'

She tried to light her cigarette. He took the lighter from her and did it for her. She inhaled nervously and fidgeted with her cigarette case.

He took it from her and, grasping her hands, squeezed them gently. 'I understand, really.' He smiled at her then added simply, 'Carrie, I think I am falling in love with you.'

She tried to compose herself. She pulled a handkerchief from her bag and dabbed at her neck with it nervously. 'My God, Sammy...' she said, but he interrupted.

'Look love, I'm sorry if I've embarrassed you, truly I am, but I can't do anything about that. I think you have a right to know how I feel. I can't stand equivocation and I don't intend any of that worshipping from afar bullshit. So you must tell me either to piss off or that I have a chance.' He squeezed her hands again. 'Fancy a beer?'

She looked at him, incredulous, struggling to recover her composure. 'Well, Sammy Parker, I think infuriating rather understated things, don't you?' He smiled at her sadly and gave a contrite shrug. Her expression softened and she gently brushed his face. 'Oh Sammy, that was not the most beguiling declaration of love a girl could wish for, was it? But yes, I should love a beer.' He grinned broadly. He is going to shout Geronimo any moment, she thought.

Before he could speak, Ben approached their table. 'Well, how did it go? Did you like the Mahler?'

'Oh Ben, it was wonderful.' Lesley quickly recovered her enthusiasm. 'In fact, it was magical. You were right about the adagio, I have never heard anything so beautiful.'

Ben smiled at her then, nodding toward Sammy, asked, 'And what about Vlad? Did it touch his barbarian soul?'

She chuckled happily. 'Yes Ben, I think perhaps it did.'

He looked at her, then at Sammy. His eyes narrowed. 'Something has happened here, hasn't it? I can feel it.' He stared intently at Lesley for some moments then at Sammy who was gazing at her. Then he began to laugh. 'My God, I must be getting old,' he cried. 'Of course, I've just twigged, you are his beautiful shiksa in the Foreign Office, aren't you? The one from Hanover...my God!'

'Shut up, you prat,' demanded Sammy, desperately.

Ben, undeterred, laughed loudly. 'Pretty lady, you are his grand obsession. He never stops talking of you. About how he met you and how you saved him from going crazy. How you actually went out with him and kissed him even though he had acted like a Narr. My life, this is marvellous. Am I to take it all his dreams are about to come true?'

Lesley, embarrassed by Ben's extrovert revelations, lowered her head. Sammy glowered at Ben. 'Look, why don't you just piss off and fetch us a couple of beers, you nosy, loud mouthed old sod.' Ben backed away, chanting in Yiddish, clicking his fingers, raising and lowering his eyebrows suggestively at the couple. Sammy looked at Lesley. 'Carrie love, what can I say? I am so sorry you were subjected to that. I feel like a complete bastard. In a moment of weakness I confided in that no good Scheisser who has a mouth which is both turbo-charged and disconnected from his brain.' He shook his head sadly. 'Are you really as pissed off as you look?'

She looked up at him. 'Sammy, I'm not in the least pissed off. But I am bewildered, taken aback, if you will. Do you know you are the most unnerving, infuriating individual I have ever known? You sit there and reveal the most intimate confidences as if they were the simply mundane. You tell me you are falling in with love me with about as much emotion as if you were telling me you had just missed the last bus, "well there it is, can't be helped, not my fault, take it or leave it". In God's name, Sammy, what do you think I am made of?' He remained silent, staring at her guiltily. 'And then that loquacious friend of yours confides that you have remembered me with, it seems, some affection ever since Hanover. My God, Sammy, how could that be? We only met for a few hours and in the most appalling conditions. My recollection of you is terribly confused. I want so much to recall the gentle, humorous man with whom I spent that brief, pleasant evening. But I cannot rid my mind of the image of your vicious attack on Gräber and Höchst. You frightened the bloody life out of me, do you know that? I still feel so insecure about you, you are a very intimidating man.' She unravelled the bunched up handkerchief she had been gripping and blew her nose loudly.

'Carrie, I'm sorry.' He took her hand. 'I've obviously gone off half cock again. As for Ben, I must have been out of my bloody head to confide in that Klutz. But it is nevertheless true, I think I love you. Don't ask me to explain, I find it as bizarre as you, but when I walked into that office in Hanover and saw you for the first time, smelled that perfume; when you looked up at me and smiled, my heart stopped. I thought I was going to be sick, my stomach turned over and my guts nearly fell through my arse. But, I shall have to get over it, shan't I? I should be able to handle a little disappointment, I've had enough practice, God knows.'

Ben returned with their drinks before she had time to respond. 'Two beers for two young lovers.' He wiped the table then placed the glasses down. He smiled at Sammy. 'Do you know, I feel quite elated, poetic even. Oh by the way, Rachel...' He turned to Lesley. '...that's the missus, well, she thinks you make a lovely couple. She'll be cooking something before sundown, you see if she don't.'

Sammy scowled at him. 'I suppose there's some Hebrew proverb for all this, some ancient saw from the Torah?'

'What do I know from the Torah?' Ben laughed. 'I'm a heathen.'

'Piss off, Ben.'

'All right already, I'm going.' He danced away again, singing.

Sammy smiled sheepishly. 'He means well.'

'Oh no, he's beautiful.' She paused. 'You too can be a dear, lovely man in spite of your mercurial temper. I know that, I have seen it. I saw it tonight.' He took hold of her hands and squeezed them gently. She sighed. 'Sammy, what you have told me of your feelings has not upset me...taken my legs from beneath me perhaps, but I am not angry, I promise. But I can still hardly believe it is true, I really do not know where I am. The whole thing, finding you were here, in the same building, meeting you this afternoon, the concert, the music, the whole thing. I am so bewildered, disorientated. I really have no experience of this sort of thing. You see, I have never had a boyfriend, let alone a lover. Oh, I have flirted with chaps, often quite shamelessly...I have petted too, sometimes more heavily than I should, but it was never anything but a bit of fun...call them my little wartime peccadilloes, if you will. Sammy, I'm afraid I may lose your friendship, because I don't know if I can love you, or even if I want to love you. But I do know something happened to me today. Since meeting you again, so unexpectedly, I cannot remember having such a feeling of contentment, or of being so happy. But because of what you have said, you have become different to me and I am confused again. If I am to love a man, I must be sure it is real and not just a brief infatuation, do you see...Sammy, how will I know?'

He smiled at her. 'You will know, sweetheart, you will know, I promise.'

She chuckled. 'When my guts falls through my arse?'

He laughed heartily. 'There, you see? I knew my natural gift for poetic imagery would be rewarded one day.' He looked at her, longingly. 'I won't embarrass you any more, old girl. You know how I feel, but I shan't press you, I promise. I could never make you unhappy...' He raised his glass 'Cheers!...But we can still be mates, right?'

'Oh Sammy, of course.' She smiled. 'In fact, I insist... Cheers!'

CHAPTER ELEVEN

The worsening political situation in the territory and its crisis workload afforded Lesley and Sammy fewer opportunities to meet. She looked for him but he was rarely at his desk. She met him fleetingly, in the mess or at the club. He was always friendly, even courteous, but appeared increasingly preoccupied. She wondered if perhaps an impulsive infatuation was beginning to wane and he was avoiding her. She was surprised that this concerned her and began to feel apprehensive. She tried to dismiss the matter, to clear her mind. She read through the papers again to confirm she had omitted nothing from the report she had prepared. The two young Irgun terrorists, having lost their appeal, were duly hanged in Acre gaol. Following the executions, the three major Jewish underground organisations, the Haganah, the Stern Gang and the Irgun, began to cooperate, coordinating their effort to greater effect. Choosing the paratroops as special targets for their attacks, the Irgun carried out a series of brutal reprisals, including the kidnap and summary execution of two sergeants of the Parachute Regiment in woods close to Nathanya. The paratroops had responded swiftly and brutally, shooting at anything moving after curfew. They carried out search and patrol duties and dealt with riots, now breaking out with increasing frequency, with exceptional rigour and violence. Having thus identified the Jewish underground as their de facto enemy, the Red Berets pursued them with all the professional efficiency and vigour for which their training had prepared them and for which they had earned such a formidable reputation in the war. Lesley became increasingly concerned that the high command was losing effective control of these troops. It was a new regiment, the youngest in the British Army. It had no written history, no tradition to respect. Its usual 'rules of engagement' required it to fight independently, without the formal lines of communication typical of conventional army units. Of necessity, it took no prisoners and most opponents met in open combat were killed. Its members were selected rigorously to ensure in each a capacity to work on his own initiative as required. Sammy had inveighed frequently against the complacency of the authorities and Lesley was beginning to agree with his argument that paratroops were not best suited to the role of crowd control and public order. She had read reports that several airborne units stationed in Judea and Samaria had gone on the rampage following the murder of their comrades. If elements of this regiment decided to 'use their own initiative' on a wider scale there would inevitably be serious diplomatic repercussions...The phone sliced through her thoughts.

'Hello, Lesley Carrington...Sammy?...You're back then?... Drink? I'd love to. Give me ten minutes to clear my desk. Where are you, in the club?...Yes OK, bye love.'

She filed the report and quickly tidied her desk. She checked her face in the mirror and hurried from the room, strangely but pleasantly elated.

He rose as she approached the table. 'Hello, old sport.' She greeted him with a smile as they sat.

He pushed a glass towards her. 'I got you a John Collins.' He appeared morose.

'Thanks...you look tired.'

'I'm bloody bushed. Things have been hectic.'

'You must be glad to be out of it though, Sammy. At least you don't have any more of those beastly patrols to lead, do you?'

'No, I just have to witness a couple of kids who still have cradle marks on their arses calling for their mothers as they drop through a bloody trap with a rope around their neck.' He looked away angrily.

'Oh God! Sammy, how awful for you, I had no idea that is where you were.' She gripped his hand. 'But justice had to be done, old thing. They murdered your comrades in cold blood.'

'Stop talking bollocks.' He glared at her and she flinched at his anger. 'It didn't have to be done and it had fuck all to do with justice. They were just kids, for crisake, all of them, including our lot. They were the victims of circumstances beyond their control, being used by a bunch of cynical old bastards whose only concern is to destabilise this whole poxed up region, socially and politically. All they are concerned with is Arab oil and it is essential that the poor fucking wogs have their attention diverted from what really should be worrying them. These Jews have no place here. Germans, Dutch, Brits, Yanks, Frenchmen, and not all camp survivors either, just ordinary Jews who have decided it might be a good idea to return to the land of Abraham now that it's up for grabs. There are people from Brooklyn and Golders Green over here, did you know that? Mouthing off that crap about the Promised Land. We shouldn't be here with our bullshit mandate and the paras certainly shouldn't be here raging about like fucking storm troopers. They should have been disbanded when the war ended. They're not trained for this kind of shit. They're not coppers or the sort of bloody wooden tops who stand guard at palaces and they don't obey the orders of those regular army idiots very easily either. They're special service troops, Carrie, trained to kill, quickly and efficiently, anyone marked as an enemy. These poor misguided bastards aren't their enemy, they don't pose a threat to the security of Great Britain. We don't belong here, we should be at home with our families. Our job was done when we beat those Nazi bastards. Look, I'm sorry love, I know you're a pretty senior FO bod and have the official line to pedal, but this is me, Sammy, remember? So spare me the bullshit, please.'

Lesley had remained silent throughout his tirade, regarding him with a hurt expression. She spoke softly, trying to control her anger. 'I wasn't trying to pedal you bullshit, Sammy, but I am required to follow and implement government policy, as are you. And if you don't mind me saying, I think your analysis is flawed, over simplistic and not helped by being articulated in Old-Low Anglo-Saxon.'

'Oh, flawed is it?' he grated. 'Over simplistic? Then tell me this, do you think it right that a bunch of refugees from a European war and a ragtag and bobtail bunch of Abes, Moishes and Jacobs who can't hack it back home should come here, to a country with which they have no legitimate connection and who appeal to some old Sumerian sky god myth to force people from their homes and villages at the point of a gun and expropriate their land?'

She felt herself becoming angry. 'Sammy, your constant reiteration is reducing that thesis to the level of tedium. It doesn't matter what I think, it's the policy of my government, your government, pursuant to international agreements and resolutions of the United Nations. As it happens, I do feel sorry for the Palestinian Arabs, but as I have said, it doesn't matter what I think or feel.'

He looked at her with ill-disguised contempt. 'Ich bin doch sehr leidvoll, aber Befehl ist Befehl, nicht?' His sing-song chant was heavy with derision.

She started, her face flushed. 'Sammy, that is not fair.'

His anger subsided quickly and he smiled sadly. 'No love,' he said, sighing. 'None of it is fair...Look love, I'm sorry. I guess I'm just tired, what with the bloody war and now all this...I'm just sick of looking at lives buckled by bombs and shrivelled with hate.' He sighed. 'Let's change the subject, shall we? I've made enough enemies here and the last thing I want is a fight with you...Please?' He held up his hands in mock submission. 'Peace, pretty lady?'

She smiled back. 'Shalom, Sammy.'

He raised his eyebrows. 'You prefer Hebrew to Old-Low Anglo-Saxon?'

She laughed. 'Shut up, you hooligan and get me another drink.'

Sammy disappeared again and Lesley began to miss him. She felt disappointed if his phone rang unanswered or if he was not at his desk. She felt hurt that he did not tell her of his movements.

'Seen anything of Sammy, Ken?'

Ken Shoppee glanced up from his work. 'He's up north, the other side of Affula. He's investigating those ghastly hangings and the breakout from Acre gaol.'

Her face darkened. 'Breakout? What breakout?'

'The Irgun busted some of their cronies out last night and there was some pretty severe anal twitching, I can tell you. I am doing a report for you now.'

'Why does he get all the grotty details? Or is it the establishment getting its own back?'

The major laughed. 'Do you seriously see Sammy doing anything he didn't want? Anyway, I don't think he'll mind this one. You'll not see him before Monday.'

'But it's only Tuesday now. Do you mean he has to be up

there over the weekend?'

'No, the job should be finished today, but he has some R & R due.'

'Oh, I see. Where will he go, Beirut?'

Again, he laughed. 'Doesn't he tell you anything?'

'About what?'

'Why he's always up at Nathanya.'

'I didn't know he was. Ken, we're just pals from our time in Germany, we're not married, for God's sake. There is no reason for him to tell me anything.'

'No, of course not.' He smiled at her. 'I'm sorry, Carrie, but I thought you were perhaps, well, more than friends. After all, your reaction to finding him here was not altogether lacking in...how shall I put it...emotion.'

'Alright, you persistent sod.' She laughed. 'Why is Sammy always up at Nathanya?'

'Well, as you are not wearing your heart on your sleeve...' He paused, regarding her thoughtfully. 'I was right, Carrie, he has a woman up there.'

'Has a woman?' She laughed nervously. 'That is a funny way to put it. Are you saying he has a pied-à-terre, a ménage à deux, a secret love nest? Oh come on, Ken, that doesn't sound a bit like Sammy.'

'No! Good heavens, it's nothing like that.' He tried to sound reassuring. 'You'll remember I told you he knows some people who own a hotel up the coast?'

'What are you saying? He meets his girlfriend in this hotel?'

'Not his girlfriend, exactly...she is the missus.'

She looked at him, bewildered. 'Ken, you've completely lost me, whose missus?'

'I don't know the whole background. It seems this Jewish couple own the hotel and apparently the wife is an old flame of Sammy's...he likes to spend time up there with them.'

She sighed with relief. 'Good God, Ken, what could be more harmless? So he goes to see an old friend who happens now to be married. Not exactly a unique situation, I would have thought.' She paused. 'Isn't it funny he should have an old flame here? How do you know all this?'

'Scuttlebutt.'

'For God's sake, Ken, speak English. You mean gossip, and how bloody typical.' She frowned. 'I wonder if she is related to Ben?'

'Who's Ben?'

She smiled. 'He's a pal of Sammy's, a waiter at the Café Delilah on Dizengoff Square. He is married to a Palestinian girl, but originally came from London. I'll bet that is the connection.'

'Yes, you're probably right, it does sound plausible. You think he might have known her in London?'

'Who knows, but I'm sure it's all perfectly harmless.'

She sealed the envelope and leaned back in her chair, stretching the fatigue out of her tired limbs. The phone rang and she reached for the receiver. 'Lesley Carrington...who?... Oh, hello Doctor...What?...Ugh, I hate those damned things, are you sure I'm due again already? They inoculated me against everything but the Black Death before I left England...OK, if I must, when?...No, I can't make it tomorrow. Right, Monday at nine o'clock it is, see you then.'

As she walked to the door the phone rang again. 'Oh shit.' She stood for a moment, deciding whether to leave and ignore it, but she knew she would have to answer the call. 'Hello?'

'Carrie, it's me, Sammy. I am so glad I caught you.'

'Hello Sammy, so you're back again?'

'What?' He sounded puzzled. 'No...Look can you get away for a few days?'

'Away? Away where?'

'Haifa, I have some R & R due and I've had this great idea. Can you get away or not?'

'Well, young Parker, as it happens I can. I've just finished a report which makes the Brittanica look like a livre de poche, which is why I am still here at this hour, I wanted to catch the bag. I was going to put my feet up...alright, what is this great idea?'

'Put your feet up at the Carmel, I'll get you a room.'

'When?'

'Now, tonight.'

'Sammy, for God's sake, it's as black as Newgate's knocker out there and what about the curfew?'

'Now that you have your own official jeep impressively tattooed with Imperialist icons, who would dare stop you? Take the Nablus road, there's nothing on it at this hour, then it's all down hill, two hours tops.'

'But Sammy, why tonight?'

'Please, no more questions. Just get in that jeep...Carrie...I miss you.'

She felt her eyes smart suddenly. 'Sammy Parker, you big shit, life is never easy with you, is it?'

'No, but it's fun. Now go, you're wasting time.'

Ignoring Sammy's advice, she took the shortest route from the hills, through Ramallah to Tel Aviv, then across the Plain of Sharon to Haifa. Squat trees, laden with fat Jaffa fruit, reared up eerily out of the darkness as she sped through the miles of citrus groves. Finally, the trees gave way to flat fields of corn and as she approached Zikhron she saw the familiar row of red hurricane lamps set across the road. 'Oh Christ no, that's all I need.' She slowed as she approached the roadblock and a soldier walked towards the jeep holding his hand up to stop her.

He looked at her, sullenly. 'Roight, out o' the vehicle,' he commanded tersely.

'I beg your pardon?'

'I said out, now move!' She reached across for her handbag. 'You touch that an' I'll blow yer fookin' 'ead off.'

She looked around, shocked and angry, and glared at the soldier. 'How dare you speak to me like that, you illiterate lout. Can't you see this is an official government car?'

'I don' give a fook what sorta car it is, and if you don'...'

'Don't you dare use such foul language to me!' she screamed at the man.

Attracted by the commotion, another soldier approached the jeep. 'What's the trouble here, Manders?'

'This snotty cow won' gerr out o' the jeep, Sarge.'

The big sergeant looked quickly at the insignia on the jeep then leaned on the windscreen, smiling at Lesley. 'Good evening, Miss.'

'My God! At last, a human being. Good evening, Sergeant.'

'May I ask where you are going?'

'Haifa, government business.'

'Might I see some ID?'

'Of course, assuming you can prevail upon this imbecile not to blow my "fookin' head off".'

The sergeant glanced over his shoulder. 'Alright Manders, get back to your squad.' He took Lesley's official pass and examined it carefully. He studied the photo then smiled at her. 'Doesn't do you justice, Miss...but then they never do, do they?'

'What is your name, Sergeant?'

'Grant, Miss.' He regarded her curiously. 'Do you wish to make an official complaint?'

'No, that won't be necessary. This mission is highly confidential, Sergeant, so I would prefer we forget the whole incident. Just make sure that lout keeps his mouth shut.' She stared at the soldier for some time. 'Paratroopers, aren't you?'

'That's right, Miss.'

'Have you seen any action? Before you came here, I mean.'

'Oh yes, Miss.'

'And what about him?' She nodded in the direction of the corporal.

He smiled. 'No Miss, he's never heard a shot fired in anger.'

She nodded then, as if to herself, said, 'Yes, I am beginning to see what he means.' The sergeant inclined his head, puzzled by her remark. 'Well thank you, Sergeant Grant, now I really must get on.' She started the engine and he stood back, allowing her to pass.

'Take it easy, Miss,' he called as she drove away.

She was relieved to see the lights of the city high on the hill in front of her and as she wound her way through the bends to the hotel she checked her watch. Just over two and a half hours. She might still be in time for dinner. She was famished.

He rose to greet her as she approached his table, grinning and as excited as a schoolboy. 'Hello Carrie, drink?' He kissed her on the cheek and they sat.

'Please. Something long and cool, it's very close tonight.'

He ordered two whisky sours with ice. 'Have you eaten?'

'Don't be bloody silly.'

'OK. If I'm reading the runes properly, that's a no and that's good because neither have I.' He smiled at the waiter. 'And a menu, please.' The waiter fetched their drinks and they decided to share a dish of skewered lamb on a bed of saffron rice.

'Right, young Parker.' She glowered at him. 'I have almost broken my neck to get here tonight. I have been delayed and abused by those psychopathic comrades in arms of yours, I am absolutely exhausted and in no mood for games of silly buggers, so this idea of yours has to be a little more than just great. I'm

237

looking for something like stupendous, monumental, or sensational...OK? So give.'

He looked concerned. 'What do you mean delayed and abused?'

She chuckled. 'I exaggerate, but only slightly. I was stopped by a para roadblock.'

'And?'

'Well, I was in a rush to meet your two-hour deadline so the last thing I needed was a wretched roadblock and when that non-com Neanderthal began addressing me in language compared with which your own would sound almost demurely restrained, I became somewhat vexed...but then all went well when a very handsome sergeant came to my rescue.'

'You say they were paras?'

'That's right. Why do they have to wear those awful clothes? Those funny smock things and those black machine guns with their bandoleers of bullets? They are so murderously intimidating and they look like Corsican bandits...and when that oaf actually threatened to blow my head off, I felt inclined to believe him.'

'He did that?'

'Oh yes, he certainly did, the damned simian.'

'Did you get any names?'

'The nice one was a Sergeant Grant, and the other thing...'

'Manders.' He ground out the name through clenched teeth.

'You know them?' she asked, surprised.

'They are my former platoon.'

'Well, you didn't bring them up very well,' she said haughtily. 'Not very well at all.' She smiled at him 'Why don't we just forget the whole thing? The sergeant was extremely courteous.'

'You must put in a complaint.'

'Don't be so bloody silly.'

'That's twice you've said that.'

'So heed me. Now shut up about the roadblock and tell me about this great idea of yours.'

'Of course, I'm sorry.' He squeezed her hand. 'I've just returned from Acre. There has been a complaint about the standard of accommodation up there.' He smiled. 'I have written my report and I am now free. I have two weeks R & R due, but I do not intend spending them in Beirut or Limasol. I have had enough of concentration camps for one lifetime. Carrie, I know a quiet little hotel, just a family affair, high up on the cliffs near Nathanya, a wonderful place overlooking the sea.' He paused as the waiter served their dinner. 'It is so beautiful up there, the little white village, the cedar woods, those lovely green bluffs, it is absolutely gorgeous.'

'I take it you like the place?'

He smiled. 'I think it is the most beautiful place in Palestine. Now, and this is the good part, the hotel is owned by Rachel's family, you remember Ben's wife?' She nodded, relieved her assumption had been correct. 'Well, the place belongs to her brother and I have an open invitation to stay there any time, so...'

'You want me to spend a dirty weekend with you in a hotel owned by that nosy yiddisher matchmaker's family?' she asked indignantly.

'Good God no,' he spluttered. 'Nothing like that, bloody hell. It is all above-board and absolutely kosher, I assure you, but...' He looked at her hesitantly. 'Carrie, we've had so little time together since that night at the concert and I still cherish the hope...well, you know.' He watched her smiling at him. 'Look, I shan't be offended if you say no. Disappointed? Sure, but I will understand, truly...I just thought perhaps...' He shrugged, grinning sheepishly.

She was still smiling at him. 'You know, for a young lion you can be awfully soft. I'm pulling your leg, you dolt. Sammy, I would love to come to your hotel and I am really touched by your invitation.'

'Really, you'll come?' he bubbled enthusiastically.

She grabbed his wrist urgently. 'Now calm down, Sammy Parker. I realise it must be ages since your last jump, but if you start screaming Geronimo you'll scare the living shit out of the other patients here.'

'Oh Christ!' He laughed heartily. 'What a bloody thing to say. There are times, Carrie Carrington, when I think you are even more incorrigible than I.'

She became serious. 'Sammy, I really didn't come prepared for a long stay. I just have some overnight things, I shall need to do some shopping.'

'No problem.' He waved a perfunctory hand. 'The family work on a kibbutz, they have loads of clobber, you know, frocks, shirts, underwear, you name it. It's like a commune.'

'That sounds like fun.' She giggled. 'Sammy, you get me a clean frock and a change of knickers and I'm all yours.'

He sighed. 'Is that a promise?'

'I hope so.'

He squeezed her hands affectionately, then looking round the dining room at the other diners, most of whom were military personnel, he smiled. 'Patients...you're absolutely spot on, look at them. Finish your drink and we'll go for a stroll, I can't bear this gawping any longer.'

'You must learn to be more tolerant, Sammy.' She laughed. 'We have lifted their eyes and quickened their appetite; we have lighted their dismal lives; we are a new and glistering star in an otherwise murky and moribund firmament.'

'Don't give me all that Ptolemaic crap, they've taken a butcher's at you and they are all as jealous as shit.'

'Oh Sammy, my darling, your gift for compliment transcends mere poesy.'

240

*

To avoid the inevitable, prurient speculation attracted by even the most innocent office flirtation, they agreed Sammy should proceed alone to Nathanya the following morning, she following the next day. She paid her usual visit to the residency to see friends and to establish she was in Haifa alone. She browsed the shops and markets and spent the rest of the day reading at several of the pleasant sidewalk cafés in the city, returning to the residency later to ask the motor pool to return her jeep to Jerusalem. She explained that she had decided to visit the ancient biblical site at Megiddo in the north of the country and that she would return to Jerusalem by bus. The following day, as arranged, she collected her bags and headed for her rendezvous at the Café Rival. She ordered coffee and began again to read the Lawrence.

'I guess you must be Carrie.' Startled by his voice, she looked up into the face of a large, fair-haired man dressed in the blue drill of a kibbutznik.

'Yes, forgive me, but I...'

'Michael Berkovitz, Rachel's brother and your most fortunate host.' He smiled. 'Here, let me get your things, my truck is parked along the street.'

She gathered her handbag, feeling slightly disconcerted. 'I expected Sammy. What happened to him?'

Michael smiled. 'He wanted to, of course, but...' He paused. 'It would rather defeat the object, wouldn't it? We decided it best if I came instead.'

She saw the sense of his remarks and immediately felt better. 'Michael, please forgive me, you have driven a long way to bring me to your home and I haven't had the good grace even to say hello.' She proffered her hand. 'Hello Michael.'

He grasped it firmly, laughing. 'Hello Carrie.'

*

They took the cliff road and she was reminded of the Pacific Coast road of southern California which she had seen as a child. She gazed at the land, lush and verdant, unlike the baking hostile crags of Judea. The hills, wooded with cypress and cedar, sloped away and up, above the winding road, while on the seaward side the eye dropped dizzily to the rocks far below and to the inky blue Mediterranean shimmering, calm, hypnotic in the sunlight.

Her reverie was interrupted as the truck swung suddenly through the hotel gate. Michael switched off the engine. 'So, here we are, welcome to our home. I'll fetch your things.' He climbed from the truck calling, 'Naomi, sweetheart, we're home.' He lifted Lesley's bags from the back of the truck and walked toward the hotel entrance. Lesley followed him.

As they reached the entrance a woman came out wiping her hands on her apron. She approached with the easy grace of a Bedou girl, erect, moving only from the hips. She stopped before them and fixed Lesley with an imperious look. She nodded as if confirming her approval and as suddenly, her face was lit by a broad, warming smile. Her dark eyes glistened with laughter and her thick hair moved, black and iridescent as a raven's wing reflecting the sun. Lesley's heart started in her breast. She felt her stomach turn over and she knew in this instant that she would come to love this woman.

'So at last, Mädl, he made you come.' She embraced Lesley warmly, kissing her. She stood back, smiling, still holding her by the arms, regarding her as a much-favoured child. 'Just look at you...so beautiful.' She turned to Michael. 'Was I right?' she asked sternly. 'Didn't I say she was beautiful? You got eyes in your head, look at her.'

'She is very beautiful, sweetheart,' Michael confirmed, winking at Lesley.

'So, I was right.'

Lesley began to feel both embarrassed and perplexed, yet

strangely elated.

'You are saying we have met?'

'Met? What do you mean, met? We met already?'

'Well no, I don't think so.'

'So there you are then.'

'But you said...'

'I didn't say anything. Sammy said it all, he never stops saying it and he never lies to me.' She hugged Lesley, kissing her again. She turned suddenly and entered the hotel, beckoning them to follow. 'Anyway,' she called back, 'good taste he's got, that Sammy. He loves beauty, doesn't he love me too?'

Michael looked at Lesley and began to laugh. 'Poor Carrie. Now that I can get a word in edgeways, that is Naomi, my dear and darling wife.'

They followed and Naomi showed Lesley to her room. She opened the shutters. 'Come, look at this.'

Lesley stood beside her and they gazed out upon another breathtaking panorama across the cliffs to the sea. 'This is so beautiful, you must be very happy here, Naomi. May I call you Naomi?' The older woman regarded her, unsmiling. She nodded her head. 'Thank you.' Lesley felt embarrassed again, averting her eyes. 'Your husband is such a nice man,' she said, breaking the silence.

Naomi regarded her pensively. 'Ja, Michael is a good man.' She turned as if to leave. 'I'll send Sammy up to you as soon as he gets back.'

'He isn't here?'

'No, he had a call, left suddenly. Always schlepping somewhere, the man.'

'Where has he gone?'

'Haifa.' She frowned. 'I think he said Haifa. He had a call.'

'But I have just come from Haifa.'

'So you passed him. He didn't want to see you in Haifa. He

wants to get you a gift, a house-warming present, is that right, house-warming?'

'I think you mean a welcome present, ein Wilkommen Geschenk. But a present, really? How very sweet and thoughtful of him.'

Naomi looked at her seriously. 'You don't know how much he loves you?'

Lesley felt herself blush. She lowered her eyes to avoid Naomi's penetrating stare. 'He told me once, blurted out that he thought he was falling in love with me. Since then, nothing.'

'You rejected him.' It was not a question.

Lesley looked up quickly. 'No, I didn't. I said I wasn't sure...no, you are right, of course.' She bit her lower lip and turned her head away to stare through the window. 'You see...I hardly knew him, I don't know him even now...' She paused and looked at Naomi. 'And yet there is something about him...it is hard to explain. I am attracted to him, I think of him constantly. I wait for his calls, I am never content unless I know where he is...but...I find him very disconcerting.'

Naomi smiled. 'So, you love him,' she stated.

'Do I? I wish I could be as sure. I need time to discover him, to discover myself. That is why I agreed to come here with him. But Naomi, I am so terribly bewildered.'

'Well, he's in love with you, believe me and I think you love him too. So find out for yourself and when you are sure, tell him and then go to each other. You can't have time, time you don't have, so stop wasting it.' She inclined her head. 'Why bewildered?'

Lesley looked at her. She struggled to find the right words but there was no easy way. 'There is gossip, at the office, they say there is another woman.'

Naomi's eyes locked upon her. She shook her head slowly but did not speak. After some moments, Lesley was forced to lower her eyes to avoid the intensity of Naomi's gaze. Then she turned suddenly and walked from the room. Lesley watched the closed door for some moments then, turning slowly, began to unpack her overnight things. She gazed out of the window trying to calm her unquiet senses. She heard a gentle knock and turned to face the door. 'Come in.'

He closed the door behind him. He was wearing the blue denim shirt and shorts of the kibbutznik. She thought how different he looked out of uniform and without his shrunken red beret. His fair hair was thick. Sammy was not one for regulation and his bright blue eyes shone happily out of his tanned face. Even with his pugilist's nose she thought him quite good looking. He grinned widely at her. 'Hello pretty lady.'

'Hello handsome.'

They stood for some moments regarding each other. 'Well, don't I get a kiss?' she asked puckishly. Laughing, he placed his hands on her arms, bending forward to kiss her cheek. 'Oh no you don't, young Parker.' She pushed herself into his arms, clinging to him. 'You are going to kiss me properly for once in your misspent life.' She raised her face and looked into his eyes. They kissed, lingeringly.

'God,' he whispered as they drew apart, 'I have waited more than a year to do that and if it's all the same to you, Madam, I am going to do it again.'

As their lips parted for the second time she took his face in her hands and smiled at him. 'But we have kissed before, in Germany, or had you forgotten?'

'Forgotten? How could I forget? I had been utterly bewitched by the most beautiful woman I had ever seen and in my emaciated, brain damaged and confused state, this vision kissed me. How could I forget?'

'Not quite like this, Sammy, was it?'

He laughed. 'Not quite. I could barely stand, let alone kiss.'

He looked at her, longingly. 'But you were exceptionally kind to me, you made me feel human again.' He began to chuckle. 'You had some guts, though. Tell me, was it as bad as it should have been?'

'Oh God, yes.' They laughed. 'You were not entirely wholesome and as I recall, your breath was a trifle high.'

He suddenly became serious. 'I was quite concerned for a while, you know. None of the unctions or other remedies they poured into me seemed to make much difference. I was convinced I had developed a serious physical dysfunction.'

She looked at him anxiously. 'What do you mean?'

'Well, I thought somehow my mouth had become directly connected to my arse.'

'Oh, you shit, Sammy,' she screamed, 'that is awful.' They fell into each other's arms. She looked up at him. 'Sammy, why did you have to go to Haifa?'

'Haifa? I haven't been to Haifa, I went into Nathanya.'

'But Naomi said you had a call from Haifa.'

'I did.' He looked at her steadily. 'It was from the bureau, it seems there are new orders for me.'

'Orders? What sort of orders?'

'I'm not sure. Bradbury was thinking of sending me down to the Negev for a spell.' He nodded towards the door. 'These sods are sneaking up the Gulf of Eilat and coming in via the tradesmen's entrance, it's probably that.'

'Oh, Sammy, no, what rotten luck. Shall you go back early?'

'I shan't know until I've seen the orders, that's why I'm popping into Haifa now. I shouldn't be more than a couple of hours.'

'Mayn't I come with you?' He inclined his head. 'No! Sorry darling, not thinking.'

'I wouldn't return immediately, anyway.' He tried to reassure her. 'We still have a weekend to enjoy.' She smiled. He took her into his arms and they began at once to kiss.

Naomi burst into the room bearing clean bed linen. She looked at Sammy, unsmiling. 'You've got a good sensible girl there, Sammy, not too high and mighty to take advice. You be nice to her, she deserves better than you, mind, so be grateful.' She turned to Lesley. 'Am I right? You're telling me I'm wrong? So get on with it.' So saying, she left the room as abruptly as she had entered, leaving Sammy shaking his head.

'What the hell was all that about?'

Lesley chuckled. 'She has confided to me how you love me, oy vey. That although I don't yet know it, I feel the same about you, please God. That time is the one commodity we don't got, already. So get on with it, yet.'

'You noticed,' he laughed. 'She speaks English like Beppo Marks. If you want to avoid confusion I advise you to speak German. But it's this bloody family, I don't believe them sometimes. If you were to write about it, as it is, nobody would believe you.' He looked at her for some moments then asked, 'And?'

'And what?'

'Is she right?'

She smiled. 'Kiss me again.' She looked at him, gently caressing his face. 'You know, old sport, I do believe she is.'

He pulled her to him. 'You will never know how that makes me feel.'

She snuggled into him. 'Sammy.'

'Yes?'

'Why did you go into Nathanya?'

'Shopping...OK, I got you a present.'

'I know,' she giggled, 'Naomi told me...where is it? What did you buy me?'

'Later.'

'No Sammy, please, tell me now.'

'I, er...I bought you some drawers...you said if I got you a change of knickers you would...' He shrugged. 'Look, a deal is a deal, right?'

'Oh Sammy!' They fell laughing into each other's arms. She pressed her face against his chest. 'I love you so much, my darling...but...slowly...please.' She closed her eyes and sighed. 'I realise now I have loved you since Hanover, but I needed time. Sammy, darling, I have never felt like this before. It is wonderful, yet somehow strange and moving...I must have time to get used to it.'

He gently kissed her neck beneath her ears. She sighed, pressing herself against him. 'We both have to get used to this, my love,' he whispered. 'Neither of us has been normal for six bloody years.' They lingered for a while then he kissed her cheek quickly. 'OK, unpack and have a siesta. When I get back I'll try and rustle up some fresh clothes for you.' He chuckled. 'At least you will have a change of knickers.' He closed the door, shutting in her laughter.

CHAPTER TWELVE

Lesley sat up suddenly, startled from her sleep. She checked her watch to find her nap had lasted almost three hours. She stood, stretching upwards, throwing her head back, eyes closed. A contented smile moved her lips as she crossed to the window. She pushed the shutters wide and gazed out, beyond the shimmering sea. Removing her clothes, she refreshed herself in the still chill water from a large terracotta jug. She began to towel herself dreamily and as she caught sight of her image in the mirror, she smiled thoughtfully. She let the towel slip slowly to the floor, revealing her naked torso. She cupped her breasts then moved her hands slowly downwards over her hips to the front of her thighs, running her fingers into the tight wiry hair. As she regarded herself she supposed another's eyes shared her contemplation. She felt apprehensive yet eager to yield to her desire. She dressed quickly and left the room.

The hotel lounge was quiet and cool, its blinds drawn against the sun. Crossing to the door, she looked out across the courtyard. Michael's truck was missing but as she crossed the yard she saw Sammy's jeep parked in the shade of the dark fig. She smiled, pleased he was already back and wondered why he had not come to wake her. Perhaps he had just returned or found her sleeping and decided not to disturb her. It was very hot without shade but a breeze rose from the sea and she heard the surf far below, hissing among the rocks in the little cove. She was attracted by voices, low yet urgent and she slowly followed their sound round the building. The voices grew louder, then suddenly stopped. A window stood open, its shutters thrown back. She wondered which room it was and thought to look inside. She peered through the window, then drew quickly back, startled.

He held her in his arms, his cheek resting on her head. Her face was pressed tight against his chest. They stood quite still then she lifted her face to him and they kissed.

'Do you remember when you came back to me, Sammy, after so long and we came here alone? I was so happy and I craved for you to take me. If you had wished it, if you had asked me to go with you, I would have said yes. I would have gone anywhere to be with you.'

He kissed her forehead tenderly. 'I know, my love, I know.' He looked away toward the window and Lesley flinched lest he saw her. But he saw only Naomi. 'And I almost did.' He sighed, caressing her face. 'My love, you were a married woman with a husband who loved you. For a time I thought my heart would break again...but then...' He smiled.

She pressed herself into his arms and they remained in silent embrace until she asked, 'Do you love her very much?'

'Yes I do, very much.'

She nodded. 'She is very beautiful.'

'Yes she is.'

'Will she make you happy?'

'How can I know?'

She reached up and gently ran her fingers into his hair. 'I want you always to be happy, Sammy.'

'Yes, my love, I know you do.'

'And you will always love me, won't you?'

'Always.'

'Promise to love me always, Sammy,' she pleaded urgently, 'for as long as you live.'

'Naomi, no more, my love. Please, don't cry. You know my life is yours and I shall always love you.'

They stood quietly holding each other as she had found them. She turned away quickly and returned to her room.

She threw herself on the bed, distraught and resentful, her mind a chaos of raging emotions. She heard a knock and tried desperately to regain her composure. The door opened slightly.

'Carrie love, are you decent?' He peered round the door, smiling. 'So, you have come to at last.' He waited for her to speak. 'May I come in?' She still did not reply but stared at him with an angry, bewildered expression. 'Carrie? What's the matter, what did I do now?'

She held him in her gaze for some time then asked, 'Sammy, what sort of people stay here?'

'What?' He felt confused.

'It's a simple enough question. Who stays in this so-called hotel? Are they travellers, commercial people, holiday makers, honeymoon couples, who?'

He laughed nervously, bewildered. 'I don't know. I wouldn't think so, times are not normal, most of those who stay are family, friends, people like us, I guess.'

'You mean we are not paying guests?'

'Of course not.'

'Why of course not? It must cost money to run a place like this.'

'Who cares? It's none of our business, we're guests here...Jesus!'

She persisted angrily. 'I agree Michael and Naomi's financial affairs are not our business, but don't pretend, don't be obtuse.

We are not just guests. They appear to treat you as one of their own, as a Jew, as a most favoured son. Dear God, they even refer to me as your shiksa. What I am trying to ascertain is, are we being compromised?'

'Carrie, what has come over you all of a sudden? What's with the bloody third degree? How would we be compromised?'

'Sammy, in heaven's name,' she snapped at him angrily, 'stop prevaricating. You are a serving officer in the British Army and these people are in open rebellion against your government, a government of which I happen to be a pretty senior representative.'

He tried levity. 'You're certainly pretty, I won't argue with that.'

She appeared to soften. 'Sammy, be serious.'

'OK, but I think you are worrying too much. These people are not in open or any other sort of rebellion, they are farmers, for heaven's sake.'

'So were the Boers, darling. You say these people, those who are constantly in and out, are simply relatives or friends from the kibbutz?' He nodded. 'Fine, this may be their local for all I know. But they have been asking me some pretty direct questions, they are extremely and persistently inquisitive. Not to put too fine a point on it, they are nosy sods.'

He shrugged. 'They're Jews.'

She smiled. 'I'm sorry, darling, I don't mean to be a boor, but we really should be careful.' He made no reply. She looked at him and knew she loved him. She knew also that she could no longer avoid the matter of his liaison with Naomi. 'Sammy, what exactly is your relationship to these people?'

He turned and regarded her seriously. 'What do you mean my relationship?'

'You mentioned having helped one of Ben's relatives who was in some trouble and soon after I arrived, Naomi said a very funny thing.'

'Naomi? Not a bloody chance.'

'Sammy!'

'All right, what did she say that was so funny?'

She looked at him closely to gauge his reaction. 'She intimated that you love her.'

He stared at her, unsmiling for some time and she was reminded how disconcerting that fixed, unblinking gaze could be. Then suddenly he grinned broadly. 'And you find that funny?'

'Sammy please, I am serious.'

'So what made her say such a thing?'

'She decided to tell me how much you loved me and how you had confided this to her. She said, and this is the funny peculiar part, "and he never lies to me...doesn't he love me too". I thought that oddly presumptuous.'

He tried to laugh. 'She's Jewish, for Christ's sake. You know what they're like and anyway, her English is not that perfect.'

'No, but my German is.' She felt again the hurt and anger. 'Sammy, please stop trivialising everything by saying they are Jewish. I am not a complete fool.' He stared at her for some moments then shrugged indifference. 'Do you still love her, Sammy?' she asked.

'What do you mean, still?'

'I have learned you knew her in the past. It seems everybody knew but me.' He looked away again, silent, lost in thought. She watched him for some moments then she reached out and touched his arm. 'Sammy, I saw you.'

He turned his head back quickly, his gaze cold and penetrating. 'Saw me? Saw what?'

'I saw you with her, with Naomi. Sammy, I wasn't prying, you must believe that,' she added quickly. 'I was looking for you and I heard your voice...I saw how you held her, how you looked at her. I heard the things you said to each other...I could not help myself.' He turned away again. 'Sammy, do you love me?'

He faced her. 'Of course I love you. Carrie, how can you ask such a question?'

She shook her head. 'How can I ask such a question? Can you possibly be serious? Sammy, speak to me, for God's sake. Who is this woman? What is she to you?'

He closed his eyes briefly, sighing heavily. 'You are right, I can't think why I haven't told you before. You have every right to know and you were bound to find out.' He hesitated, struggling with feelings too strong to suppress and as she looked at him she felt fear, a terrible apprehension that she could lose him at the very moment she had come to love him.

'Sammy, please,' she entreated, but he would not look at her.

He said softly, 'Matthausen.'

Her anguish immediately gave way to bewilderment. 'What?'

'Matthausen.' As he spoke the name he slowly shook his head, hating this moment which had come to reawaken those terrible memories. He looked at her now. 'Naomi was the woman I met in the camp, the one who saved my life.'

'Naomi was in Matthausen?' She shook her head, unable to grasp the significance of his words. She glanced towards the door, expecting Naomi to come, to resolve her confusion. 'But she is married to Michael, they own this hotel, they have lived here for years.'

'Michael has lived here for years. He was born here. But he was also a member of the Jewish Council for Refugees. He brought Naomi here from a DP camp in Germany.'

'You mean she is an illegal immigrant?'

'No, he married her in Greece before she came...to give her citizenship.'

Lesley felt her anger return, compounding her fear and confusion. 'Sammy Parker, you frustrating man. I have behaved like a lovesick adolescent. I just cannot believe this is happening to me. At the age of twenty-six I fall in love for the first time only to find myself playing second fiddle to a middle-aged concentration camp survivor who married a Palestinian hotelier in Greece after saving my lover's life. I discover them in each other's arms, swearing undying fealty even though he swears he loves me. How can I ask? You want to know how I can ask? I'll tell you how I can damned well ask, Captain Parker, because I don't know what the hell is going on, that's how. Here am I, a senior British government official, staying with people from the Jewish Council for Refugees and illegal immigrants, maybe terrorists even, are coming out of the woodwork. For all I know I have been breaking bread with the Haganah, cracking matzos with the Irgun and singing "We'll Meet Again" with the wretched Stern Gang. You bring me here, to your...your...your tryst house...and for what? To do what exactly...dance an "excuse me" with your Jewess? Sammy, you deceitful bastard...Oh Christ.' Her tirade became increasingly incoherent and she began to cry. He tried to take her in his arms. 'Don't touch me.' She pulled away violently but he persevered.

'Carrie, stop it. Please stop it, sweetheart, you are jumping to all the wrong conclusions and making yourself ill. Carrie, I love you.'

'How can you say that?' she shouted, her anger unabated. 'Do you deny you love this woman? If she is the woman you encountered in Matthausen, of course you love her. You almost died in her arms, she saved you. Sammy, you owe her your life. You turned half of Europe upside down to find her. I remember how you looked when you spoke of her. I remember telling you not to give up until you had found her. Well you did, didn't you? You found her here. It is the reason you came. You could have had a deferment, a discharge. You were half dead when you left Germany. But you came here, the better to find her, didn't you?

And now you have found her.' She looked down at the floor and her shoulders drooped as her anger gave way to grief. He took her in his arms and this time she did not protest. She looked up into his eyes. 'And yet you have told me that you love me, you have told Ben that you love me, I even heard you tell her that you love me.'

He smiled and kissed her gently. 'And I have never lied to her.'

She looked at him for some time then she clung to him desperately. 'Oh Sammy, I do so want to believe you, but I am so bewildered, I just do not understand.'

'Neither do I.' He sighed. 'Carrie, I cannot explain it, either to myself or to you. Naomi will always be special to me, but she is Michael's wife. He loves her, they are happy together and that makes me happy. She knows I love you and want to be with you and that makes her happy.'

'But Sammy, how can you know that?'

'Because she has told me.'

She smiled. 'And she never lies to you?'

'Never.'

'Sammy, do you promise she will never come between us?'

'That would not be possible, I love you too much.'

'But what of her?'

'She loves me as I love her, she would never hurt me.'

'And how do you love her? Tell me Sammy, I have to know.'

'Carrie, please don't ask me again, I can't explain. It is not like us, not a lovers' sort of love. I guess there are many different emotions which we call love. I love my mother, I love my father, I love my sister, but not the way I love you. I could not love anyone the way I love you.'

'Are you telling me you love Naomi like your mother? Like a sister?'

'No, I cannot lie to you, it is not like that. But it is different, so different that I am able to love you both...I am sorry, I am not being very rational am I?'

'No, not very.' She kissed him and he held her tight against his body. 'But if that is all you have to offer, I suppose I shall have to settle for a different sort of love.'

He laughed. 'There, you see. Another mot historique. Aren't you just bewitched by my eloquence?'

She began to laugh through her tears. 'Oh Sammy, I do love you so much.'

'Then why don't we stop babbling and start enjoying ourselves?'

'Why don't we, Sammy? Why don't we do just that?'

The four friends had gathered on the terrace to eat. Throughout the meal Lesley felt her gaze repeatedly drawn to Naomi, watching her every gesture. How she had eyes only for Sammy, how she spoke to him, how she moved to him, how she constantly touched him as they spoke and laughed. She wondered if she always behaved in this way. Affectionate, tactile and effusive. 'She's Jewish, for Christ's sake.' The thought caused her to smile...she looked at Sammy. He was totally at ease with Naomi, laughing and hugging her as they shared a joke. She wished with all her heart to see two old and dear friends together, each enjoying the other's company, but her eyes revealed two people in love rejoicing in their reunion. She tried to turn away, to rid herself of the jealousy and apprehension she felt, but the image of them in each other's arms persistently and painfully obsessed her.

'Sammy, why don't we take Carrie to visit the Rosh tomorrow? I'm sure she would find it interesting.' Michael's voice cut into her thoughts.

'Great idea. Would you like that, Carrie love?'

She smiled. 'If I knew what the Rosh was I could probably

tell you.'

'The kibbutz,' said Naomi. 'Michael teaches there.'

'Oh, yes please, that sounds like fun.'

The three burst into laughter. 'Fun? Your feet won't touch, they will put you to work before you have time to hang your coat.'

The kibbutzniks gave her a welcome appropriate to 'Sammy's shiksa'. They did not, however, put her to work. Instead they proudly showed her all they had achieved in turning the desert into a garden. She looked across the neat fields and groves to the coiled razor wire around the distant perimeter. Simon followed her gaze. 'When we establish Eretz Israel, Carrie, all that will come down and we shall be a free people again.' She nodded and smiled at his naive enthusiasm.

Walking back to the central hall, she determined to approach Michael on the subject that was causing her so much anxiety. She entered the hall to find him there alone. 'I guess we are the first back. Would you like some cold lemonade, or perhaps some coffee?'

'Lemonade sounds good.'

'Right, I'll fetch a jug. Won't be a jiff.' He shouted from the kitchen, 'Have a look at the murals, Carrie, some of them are quite good.' She walked round, finally stopping before the painting of Naomi. As she contemplated that sad, beautiful face she felt her heart would break. 'It's very good isn't it?' Michael stood beside her. 'That is the picture which caused Sammy's heart to stop.' He laughed.

She turned to face him, her eyes moist. 'Then you know they are in love?'

He regarded her curiously. 'I know they love each other, of course.'

'And you are happy with this.'

'I am happy now. What else can I do?'

'I don't understand '

'You will.'

'I don't think so. I love him too much and I cannot bear to think of him loving anyone else. I want him to love only me.'

'But he does, Carrie. In all that is necessary to you, in all that you want from him, he loves only you. What they have, what they feel for each other is different.'

'How do you know that?'

'Because I understand it now, as you will come to understand it. But Lesley, you must want to understand, otherwise your jealousy will destroy the wonderful thing you have. He can never give her up, nor she him, they can not. What happened to them in that camp bonded them, they are indivisible. They survived with and through each other and now their lives belong to each other.'

'You know they see each other, don't you?'

'What an extraordinary question. Why do you think he comes here?'

'Are they lovers?'

'No.'

'How can you be sure?'

'Because they have said so.'

'You asked them?'

'Why do you sound so surprised? At first I was exactly like you. Carrie, you should have been here the day he came. I thought I had lost her forever and I felt helpless. At first I was filled with rage, but their joy was magnificent, so beautiful, transcendent almost and I could not but be happy for her because I saw how she loved him. I would have let her go to him if that had been his wish.'

'His wish?'

'She would have gone to him had he asked her.'

She recalled Naomi's words. 'But how do you know this?'

'Because she told me. I would not believe at first that two people could love each other so much, yet not want to celebrate and to consummate that love. Only later did I come to understand. Sammy is a man of great integrity. He is content, now that she is safe and happy, to...' He paused. 'I am certain that though he loves her still, he no longer desires her. I do not even know whether he ever desired her. He said to me once, "We were never really lovers, you know". It was a strange remark and I have never been able to resolve its ambiguity.'

'And does that go for her?'

He looked away, weighing the question to which he knew he had no easy answer. 'Until you came, I was not sure. But I know she would never do anything to hurt him and I believe she is finally reconciled to the fact that she can never have him and she is content with his happiness.'

Lesley regarded him thoughtfully for some moments. 'I want to believe your answer is not wishful, not naive. My heart tells me that they love each other in a different, if you like, spiritual way. But my cynical, practical head insists their love is real, that only convention prevents its consummation and that we get what is left. But I love him so very much, I prefer to believe my heart.'

'I am more than satisfied with that and so should you be.'

They fell silent, contemplative, then she asked, 'Do you want children?'

'Very much.'

'She won't let you have them?'

'I shall never know. Naomi cannot have children.'

'But she had two daughters.'

'That was before the Germans sterilised her.'

'Why did they do that?'

'She was beautiful and Gräber desired her. But as the commandant of an extermination camp he knew it was his duty to kill all Jewish babies born in the camp, so...'

'Bloody hell! Michael, I had no idea. My God, that poor woman. Those damned rotten hypocritical swine.' She looked at him. 'Does it bother you she was a concubine?'

'Concubine?' He laughed quietly. 'How very English.' The smile faded gradually. 'She was a slave whore, Carrie, and Alfried Gräber would have killed her without compunction had she refused him. She was not a concubine, she was a victim.' He regarded her sadly. 'Does it bother me? I do not like to think about it but I like even less the thought that she might have been murdered like all the others.'

'She almost was, wasn't she?'

'Ah! But they did not figure on the redoubtable Sammy, did they?' He placed his arm round her and hugged her gently. 'I have seen your fear and, God forgive me, shared your jealousy, Carrie. I have felt your anxiety but have not known how to help you. I am glad you decided to speak to me. He is yours, you have nothing to fear from any of us. So go to him, make your life together. He deserves the love you will give him.'

They were in love and they came together avidly, greedily and with all the passionate intensity of those denied by the fortunes of war, those painful, bewildering and awesome excursions of youth. Now they had the time to explore, to discover each other. They roamed the woods and hills, picking wild berries. They made their tortuous way down the cliff path to the shore and swam in the gentle, almost tideless sea. They fished for crabs in the warm rock pools, Sammy in his shorts and Lesley with her dress hitched up in her knickers, she screaming with delight as he playfully thrust the writhing animal at her.

They laid side by side on the gentle slope, the haze lazy upon them as they listened to the cicadas in the warm cliff top grass. The refracting sea, scintillating in the afternoon sun, was almost hypnotic and they drowsed contentedly. She rolled slowly on to one elbow and lowered her eyes to him. She laid her head on his chest and, moved by the slow beating of his heart, felt her need grow within her. She reached up with her body and kissed him on the mouth. He stirred sleepily.

She sat up and looked down at him. 'Sammy, I want to go back now.'

'Back?' He looked bewildered.

'To the hotel, darling.'

He became concerned. 'Are you alright?'

'No Sammy, I'm not alright, that's why I want to go back.'

He stood up and lifted her to her feet. They hurried in silence back to the hotel where they went straight to her room. He looked at her anxiously. 'What is it, love? Would you like me to fetch Naomi?'

'No, I would not like you to fetch Naomi.' She smiled at him. 'Sammy, lock the door.'

'What?'

'Lock the door, darling, please.'

He turned and did as she bade then came back and stood before her. She held out her arms. 'Come here, Captain Parker.' They came together. She started to slowly unbutton his shirt and he felt himself aroused. He looked at her, longingly. 'Carrie, are you sure you want to do this?'

She smiled at him. 'Shush, darling, help me with my dress.'

They stood quietly as they slowly and deliberately undressed each other. They stood naked, in mute wonder. He lifted her in his arms and kissed her gently. As he carried her to the bed she said, 'Sammy, can you reach that towel?'

'Towel?'

'Just in case, darling.' He spread the towel on the bed and she laid upon it. She held out her arms to him. 'Now, Sammy, please darling, now.'

She had taken no real sexual pleasure in her life before and she was not prepared for the intense desire she felt as he kissed her breasts. She wanted to take pleasure but did not yet know how. She looked up at him and as he pressed himself into her, she knew for the first time what it was to be a woman. She cried out, incoherent, arching her back against the pain and in his excitement he could not hold himself. He rolled over and lay beside her. They could not speak. After a while he felt her take his hand and squeeze it gently. He did not turn to her but stared at the ceiling as he spoke. 'Carrie, I am so sorry. I had no idea I would be the first and I could not help myself...I feel such a shit.'

She sat up, gazing down at him. 'No Sammy, don't. Darling, it was not your fault, how could you know, a woman my age? I did try to tell you I wasn't very good at this sort of thing. I am a flirt, not a lover. It will be better next time, you'll see...I promise. Darling, kiss me, please.'

He turned to her now, wide eyed. 'Next time? After the balls up I made of this?'

'Sammy, stop this at once. Let's face it, darling, we're both freshers on this course, aren't we? Tell me honestly, how many women have you had?'

He smiled at her. 'So, green light on, eh? Moment of truth.' He bent down and kissed her. 'Not many.'

'I said honestly, Sammy. How many?'

He laid back again, staring upward. 'Only one.'

She glanced sideways at him but he did not move. She knew at once who it was and it aroused within her an inexplicable pleasure. She felt no envy, no malice. She knew now, at last, that he loved her, but she chuckled. 'Oh come now, Captain Parker, surely you jest, Sir. The most eligible of all the Young Lions and you expect me to believe you have deflowered only one maiden before me?'

'I have not deflowered any maidens before you and I have

only known one other woman.'

'What about your English Teacher?'

'Sarah?' He fell back laughing. 'Are you serious?'

'But why?'

'Well...you know. Anyway, it would have been tantamount almost to incest.'

She fell across him and as they laughed they fell into an embrace and their kissing became urgent again. She straddled him, running her fingers into his hair. She lifted his head. 'Sammy, I do love you and I know now that you do love me. Oh Sammy, I love you,' she sang out, 'Ich liebe dich, je t'aime, ya lublu tebya.' She gazed at him longingly then frowned. 'Darling, what's the matter?'

'Bloody show off,' he sniffed.

She laughed and they hand wrestled, she wriggling on him. Suddenly she felt him inside her again and she was quickly overtaken by a depth of passion she had not known before. She could not attempt any rational description of what she was feeling. She would need a new and unique lexicon or an entire silver poesy to describe the sensation. She only knew that the experience was central to her life. She cried out, repeating his name. 'Sammy, Sammy, oh God, Sammy...'

He put his hand up to cover her mouth. 'Shush, darling, not so loud, do you want the whole world to know what we are doing up here?'

She bit his hand in her ecstasy. 'Oh yes, yes, Oh God, Sammy, tell me you love me, love me Sammy, love me.' She heard him cry out and as he thrust upwards in his release, she screamed. 'Oh God...' As her passion subsided she fell on to him and lay still.

They shared a cigarette and remained silent for some time then he said, 'They say it's like riding a bike, you know.'

'What is?'

'Making love. Once you've learned how to do it, you never forget, you just get better at it.'

'Well, all I can say is if it's like that every time, I won't want to forget. But how could it possibly get better?'

'Trust me, it gets better.'

'Oh yes, the expert after only two Geronimos? Alright Mister, show me.' They fell back again and lay in each other's arms. After a while she said, 'Good job I thought of that towel.'

'Oh Jesus, the towel. Is it bad?'

She pushed him over and pulled the towel from under him. 'Not too bad, I'll rinse it. It will soon dry in the sun.'

He turned to her. 'Mind you don't break it.'

'Oh Sammy, you dirty minded sod,' she shrieked. 'How did I ever get mixed up with a lout like you?'

'Lout? Lout? I thought I was just a plain and simple thug.' She hung the towel from the window ledge. 'For Christ's sake, don't hang the bloody thing out of the window, this is the Middle East, remember? You'll have them all clapping and cheering an ancient virgin nuptial.'

'Why not, Sammy darling?' She chuckled. 'After all, that's exactly what it was.' He lay watching her every movement and he knew he had never been happier. She turned from the window and looked at him then lit two cigarettes and handed one to him.

He smiled at her. 'Who do you think you are, Bette Davis?'

'No, I'm better looking.'

'So am I,' he agreed emphatically.

Giggling, she laid down beside him, utterly at peace. She shot up suddenly. 'Oh Christ!'

'What? What's the matter?'

'I forgot to go for my bloody jabs.'

'Jabs?' He looked at her with a shocked expression. 'Jabs? For Christ's sake, Carrie, I know I'm a bit on the rough side, but jabs you need?'

'Oh, you idiot!' she shrieked as she fell back.

He sat up and stubbed out his cigarette. 'Shall we go down for some grub?'

She smiled. 'Not yet.'

'Aren't you hungry?'

'Famished, but it's a matter of priorities and I have other, more urgent appetites to assuage right now.'

'Bloody wars! Couldn't we skip the foreplay and just light another fag?'

'Oh, come on, Sammy, please,' she pleaded, trying to pull him up.

'Sweetheart, don't you understand? The spirit is willing but the flesh is weak.'

She lifted the sheet slowly and peered beneath. 'No it isn't,' she asserted.

'Carrie! Jesus Christ.'

She punched him playfully. 'Shut up, Parker. Lie back and think of England.'

She took him again, passionately and noisily. He knew any attempt to quell her ululations would be entirely in vain. Finally she rolled over and laid beside him. 'My God, Sammy,' she said, recovering her breath, 'I can't believe how wonderful that is.'

He kissed her. 'As the rabbi said to the priest, "Better than bacon, ain't it?"'

She squealed with delight. 'Speaking of which,' she said, 'let's go eat.'

He looked up at her. 'Eat? I don't think I have the energy to lift a butter knife. Jesus H. Christ, I'm knackered.'

'Knackered?' She chuckled happily. 'I'm sure I have heard you use another more apposite expletive to describe your present state.'

'Lesley Carrington! You are an incorrigible little whelp.' He leapt from the bed. 'Come on, before the natives get suspicious.'

He began to gather up her clothes. She looked at him mischievously.

'Sure you don't want to try for five?'

'Do you want to kill me?' He threw the clothes at her. 'Get your clobber on.'

The 'family' sat around the large stone table. The customary cacophony of umpteen simultaneous conversations, all at maximum volume, smothered the sound of their approach but as the couple drew near, all became quiet. They looked at Sammy and Lesley wide-eyed and expectant. Naomi fixed Sammy with a severe look but then closed her eyes and lifting her head, turned away disapprovingly. Daniel smiled knowingly at the two lovers. 'Good siesta?' They all laughed at Sammy's embarrassment but Lesley responded unabashed.

'Great, thank you, Daniel. Wonderful, in fact, the best siesta I've ever had.'

Daniel laughed. 'Then you must be hungry.'

'Absolutely starving.'

Naomi looked at Lesley. 'So now you want to eat?'

'Of course they want to eat,' said Joseph. 'Everybody knows it gives you an appetite.'

'What does?' Naomi demanded.

'Sleeping, what do you think?'

She snorted at their laughter and headed for the kitchen. Lesley followed her into the house.

'I'll give you a hand,' she called after the older woman. In the kitchen Naomi began to prepare the evening meal. She ignored Lesley as she busied herself collecting the pans and ingredients she was going to need. Lesley watched her for some time and then said, 'Naomi, please let me help you.'

Naomi turned and looked at Lesley. She nodded slowly then her face broke into a broad smile. 'Well, he certainly brought a bloom to your cheeks, that Sammy. I take it he knows now that you love him?'

Lesley's heart went out to her joyfully. 'Oh yes, Naomi, I think he knows at last.'

'Good, so now you can live.' Naomi regarded Lesley gravely for a while then came forward and hugged her, almost desperately. 'Be careful, Mädl, these are funny times, bad times, don't be hurt.' She kissed Lesley affectionately. 'Listen, you must take love while you can, believe me, I know.'

Lesley detected a hint of pathos in her voice. 'But you have Michael who obviously adores you, don't you have love enough with him?'

Naomi nodded. 'He is a good man, Michael, he is my husband.'

The two women regarded each other for some moments then Lesley said, 'Naomi, I know about you and Sammy, he has told me everything.'

Naomi stared at her. 'Everything? You know about me and Sammy, everything?'

'Yes. He has told me how you met in that horrible camp, how you came to him when he was so desperate and how you saved him from going mad. He says you saved his life. He has told me how you feel for each other because of what you endured together. Oh Naomi, I think the relationship you have is so beautiful.' Naomi looked at her, expressionless. Lesley went on. 'When I discovered he had known you I did not know what to think. There was gossip at HQ that he had a lover in Palestine, an old flame, they said, and I couldn't understand why he would bring me here. Then I met you and almost at once you told me he loved you. I was desperately jealous because I love him so much. But he explained everything to me and now I understand.'

Naomi remained impassive. 'You do? You understand everything? Well, that's good.'

Lesley looked at her and felt a distinct unease. 'Naomi?'

'You understand everything Sammy tells you, that's all,' she said curtly. 'How can you ever know what I feel?' She closed her eyes and sighed deeply then sat at the table, her head bowed.

Lesley saw that she was crying now. She tried to hang back as Naomi wept but she felt herself drawn to her. She rounded the table and took her in her arms. 'Oh Naomi, darling, I am so sorry, I should have realised. I was jealous to think he loved you. It simply did not occur to me...what are we going to do?'

Naomi recovered quickly. She blew her nose on her apron, causing Lesley to wrinkle her nose slightly. 'Has he told you how we know each other?'

Lesley was slightly confused by the question. 'You met in the camp.'

'Met in the camp?' Naomi's tone was peremptory. 'Met in the camp? There were twenty thousand people in that camp. We didn't meet in the camp, I went after him.'

'You went after him? I don't understand, why did you go after him?'

'It was Christmas.'

'What?' Lesley could not restrain a nervous laugh.

'I had been watching him for weeks. I was in Gräber's house and he worked in the dispensary, across the compound. He was always looking through the window at me. It was Christmas, all the Germans were blau, so I thought I would have some fun with him, you know, try to drop him in the shit.'

Lesley started in surprise and looked at Naomi. 'But in God's name why?'

'I thought he was a Russian.'

'A Russian?' Lesley was nonplussed. 'Sammy? Why would you think he was a Russian?'

'He had a red hat.'

Lesley's expression betrayed her increasing bewilderment.

'Do Russians wear red hats?'

'I should know what hats Russians wear?'

'Then I don't understand, what had his red hat to do with it?'

'Red is a communist colour, right?'

'Right.' Lesley nodded. 'But why would you want to drop a Russian in...weren't they winning the war to free you?'

'Winning the war to free us? Ney!' Naomi waved a dismissive hand. 'Don't you know what the Russians have done to the Jews? Have you never heard of a pogrom? You think Hitler was the first?'

'And did you drop...did you get him into trouble?'

Naomi lowered her gaze for a moment then looked straight at Lesley. 'I didn't get the chance, he wouldn't take me.'

'Take you?' Lesley asked, puzzled, then began to comprehend. 'You mean you...you wanted to but...then who...?'

Naomi frowned, unable to follow Lesley's questioning. 'It was forbidden. I was only for Gräber, you understand, he would have been beaten, but...' She shrugged. '...he wouldn't take me. He washed my face and dried my eyes and comforted me. He spoke to me in kindness, as a human being. He made me feel like a woman again. He gave me back my self respect, he wept for what they had done to me.' She looked up into Lesley's eyes. 'He loved me, that man, like no other had ever done before. Simply, unselfishly, for myself and he almost died for it.' She recited the whole story and when she had finished she lowered her head and stared at her hands.

Lesley bent and kissed her hair. 'Dear God, I had no idea he did all that for you. No notion of what went on. I had reports, of course, about what he had done to Gräber and Höchst. I myself witnessed his terrible rage, but the detail was confused...Do you love him still?'

Naomi smiled. 'You want I should make you jealous again?'

Lesley sat before her and took her hands in her own. 'Naomi,

I could not be jealous of you, my darling. I simply did not know. He never speaks about the camp. He made his report to me in Hanover, of course, about the conditions and about Gräber and Höchst, but he refuses to discuss his own part in all of this. We knew that he met a woman in there, he told us that much to elicit our help to find you. He even spoke of you to me. But Naomi, I had no idea just what you meant to each other and why. I thought it was just another tragic, desperate affair.'

'Some affair you can have in Matthausen. We should walk hand in hand to the gas chamber? Kiss and cuddle in the doorway of the crematorium? He didn't give me no affair, he gave me my life.'

'Did you never make love?'

'Why do you ask that?'

Lesley squeezed her hands. 'He told me he has had only one woman before me.' She paused and looked at Naomi. 'I could not bear it to be anyone else.'

Naomi smiled, shaking her head. 'You English...You are all mad, do you know that? How did you ever win the war?'

'With a little help from our friends...Well?'

'You are telling me I was his first?'

'And he never lies to me.'

Naomi grinned with an uncharacteristic glint of mischief in her eyes. 'I should have known.' She dropped her gaze, almost modestly, looking into her hands. 'Er war schön, aber...' She raised her eyes, smiling. 'He was not very good...well, not at first.'

Lesley, shocked at first, began to laugh. 'Well, he hadn't been well, had he, my poor pet.' The two women were laughing heartily now and fell into an embrace. Lesley kissed her, fully, upon the mouth. 'I love you, Naomi, and not just for saving him for me.' She gazed at the older woman poignantly.

Naomi smiled at her then stroked her cheek. 'Keine Angst,

Mädl. He is yours now. He loves me, I know that, but not like you, you are what he lives for now. So take him and be good to him, he is the best of men.'

'But what shall you do?'

'Do? Me? Dinner is what I do. Come, help me with these vegetables.'

CHAPTER THIRTEEN

There were twelve of them, elbow to elbow around the table under the tree, everybody speaking at full throat, regaling all with their opinion and with little regard for any other point of view. They had gathered to eat and eating is ever a rumbustious affair in a large Jewish 'family'. Lesley was both bewildered and fascinated, her attention switching frantically from face to face as she tried to decant this noisy, obstreperous concoction. During the afternoon Naomi and Lesley had been joined in the kitchen by several other women. Rachel arrived with Ben, accompanied by another sister, Esther, then Belle and Netta with their men from the kibbutz. Simon, a large-framed old man with sad, rheumy blue eyes, stared at the table approvingly.

'My God, look at this spread. Do I see Naomi's potato kügel?'

'And Netta's Kartoffelsalat.'

'And Belle's noodle pudding.'

'Carrie made the matzo balls,' Naomi announced.

'What?' Sammy was dumfounded.

'Under her expert guidance, of course,' Lesley assured everyone.

'That's my beautiful almond honey cake,' Rachel boasted shamelessly.

'Please God you are all square with your dentist,' Ben offered helpfully.

Simon reached across and began to serve himself with copious helpings of food: chicken wings, string beans, salt beef, noodle pudding. 'If you're figuring on eating today, you'd better get your forks busy before Goliath of Gath clears the table,' shouted Ben.

Naomi stood and at once began to fill Sammy's plate. 'Thank you, sweetheart.' His lips gently touched her arm. 'Come and sit here with me.' He shuffled along the settle to make room for her. Lesley, trying desperately not to notice, listened patiently as Esther regaled her with stories of shopping expeditions to Haifa and Tel Aviv in search of elusive crochet hooks and even rarer cotton.

'So, what's new?' Daniel looked at Michael.

'He's writing a book,' said Rachel.

'What about?' Simon looked suspicious.

'The Jewish tragedy,' said Michael. 'It's not exactly a...'

'Whose?' demanded Simon.

'Whose what?'

'Whose Jewish tragedy?'

'Well, ours, of course.'

'It's a book about being Jewish,' explained Rachel.

'What does he know about being Jewish?' Simon snorted. 'He was born right here, in Palestine.'

'Oh Christ,' Sammy guffawed, 'that's bloody marvellous. You tell 'em, Simon, old son.'

'Simon, listen already,' Rachel adjured, 'it is about being Jewish in Israel.'

'Not yet, it ain't,' said Ben.

'Well, Palestine then.'

'I've been Jewish in Palestine longer than he has.' Simon threw down the gauntlet. He glowered across the table. 'What's that?' He pointed to a large bowl.

'It's your favourite,' said Naomi, 'potatoes mashed with chicken fat and onions.'

'If it's my favourite, why is everybody else eating it?'

'Please God he should never go hungry.' Netta pushed the bowl toward the old man.

'How much you getting for this book?'

'Nothing.' Michael scowled at Simon impatiently. 'I'm trying to tell you, I am just jotting down a few ideas...for myself.'

'For yourself? For yourself is going to put food on the table? Don't be a nar all your life. Sell it, make money, you always gotta make money.' He turned to address the gathering. 'That's the one useful thing I learned from the goyim, here.' Sammy roared again, this time joined by the others. Simon glared at them then plunged his spoon into the bowl and fell silent, much to everyone's relief. The conversation inevitably turned to the political situation and the future of Palestine, the kibbutzniks losing no time directing their attention to their captive British diplomat.

'Sammy tells us you are at the centre of things, Carrie.' Daniel smiled at her disarmingly. 'I for one would be interested in your comments.'

'Daniel, I fear my comments would be singularly ill informed, so I think perhaps I should claim diplomatic immunity.' She laughed.

'You are much too modest, Carrie,' said Michael. 'We understand you would not wish to be compromised and we would not wish to press you on current British policy, although perhaps some might say it becomes clearer by the day, but you are a senior official and were not chosen for the job because you are "ill informed". Like Daniel, I would like to hear your own, personal opinion.'

'That's right, tell us what you think about the Palestinian

problem, Carrie,' Daniel said to a chorus of encouragement.

'You appreciate, of course, that officially I cannot have a personal opinion on any matter arising from British foreign policy.' Lesley looked to Sammy to assist her in her dilemma.

He winked broadly at her. 'Don't discuss official policy with this bunch of no good yids,' he advised. 'Just give them the published facts. The "Not the Jewish Chronicle" version. They might not like what they hear, they detest facts, they are confused by them. They won't actually listen, of course, but maybe, just maybe, if you shout loud enough, one of them might get the gist.'

'Shut it, Attila.'

'Yeah, stumm, you no good goy.'

'You're a paratrooper, Sammy, go take a jump.' He laughed with them.

Lesley smiled. 'Alright, if you insist, the Gospel according to Carrie Carrington, although I fear the news might not be all good.' She looked at their expectant faces. Sammy moved to the window, seemingly unconcerned. She looked at Naomi who smiled at her gently, giving a little nod of encouragement.

'When the department sent me to Palestine I really had no idea what to expect. My knowledge of the region was superficial. Its history, its geography, its social and ethnic fabric were, in most respects, a closed book to me. You see, my training and what little experience I had were substantially concerned with the procedures and protocols of international diplomacy. My brief here was firstly to advise H. M. Government, both locally and nationally, during the negotiations of the various United Nations resolutions, and secondly, to advise them on the implications for British foreign policy of those resolutions, as, for example, to their effect upon security within the region and also upon migration to the region.' She looked at their intense faces. 'I know you will forgive me, therefore, if I do not discuss those particular aspects in any detail.'

They all nodded their affirmation 'Oh, absolutely!'

'Sure, no problem.'

'Understood!'

'OK, fine. All I can do is give you my thoughts on the subject with the all important and necessary caveat that, as I have remarked, they are based only upon very recent consideration and entirely incomplete and superficial reading and observation.'

'That's classic F-off-ese,' said Sammy. 'It means, if you don't like what you hear, tough shit.' They all laughed.

'Thank you, darling, I knew I could count on your support.'

'Ignore him, Carrie,' Daniel advised, encouragingly.

She smiled. 'Before I left England I had a briefing by my section head during the course of which he made the offhand remark that it was a pity Balfour had not kept his mouth shut. The words did not mean a great deal to me at the time. As I have explained, I knew little about Middle Eastern politics and I was still recovering from a rather traumatic experience in Germany.' They all laughed as Sammy raised his eyebrows indignantly. 'Of course, I later came across the famous, or according to one's point of view, infamous Balfour Declaration. The more I read it the more I began to wonder why a British Foreign Secretary should have made such an ambiguous and, as it seemed to me, totally provocative pronouncement. After all, the British, in particular the upper class, are not entirely free of anti-Semitism and the British government is not subject to the same pressures as the United States. For example, there is no powerful Jewish lobby to affect the electoral prospects of either of the main political parties. So I looked for other reasons and I am afraid I may have found them. In 1919, two years after his Declaration, Balfour was opening his mouth again. He said, and I don't think I paraphrase, I read the statement so many times I virtually committed it to memory: "In Palestine we do not propose even to go through the form of consulting the wishes of the present inhabitants of the country, although the American Commission has been going through the process of asking who they are." I was intrigued by that particular passage, containing as it did the implicit question, "how and by whom is the population of Palestine made up?" He went on: "The Great Powers..." and I presumed by that he meant Britain, France and the United States, "...are committed to Zionism. And Zionism, be it right or wrong, good or bad, is rooted in age-long traditions, in present needs, in future hopes, of far profounder import than the desires and prejudices of the 700,000 Arabs who now inhabit that ancient land. In my opinion that is right".'

'Well, the anti-Semitic British upper class has always had a vested interest in age-long tradition,' said Sammy cynically.

Lesley smiled wryly then continued. 'You see, what I found particularly surprising was the profoundly undiplomatic tone of this statement. It is so value-laden as to destroy, in my view, any worth it might have as a basis for intelligent analysis or discussion. To what extent, I asked, is Zionism rooted in age-long tradition? It dates only from 1897 and despite the eloquence of Herzl and Weizmann is, in my view, based upon an extremely questionable political and historical agenda. Further, with regard to what criteria is it of profounder import than the desires and prejudices, not aspirations or hopes or beliefs, you will note, but prejudices, of the Palestinian Arabs? The significant phrases for me are those which refer to present needs and future hopes. I asked myself, whose hopes? And what are they? It became increasingly clear to me that despite an ancient, almost endemic anti-Semitism, the Western powers, in particular the Anglo-Saxons, regard Jews as essentially European and Arabs as basically oriental, or, if you like, congenitally different and that this differentiation contains a quite overt racism. They view Arab culture as essentially anti-democratic, violent and regressive.

This regard, of course, underscores the perceived value of 'our' Judeo-Christian, i.e. Western liberal democratic heritage as opposed to the nefarious, evil and cruel immaturity of the Islamic world. It was clear to me from Balfour's statements and the subsequent policy outcomes of the British and other allied governments that undertakings given to the Arabs after their victorious desert campaigns against the Turks under Lawrence during the First World War are not worth the paper they are written on. I believe further that the Western powers do not regard Arabs as fit to govern, in this, or any other region.' She looked round at her audience. 'You see, the commercial interests of the West demand and require that the region be kept in a state of permanent political instability and its various regional ambitions polarised between competing and structurally irreconcilable factions. Now, how best to achieve this? Well clearly, essential to that polarisation is an independent, quasi-European state within the region. Zionism gave them a cause to endorse, the Holocaust the justification they would otherwise have had to invent and Palestine a convenient arena in which to place the protagonists.'

'But Carrie, if what you say is correct, why on Earth would the British government obstruct immigration so brutally? Why are they forcing our brothers and sisters into concentration camps on Cyprus just when they are in sight of their homeland?' Daniel shook his head. 'No, the British are dead set against us coming here to settle our own land.'

'Whose own land?' Sammy challenged. 'Half you sods haven't been here five minutes.'

'Now come on, Sammy.' Daniel's protest rose above a general chorus of dissent. 'Of course it's our land.'

'It's God-given.'

'It is in the Bible!'

'Is it?' shouted Sammy, defiantly. 'All I can find in the

bloody Bible is a story about how an ancient tribe of sheep-shagging Semites from the Sinai desert fell foul of an Egyptian Pharaoh, got thrown out on their arses and moved in here at the expense of the locals who had been here for hundreds of years. It seems every time you drop yourselves in it with your "chosen people" bullshit, you dump on these poor buggers. So please, spare me the Bible.'

'Sammy, Daniel, all of you, please.' Lesley's voice cut into the fracas. 'You are not listening to Balfour's words. The establishment of a national home for the Jewish people in Palestine is a British initiative. But you ignore the realities of the post-imperial future facing Great Britain. We are about to surrender the greatest overseas empire in the history of mankind. The ultimate defeat of British imperialism has been occasioned, paradoxically, by the cost of its victories over Germany in two wars. The United States is about to wrest the imperial crown from us and there will inevitably be a sort of post-imperial inertia, an interregnum of reluctant acquiescence, if you will permit me a mild tautology, on the part of the British establishment, to the surrender of what is left of its influence in world affairs.'

'That will be good for us,' said Michael. 'The Americans are our friends. Once they have convinced the United Nations to accept the partition of Palestine, Israel will return to its rightful place in the world.' He looked apprehensively at Sammy but there was no response.

Lesley smiled sadly as she looked round the table at the confident faces, each confirming a belief in a future filled with hope. 'I fear, Michael, the dream may be somewhat different from the reality.'

'Why should that be?'

'Michael, as we speak, the United Nations is meeting at Lake Success to consider a resolution, promoted by the United States, for the partition of Palestine and the founding of a Jewish state within its former territory. It is almost impossible to believe this resolution will not be adopted. The only thing which could prevent it would be for either Britain, France or the Soviet Union to exercise their veto in the Security Council. My belief is that France will support the resolution and that Britain will abstain. Russia could be a problem, but I do not think their interests in the region would be best served by opposition.'

'I don't understand.' Daniel looked at Lesley. 'How would Russian interests be served if a Jewish state is established in Palestine? The Russians have no love for the Jews, particularly the Zionists, and we don't like them either.'

'That is precisely the point,' Lesley stressed. 'If a Jewish state is established in Palestine the region will be thrown into turmoil, the Arabs will rise up to attack you and the United States will back the Jews to the hilt, militarily that is. If the Arabs are victorious, you will be driven into the sea and your national dreams shattered forever. If they lose, your victory will drive the Arabs into the arms of the Soviet Union.' She smiled. 'Heads they win, tails the Yanks lose.'

'But surely Great Britain still has considerable interests in the region, as does France,' Michael interjected. 'I mean, the deal they struck in secret at the end of the First World War showed they have no intention of surrendering their position.'

Lesley nodded. 'There is no doubt they will be extremely reluctant, but they still have to face the realities. Neither have the resources to sustain a prolonged military presence in the region. However, their investment of the region is still considerable and will have to be reckoned with, certainly as it affects American policy.'

'Investments? What investments?' Simon looked puzzled.

Lesley smiled. 'One of the disadvantages of a language as comprehensive and encompassing as English is that it can confuse. I said investment, Simon, in the sense of occupation, influence, presence. Of course, such investment is an essential concomitant of their investments.'

'Now you've completely confused the poor old sod,' said Sammy. He placed his arm around Simon and hugged him affectionately. 'Don't worry about it Simon, son, you just keep eating the pies.'

'Pies?' He gazed around the table then laughed with the rest without knowing quite why.

'Carrie, please go on,' said Michael. Sammy turned and looked through the window. He gazed out at the sea beyond the cliffs. Lesley watched him for a moment, longing to be with him. 'I should be brief,' she said, smiling. 'My lover is impatient.'

'No, you go ahead, love.' Sammy looked round. 'It will do this lot good to understand what the score is here. Anyway, I'm finding it interesting too.'

'OK. Let's consider the imperial legacy inherited by France and Britain after the defeat of first the Ottoman and then Italian overseas Empires. This created a region of quite unusual homogeneity. Even today it is still possible to travel overland from Lebanon to Syria, through Palestine to Egypt and points west to Algeria and Morocco. A large, substantially non-democratic, and despite the vestigial interests of Great Britain and France, Arab world. It is also an area which contains the bulk of the world's surplus oil supply and which seems to many, particularly in the United States, to be susceptible to Soviet penetration and toward which a powerfully organised domestic lobby presses for unflinching support for an isolated but militarily efficient Jewish state. Israel? Let's call it Israel. The immediate consequence of the establishment of a State of Israel in the region will be the expulsion of the indigenous Arab population living within its defined borders.'

'Expulsion?' Michael said, surprised. 'Why would we expel

them? We have lived alongside Arabs for years, they are an essential part of our economy.'

'Michael, think. You are a native Palestinian, you were born here, your family has lived, first under the Turks from whom I assume your ancestors bought the land you now work, then under a reasonably benign British mandate. But it will not be the same. Even if the whole of Palestine was available to you it still would not be big enough to accommodate the more than one million Arabs as well as all the Jews who would flood into any new Israeli state. It is already a Zionist promise that no Jew will be denied entry into a new Israel. Your people are already expropriating Arab lands and expelling them from their villages in order to pre-empt the UN and pre-determine boundaries. No, Michael, I fear the native Arab Palestinians will be forced to embark upon their own tragic Diaspora.'

'But where will they go?'

'Good question. Until we know what the boundaries are to be, it is possible only to speculate. But the existing regional geography suggests they will become refugees in one of the neighbouring Arab states, almost certainly Trans-Jordan and probably also the Lebanon.'

'But suppose those countries will not accept them.'

'Isn't that the whole point of destabilisation? The new militant State of Israel will actively contribute to the polarisation of the region in which native Palestinians, dispossessed and exiled by Israel, will come to represent little more than "terrorism". State nationalism will fracture into clan or sectarian regimes. There will be rigid cantonisation in one form or another nearly everywhere, with bureaucracies and secret police. Rulers will be clan families, cliques, closed circles of aging oligarchs, such as the Saudis and the Hashemites, conservative, fundamentalist reactionaries congenitally immune to change. The region will be controlled either by the major industrial powers directly or indirectly through the establishment of armed surrogates. Iraq, Iran, Syria and Egypt already exercise such a form of control on behalf of Great Britain and France. Israel will become the surrogate military arm of American "Realpolitik" in the Middle East. Your new country will be in a permanent state of siege, with rigid military conscription which, because you are so few, will, of need, apply to both sexes. Traditional Jewish culture will decline and you will be constantly in conflict with your neighbours. You will not find your Promised Land, I fear. You will simply become a new Sparta.'

Michael looked sadly at Lesley. 'Your politics is well informed and your analysis eloquent, but I think you paint too black a picture, Carrie. I do not think the cause of Zion will admit such an outcome.'

Sammy turned from the window and rejoined the discussion. 'As a "warfare state", your new Israel will be economically non-viable, you will be financially dependent on the United States to finance the territorial wars you will have to wage to occupy most of what is now Palestine and Trans-Jordan, as well as southern Lebanon, Galilee and Sinai.'

'Why would we need to do that?'

'Because, Michael, they contain both the commanding geographical heights in the region and are the well-head for the major water supplies. You will have no choice. Anyway, what is this cause of Zion you find putatively so altruistic? I think Zionism is, if anything, an ungenerous doctrine.'

Michael smiled at him. 'Why ungenerous, Sammy?'

He thought for a moment. 'Michael, I think you might agree that no race has received so much attention from historians, philosophers and theologians as the Jews...' Michael nodded. '...yet for all that, their ethnic and cultural origins remain shrouded in mystery, largely because the main source of information, the Bible, is so self-contradictory in this regard.

Take the word itself, bible simply means library, a large corpus of work gathered from a wide area of space and time. The myths, legends and traditions contained within it are extremely ancient. They were already very old before they were even collected and written down in their present form and stem in large measure from the pre-Semitic strata of Near Eastern culture. The task of sifting fact from fancy and history from pious hero-worship becomes increasingly difficult as the heterogeneous nature of biblical traditions becomes more evident. Any unity that has been impressed upon them is, I fear, largely rabbinical, deriving from the wishful thinking of Jewish theologians of a comparatively recent date...' He was interrupted by a chorus of disapproval.

'Myths and legends? You call the word of God myths and legends?'

'You are saying the writings of the prophets and the rabbis are wishful thinking?'

'...I'm not saying anything, Daniel, I am simply quoting from recent theological and historical criticism. Let us consider, for example, the history of the Jews in Europe. They have existed as a sort of subculture within the societies into which they were born. They have consistently refused to integrate into their national communities, generally refusing to marry outside their own closed social and religious group. From the time of the Seleucid conquest and their return from exile in Babylon, the Jews have chosen the ghetto as a means by which they could insulate themselves from the wider society to ensure their separate identity.'

'My God, Sammy, it's outrageous to say the Jews invented the ghettos.'

'I didn't say they invented ghettos, Mordi, I said they chose them. Look, let's face it, you are a stiff-necked, arrogant and insular bunch of sods who claim some beneficial relationship to the one true God of the universe, the "chosen people". This is an intolerant belief and whatever you may say, it is resented. The result is the Jews have become marginalised. This was entirely their choice. This marginalising inevitably turned to alienation and the Jews found their own intolerance to Gentile society turned against them as they were subjected first to increasing discrimination then actual persecution. Naturally there began to grow within the Jewish communities a resistance to this persecution and a desire for national liberation. Now, I say Zionism is an ungenerous ideology because it has betrayed that liberationist ideal in favour of a crude militant Jewish nationalism, intolerant, atavistic and cruel. Like fascism, it has institutionalised marginality into separatism and hardened resistance into dogma.'

'Now he's calling us fascists, my God,' Daniel shouted.

'I am not calling you fascists, Daniel, but I am saying that Zionism in practice is coming to resemble fascism.'

Michael raised his hand and the rising anger quickly subsided. He smiled at Sammy. 'You refer to a crude nationalism. Why should our form of nationalism be cruder than any other?'

'OK Michael, that's a fair question. But it is an important one and ironically bears on the resistance to integration to which I have just referred and to the original arguments for Zionism. Zionism is an invention of the Ashkenazim. Although some Sephardim have adopted its aims and ideals, it is not an issue of their collective consciousness. Zionism pretends a unique claim for European Jewry to a biblical origin, conferring rights upon them to biblical lands, from which they claim they were expelled by a coercive imperial power, Rome, and condemned in perpetuity to wander a hostile world. In other words, the Diaspora. Now you tell me, where is the hard evidence for this? Or that the Ashkenazim are or were in any way related to or otherwise associated with the ancient Twelve Tribes of Israel?'

'There he goes again, my God. First the Bible is a book of fairy stories and now he's telling us we're not Jewish.'

'Did you never hear of Josephus?'

'No, no, let me finish.' He held up his hand to quell the dissenting voices. 'By far the largest proportion of the world's Jews have been in Europe since before the Middle Ages. Almost their entire cultural Jewish identity has its origins in the life they have led among the European Gentiles.'

'And look at the way they have treated us. Why do you think we want to come home to our God-given lands?'

'For God's sake, listen to me, Mordi. You are confusing your long European history with the twelve years of Hitler's reign. If that evil bastard had never existed, if his twelve terrible years could somehow be expunged from your memory, then I think it would seem to you no more unthinkable that Jews should be Europeans than that they should be Americans. You might even see a closer connection between the Jew and Budapest, the Jew and Warsaw, the Jew and Kiev than the one between the Jew and New York or the Jew and Los Angeles. Look, there is a lot of serious historical scholarship on the matter of European Jewry which tends to support the thesis that the Ashkenazim are a people of Caucasian origin who, in the twelfth century, under threat of extinction from the opposing forces of Christianity and Islam, assumed Judaism as a national religion in order to survive...a sort of Caucasian thirteenth tribe. In other words, my friends, the probability that you are Caucasians is just as valid as your claim to be Semites. This assumption, in those circumstances, may have been seen as necessary at the time, but it was entirely facile...Hold on, hold on,' he shouted above an uproar of fresh dissent, 'the Arabs, on the other hand, are Semites, some may even be the direct descendants of ancient Hebrews, converted to Islam at the point of a scimitar. They are much closer to the Sephardim than to you Europeans and in all probability, they have closer ethnic ties with the original twelve tribes than you lot.'

'That is outrageous.'

'You're very big on outrage today, Mordi, but little on argument.'

'But this is our country.'

'Why?'

'Because it is.'

'Well that's convincing. It's the sort of argument which requires a machine gun to succeed...' Mordechai lowered his head sulkily. '...I happen to think all nationalism is crude and stupid, often lethally so. But in most cases it is not difficult to see that claims to a national identity are valid. I looked it up in the O.E.D. They define it as a property attributed to a people by virtue of a common ethnic and social identity and of the durable settlement of an area within defined boundaries. The case of the Jews is quite obviously not that. I do not accept the existence of a Jewish race, per se. It is a religion. Your claim to a racial identity is as irrational as claiming to be a member of the Catholic race as opposed to being Irish or Spanish or French. Or to being racially Muslim rather than Turkish or Persian. So your claim to a Zionist national identity in order to occupy this territory and expel its people is, I believe, crude, opportunistic and cruel.'

'You may be right, there has certainly been cruelty, but from all sides, including yours, Sammy. I don't like what you say. It may be your argument can only be refuted by an appeal to faith, but Sammy, you saw at firsthand what they did to our people. You felt it, it touched you. Where are we to go now that we have been expelled from Europe, too? We have wandered too long and suffered too much, we will take no more.'

'Michael, that's fine.' Sammy nodded. 'I can understand that.

But at least be honest about what you are doing here. You are carving a homeland out of another people's country and in the process creating a dispossessionist state. This is territorial annexation, plain and simple. Not exactly an original idea, we British have been doing it for years. But don't keep tarting it all up in this "God's chosen race" bullshit to justify a good old-fashioned invasion. You've been collectively fucked for the umpteenth time and have decided that enough is enough. So with the help of the Americans and the acquiescence of the French and British you are going to dispossess a bunch of powerless ragged-arsed Arabs who happen to have lived in the land of milk and honey for the last nine hundred or so years. Michael, these poor bastards didn't stick it to you, it was the Nazis. If you want revenge for what the world has done to you, go fuck the Germans...go home.'

'Where, Sammy?' Ben asked quietly. 'Where is home?' Sammy looked at him intently. Ben smiled. 'You're a lovely fellow, Sammy, a Mensch, and we all love you. But you are like so many people in England and the States. You tend to think that the holocaust was sui generis, that Nazi ideology centered around Jew-bashing and that it was they, the Germans, who alone set about the final extermination of the Jews. Hitler did exist and those twelve years cannot be expunged from our history any more than we can wipe them from our memory. The murder of six million of our people cannot be ignored and the destruction of European Jewry simply be written out as some kind of aberration because it only took twelve years to accomplish. Can't you see it's in the very blood of the masses in Europe and is used over and over as a pretext for winning them over and for diverting their attention from what really ails them? Sammy, old mate, it is only the horror, the catastrophe of this so-called "Final Solution" and even more the hopelessness and uprootedness of its survivors which has made the Jewish question so prominent today. Did you really never stop to consider why it should have been a small and seemingly unimportant Jewish problem in Germany that set that whole fucking obscenity in motion?' Sammy regarded his friend sadly, unable to reply.

'Come, enough of this, let us drink more wine.' Daniel filled the glasses from a large stone jug. He turned to Sammy. 'So, old friend, when do you go home?'

Sammy fidgeted slightly with embarrassment. 'My group is due to come up in about two months. But I may get deferred.'

'Deferred you don't need. Go home, get away from this madhouse.'

Michael nodded agreement. 'Anyway, the British are finished here now, there's little they can do to stop the immigration even if they wanted to. The Yanks have them by the throat.'

'And the Jews have the Yanks by the balls,' attested Simon.

'Daniel is right,' Michael went on above the laughter. 'Go home, Sammy, you're not happy here, you do not agree with what's going on and you constantly criticise us. God only knows why we tolerate you with your blonde hair and your blue eyes, you Aryan bastard.'

'What about you, you cheeky sod? You are not exactly the Jew Suss are you?'

'It is this beautiful black-haired shiksa, she's the only reason we have him up here.'

'No, we must be fair, it is his natural charm.'

'And his beautiful black-haired shiksa.'

'I can't think what she sees in this meshuggener, the sun must have boiled her brain.'

'She's brilliant as well as beautiful, too. What a waste, it's criminal.'

Sammy laughed at Lesley's embarrassed expression. 'Have you finished? You bloody bunch of lowlifes.' He looked at

Lesley. 'Take no notice, love, it's one of their Sammy-bashing days.'

Lesley was both amused and bewildered by the banter but before she could respond Naomi's commanding voice quelled all further badinage. 'Enough already,' she commanded, 'finish this food.'

Replete with the huge repast and warmed by the sun and much local wine, the two lovers settled beneath a cypress tree at the top of the cliffs. He leaned against the trunk and she against him and they gazed out at the darkening sea below. 'Sammy, this has been so wonderful, they are such lovely people.'

'Well, you have certainly captivated them.' He smiled. 'Seriously love, you gave a very impressive performance. You have clearly done your homework on this region.'

'Well thank you, Sir.' She smiled. 'But you were not so bad yourself and they do all love you so much.'

'Love me?' He laughed. 'They called me a Nazi.'

'No they did not, they said you are an Aryan, and so you are.'

'Aryan bastard,' he corrected.

'Don't quibble.'

He cuddled her. 'I'm glad we came too, sweetheart, but I'm not sure wonderful is enough to describe my experience.' He kissed her face gently. 'As it says in the twenty-third Psalm, "my cup runneth over".'

'It certainly did, my darling,' she giggled. 'Several times.'

'Carrie! Jesus.' They embraced, laughing happily together then she asked quietly, 'Sammy, when are you going home? You said something about two months to Daniel.' She sat up and regarded him sadly. 'What is going to happen to us? Will that be it, two months then "finis"?'

He hugged her. 'God Almighty, girl, I love you, I want to be with you always. Do you seriously believe I could leave you? Do you think I waited almost two bloody years just for two months? If I can't get a deferment I'll just stay on. There's no rule says I've got to be demobbed in Blighty. Ben wasn't. I'll work on a kibbutz, if necessary I'll even work for that old sourpuss Naomi.'

She hugged him excitedly then she gazed up at him. 'Sammy?'

'What?'

'Do you really want to be with me always?'

'Of course.'

'And will we be married?'

'Absolutely.'

'Here?'

He laughed. 'You want me to wear the yarmulka and dance around jumping on the glassware?'

'Of course not. Anyway, you're a Christian.'

'I am?'

She laughed at his feigned surprise. She became suddenly excited. 'I know, let's do it in Bethlehem.'

He shook his head disapprovingly. 'Mary did it in Bethlehem and look what happened to her.'

'Who's Mary?'

He fell back laughing. 'Bloody wars, she wants to be married in the well-spring of Christianity and she doesn't even know who Mary is. Mary, you dumb shiksa, the broad in the Jesus, Mary and Joseph routine, got to know a ghost. Biblically, that is.'

She squealed with delight. 'You blasphemous sod, Sammy Parker!' She sat back on her heels facing him, her face aglow with excitement. 'I'm going to tell everybody I love you and that we're engaged.'

'Engaged?'

'Of course engaged, you just proposed to me.'

'I did?'

'Sammy, you shit! After what you have done to me, can you

possibly believe I shall allow you simply to walk away?'

'After what I've done to you? My God, the effrontery. Carrie Carrington you are a one woman orgy.'

'Sammy!' she shrieked. 'How could you? What a rotten thing to say.' She suddenly became serious. 'But darling, it is all so wonderful. You have awakened a passion within me I did not think possible. I had always been, well you know...indifferent to sex...I sometimes wondered if perhaps...well, you know what public schools are like? Anyway, I no longer have misgivings on that score...Sammy darling, am I really too much for you?'

He smiled at her. 'Let's put it this way, love, you've given a whole new slant to the term "serving officer".'

She began to pummel him with her fists, howling with laughter. 'You rotter, you will pay for that and I mean it, I am going to tell everyone about us. I want the whole world to know you belong to me. I am not having any of those army floozies getting ideas, I have seen the way some of them look at you.'

'So have I, that's why I am constantly sniffing my armpits.'

'Oh God, you are absolutely disgusting, you pig. But I love you, so come here, right now.'

'Put me down, I've got a headache.'

They fell into an embrace. She turned, snuggling into him. 'I am serious, Sammy, I mean to tell everyone about us.'

'Well that's cute and you'll be on the next boat home.'

'In heaven's name why?' She sat up quickly.

'Carrie, think! You're the diplomat, do you really see that bunch at the King David even beginning to understand what we are doing here?'

'Understand what? That we love each other?'

'Darling, you're still not thinking. We came here separately to avoid gossip. Our hosts are Jews, Michael works for the Committee for Refugees, the hotel does not take normal guests but practically services the biggest kibbutz in the territory. You and I know these are decent people, simple farmers who just want to be left alone to get on with their lives. They love us and have us in their home because of what happened to Naomi and me. But sweetheart, they break our laws every day, laws you and I were sent here to enforce. Now, can you see our masters understanding that?'

She kissed his cheek. 'I am sorry, my darling, these few days have addled my brain. Of course you are right. God knows, I have lectured you enough about it.' She looked at him intently. 'Do you think we should stop coming here? We could always find somewhere else to stay.'

'That would be a first, cohabiting at the "Y". No love, it wouldn't be the same. We love it here. I know I do and they've taken you to their hearts as well. It isn't just Naomi, although she is important to me, as you know. It's because we feel so happy here. It's gemütlich, it's the nearest thing we will ever get to home. We just have to be careful, exercise some discretion. These people will look after us, so if we are tumbled it will be our fault. So, no shouting from the rooftops, versteh'?'

'Versteh', Captain.' She looked at him. 'Sammy, must you go back?'

'What do you suggest I do, refuse?'

'How did they know you were here?'

'They didn't, orders were left for me at the Carmel.'

'Alright, how did you know that?'

He winked. 'Contacts.'

She laughed. 'My God, you are a devious sod,' then sighing, added, 'it is such a damned pain though, when everything is so wonderful for us.'

'I know love, but they will still owe me that week's R & R. The family are having some sort of party the weekend after next, starts on the Saturday, after Shabat, so I guess it's some feast day or other. They are absolutely insisting we be here, won't take no for an answer. So, when we come back we can pick up where we left off.'

'Then it is vital we know exactly where that was, so begone with discretion, Parker, come here, now.'

CHAPTER FOURTEEN

Major General Bradbury received the Major's report without comment. He leaned back in his chair and regarded his adjutant. He suspected he did not approve of Captain Parker. Not Ken Shoppee's kind of soldier. But because, like most things, it didn't appear to bother Sammy, he had not pressed the Major on the matter. 'Who is this spook?'

'A Major Palmer, Sir, military intelligence.'

'Hmph!' He felt annoyed and not a little suspicious. 'You think I should talk to him?' The adjutant nodded. 'Show him in, will you please Major.' Ken left the room, returning moments later with a man dressed in civilian clothes. Bradbury regarded the man. I don't know why the bastards bother with mufti, he thought, they may as well be in uniform for all the distinction it makes.

'Major Palmer, Sir.'

The general nodded then flicked his hand irritably. 'Sit down, Major.' He waited. 'Major Shoppee has told me of your interest in our Captain Parker. It seems he has taken to spending his free time at a hotel owned by Jews and appears to be on friendly, some might say intimate, terms with at least one of them.' He paused but the intelligence officer remained impassive. 'I have to tell you, Major, that I have personal knowledge of Captain

Parker's relationship with a Mrs Berkovitz, the wife of an hotelier in Nathanya. I know that Captain Parker and Mrs Berkovitz came to know each other during the time they were incarcerated in the terrible concentration camp at Matthausen. I know Mrs Berkovitz's family and a wide circle of their friends hold Captain Parker in a very special regard because of what he did to help her survive that ordeal. I am also aware, as you must be, that almost all the hotels in Palestine are owned or run by Jews and that nothing I have heard from Major Shoppee adds in any way to what I already know. Perhaps you have something more?'

The major ventured a weak smile. He reached into his briefcase and withdrew a thin file which he handed to the general. 'You might care to glance through that, Sir.' He paused as the general opened the file. 'We are also aware of Captain Parker's outstanding war record and we have a great deal of anecdotal evidence, from former inmates, about his time in Matthausen, during which it appears not only his courage but also his impetuous, some might say contemptuous, disregard for authority were undiminished. However, his association with certain individuals since coming to Palestine has become a matter of more serious concern...there could be grave security implications.'

'Who exactly are these "certain individuals"?' the general asked.

'Sir, the hotel owned by Mr & Mrs Berkovitz is very close to the kibbutz at Rosh Pinnah. This is the largest collective in the mandated territory and is very active in support of the "Eretz Israel" movement. We have agent's reports which appear to indicate that several senior members of the kibbutz council are themselves active service members of the Haganah and we believe also that others are either members of Irgun and the Stern Gang, or support them directly through the not inconsiderable resources of the kibbutz.' He paused, watching the general closely.

As he listened to the major, Bradbury skimmed through the report. He looked up. 'As far as I can see, most of what you have told me is in this report, would that be correct?'

'Yes Sir.'

'Yes. Clearly, Major, if your suspicions are well founded, and I'm sure your agents have done their homework, there is some cause for concern here. However, knowing Captain Parker as I do, I am confident that he is innocent of involvement in any covert or seditious activities. Despite his apparent contempt for authority to which you have referred, Captain Parker is a loyal officer who would be entirely naive about such matters. If he regards these people as his friends, as I'm sure he must, he would trust them to behave with the same propriety towards him as he to them. However, it is obvious I must speak with him and advise him in the matter.' He looked at the major. 'Now, do I have everything here?'

'Not quite, Sir.'

The general smiled wryly. 'I suspected as much...so?'

'There is a much more serious matter, Sir. You will see from the file I gave you that we are also aware of the captain's association with Rosh Pinnah. We were at first concerned, but like you, we are now of the opinion that his relationship with them is an entirely innocent one. What is causing us greater concern is the clandestine affair between Captain Parker and a senior Foreign Office official on the staff of the High Commissioner, Sir Alan Cunningham.'

'Clandestine affair? Foreign Office official?' The general leafed through the report. 'I recall no reference to that.'

'No Sir, the matter is much too delicate to be committed to paper...as yet.'

'Well who is she, for God's sake?' He paused. 'I suppose it is a she?'

Major Palmer smiled. 'Yes Sir, it is a lady, no mistake about that. But the High Commissioner does not wish her identity revealed...yet.'

'Thank God for that. But what has this affair, as you call it, to do with Sammy's, er Captain Parker's friends at Nathanya?'

'Sir, we have a serving officer of the Parachute Regiment, a member of your own staff, plus a high ranking diplomat on the staff of the High Commissioner in an intimate relationship, keeping their trysts in what we suspect is a nest of Jewish activists who are probably involved in terrorist activity. Do I really have to spell it out?'

'Bloody hell!' The general banged his fist on his desk. 'That crazy maverick sod, why didn't he bloody well stay in England?' He glanced quickly at the officer. 'My apologies, Major Palmer. No, you do not have to spell it out.' He turned to Ken. 'Is he finished at Eilat?'

'I can't say for sure, Sir. As you know we sent him "out in the cold", if one can say that about the Negev. But he won't be back here until next week. You remember, we interrupted his R & R.'

'Bugger his R & R. Can we contact him? Do we know where he is?'

'Not exactly, Sir. He went walkabout with the Bedou looking for sites of possible illegal landings. He could be anywhere in the desert.'

'He wouldn't be going back to his love nest, would he?'

'He is mobile, Sir.' He shrugged. 'Who knows?'

The general looked at Major Palmer. 'What about the woman?'

'Our information is that she has also taken leave.'

'Where?'

'She took a room at the Carmel in Haifa, Sir, but she left word with the residency office that she was going up country...to spend a few days at the Cedars...a pleasant resort in the Lebanon.'

The general glared at the major. 'And did she, or did she not go to Nathanya?'

'We have no recent intelligence, Sir. But then our resources are stretched pretty thin. We have been occupied with Begin and company following the breakout at Acre.'

'Ken?'

'No idea, Sir.' Ken surprised even himself. He knew Sammy and Lesley were seeing each other, that she was undoubtedly the 'diplomat' whose identity was being protected and that they were almost certainly together at their hotel. But inexplicably he felt himself forced to protect a fellow para. He disapproved of Sammy's attitude to the army and to matters of discipline but he still had a quiet regard for a brave man and he was not about to surrender him to the tender mercies of military intelligence until he had an opportunity to forewarn him. 'There is always the possibility that he'll go to one of the R & R centres. I'll check with the EFI people at Nicosia. If he's not there, I'll try Beirut.'

'That's not bloody likely, is it, Shoppee?' the general asked scornfully. 'In any case, he will be back before you get a reply. Why don't you get on to this damned hotel?'

'There would be no point, Sir,' Major Palmer interjected. 'We are persona non grata amongst that lot but he is treated as one of the family. If we start sniffing around, asking questions, they will just close ranks to protect him. Furthermore, I doubt there is any record he has ever been there.'

'So how do you know so much about him?'

'We have an agent at the kibbutz.'

'Can't you ask him?'

'Her, Sir,' the Major corrected. 'We believe something big is being planned. We simply cannot risk blowing her cover, she would be dead within the hour.'

'A Jewish woman?' the general asked, surprised.

'Yemeni, Sir...Sephardim...there is friction.'

'Jesus Christ! What a situation. God save us from bloody religion.' The general turned to his adjutant. 'Major Shoppee, do whatever it takes to find him. I want him back here and on the bloody double.'

'Right, Sir.'

After what had been the most exhilarating four days of her life, Lesley returned to Jerusalem. It had been a time of anguish, of expectation, of joy, of love, more, it had been a time of knowing. She had finally given of herself and had known a passion so overwhelming to be almost beyond imagination. The flirting and the petting with a procession of vacuous young men had at last ceded to a magical new experience. She had discovered the wonder of being a woman and she exulted in her newly awakened sexuality. Her impetuous, awkward, painful hymeneal had yielded to the ecstasy of bursting physical pleasure and she knew at last what it meant to be in love, truly, wildly, unimaginably in love. She tried to concentrate on work but her thoughts returned again and again to Nathanya. To the hotel, to the cove with its quiet strand, but most of all to Sammy. She rehearsed over and again all they had discovered together. Sammy had proposed marriage but before she had time to recover, was immediately summoned back for a special assignment. Ben insisted they both return to Nathanya to celebrate their betrothal and she could not wait for the weekend. She prayed the time would pass, impatient to be with him again. She wanted everyone to know how wondrously happy she was. She wanted to tell Maggs, to share her elation with a friend. But she knew she must not. Sammy was right. She was startled from her reverie by a knock.

'Come in.' She looked up as the door opened. 'Oh, hello

Ken.' She regarded him suspiciously. 'Not more reports, I hope, I have more than enough to keep me going until I go to the Hill on Friday.'

He placed the armful of manila files he had been carrying on the table. 'Don't fret, this lot is mine, I hate to say. As it happens, I wanted to see you on another matter, can you spare a few minutes?'

She leaned back in her chair, a slight frown creasing her brow. 'Of course, take a pew. What's up? You look like bad news.'

He sat and faced her. 'I hope not. Carrie, do you know where Sammy is right now?'

Her frown deepened. 'No, I assumed you did. It was, after all, your office who interrupted his leave for this assignment.'

'How do you know that?'

'He told me, of course. Look, what's all this about?'

He sighed. 'So it is you?'

She arched her brows. 'What is me? For heaven's sake, Ken, will you stop being so bloody cryptic and get to the point.'

He looked at her for some moments then said, 'Carrie, the MI bods are on to Sammy. They've been to see Bradbury and he's hopping mad. I think our boy's for the high jump this time.'

'Sammy?' He nodded. 'But why, for God's sake? What do you mean "on to him"? What did he do?'

'That is what the General wants to know and why I have to find him. The spooks have a file on him. They are worried about the company he is keeping.'

'Company?'

'Nathanya. Carrie, they know about Nathanya.'

She felt fear grab at her stomach but she retained her outward composure. 'I don't understand. He has some very close friends in Nathanya, the woman whose life he saved in Matthausen lives there, her husband owns a hotel. You make it sound as though he

302

keeps it a secret. Jesus, Ken, you know he goes there to see her, it was you, after all, who told me about it, so why all the secrecy? Are you telling me military intelligence is getting itself into a lather about an acquaintance which is common knowledge? You know these people are his friends.'

Ken regarded her anxiously. 'Carrie, that is not the acquaintance which is exercising them at the moment.'

'What do you mean?' she asked needlessly.

'They know about you two. They know you meet there, at the hotel, I mean, in secret.'

'Know about us? What do they know about us? What do you mean, "meet in secret"? Some secret. It seems to me the whole damned world knows about it.' Her rising anger made her incoherent. 'How dare they spy on me. Who the hell do they think I am? Who do they think they are, come to that? How bloody dare they.' She stared angrily at Ken. 'Are you involved in this contemptible deceit, Ken? I know you dislike Sammy, but my God, this is a bit thick.' She began nervously shuffling the paperwork on her desk as she became more overwrought. She looked up and the Major saw her eyes were moist. 'Ken, they do not know a thing about us. Do they...do you...really believe we are up to something rotten?'

He looked down quickly to avoid the reproach in her eyes. 'No, of course not, old girl. But that is not the point, is it? Carrie, you are a senior member of the High Commissioner's staff and you are having an affair with an army officer at an establishment suspected of being involved with known dissidents. Surely you see the implications?'

She looked away as she recalled Sammy's admonition. 'Ken, why have you come to see me?' She turned to face him. 'You could easily have let this lot drop on us without warning. I presume they will wish to question us about it.'

He tried to smile. 'That's why I came, old thing. I couldn't just let this lot drop on you without warning.' He directed his gaze at her. 'You're wrong, you know. I don't dislike Sammy and I certainly don't dislike you. I admit I have disapproved of some of his methods, his lack of discipline, but he is a good active service soldier.' His face suddenly assumed a defiant expression. 'Correction, he is a first class active service soldier, the best, and he doesn't deserve all this fucking hole-in-the-wall bullshit.' Just as suddenly he dropped his gaze, sheepishly. 'I'm sorry, Carrie, language a bit strong there. Not like me, forgetting myself. Please forgive me.'

She felt herself choke. She reached out and touched his hand. 'Oh Ken,' she said, 'you soppy, lovely old thing. The famous paras' esprit de corps got the better of you at last, has it?'

He looked up with a wry smile. 'Something like that.' He stared at her for some time then asked, 'What will you do?'

'What can we do? We shall have to face the music, I suppose, confront them. We really have nothing to hide. The worst they can say of us is that we have been perhaps a bit indiscreet.' She looked at him. 'But Ken, they've got it all wrong. Sammy and I are not having an affair, we are engaged to be married, we love each other. Ken, we stay at the hotel because it is quiet and isolated. We can be together undisturbed, among people who love us. Well him, anyway.'

'Engaged? You and Sammy? Really?' She nodded. 'Why that's marvellous, old girl. The lucky sod.'

She smiled. 'Thank you, Ken, that's sweet. But love, they couldn't be more wrong. That hotel is not a hotbed of dissidents. They are certainly all for their State of Israel and want the British out, but that hardly makes them unique, does it? And you know Sammy's views about that and he makes no secret of it with them. They fight like cats and dogs most of the time. I think they enjoy baiting him. But Ken, they would not betray him or use him in any underhand way. Unless you have been there, seen them together, you cannot know how much they love and respect him. He committed the most amazing acts of bravery in that camp to save that woman's life.'

'What is she like?' Ken watched Lesley closely.

'She is the most extraordinary woman I have ever known. She has an aura of nobility which is almost impossible to define. She is, quite simply, beautiful.'

'So they weren't having an affair, after all?'

Lesley smiled. 'No Ken, they have far too much respect for each other.'

'I'm sure you're right.' He nodded assent. 'Listen, I'll talk to the General. He likes Sammy. We must hope the spooks don't have anything concrete on any of the people at Rosh Pinnah. Sammy is bound to call you when he gets back. Try to make him understand the necessity of coming clean on this one. If he tries to bullshit Bradbury, and he just might to protect you, his feet won't touch. You do see that?'

'I don't know where he is Ken, really.' She paused. 'Look, his Jews are throwing a party in honour of our engagement at the hotel and we are to stay for the weekend. The plan is I drive up and meet him there. He still has R & R to come and I think it was his intention to go to Nathanya as soon as he had finished whatever it was he was doing for you.'

'Well, you will have to rearrange your schedule. If the General doesn't see him by Friday, or he doesn't present a report on his assignment by then, the old boy might just have the bugger arrested...he's that brassed off. Make him come in on Friday. If he explains what you two have been doing, as you have to me, I'm sure all will be fine. Old Bradbury might give him a mild rocket for not using his head, he might even send the bugger home, but that would be no bad thing, would it? You could ask for leave to get married, then you would both be shot of this damned place for good. What do you say?'

She nodded. 'You're right, of course. Rely on me, I will see to it. Once I have explained everything to Sammy he will report back, I know he will. And thanks, Ken, you didn't have to warn us. I appreciate it, you're a good friend.' She stood up, gathering her bag. 'Right, Major Shoppee, on your feet. I'm going to buy my good friend a drink.'

Wing Commander Bromley stood as Lesley entered his office. He smiled. 'Good morning, Miss Carrington, thank you for being so punctual. Do please sit down.' She sat on the small settee and waited for him to join her. He crossed and sat beside her then addressed his secretary. 'Perhaps we might have some tea, Frances...' He looked at Lesley. '...unless you prefer coffee?'

'Tea is fine.'

He nodded and the secretary left the room. He smiled at Lesley. 'Miss Carrington, the HC has asked me to speak to you on a highly confidential matter.' He paused, watching her carefully. She smiled at him, curious, not betraying the anxiety she felt. 'As you know, a proposal is presently before the Security Council of the United Nations, tabled by the United States, for the partition of Palestine into two discrete areas, one of which is to be designated as an independent Jewish state. Should the Security Council approve the proposal, it will be submitted to the General Assembly for final resolution. I have to tell you that His Majesty's Government intends to abstain on the proposal and we believe the remaining four permanent members will almost certainly approve it.'

The secretary returned with the tray of tea and placed it on the table before them. 'Thank you, Frances, hold any calls and please see that we are not interrupted.' She nodded and left.

The Wing Commander lifted the pot and began to pour. He offered the cup to Lesley. 'Please help yourself to milk and sugar.'

'Thank you.' She took the cup. 'I rather thought that would be the position the Cabinet would take. So...that just about settles matters as far as the mandate is concerned, but I do not see what...that is how...'

He interrupted. 'The HC wishes you to go to New York.'

'In what capacity?'

'A purely assistive role, as I understand. Your brief is being prepared. The General is concerned the transition proceeds as smoothly as possible. Some extremely delicate diplomacy is required to ensure this and you are to represent the interests of the High Commissioner who, until the mandate either expires or is rescinded, still has responsibility for the governance of the territory. The purpose of these negotiations will be to ensure the cooperation of the parties concerned, namely the United States, the Jewish Council and ourselves.'

'And the Arabs?'

'Arabs?'

She nodded. 'I see we have not yet determined what the population of this country is.'

'I don't understand.'

'And neither will the Arabs.' She considered his perplexed expression. 'But then it will no longer be a matter of concern for us. So, when am I to leave?'

'What?' He still seemed perplexed.

'When do I leave and for how long?'

'As soon as your brief is complete. Following the resolution we expect the negotiations to take about a month, but you may wish to return periodically to report. My advice is clear your desk.'

She nodded. 'I shall be away for a few days. I shall of course report daily by telephone.'

He regarded her firmly. 'You may prefer to stay in Jerusalem.'

'Why?'

'Very well, we would prefer that you did.'

'I am to be confined?'

He smiled. 'By no means, I simply suggest it might be better if you did not leave.'

She nodded. 'Thank you for the suggestion and the tea, Wing Commander.' She looked at her watch. 'I shall return in two hours, kindly see that my brief is ready. I shall take it with me to read over the weekend.'

'But you must fly to New York at once.' He appeared agitated.

'Wing Commander Bromley, kindly do not take me for a fool. It is quite impossible for you to know which way the vote of the Soviet Union will go. Therefore there seems little point my going to New York to discuss the consequences of a resolution of the General Assembly before the enabling proposal has been approved by the Security Council. On the most optimistic expectation, this process will take at least two weeks, perhaps a month. In which case, if you insist I fly to New York sooner, I shall be forced to conclude you want me out of here for an entirely different reason.' She hesitated but he made no response. 'I have no intention of clearing my desk. I shall, of course, liaise with Washington and when I deem it appropriate, I shall leave for New York. In the meantime, I shall reconcile my files.'

He smiled approvingly at her self confidence. 'Please keep in touch, Miss Carrington.'

'Goodbye, Wing Commander.'

She showed her pass to the sentry who nodded then opened the gate. She passed into the bustling crowd on the Hill of Evil Counsel. After a few paces she stopped. She closed her eyes and breathed a heavy sigh of relief, thankful the Wing Commander appeared to have a sense of humour. The involvement of military intelligence made her especially anxious and she tried to think how she could avoid going to Nathanya again. She was concerned that Sammy should do nothing which would confirm their suspicions, or cause him to loose the confidence of General Bradbury. She made her way back to the King David, picking her way through the throng as if by reflex, her mind rapidly and anxiously considering the situation and the possible alternatives. She knew that if she went to New York the high commission would make sure she would not return. She determined to warn Sammy of the danger. She turned into Princess Mary Way and walked quickly to the King David Hotel where she made straight for the desk.

Maggs looked up, smiling. 'Hello Lesley, your jeep is it?'

'Please, is it here?'

'Of course, would I let anyone else have it?'

'Great! Maggs, I'm going away for a few days. I shall let the residency in Haifa know where I can be contacted, OK?'

'No problem, love. Where you going, somewhere nice?'

'I've been toying with the idea of taking the train up to the Cedars of Lebanon. I am told it is very beautiful there.'

'Train? What about the jeep?'

'Oh God. Look Maggs, I will leave it at the Residency. Can you arrange to have it collected?'

'I'll fetch it back for you. Gives me the excuse to skive off for a trip.' She crossed to the wallboard and took down the keys which she threw to Lesley. 'Have a good trip, lovey, and don't do anything I wouldn't do.'

'Well I couldn't wish for more latitude, could I Maggs?' She left her friend laughing raucously.

She drove at speed to Tel Aviv, hardly noticing the shimmering Judean passes through which she threw the jeep. Through Petah

Tiqva and Ramat Gan she passed several road blocks but was waved quickly through when the paras saw her vehicle's insignia. She raced along Allenby Street to Dizengoff Square and screeched to a stop outside the Café Delilah. A surprised waiter approached her. 'Something in a hurry, lady?'

'What?' She looked past him, frowning. 'Oh...yes, coffee please, black. Is Ben around?'

'Ben? Sure, he's out back with Rachel, the cook. She's his wife.'

Lesley turned to him impatiently. 'Yes, I know. I want to see him at once, tell him it's Carrie.'

'You sure you want me to tell him in front of Rachel?' He grinned suggestively.

'Look, will you just do as I ask and stop fucking me around?' she snapped, surprised and shocked by her own profanity.

The man, visibly shaken, raised his hands submissively. 'OK. Right. Hey, shalom lady, keep your hair on.' He withdrew through the service door, shaking his head.

After some moments Ben appeared, his brows raised in surprise. He took her hands and kissed her cheek affectionately. 'Carrie, what brings you to Tel Aviv in the middle of the week? And what did you do to Mischa? He says you have the manners of a paratrooper, which I thought was laying it on a bit thick, but he is most put out.'

She laughed. As usual, Ben began to make her feel better. 'Ben, I'm sorry, I guess I'm not in the mood for jokes.'

He still held her hands as he sat at a table, pulling her into the seat beside him. 'What's up, love? Trouble?'

'They are sending me to New York, to Lake Success to cover the Jewish Homeland debate, but I have this awful feeling that once I leave here I won't be back.'

'Why?' He frowned, puzzled.

'I've been warned, Ben. They have been watching Sammy

and me. They know we meet at the hotel.'

'So what?'

'Ben, they think it is a hotbed of sedition, a haven for terrorists.'

Ben stared at her for some moments then began to laugh. 'Terrorists?' He guffawed. 'That lot couldn't terrorise gefüllter fish. Does Sammy know about this? He'll do his nut.'

'Ben, that's the problem, I don't know...'

'One coffee, black.' The waiter placed the steaming cup before her, unsmiling.

She looked up at him and gave a contrite shrug. 'Mischa, what can I say? My manners were unforgivable...' She took his hand, smiling sadly. 'But like a paratrooper? Mischa, really.' He could not restrain his laughter as she squeezed his hand. 'Forgiven?'

He nodded. 'Yeah, you're forgiven.'

She turned back to Ben. 'I don't know where he is, Ben. He had some sort of assignment in the Negev.'

Ben looked at her, surprised. 'But he's at the hotel, Carrie. I assumed you knew, he arrived yesterday. You haven't forgotten you are coming for the weekend?'

'Why didn't that wretch let me know? I have been going frantic. I swear to God I shall kill him when I see him.'

'Not before Sunday,' Ben said, amused by her anger, 'or you'll have Naomi to answer to. She's been cooking all week. Kill him on Monday.'

'Ben, I am not sure it would be wise for us to come up.' She regarded him seriously. 'I think it...'

'No, out of the question,' he interrupted nervously, 'you have to be there.' He looked at her anxiously as she regarded him, bemused by his demeanour.

'I think we should wait until things cool down a bit, Ben.'

He recovered a little and smiled at her. 'Carrie love, you'll have to wait until hell freezes over before things cool down.' He laughed. 'You have a choice. Who would you rather face, the Brits or Naomi?'

She shook her head. 'Ben, I simply do not know what to do.'

'Well, you can start by drinking that coffee.' He squeezed her hands. 'Talk to Sammy. It's probably just a storm in a teacup, some officious sod at HQ with time on his hands thought he'd stir the shit. I mean there's no love lost between Sammy and that lot, is there?'

She sighed loudly. 'Yes, of course, that is the best thing. Thank you Ben, you always make me feel better, don't you?'

'I hope so, sweetheart.' He smiled at her. 'And don't even think of cancelling this weekend or Naomi will kill all of us.'

She drove to Haifa and booked a room at the Carmel. She bathed, changed then drove to the residency where she left the jeep with the MT sergeant. She stopped for her usual Kaffeeklatsch to establish an alibi then took a cab to Nathanya.

Sammy was seated beneath a parasol at a small table in the courtyard, busy compiling his report. He looked up, surprised as the taxi drove in. He saw her alight and stood smiling as she paid the driver. She ran to him, flinging herself into his arms.

'What a lovely surprise, sweetheart. I didn't expect you until tomorrow.' She clung to him desperately. 'Well, don't I get a kiss?' She looked up at him and he saw her tears. 'Carrie, what is it, love?'

'Oh Sammy, I am so frightened and unhappy. Ken Shoppee came to see me. The MI people have been spying on us and they want to separate us. They are sending me to New York and I am sure I won't be back, I just know it. What are we to do?'

He smiled at her but his eyes had that too familiar icy glint. 'Now slow down, old girl, one thing at a time. What has all this to do with Ken Shoppee?'

'Sammy, he was so good. He came to warn us, that we should not be taken unawares. He says General Bradbury is angry with you and wants to see you.'

'Why is Bradbury angry with me?'

'Military Intelligence have been watching us here. They say this hotel is a meeting place for dissidents and that you are over friendly with the Jews.'

He laughed wryly. 'Of course it's a meeting place for dissidents, it's full of Jews, for crisake. The buggers are all dissidents, or haven't those prats noticed? What the fuck do they do all day, stand around with their heads up their arses?'

She looked at him, confused. 'Sammy, we should leave here, darling. Perhaps it was a mistake to come here at all. I know how much you love these people and why, but the army does not know that, do they? And it is bound to raise their suspicions. We must avoid anything which would embarrass Naomi and Michael. Let us wait until we have cleared this thing up. We can leave now, go to Haifa. Darling, we cannot afford to take unnecessary risks.'

He looked at her, shaking his head in frustration. 'Carrie, you know they've arranged a special party for us to celebrate our engagement. We can't let them down now. Besides, I have been going nuts wanting you. We can't leave, not now.'

'Oh Sammy, I want you too, my darling, and I am so touched that they would want to share our happiness.' She kissed him anxiously. 'Darling, go back tomorrow, talk to Bradbury. Ken says he still has a soft spot for you. I am sure he will understand when you explain that we are in love and engaged.'

He snorted loudly. 'Mark Bradbury doesn't have a sentimental bone in his body. If he's demanding my presence, it's to give me a bollocking. Remember, I'm still on probation after my last fuck up.' He threw himself angrily into a chair. 'Let him wait until Monday, I'm still on bloody R & R.'

'But what about the intelligence people, Sammy? What will we say to them?'

'Fuck 'em!' His chin jutted defiantly. 'We are not doing any harm and neither are the Berkovitzes. I am not going to deliberately upset our friends just because a bunch of paranoid, prick skewered public school fags have got their drawers up the crease of their arse. Let the snooping bastards wait. Fucking voyeurs.'

She gave a sad laugh. 'I can always tell when you're vexed, Sammy my sweet, your eloquence knows no bounds. But darling, be sensible, if you refuse to go back you will only confirm their suspicions and they will have you arrested. Tell them the truth. What can they do? As you say, we are not doing anything wrong.'

He sat for some time, quietly seething, drumming his fingers angrily on the table. Then he looked at Lesley. 'Alright, I'll go back tomorrow. I'll see Bradbury then I'm coming straight back, right? And listen, I don't want these people to know what's going on, I don't want them to know they have been under surveillance. Tell them I've gone to Haifa to check my pigeon hole at the Carmel.'

She watched him for some time, his cold gaze directed out toward the cliffs. She reached out and touched his hand. He did not move. 'Sammy?'

'Hm?'

'I feel a bit grotty after that drive. I am going upstairs for a nice bath.'

'Hm!'

She began to trace small circles on his hand. 'Don't suppose you feel like scrubbing a girl's back, do you?'

He shook his head angrily. 'I'm not in the mood,' he spat 'For two pins I could strangle those bastards.'

She choked back at the venom in his voice, her eye

314

brimmed. 'Sammy, don't darling, please. You make me so afraid when you are angry.'

Her entreaty calmed him at once. He gave a short, resigned sigh. He stood up suddenly, pulling her to her feet. 'So, you want your back scrubbed, do you?' He shoved her towards the hotel. 'Right, get up those bloody stairs.' She ran from him squealing, through the lounge and toward the staircase. He pursued her, shouting. 'I'll scrub a little more than your back, Miss Diplomat. I'll teach you to scare the shit out of me like that.'

She closed the door and leaned against it, gazing at him, her limpid eyes betraying her desire. He laid his head upon her breast and felt the aggression and discontent rapidly melt away. 'Why am I so happy when I should feel so unbearably frustrated?' She kissed his head. 'Carrie, I want you so much,' he whispered.

She stood quite still. 'And so you should.' He looked up, surprised. She brushed the end of his nose with her lips. 'So...what are you waiting for?'

Taking her in his arms, he carried her bodily into the bathroom.

She laid back on the bed, utterly content. He stood over her, sprinkling her still-warm body with talcum powder. 'My mum used to do this to the turkey every Christmas,' he said.

She opened her eyes. 'What, sprinkle it with talcum powder? Didn't it taste peculiar?'

'I don't remember, let's see.' He leapt upon her and began to softly bite her stomach and breasts. 'Tastes pretty good to me.' She groaned with pleasure as they moved upon the bed and they made love again. She curled up in his arms and they slept quietly.

Sammy roared into the car park beneath the King David Hotel.

He was forced to brake sharply to avoid a collision with a large truck obstructing the entrance. He climbed from the jeep and approached a group of workmen standing beside the truck.

'What's going on here? Why are you blocking the car park like this?'

One of the men detached himself from the rest. 'Excuse me, Effendi, we have been called to attend a gas leak.' The man spoke perfect English, too perfect, thought Sammy, for a gas worker.

'And who sent for you?'

'I don't know, Effendi, we have to ask at the reception.'

Sammy nodded. 'Right, you do that and get this bloody lorry out of the way, nobody can get either in or out.'

'Right away, Effendi.' The man climbed into the truck and pulled it to one side. Sammy parked the jeep and headed for the stairs. When he was out of sight, the driver repositioned the truck across the car park entrance. He climbed from the vehicle and signalled to his colleagues whereupon they all followed him from the building.

Sammy tossed the keys to Maggs. 'Get her filled up, Maggs. I shall be going out again shortly.'

'Right Sammy...how's the oil?'

'What do I know about bloody oil? Who am I, Gulbenkian? I just drive the bloody thing.' Maggs laughed as she watched him head for the lift. He stopped suddenly, turning. 'Maggs, do you know anything about a gas leak?'

'Gas leak?'

'Yeah, there's a bunch of wogs in the car park with a bloody great lorry. They say they've come to fix a gas leak.'

'Gas leak?'

Sammy regarded her thoughtfully then he said, 'Gas leak.'

'Gas leak?' she answered.

Sammy nodded. 'Just as I thought. Maggs, you are suffering

from chronic Pavlovian reflex echo syndrome, triggered by the phrase "Gas leak".'

'Gas leak?'

'There you go, QED.'

'What are you pratting on about, Sammy?'

'A gas leak.' He raised an admonishing hand before she could reply. 'No Maggs, please, enough already. Be a pal, just look into it.'

CHAPTER FIFTEEN

Lesley awoke gradually, roused by the chatter rising from the courtyard below her window. She ran her hand across his pillow but he was already gone. She vaguely recalled his farewell kiss as she drowsed contentedly between sleep and waking. Having shorn his rage, briefed him and persuaded him to attend the general, she prayed everything would now be resolved, that she had not dispatched him 'eyeless' to Jerusalem. She smiled sleepily as she felt her confidence return. She swung her legs from the bed and, crossing to the window, looked across the cliffs to the sea beyond. The sun blazed white and formless, a diffusion of intense brightness in a cloudless sky; it would be another scorching day. She thought of Sammy in the pitiless heat of the city and longed for the day to pass, to be with him again. She washed quickly then, dressing casually in shorts and blouse, went down to join the others.

'Shalom Carrie.'

'At last, Sammy's beautiful shiksa is here.'

'He's the shiksa. She's dark and gorgeous like a nice Jewish girl. He looks like a Nazi.'

'The Nazis wouldn't tolerate him, he's too crude.'

'Here comes the bride,' someone sang.

'Can you believe that Teuton is to marry this vision?'

'Is there no justice left in this world?'

Amused by their teasing she took their hands, kissing each in turn, chatting happily, enjoying the banter. Looking up, she spotted Ben at the hotel entrance talking to a small dark bespectacled man. Their conversation was animated and Ben gesticulated violently to emphasise a point.

'Shalom Carrie.' Naomi came to the table and kissed her affectionately.

'Hello my love.' She smiled warmly at Naomi then looked back towards the door. 'Who is that man talking to Ben?'

'That's Minny, he's from the kibbutz and he and Ben don't talk, they squabble.'

'So I observe, but why?'

'Ben hates him, says he's a gangster.'

Lesley's brow furrowed. 'And is he? A gangster, I mean.'

Naomi ignored the question. 'You want some breakfast?'

'Is it not too late?'

'Late? What's late got to do with eating? Are you hungry?'

'Starving.'

'What do you know from starving? You're hungry, listen to me. Come.' Naomi took her hand and led her into the kitchen. She cut freshly baked bread which she served with cheese, pickled eggs and black olives. Lesley tucked in to the food with gusto, Naomi smiling approvingly. 'So, you were starving, Mädl. I am not afraid to admit when I am wrong.' She watched Lesley as she ate. 'So, you are going to marry him.'

Lesley closed her eyes, sighing pleasurably. 'Oh yes, yes and I feel wonderful. I still cannot believe it. Naomi, I've known him such a short while, yet I feel it is right. I love him and I know he is right for me. He is my man.' She glanced guiltily at Naomi, fearing her exuberance might have been tactless.

But the older woman smiled back. 'Will you both return to England when the army has done with him?'

'Has he not told you? We are to be married here, in Palestine. He is going to stay after he is discharged, as Ben did.' She nodded toward the window.

'But Ben is a Jew,' Naomi stated. 'Why would a Goy want to stay here? The British are not exactly popular, are they?'

'To be with me, of course.' Lesley chuckled happily. 'But you love him too. You all do, don't you?'

Naomi nodded. 'To us he is very special, yes, but do you want to be with us for the rest of your lives? No Liebchen, get away from this terrible place, go home.'

'Oh Naomi.' Lesley laughed. 'It is so we can be married in Bethlehem, it will be something special, then we shall of course go home.' She contemplated Naomi's sad, wistful expression. 'Why do you call this a terrible place? Isn't this your homeland? Don't you like it here?'

Naomi regarded her solemnly. 'No, I don't like it here. And it is not my homeland. I am a German.' She gazed away, lost in thought. 'Have you ever been to Dresden?'

'No, I'm afraid not, but I hear it was a beautiful baroque city. I am sure they will rebuild it,' she added reassuringly.

Naomi nodded. 'Ja, I think it is the most beautiful city in Germany. My father has a bookshop. He sells old maps and charts...how do you call it?'

Lesley frowned, embarrassed by the question. 'Cartography.' She wondered if she knew about the bombing.

Naomi nodded pensively, seeming to recover. 'Where is Sammy? I saw him leave early this morning.'

'He has driven to Haifa, there are new orders for him. He also has to see a couple of people.'

'He went the wrong way.'

'What?'

'If he was going to Haifa, he went the wrong way. He turned toward Nathanya.'

Lesley laughed. 'You know Sammy.'

Den appeared in the doorway, his expression stern, but when he saw the two women his scowl cleared. He crossed and sat at the table with them.

'What were you and Minny arguing about this time?' Naomi fixed him with a disapproving eye.

'Nothing serious.' He laughed. 'You know how I am with Minny, if the poor sod says good morning I look out of the window to check. He is such a charmless, bigoted bastard.'

Naomi stood up. 'Well, I can't sit here gossiping all day, it's shabbat and I have things to do.' She crossed to the door.

Ben smiled at Lesley. 'Where's Sammy?'

'Haifa, he promised to be back before sundown.'

'I told you, he went the wrong way.' Naomi called back over her shoulder.

Ben watched as she disappeared through the doorway. 'What did she mean?'

She glanced around furtively, ensuring no one was within earshot. 'He was called to Jerusalem, Ben,' she whispered. 'About the matter we were discussing yesterday. It appears the general has let slip the dogs. He made me lie about Haifa, he did not want the people here to know that security had been poking about.'

'When you say Jerusalem...' Ben's eyes narrowed and he appeared agitated. 'Where exactly in Jerusalem...does this General "What's His Name" hang out on the Hill?'

'No, Ben.' Lesley laughed. 'General Bradbury is the Military Governor, not the High Commissioner. His office is in the King David Hotel, Sammy is on his staff.'

'And Sammy has gone to the King David?'

'Yes, he is probably there already...Ben?' She looked at him quizzically. 'Why are you so interested in his movements?' She grinned. 'Don't worry, you know Sammy, he will sort it out quickly and be back before tea.'

'Yeah...right.' He seemed preoccupied, tense. 'Look, I've one or two things to do, Carrie. I'll catch you later, OK?' He stood and left abruptly, leaving her feeling a twinge of apprehension.

Naomi returned bearing a basket of vegetables from the garden together with an assortment of jugs and jars of various preserved foods: fruit, fish, olives, conserves. She heaved her load on to the table then, wiping her hands on her apron, reached up and switched on the radio. She grinned at Lesley. 'A little decadent Yankee music while you help me with this lot.'

'Decadent?' Lesley chuckled. 'I will have you know this is Frank Sinatra. This boy's voice is one of the world's great aphrodisiacs. Ah! "Try a little tenderness". I hope my lover is listening to this.'

'You want tender as well as athletic?'

'Oh God, Naomi,' Lesley whooped, her face flushing with joy and embarrassment. They worked together, preparing food for the evening meal, gossiping happily and singing along with the music from the British Forces Network.

'If you are to be married here we must get you a wedding dress, I'll talk to Esther.'

'Who's Esther?'

'Michael's other sister. You met her here at the party, the queen of the crochet hooks, remember?'

Lesley chuckled. 'She knows a good dressmaker?'

'Esther is a good dressmaker, the best.'

'Oh Naomi, I am so excited, that would be so lovely.' She frowned. 'But can I be married in a white dress? I am no longer a virgin, you know. The good captain has seen to that.'

'So who is?' Their pealing laughter echoed around the large kitchen.

'You are surely not suggesting my Sammy is entirely responsible?'

'Well...perhaps not entirely'

'God, the mind boggles.' They leaned into each other, squealing with joy. Suddenly Naomi straightened. 'Shush, listen.' She raised a hand, concentrating on the radio announcer's voice.

'...the resulting explosions have virtually destroyed the hotel and caused widespread damage to adjacent buildings. Casualty figures are not yet confirmed, but it is feared the loss of life may be high. That is the end of this special bulletin, now back to Forces Favourites and BFN.'

There was a brief pause then the announcer's voice, solemn and measured. 'I'm sure all our listeners will agree it would not be entirely appropriate to continue normal programming at this time. We will not be closing down however, but will play a continuous programme of solemn music. We will bring you more information about the atrocity as it comes to hand.'

Lesley looked at Naomi, her expression one of bewilderment and fear. 'I don't understand, what does he mean, atrocity? Has a hotel been attacked?...What?'

'I don't know, Mädl. I didn't hear any more than you. Perhaps they had the radio on in the lounge.' As she stood, Ben appeared in the doorway, his face ashen. He was weeping. Naomi's hands fell to her side as she stared at him, her eyes cold.

He came to her and took her in his arms. 'Dear God! Oh dear, sweet God,' he cried.

She pushed him slowly back, holding him at arm's length. 'What have you maniacs done?' Her voice was soft but edged with a terrible anger.

He looked at her hopelessly. 'Sister, you must believe me, I didn't know...it was the Irgun...they say it was the Arabs...I swear I didn't know,' he babbled incoherently.

She held him in her gaze for some moments then struck him viciously across the face. The sound of the blow seemed to arouse Lesley who began to weep silently. Naomi shook Ben violently. 'Don't lie to me, you bastard. The radio said a hotel has been attacked...Which hotel?...Where?'

'Jerusalem, the King David.' He looked at her, shaking his head helplessly. 'I didn't know he would go back. How could I know that? He was supposed to be here. I arranged everything so they would both be here. He should have told me.' He pointed a finger accusingly at Lesley. 'She should have told me. How could I know?'

As the import of his words began to penetrate her consciousness, the blood slowly drained from her face. Naomi realised now that Sammy had not driven in the wrong direction, but to Jerusalem, to the King David. That it was the King David that had been destroyed, and that Sammy, her Sammy, her heart, her soul, her only reason for living was probably dead, killed by her own people. She looked at Lesley who sat motionless, shocked into silence. Her eyes filled with tears and she began to thrash her head from side to side as she suddenly gave voice to a terrible cry of anguish. 'Sammy...Sammy...Oh God, no.' She sank to her knees and began to pound the hard floor with her fists. She rocked back and forth on her heels as she cried out. 'No...no...no...Sammy...what have they done to you?...No...no... Please God, let it not be him.'

Michael and Daniel appeared in the doorway, summoned by her cries. They rushed to her side and attempted to lift her. 'Come, my darling.' Michael grasped her arms.

She lashed out at him, knocking him back on his heels. 'Murderers!' she screamed. 'Keep your filthy hands off me, you Nazi swine. Don't touch me.' They fell back in horror before her rage and stood aghast as she hurled insult after insult at them. Possessed by the intensity of Naomi's excoriation they did not heed Lesley who, having sat in silent witness to the violence of Naomi's reaction, slowly stood and walked past them and out of the room.

She came out into the bright sunlight and lifted her head to the sky. She closed her eyes and stood quietly for some time then calmly climbed into Michael's truck. She sat motionless, gripping the steering wheel and staring straight ahead. She tried to collect her thoughts. She must go at once to Jerusalem. The news had been sketchy, there will be survivors, the bulletin had mentioned some loss of life. She must maintain her composure until she knew for sure whether Sammy was a casualty. Naomi's cries still rent the air and she tried to blot them out by closing her eyes tightly. She was reminded of the images of war portrayed in the newsreels from Russia, from Greece, from the camps. Images of women on their knees wailing over the bodies of their dead loved ones, beating the ground with their hands. Why does she assume the worst? Why does she behave so irrationally?

'She's Jewish, for Christ's sake.'

As his voice cut into her thoughts she began to laugh, quietly at first, but then without restraint until finally she was gripped by an uncontrollable hysteria. She tasted the salt tears in her mouth and she shuddered suddenly to silence. She tossed her head back and snorted loudly, swallowing saliva and mucus. She pulled the starter and the engine shook noisily to life. She drove away toward Haifa. She did not look back.

She left the truck on Carmelite Road and walked the short distance to the Residency. Since leaving the hotel she had wanted to cry, to ease the torment out, to relieve the pain gripping her heart but she resisted her anguish, pushed it deep within her. Outwardly she remained calm. Accomplished in her profession, she maintained a composure which concealed the agony which raged inside.

'Good morning, Miss Carrington. Did you have a nice trip?'

'Fine, thank you.' She smiled at the receptionist. 'Are there any messages for me?'

A slight frown flickered across the woman's face. 'No, but then things are a bit chaotic.'

Lesley tilted her head inquisitively. 'Chaotic?'

'Yes, of course.' She gasped, placing her hand to her mouth. 'Oh dear, you won't have heard will you?'

'Heard what?'

'Oh, Miss Carrington, it's terrible. They've blown up HQ, the King David. It's been destroyed. A huge bomb in a truck in the underground garage blew up the gas mains. The whole place has gone. They're nearly all dead, very few got out alive.'

'Dear God!' Lesley began slowly to release the agony within her, she began to cry. 'Oh dear God, not Sammy, please let it not be Sammy.'

The receptionist left her desk and placed an arm around her. 'Come and sit down love, I'll get you some coffee. Who's Sammy? Your boyfriend is he?' She was sobbing freely now and several of the staff gathered to comfort her. 'I think her boyfriend was in the King David,' the receptionist confided. 'Poor thing knew nothing about it.'

Lesley recovered slightly. 'Has my jeep been returned to Jerusalem?'

'No Miss. Well I mean, it wouldn't be, would it?'

'Then I must return at once.'

'But you can't go back to HQ, Miss.'

'Then I must go to the High Commission.'

'Are you sure you'll be all right to drive, Miss? I mean you've had quite a shock.'

Lesley forced a smile. 'I shall be fine, thank you. You have all been very kind, but I must leave at once.' She stood and walked away, erect, her face bathed with her tears. They backed away as she passed, watching until she disappeared through the door.

'Isn't that sad?'

'Poor girl, fancy finding out like that.'

'I didn't know she had a bloke, she always kept herself to herself.'

'Didn't she take it well though, I mean she was obviously cut up, but she didn't fall apart, did she? She was so proud.'

'That's breeding for you. She's upper crust all right, that one.'

'If she had a bloke at the King David, why did she always go off on her own?'

She felt the sand, course and violent on her tongue and the wind in her hair, for a breeze had blown in from the sea bringing a salty tang and a faint air of melancholy. She did not know how she came to be walking along the seashore. The late afternoon light was gentle and honeyed, casting a strange golden glow on the few semi transparent clouds which passed overhead on their way from the sea to the mountains. The soft breeze rustled the dune grasses, spraying her breasts with tiny droplets from the surf till her nipples squinted beneath the clinging cotton blouse. She heard her own cries, formless, incoherent, wrenched from her body and borne away upon the warm vagrant wind. She turned to face the sea and as the sun dried her tears, she became quiet. She stood, desolate and silent. Her body shook as each sob rose from deep within her. Slowly, she removed her clothes, dropping each item absently on to the warm sand, then head bowed, she walked into the water. The swell was gentle and warm and as it gradually covered her body she cried out for him again.

He watched her from the dunes, ready to plunge after her should her anguish drive her to madness. He saw her jump and whirl like a dervish in the water, just as she had with him that fateful day. He watched her smash her hands on to the surface of the sea in the terrible anguish of her loss. He could hear her cries carried faintly on the breeze and he wanted to comfort her, but he knew he would not find the words to assuage her grief.

Suddenly she was still. She turned to look toward him. She stood motionless for some time then began to wade toward the beach. She stopped, waist deep in the warm sea and gazed at him. The swell rose to cover her breasts then fell away again. He knew in that instant that though he loved her still, he had lost her and he too began to weep. As she began to move again, he walked to the water's edge to meet her. He raised the beach towel to cover her nakedness then took her into his arms and kissed her hair to comfort her. Her salt-wet hair and tears soaked his shirt and he gripped her more tightly until her grief stilled. He wiped her eyes with the hem of the towel and tried to smile. She looked at him, desperate to deny what had been done.

'Michael, tell me it isn't true. Please Michael, tell me it didn't happen, wake me from this nightmare, tell me he's coming back.' Her sobs began to wrack her body again and he pulled her to him.

'My love, what can I say to you?'

She eased away from him and sank slowly to her knees. The towel fell away and she sat back on her heels, head low, her hands laying limply in her lap. Michael stood helpless, staring down at her. He wanted to reach out to her, to ease her pain, but could not. He watched the beads of water gather into a trickle on her still firm breasts, then drip on to her arms, watched it form again to move over the tight white scar, a shiny witness to numbers once there, showing faintly like the marks of teeth. It reminded him of the love which had so tormented her and which had now finally broken her heart. She sat, motionless, as the breeze heaped the fine sand against her thigh. Then she spoke softly, without emotion. 'I shall leave you now, Michael.' She raised her head to look at him. 'I should not have come. I should have returned to my home. That is what I wanted, but you told me I could not. You are a good man, Michael and though I could never love you, I thought we could make a life here together. But it was never real, not for me. Only one thing was ever real for me and now that is gone.' Her head fell forward and she shook it slowly from side to side. 'To think we survived that madness, the cruelty, the death and now you have killed him, you Michael, with your hatred.' She closed her eyes briefly and sighed, resigning herself to her sorrow. 'Only I know how he suffered. Not even God himself could know because he too died in those ovens. Not that I believe in any God. While he lived I had hope and when he found me here, I knew what it was to live again. But now he's gone, dead, and I shall know only loneliness.' She reached forward and touched his hand as if to be sure he understood. 'You see Michael, this is my real exile, my real despair. It begins here, now. While he lived I could hope he would one day come back to me. You knew how many times I wept for him and how I would wake in torment from my dreams.' She looked away and a faint smile softened her face. 'Sometimes I would dream that he came to me in the night and I, sweetly perfumed, would touch him. I would put out the fires of his anger and give him peace. I would hear him and feel him within me, then resting peacefully, I would close his eyes with my lips and lull him to sleep as I had done so many times before.' She shook her head. 'It is no use looking at me like that Michael, it will do no good. I want you to know how much I hate this terrible, arid, philistine place, this Promised Land of yours, where one group of madmen attacks another in the name of sanity and reason. I want you to know once and for all how much I loathe all of you and what you stand for. Yes loathe, Michael. Your Zionism, your Herzogs, your Ben Gurions, your Miers, your Weizmanns, all of them. I wish your terrorists, your Begin and your Shamir, who took my Sammy from me, would blow them all and themselves sky high.'

Michael looked at her, his expression hard. 'You do not know what you are saying, Naomi. You are distraught. Now, that will do, cover yourself, that is enough.'

She smiled at him sadly. 'You're right Michael, that is enough and I'm going home.'

'What do you mean, home? This is your home.'

She stood and began to gather her clothes. 'No Michael, this is your home. My home is in Germany. Sammy was right, he was always right, I don't belong here. You might, but not me. I am a German, not a Jew. I am just an ordinary German Hausfrau who happens to be Jewish and I am going home.'

A cordon had been thrown around the stricken hotel. Lesley drew up at one of the checkpoints established to control access to the area. The paratrooper regarded her impassively. 'I'm sorry Miss, you can't come through here and we don't want no sightseers.'

She proffered her pass and looked past him, horrified by the scale of destruction. The entire frontage had been sliced away by the explosion and the floors lay one upon the other in a grotesque, curving shingle. Wisps of smoke still rose sullenly from the wreckage and the acrid smell of fire filled the air. Rescue and demolition squads from the Royal Engineers picked away busily at the debris, still hoping to find survivors. She turned her gaze to the soldier. 'Who is in charge here?'

'Captain Fry, Miss.'

'And where is he?'

'That's him over there, talking to the sappers.'

As she looked at the officer he turned his gaze in her direction. He said something to the sapper sergeant then approached her. He looked at her without smiling. 'May I help you?' His voice was deep and refined.

'Captain Fry?' He nodded. 'My name is Lesley Carrington, I am with the High Commission, I had an office in there.' She nodded toward the hotel. 'I only learned of this outrage this morning when I returned from leave and I am naturally concerned about the fate of my colleagues.'

The officer's expression softened. 'Miss Carrington, I am truly sorry you have returned to such horror. How fortunate you were not yourself in the hotel.'

'Thank you, Captain.'

'I fear, however, I can be of little assistance to you in this matter, my job is largely to keep the ghouls away.' He paused to look at her and realised she was struggling to control herself. 'Did you have many friends on the General's staff?' She shook her head as her eyes brimmed with tears. He looked away briefly, embarrassed by her grief. 'There is an officer from the Military Governor's staff in that tent over there.' He pointed towards a large supply tent which had been erected on the forecourt of the hotel. 'He has been given the unenviable task of identifying the bodies as they recover them. If you are ready for some real grief, I suggest you speak to him.' She looked at him dejectedly then her tears began to flow unchecked, tracing through the dust on her face. He pulled a large olive green handkerchief from his pocket and began to wipe her face. 'Don't cry, love.' He lifted her hand and pressed the cloth into it. 'Here, wipe your eyes and have a good blow.' This simple, almost involuntary gesture, so reminiscent of Sammy, released the full flood of her grief. The Captain took her into his arms and held her tight until her weeping stopped.

She lifted her head and began to wipe her eyes. 'Please forgive me Captain, I am not very good at this sort of thing. I have seen many horrors, but it is always the same, I simply cannot understand why men do such things to one another.'

'It is not easy to understand the irrational, Miss Carrington, but please do not apologise, I realise what a shock this must be. Come, allow me to walk you to the major's tent.'

He pulled the flap aside for her to enter. She squinted slightly, waiting for her eyes to adjust to the gloom inside the tent. Ken Shoppee looked up, dreading the moment. He stood to face her, desperately reaching for the words he needed to ease the pain of what he knew he must tell her. But none were needed. She saw the torment in his eyes and knew at once that Sammy was dead. She turned and walked out, back into the sunlight. She stood very still, her eyes pressed shut. Captain Fry moved to touch her but hesitated. He peered back into the tent. Ken stood motionless, staring out at Lesley. 'Give her a couple of minutes, Ken,' Peter said softly. 'She has just returned from leave into this lot, I don't think she is used to this sort of thing. She will be OK in a minute.'

'I don't think so.' Ken's voice broke as he tried to fight back his own tears. 'Peter, that is Carrie, Sammy's fiancée.'

'But she said her name was Lesley Carr...oh Christ, oh dear, sweet Jesus Christ.' He turned and stared at Lesley's forlorn figure. They watched her for some time in uncomfortable silence. Finally she turned and came back into the tent. Peter stood back, allowing her to pass.

She sat and looked up at Ken. 'What about Maggs, Ken?...Is she...did she...Oh God, no.' Her head fell and she remained motionless. Peter looked down at her, wanting to reach out to her, to ease her pain. Then her voice came, soft yet steady. She was now beyond tears. 'Where is he, Ken?'

He cleared his throat painfully. 'They are taking them to Sarafand, to the Command Hospital. They have a cold morgue up there.' He shuffled uncomfortably as he spoke.

'Was he badly hurt?...Oh Christ, what a bloody stupid thing to ask...I meant, did he suffer?'

'I don't think so. He was caught in the blast, he probably...'

'He died instantly,' Peter intervened. Lesley turned to face him. 'His body was handed over to us, he was one of ours, you see.'

She smiled wistfully. 'Yes I know Captain, and you always look after your own, don't you?' He nodded. 'How do you know he died instantly?'

'The MO examined him in my presence. There was not a mark on him except a few abrasions from debris. The blast killed him, a massive concussion...asphyxiation...he would not have known a thing.' He touched her arm gently. 'Miss Carrington, no words of mine can possibly ease the pain you are suffering at this moment, but you should know that we who knew him, who had the privilege to serve with him, loved him too. He was a fine man and a magnificent soldier. After such a war as his it is tragic and inconceivable that he should have died like this, here and at the hand of these, of all people.'

'Thank you, Captain Fry.' She turned to the major. 'Can I see him, Ken?'

He looked uncomfortably at Peter. 'I don't think that would be a good...'

Peter intervened again. 'Of course, Miss Carrington. I shall be pleased to drive you to Sarafand myself.' He glanced aside. 'You don't have a problem with that, do you Ken?'

'No, no, absolutely not. I merely thought, in the circumstances...No, no problem at all.' Lesley stood and went to Ken. Putting her arms around him, she laid her face against his chest. He looked uncertainly at Peter then he embraced her firmly, almost desperately. 'I'm so sorry, old girl. It's such rotten luck. If we hadn't made him come back to see those damned spooks...' His voice trailed away.

She reached up and kissed his cheek. 'It is not your fault Ken, it is this wretched country. There is no trust, no honour, just hatred.' She looked at Peter. 'May I beg a lift to the palace, Captain? I do not appear to have a room here any more and I should like to clean up.'

'Yes, of course.' He frowned slightly. 'But what of your jeep?'

'What? Oh yes, I had quite forgotten...Can I leave it with you Ken?'

'No problem.' He looked at her, concerned by her apparent calm. 'Are you sure you will be all right, old girl?'

She smiled. 'I just want to bathe and be alone for a while.' She turned to Peter. 'Ready, Captain?'

She gazed down at the face. It had been cleaned until it shone. It had a slightly blue tinge. 'Cyanosis, lack of oxygen,' Peter explained.

She reached out, but immediately withdrew her hand. She knew she could not touch this body which smelled of ether and formaldehyde. She wondered why the feet were exposed. She tilted her head to read the tag tied to a toe. 'Parker, S. A. M. Captain. The Parachute Regiment.' She looked again at this face and tried to remember how joy and mischief and anger and love had once so animated it. She looked at the hands and tried to recall the firmness of their grip, the gentleness of their touch, the excitement of their caress. She looked at this body, still firm beneath the shroud and she tried again to sense its warmth and its energy. But she felt nothing now, nothing of him. He was gone and she would not know him again. She closed her eyes upon this body, turned and quickly walked away.

IT NEVER WAS YOU

Part 2 of the *Cypress Branches* trilogy

by

WILLIAM E. THOMAS

COMING SOON

acuteanglebooks.co.uk/itneverwasyou

JOIN THE CONVERSATION

Loved the book?
Can't wait for Part 2?
Have something to say?

Share your experience of reading *Pegasus Falling* with other
readers by joining in the conversation on the forum.

It's free to join up and if you'd like us to, we'll send you the
latest news by email so that you'll be the first to hear when
It Never Was You is released.

acuteanglebooks.co.uk/forum